SOHO GHOSTS

THE SOHO SERIES BOOK TWO

SOHO GHOSTS

THE SOHO SERIES BOOK TWO

GREG KEEN

THOMAS & MERCER

Text copyright © 2018 by Greg Keen

Published by Thomas & Mercer, Seattle

www.apub.com

Amazon, the Amazon logo, and Thomas & Mercer are trademarks of Amazon.com, Inc., or its affiliates.

ISBN-13: 9781542048361
ISBN-10: 1542048362

Cover design by @blacksheep-uk.com

Printed in the United States of America

For Kiare

Tempus Omnia Revelat
(Time Reveals All)

Hibbert & Saviours School motto

PROLOGUE

Highgate Cemetery, 1979

The boy surveys the moonlit necropolis. Some gravestones are perfectly straight; others have listed, and several monuments have collapsed entirely. A marble column rises like an admonitory finger from the foliage at its base. Carefully the boy manoeuvres his legs until he is perched on the top of the wall. In his mid-teens, he has side-parted hair and an athlete's angular shoulders. Pulling a torch out of his jeans, he examines the ground below. He switches off the torch, braces himself, and makes the twelve-foot drop.

Rolling like a man after a parachute jump, he gets to his feet and brushes off a couple of burrs. Damp streaks mottle his grey shirt. He switches the torch back on. The beam falls on a monument encircled by a black railing. Ivy has festooned the grave and is creeping up the chubby legs of a trumpet-toting angel. The only text the boy can make out reads: *Agnes Car*** beloved wife of Antho** and much-missed mother of ***mas. Born Jan**ry 9th 187*. Fell a*leep *ug*st 7th 1922.*

He tracks past a dozen other tombs. Some are grand affairs with elaborate masonry and architectural flourishes, others the final resting places of those of more modest means. Albert Creswell of Caledonian Road's memorial has been smashed at its base. Pale inner stone contrasts sharply with the grey exterior.

The boy stops at a granite ossuary that rises to his chest. The length of a family car, it has either been spared the ravages of the ivy or had the vegetation stripped away. From the back of the tomb he carefully slides out an aluminium ladder.

Back at the wall he sets the ladder and makes sure its feet are rooted firmly in the ground. He ascends and peers over the barricade between the living and the dead.

'Okay, it's all fine,' he says in his Yorkshire accent.

A second teenager appears. Dark curly hair falls to the collar of his shirt. Around his chin is a corona of acne. The first boy helps him off one ladder and guides his feet on to the rungs of the second.

'Thanks, Clarkey.'

The third boy over the wall is slight. Wire-framed glasses are tucked into the breast pocket of a Levi's jacket. Badges bearing the logos of Led Zeppelin, Deep Purple, Black Sabbath and Judas Priest are pinned to the denim. The boy descends the ladder in seconds.

'Bloody hell,' he says. 'Even more amazing at night, isn't it, Timms?'

'Yeah, brilliant,' Timms replies, although his acned features tell a different story.

'You're not getting the shits up, are you?'

'Course not, Paxo,' Timms says.

Another face appears over the wall. 'Can you take your bag, Paxo?' this boy asks. He is holding a plastic bag containing something bulky. He looks a year or two younger than the other three. In some part this is due to ears that stick out at right angles.

Paxo ascends the ladder and takes the bag from him. The boy contemplates the drop. 'Is it safe, Paxo?' he asks.

'Of course it's safe, Dent. Clarkey *jumped* it, for fuck's sake.'

Dent bites his bottom lip and frowns. These actions remove another year or two from his age. He could be twelve instead of sixteen. He straddles the wall and descends the ladder.

Paxo has removed a book from the bag. Its cover carries a symbol – a diamond piercing a square. 'This is it,' he says, gazing at the book. 'We're really doing it.'

'How far away is his grave?' Dent asks.

'Two minutes,' Paxo replies. 'And it's a mausoleum, not a grave.'

'You do know the way?' Dent asks, and peers into the gloom of the necropolis. 'I mean, it's pretty . . . dark.'

'Of course I know the way. And we've got three torches between us. The main thing is not to split up.'

The boy Timms's eyes widen and he swallows. The thought of separation is not a happy one.

Someone else is climbing the ladder on the other side of the wall. The fifth boy has a bulky torso and a flop of blonde hair falling to his jaw. 'Hide the ladder and keep an eye out for us, Blimp,' he calls to someone streetside. 'And whatever happens, do not piss off.'

'What if someone comes, Will?' a falsetto voice asks.

Will emits an exasperated sigh. 'Just make sure you're here when we come back, you fat oik,' he says. 'Anyone finds out about this and we're all sacked, you included.'

There is the sound of one ladder being removed while Will descends the other. He is two inches taller than the boy called Clarkey. He is sleek and rangy; the latter has the compact build of a cruiserweight boxer.

'Maybe we should get a shift on,' Clarkey says.

'Does tha think so, lad?' Will says, parodying his accent. 'And we'll have to be reet quiet like if we're not going to be nabbed by t'cozzers.'

Clarkey looks evenly at Will, no sign of anger or humiliation on his face. Indeed, it seems that the taller boy is the marginally less comfortable of the pair.

'He's right,' Timms says. 'The sooner we get this over with, the better.'

Maliciously, Will directs the beam of his torch into Timms's face. The boy extends a hand to block the light. He's saved the bother when it dwindles and dies. Will shakes the torch before toggling the switch. A faint glow lasts less than five seconds.

'Didn't you put new batteries in?' Paxo asks, incredulity in his voice.

'Course I did. There's something wrong with the fucking thing.' Will flings the torch away. It strikes the trumpeting angel, knocking off part of a wing. 'Give me your torch, Paxo. You can't hold that and the book. I'll go on point and you bring up the rear, Clarke.'

The tone in Will's voice echoes that his forebears used when marshalling the troops at Bosworth Field. Paxo lines up behind him, as do Timms, Dent and Clarke. The boys tack east along a gravel path that has not been raked in thirty years.

Five minutes later they reach a building set in a patch of open ground. Its white walls appear almost phosphorescent in the moonlight. The roof is pointed and stepped, giving the structure a vaguely oriental aspect. On each wall is an arched window of latticed metal strands. Above a pair of imposing zinc doors, two words have been carved.

MAUSOLEUM PORTEUS

'So, Alexander Porteus is in there?' Dent asks. Paxo nods. 'Is he buried, or just . . . lying on the floor?'

'He's in a coffin resting on a shelf.'

'I'm not going inside,' says Timms. From his reaction, it's clear the word *coffin* has had a visible effect. 'The rest of you do what you like. I'm staying out here.'

'No one's going in, tithead,' Will says. 'You couldn't get through those doors with a battering ram. Mind you, it looks like someone's had—'

Will is interrupted by rustling from bushes at the base of a tree. 'What was that?' Timms almost shrieks. Even the phlegmatic Clarkey jumps an inch or two.

'Where did it come from?' Clarkey asks.

'Over there.' Dent points at the poplar. Clarkey directs his torch. Several moths are illuminated in the beam. It does not, however, reveal the source of the noise.

'Please let's get out of here,' begs Timms.

'Probably just a bird or something,' Dent reassures him. 'You know what that chap who took us round said – the place is full of wildlife.'

Bang on cue, a dog fox trots out of the bushes. He regards the five visitors with mild curiosity. Deciding they present neither threat nor opportunity, he lollops over the grass and goes to earth behind an obelisk.

Will guffaws. 'A fox! You were wadding it over a fucking fox!'

If any boy detects a hint of relief in Will's laughter, he keeps it to himself.

'Get on with it, Paxo,' Will says. 'I told Blimp we'd be half an hour.'

'I need a torch to read,' Paxo says. Clarkey trains the light over Paxo's shoulder while he finds the relevant page. 'Okay, while I'm doing this, each of you take a candle from the bag and light it. That's the first thing.'

Starting with Dent, the boys each take a blue candle from the plastic bag and light it with a brass Zippo. The flames flicker in the breeze but remain alight. Paxo collects the bag from Clarkey and removes a small cloth pouch.

'I'm going to give you something to chuck into the middle. The important thing is to hang fire until I say so.' Paxo pours pale powder into the left hand of each boy. 'We need to arrange ourselves properly,' he says. 'Dent, if you stand about ten feet over there. Will, opposite me. Timms and Clarkey, nearer the tree.'

Paxo modifies his formation like a cricket captain adjusting the infield. The boys are in a lopsided circle before the mausoleum, a single candle illuminating each youthful face. A cloud passes over the moon, deepening the darkness.

'I'll recite the incantation now. Make the responses we rehearsed and, when I nod, throw the powder.' Paxo closes his eyes and tilts his head upwards. A distant car horn punctures the silence. Then, in a voice an octave higher than its usual register, he begins. 'Great Daemon, those who worship you have gathered in your garden.'

'We worship you,' the boys respond.

'We renounce those who mock the path.'

'We renounce them.'

'Yours is the one true way.'

'The one true way.'

'We five disciples have brought you brimstone and fire.'

Paxo nods and the boys throw the powder into the circle.

'In the name of your great book,' Paxo continues, raising the volume above his head, 'we beg to share in your triumph in this world and the world to come.'

A sudden gust extinguishes the candles.

'Sod it,' says Dent.

'Bollocks,' says Will.

'Turn a torch on,' says Timms.

Will and Clarkey fumble on the ground for their torches. Clarkey is first to the switch. He plays the beam on the mausoleum, from where the wind seemed to emanate. The doors remain closed. Nothing has changed.

Another rustling sound.

'Oh, God,' Timms groans.

Will laughs. 'Don't crap your knickers, sport. It's only the bloody fox.'

He flashes the beam of his torch around the bushes where the animal first appeared. Nothing. He redirects to the obelisk where it was last seen. It illuminates a bulky figure over six feet tall, wearing a cloak. Although his face is in shadow, it is clear the man is entirely bald. He extends an arm and points towards the group.

Will screams and disappears across the clearing, brandishing the torch as though it were the baton in a relay race. Dent follows his lead, with Timms hard on his heels. Paxo continues to stare at the cloaked man, who is now walking towards him and Clarke, arm outstretched.

'It's him,' he says in a stupefied voice. 'Alexander Porteus . . .'

'Paxo, we've got to get out of here,' Clarkey says.

'It worked. It only bloody worked.'

Clarkey shakes Paxo. The book falls from his hands and lands with a muffled thump on the grass. 'Come on!'

Paxo retrieves the tome. He takes a final look at the man, now only twenty feet away, and runs after Clarkey. By the time they reach the path leading back to the ladder, the cloud has passed and the cemetery is once again flooded with moonlight. The boys reach the ladder to find that Will has scaled it.

'Is Blimp there?' Dent asks.

'What do you think?' is Will's bitter response. 'Look, we can't wait any longer. I'm going to jump, which means we're all going to jump. Agreed?'

The other four boys look at each other and nod. Will positions himself on the top of the wall. He takes a deep breath and disappears from sight.

'You next, Timms,' says Dent.

The terrified boy requires no encouragement. He scales the ladder and, after one last look at the cemetery, pushes himself off the wall. Dent is third to make an exit, while Paxo stares down the gloomy path.

'He's still coming,' he says matter-of-factly.

The figure's rolling gait makes it look as though he is struggling against a headwind. Nevertheless, in another thirty seconds he will have reached the remaining two boys.

'Now!' Clarkey shouts. 'Go now!'

Paxo ascends, with Clarkey directly behind. The ladder bows under their combined weight. It shifts on the crumbling brickwork but remains in position. Paxo struggles to lever his left leg over the apex of the wall. Clarkey grabs his foot and pushes it into place. By the time his companion has made the drop, the figure has arrived at the base of the ladder. Pallid hands emerge from the cloak, fasten on to it and begin to shake.

When the ladder crashes into the undergrowth, Clarkey is left hanging, arms fully extended. With an animal cry, and scrabbling with his feet for purchase, he succeeds in pulling his body upwards. He cannot stop himself from looking into the figure's face. The only thing he will remember – although it will be for the rest of his life – are the eyes: two dark portals willing him to fall.

In the street, Will, Timms, Dent and Paxo are in a huddle. Timms is rubbing his elbow, Will looking at his watch. Paxo is examining his book for signs of damage.

'Quick, Clarkey,' Dent says in a hushed voice. 'Someone heard us.'

On the opposite side of the road is a three-storey Victorian house. A light is on in one of the upper windows. The front door opens and an elderly female voice shouts, 'Whoever you are, the police are on their way.'

'Christ,' Will says. 'That's all we need.'

Clarkey pushes free of the wall. He lands awkwardly and shouts in pain.

'What's up?' Dent asks.

'I've done something . . . to . . . my ankle.'

'Try to stand.' With Dent's assistance, Clarkey gets to his feet. 'Put your weight on my shoulder and see if you can walk.'

Together they take a few awkward steps. Given ten minutes to escape, their collaboration may well prove successful. But if the woman is to be believed, there are only a matter of moments, a fact that is not lost on Will. 'We can't hang around until the police arrive,' he says.

'What else can we do?' Paxo asks.

'Look, there's no point in us all getting caught. Clarke can say he was acting alone. He's a skimp. All they'll do is gate him for a month.'

'Will's right,' Clarkey says. 'The rest of you go.'

'There's a car coming,' Dent says, and indeed there is. It could be a taxi ferrying someone home from a late-night party. It could be the police on their way to investigate. Either way, the boys are forced to make a decision.

'Maybe it's for the best,' Timms says.

With this observation, the die is cast. Will, Timms and Paxo begin running. Dent hesitates. His and Clarke's eyes meet. It seems as though Dent might be about to change his mind. Then he turns and sprints after his schoolmates.

Thirty seconds later, a patrol car rounds the bend.

Evening Standard, 2 September 2016

The funeral of George Dent, former Shadow Minister for Urban Development, is due to take place at St Mark's Church in his hometown of Mavering on 16 September.

Dent died following a fall from his London apartment in Mermaid Court last week. The coroner's report delivered a verdict of accidental death, although a post-mortem report indicated high levels of alcohol in the MP's bloodstream.

A Labour Party spokesperson said that its thoughts were with Dent's family at this difficult time. The party had suspended Dent pending the outcome of a trial after police discovered quantities of cocaine and child pornography in his Pimlico flat. It is not thought there will be official representation at the funeral.

A date has yet to be set for what will be a hotly contested by-election in the former MP's constituency of Dartford West.

ONE

'It's creamy Zummerzet milk wot probably makes Budfield butter taste the best!'

'Excellent effort, Sir Liam,' said the woman behind the console, 'but I'm wondering if we could make it a touch less regional.'

'You just said you wanted it more regional.'

'*Cider With Rosie* is the space we're after. We're in danger of drifting a teeny bit towards The Wurzels at the moment.'

Behind the glass the greatest thespian of his generation, and one who had delivered what many critics considered the definitive Lear, looked as though he considered himself to be more sinned against than sinning.

'For fuck's sake,' he muttered into his beard.

The booth mic picked up the comment but the director opted, wisely in my opinion, to ignore it. 'Could we go one more time, Sir Liam?' she asked.

'I've got lunch at the Garrick in half an hour.'

'We're so close to nailing it.'

Sir Liam was a trouper. He set his shoulders, took a couple of steadying breaths and inclined his head towards the microphone. 'It's creamy Zummerzet milk wot probably makes Budfield butter taste the best!'

'Little bit slower . . .'

'It's creamy Zummerzet milk wot probably makes Budfield butter taste the best!'

'Tiny bit more emphasis on Somerset.'

'It's creamy *Zummerzet* milk wot probably makes Budfield butter taste the best!'

'Slightly warmer this time.'

'It's creamy Zummerzet milk wot probably makes Budfield butter so good for lubing your boyfriend's arsehole with.'

My brother rose from an L-shaped sofa. 'I think we'll leave it there, Suzie,' he said before speaking into the connecting microphone. 'Thank you so much for your hard work this morning, Sir Liam. I'm sure we can use one of the takes we already have. If not, we'll get back to your agent.'

The national treasure pulled off his headphones, hung them on the mic stand and exited the sound booth. Craggy features were a little craggier today after his attendance at the previous night's BAFTA party. It didn't appear that celebrating the best in British cinematic talent had done much to sweeten his disposition.

'Sorry about that last one,' he said to Malcolm. 'But you can only say the same damn sentence so many times.'

'I completely understand.'

A studio lackey appeared carrying a black overcoat. With her assistance, Sir Liam slotted his arms into the sleeves and buttoned it up.

'Obviously I'll return if you haven't got exactly what you want,' he said.

'Oh, I think we'll probably be okay, won't we, Suzie?' my brother replied.

The director shrugged, indicating that this may or may not be the case. Grey hair and a pinafore dress made her look like a primary school teacher, although if she had been at all nervous working with the great man, it wasn't showing.

'I'll be on my way, then,' Sir Liam said. 'So nice to meet you, Malcolm.'

He shook hands with my brother and nodded at a middle-aged man who was sitting on the sofa. The director may as well have been invisible for all the attention she received. The lackey led the actor past me and out of the studio. Malcolm released a long breath.

'Christ, Suzie, you rode him a bit hard, didn't you?'

'Just trying to get the best out of the old boy. Not my fault if he turns up half-cut.'

'Well, if we have to get him back, we have to get him back,' Malcolm said. 'Thanks for a great job under the circumstances. He's not the easiest.'

'No problem. Need me for anything else?'

'Not right now.' Malcolm looked at his watch. 'I'll ask the office to get in touch and we can go through the takes tomorrow. That suit you, Peter?'

The guy on the sofa nodded. Malcolm and Suzie embraced briefly, after which she left the studio. Having arrived while the commercial was being recorded, I hadn't had the opportunity to greet my brother. We gave each other a backslapping hug.

'Thanks for coming, Kenny,' he said. 'How have you been?'

'Not bad,' I said.

Malcolm was three years older, two stone heavier, and thirty-one million pounds richer than me. That aside, there wasn't much difference between us.

'I'd like to introduce you to Peter Timms,' he said, gesturing to the guy who had now risen from the sofa. 'Peter's the CEO of Dairy Vale, the people we're making the commercial for.'

'Pleased to meet you,' I said, and we shook hands.

Peter's suit was immaculately cut, and an Audemars Piguet Perpetual Calendar watch peeped out from his shirt cuff. He was pot-bellied and in his mid-fifties. No wedding ring. Not much hair.

'Peter knows you're a private detective,' my brother said.

'Skip-tracer,' I corrected him.

'What's the difference?' Peter asked.

'About a hundred quid an hour.' He looked blank in the same way everyone looked blank when I outlined my job description. I should have become a life coach. 'Usually I'm hunting down people who've reneged on their child support or haven't returned a hire car,' I explained. 'If things get really glamorous, I might pull an insurance case.'

'What about last year, Kenny?' Malcolm said. 'That was . . . off the beaten track.'

That was one way of describing it. An ex-employer had asked me to trace his runaway daughter. A week later, four people were dead. Sometimes I wondered whether I could have handled things differently. Mostly I just tried to forget about it.

'Are you busy at the moment?' Peter asked.

'I've got a few irons in the fire.'

'You wouldn't be able to take something on, then?'

'I might. Depending on what the something was.'

'Have you heard of George Dent?'

I had. But then everyone had. 'Disgraced Shadow Minister for Urban Development,' I said. 'The cops found a load of coke and kiddie porn in his flat. Two weeks later he took a header out of— what's the place called?'

'Mermaid Court.'

'George was a friend of Peter's,' Malcolm said.

'Not a friend exactly,' Peter clarified. 'We were at school together and kept in touch. A week or so before he died, I received a call from George. He was very agitated about someone who'd been standing outside his flat.'

'He had a stalker?'

'I suppose that's one way of putting it.'

'D'you know his name?'

'Alexander Porteus.'

'Has anyone talked to the guy?'

'That would be difficult.'

'Why's that?'

'He died in 1947.'

◆　◆　◆

Sir Liam's early departure meant there was another twenty minutes on the clock to interview Peter in the studio. We helped ourselves to coffee out of the machine and settled on the sofa. The windowless room with its padded walls lent a confessional quality to the conversation. It turned out to be appropriate.

'You're telling me George Dent was being doorstepped by a dead man?' I said.

'That's what *he* said.'

'Which is impossible.'

Peter took a sip of coffee. He stared at the carpet for a few seconds and took another sip of coffee. 'I suppose it is,' he said.

'You don't seem entirely convinced.'

'Whatever you say will be treated in complete confidence,' Malcolm assured him. 'Isn't that right, Kenny?'

I nodded, and Peter laid the coffee cup down. He placed his elbows on his knees and interlaced his fingers. They were slender with beautifully manicured nails. More like a woman's than a man's.

'George and I attended Hibbert & Saviours in Highgate. You may know it . . .'

Indeed I did. H&S was one of the best-regarded public schools in the country, the kind of place that you paid fifteen grand a term to send little Johnny if you wanted him to emerge with immaculate vowels and armour-plated self-esteem.

'When we were in the lower sixth, I and some other pupils played a bit of a prank.'

'What kind of prank?'

'We broke into Highgate Cemetery.'

'Okay, and what happened?'

'One of the boys had become obsessed with the occultist Alexander Porteus. You don't hear of him much now but in the interwar years he was quite famous. Lord Beaverbrook called him the wickedest man in the world.'

A distant bell rang in my memory. 'Didn't he live in Dean Street?'

'That's right.'

'And there's a bookshop in Cecil Court with that name.'

'He opened it in 1928,' Peter said. 'I believe it's still in the family.'

'What's his connection with Highgate Cemetery?'

'Porteus is interred in the family mausoleum. Simon – he's the boy I was telling you about – wanted to perform some kind of ritual in front of the tomb.' Peter breathed heavily a couple of times. 'We didn't get the chance to complete it. Halfway through the ceremony a figure appeared. It was Alexander Porteus.'

The silence in the room deepened. Peter stared at his hands. I caught Malcolm's eye, looking for any indication that his friend might be off his swede. He didn't give me one.

'So what you're telling me,' I said, 'is that forty years ago you raised Alexander Porteus from the dead?'

'We all saw him.'

'How d'you know it wasn't someone else playing a prank?'

'I'd seen photographs. The likeness was too accurate for it to be . . .' Peter trailed off, shrugged and said, 'It was Porteus.'

'I'm guessing you didn't hang round to say hello.'

'We ran like hell.'

'And that was that?'

'Not quite. One of the boys damaged his knee getting back over the wall. Ray couldn't walk, and someone called the police. He ended up being sacked.'

'Sacked?'

'Expelled.'

'None of you said anything to save him?'

'I'm afraid not.'

'Have you heard from Ray since?' Peter shook his head. 'What about the other boys?' I asked. 'Are you in touch with them?'

'Apart from George, I haven't spoken to any of them in years.'

'What d'you want me to do?' I asked.

'Contact the others and see if any of them have heard from Porteus.'

Money was tight because work was slack. All the same . . .

'You want me to ask . . . how many men?'

'Four.'

'Ask four men whether they've seen the same ghost you reckon was hassling your ex-schoolmate shortly before he died. Is that right?'

Peter didn't say it was, but he didn't say it wasn't either.

'Can't you do it yourself?' I asked.

'I've no idea where two of them are,' he said. 'And one of them is virtually impossible to speak to.'

'Let me get this absolutely straight. How many boys in total went to the cemetery that night?'

'Six including me. Ray Clarke was a scholarship boy from Yorkshire. I suppose you'd describe Will Creighton-Smith as the alpha male, and Simon Paxton was the kid whose idea it all was. We used to call him Paxo, if that helps.'

'Okay, so put the late George Dent and yourself into the mix and we have five . . .'

'The sixth person didn't actually come in,' Peter said. 'Henry Baxter was in charge of the ladder. You might know him better as Blimp Baxter.'

'The developer?'

He nodded again. This information didn't whet my appetite. Blimp Baxter brought to property deals what the great white shark brought to Bondi Beach. It wasn't that he didn't suffer fools gladly – he didn't suffer them at all.

'I'm really not sure about this,' I said, which was putting it mildly. 'George Dent was probably whacked sideways on coke and Christ knows what else when he saw whatever he thought he saw out of his window. Why not just forget about it?'

'It's not that easy.'

'Because . . . ?' I asked.

Peter Timms continued to stare at the carpet as though he had lost something minute and extremely valuable in its weave.

'Tell Kenny what you told me, Peter,' my brother said.

Timms nodded. He straightened up and looked me full in the face.

'Eight nights ago I saw Alexander Porteus as well.'

TWO

The studio lackey re-entered the room. She told us that the next client was due. Malcolm thanked her and I asked Peter my next question. 'What did he look like?'

'Same as in the cemetery. Tall with a hooded cloak that fell to the ground.'

'How close were you to him?'

'About thirty yards. I was looking out of my bedroom window and he was in the garden. There was a bomber's moon and it never really gets properly dark in London.'

'How did you know he was there in the first place?' I asked.

'There was a peculiar baying sound. At first I thought it was a dog howling but it just went on and on. When I pulled the curtains open . . . there he was.'

'What did he do?'

'Raised his arm and pointed at me. After a few seconds he turned and walked towards the bottom of the garden. By the time I'd pulled some clothes on, he'd disappeared.'

'Is there any way out?'

'A gate separates my garden from the neighbour's, but the mechanism's rusted. The entrance from the street is alarmed. I checked it and nothing had been disturbed.'

'Did anyone else see the figure?'

Peter shook his head. 'My wife and I separated last year. I live on my own.'

'Who else have you told?'

'Only Malcolm. He suggested I speak to you.'

'No one comes back from the grave,' I said. 'Whoever you saw is just trying to scare you for some reason. And if it were Porteus – which it definitely isn't – why would he wait thirty-odd years before putting an appearance in?'

'Kenny's right,' Malcolm added. 'It's just some moron's idea of a laugh.'

'What about George Dent?'

'Coincidence,' I said. 'Have you ever told anyone what you saw in Highgate?'

'No. We had a pact not to mention it again.'

'Doesn't mean someone hasn't broken it.'

'I suppose not,' Timms conceded.

I fished out a notebook and flipped it open. When a bit more fishing failed to produce a pen, Malcolm passed me a Montblanc the size of a torpedo.

'So, Blimp Baxter was one of the boys,' I said after removing its cap and writing the date. 'But you don't know the whereabouts of the others?'

'Not Will Creighton-Smith and Ray Clarke, but Simon Paxton I do . . .'

I smiled encouragingly.

'After he left Hibberts, he had a lot of mental health issues. Simon's family disowned him and he was in and out of institutions for years. He lives somewhere on the east coast now. As far as I'm aware, he's a recluse.'

'Do you have an address or a number?'

'Zetland House. It's quite remote. The nearest village is a place called Middlemere. If there's a phone number, I couldn't find it.'

I wrote the details down.

'If any of them have seen Porteus, what then?'

'I'd feel a lot more comfortable going to the police.' Timms straightened on the sofa. 'George didn't take drugs and I don't believe the child abuse images belonged to him,' he said firmly.

'Even though they were found in his flat?'

'He was set up.'

'By the ghost of Alexander Porteus?'

'Look, I know that whoever was in my garden, it wasn't Porteus. I'm not an idiot. Someone's trying to rattle me for some reason.'

'Why?'

'I don't know.'

I closed my notebook and put the Montblanc in my jacket pocket.

'You hardly knew George Dent. Paedophiles don't go round advertising the fact, and half the world snorts coke these days. How often did the two of you meet?'

'We'd have dinner every six months or so.'

'There we are, then.'

'I know how that sounds, but I was pretty much George's best friend. He didn't have a partner and he wasn't close to his family. He even made me his executor.'

'My advice is step up security at your house and forget about it,' I said.

'You're not interested?'

I wasn't particularly, although I'm not interested in tracking down unreturned hire cars either, and Malcolm had recommended me.

'You know my fees?'

'I'm sure I can afford them.'

I sucked my teeth for a few seconds but it was all for show. Peter Timms might have been nuts, but his money was as sane as anyone's. 'Okay, I'll get on to it next week.'

'Actually, I'd hoped you could make it a little earlier than that.'

Most clients want you on the job as soon as possible, but there was a tension in Peter's voice that I didn't usually hear. 'Any particular reason?' I asked.

'George received a phone call on the same night he saw Porteus.'

'What kind of call?'

'A man said "Ten days" and hung up. Number withheld.'

'And ten days later, George . . . ?'

Peter nodded.

'Don't suppose you know what the guy sounded like?' I asked.

'He had a well-educated voice.'

'George told you that?'

'He didn't have to. I received an identical call. At least, I'm assuming it was the same person.'

'When?'

'An hour after I saw Porteus.'

'And that was eight days ago.'

'Yes.'

I performed the simple calculation. Time up on Wednesday.

'Why have you left it over a week to bring it to me?'

'Because I've been unbelievably busy.'

'All the same, you should go to the police. Someone *is* threatening your life.'

Peter shrugged. 'Are they? All I can say is that I saw a figure and received a call. There's no concrete proof of anything.'

'Go on holiday, then.'

'That's not an option.'

There was a hiatus in the conversation. Peter was right: the police weren't likely to take him that seriously. Everything he could tell them would be anecdotal and unsubstantiated. And my diary wasn't exactly bursting at the seams.

'Okay, I'll get on to it immediately,' I said. 'But I'd advise keeping your wits about you for the next few days.'

'Of course,' Peter said. 'Do you want to see George's apartment?'

'You've got the key?'

He nodded. 'Once I've cleared out his papers and personal effects, I'll get the removers in.' He fished a fob with a single Yale key attached to it from his pocket. 'Could you leave it at the porter's lodge when you're finished? I'll pick it up this evening.' My new client stood up and checked his watch. 'Malcolm, I'll speak to you tomorrow. Kenny, is there anything I need to sign?'

'I'll email you a couple of forms,' I said.

Peter handed me a card that looked and felt as though it had been inscribed on vellum. It read PETER TIMMS, CEO, DAIRY VALE along with a debossed logo and the usual details. Mine came courtesy of biz-cards4you.co.uk. I straightened it out and handed it over.

'What does the OC stand for?' he asked.

'Odeerie Charles,' I said. 'He's my business partner.'

Peter nodded, shook hands and headed for the door.

'Thanks for recommending me,' I said to Malcolm when he was on the other side of it. 'How long have you known Peter?'

'About five years. He's a friend as much as a client.'

'Doesn't seem like your typical CEO.'

'Yeah, well, the days of blokes chewing cigars and pounding the boardroom table are long gone. Most chief execs are accountants, which is what Peter trained as. And Dairy Vale's share price has been dropping like a stone all year.'

'He's under a lot of pressure?' I asked. Malcolm nodded. 'So all this Alexander Porteus stuff could just be a figment of his imagination?'

'It could be, but I don't think it is. Not with the phone call too.'

'No,' I said. 'Nor do I.'

'What's your best guess?'

'It's just someone pissing around. If he gets a couple of floodlights and a camera installed, that'll be the end of it. And he might want to change his phone number.'

'And the George Dent stuff? It's weird both of them got the same call.'

'Probably one of the other boys mucking around.'

'But you'll check it out?'

'Like I said: right away.'

'Actually, there is one thing before you go, Kenny.'

'What's that?'

'Can I have my pen back, please?'

◆ ◆ ◆

I had described Odeerie to Peter Timms as my business partner, although 'employer' would have been the more accurate description. After his wife ran off with her Pilates teacher, the fat man had become increasingly disinclined to accept social invitations. Ten years ago he developed a mild form of agoraphobia. These days it would require a keg of dynamite to coax him out of his Meard Street flat.

Odeerie runs his business from home. Occasionally he needs someone to visit the local chippy and enquire whether an old army buddy is still living at number 45, or provide photographic evidence for an insurance company that Rommel the schnauzer hasn't been dognapped at all. That's where I come in.

The official term for what I do is *pretexting*, although the man in the street often refers to it as lying, deceiving, or a gross invasion of privacy. Sometimes the man in the street is clutching a ball-peen hammer while the pretexter is running like a bastard in the opposite direction. It's fair to say that none of this is what I imagined I'd be doing aged fifty-eight. Thanking the Nobel Committee for its overdue award is more what I had in mind.

On the plus side, I had picked up a client when clients weren't thick on the ground. My agreement with Odeerie is that, if anyone approaches me privately, then I put it through the company's books.

Fair enough, bearing in mind that he supplies work on a semi-regular basis and that my IT skills aren't exactly sparkling.

I pressed Odeerie's buzzer on the panel outside Albion Mansions. A minute passed and I pressed it again. Still nothing. The occupant of flat 4 had either nodded off or was speaking to a client. After multiple rings, his mobile went to voicemail. A call to the landline met with the same outcome. I was about to nip round the corner for a sharpener in the Ship when the door opened and a woman in her late sixties emerged. 'Can I help you?' she asked.

'I'm visiting a friend in flat four,' I said. 'He isn't answering his buzzer.'

'Your friend may be out.'

'He doesn't go out. All I want to do is go in and knock on his door.'

The woman was wearing an orange gilet and wraparound sunglasses. As it was drizzling steadily out of a pewter sky, I suspected some type of eye condition.

'What's his name?' she asked.

'Odeerie Charles.'

'Describe him to me.'

'He's a black guy in his fifties. He's about five-eleven with short, greying hair and he's a bit of a . . . He's got a heavy build.'

I narrowly avoided the words *fat bastard*. They were a sight more accurate descriptors than *heavy build*, but weren't likely to advance my chances of admission. I couldn't see the woman's eyes through the dark lenses of her glasses, but suspected they were appraising me. I treated her to my best pretexter expression.

It worked like a charm.

Albion Mansions was built at the turn of the last century. The lift can't have been installed long afterwards. Tiny and panelled in oak, it ascends at an arthritic rate. As usual when I visited Odeerie, his door had been left ajar. Given that he hadn't buzzed me up, this was odd. I knocked a couple of times and received no reply. Probably the fat man had taken a delivery of something before hastening back to whatever he'd been working on. I pushed the door open and entered the flat.

To my left was the sitting room in which Odeerie met clients; opposite was the spare bedroom he used as an office. A cigarette end had been ground into the oatmeal-coloured carpet between the doors. Odeerie didn't smoke and he kept the flat scrupulously clean. My skin prickled as though statically charged.

'Odeerie,' I said loudly. 'It's Kenny . . .'

My employer was well overdue a massive heart attack. It wouldn't particularly have surprised me to find that he had gone to his reward. The open door and the crushed ciggie didn't point in that direction, though.

'Are you there?' I tried again.

More silence.

In the sitting room a couple of sofas had been placed at right angles to each other. Books were arranged neatly on shelves either side of the fireplace, as was a rack of classical vinyl. A pair of Bose headphones lay on a Perspex turntable cover. Nothing appeared to have been disturbed. Perhaps I'd checked the sitting room first subconsciously fearing what I might discover in the office. If so, my subconscious was firing on all cylinders.

Lying on the floor of the office was Odeerie Charles.

THREE

The left side of Odeerie's face was swollen, and his eye was partially closed. Over his lips and chin was a skein of blood. His nose wouldn't require X-raying to reveal a fracture. I laid a couple of fingers on his neck and felt a pulse.

'Odeerie, it's Kenny. Don't worry, mate, I'm calling an ambulance.'

His mouth parted and a groan emerged.

'Can you hear me?' I asked. Another groan, followed by something I couldn't make out. 'What was that?'

'Have . . . they . . . gone?'

'Yeah, no one's here. You're safe.'

One eye opened. The other couldn't.

'No cops . . . no ambulance,' he said. A deep breath caused a tiny bubble of blood to inflate and burst in a nostril. 'I'm serious, Kenny. Don't call . . . anyone.'

'Odeerie, you need medical help and whoever's done this—'

A large hand clamped itself around my wrist. 'I said no. Get me . . . water.'

Odeerie's interpretation of the Data Protection Act is fairly liberal, meaning that he can be a little wary of giving the law any excuse to examine his hard drives.

'Water and a bucket,' he repeated. 'No ambulance.'

As the fat man's blood pressure has been fucking colossal over fucking horrendous for the last twenty years, I postponed calling the emergency services. No point in agitating him further and risk finishing off what others had started. I returned from the kitchen with a pint glass and a washing-up bowl. Odeerie took a couple of sips and concentrated on his breathing.

The office contained two aluminium desks. On each was a large screen with a set of cables feeding into a central stack. Apart from a filing cabinet, a sofa and half a dozen reference books, that was basically it. Nothing had been taken. Either Odeerie's assailant had been disturbed or robbery wasn't the motive.

'What happened?' I asked after he'd taken more fluid on board.

'There were three of them.'

'How did they get in?'

'They said there'd been reports of a gas leak. By the time I worked out who they really were, it was too late to get the chain on. One of them was Billy Dylan.'

Odeerie turned his head and yakked up something deeply unpleasant into the washing-up bowl. I very nearly followed suit.

◆ ◆ ◆

Four months earlier, a woman in her late twenties had contacted Odeerie via the website. She suspected her husband of having an affair and wanted to hire OC Trace and Find to confirm her suspicions. The woman – her name was Sandra Smith – was prepared to offer full rate plus expenses and a ten per cent bonus for the money shot.

It was the kind of work for which Odeerie usually recommended a more appropriate firm. But the fee was good and we weren't drowning in clients. Against Odeerie's better judgment, he took an advance of a thousand quid in fifties. Three days later his number-one associate was sitting in a Fiat Uno outside a large semi in Chingford with a Pentax and an A4 photo of the husband resting on his lap.

Shortly after noon, a black BMW pulled up. A beefy bald guy in a fleece exited the driver's side and opened the rear door to allow his passenger out. No mistaking the bloke in the photograph Odeerie had been supplied with. Sandra's husband was in his late twenties and had dark curly hair that fell to the collar of a distressed biker jacket. His pale features had an almost feminine delicacy about them. He swaggered to the front door and was admitted without having to ring the bell.

The guy was in the house for an hour, during which time his chauffeur leant against the hood of the car, smoked his guts out and read a copy of *Heat*. When the front door opened, I pointed the camera and let the motor drive do the work.

The couple gave each other a long snog goodbye that I captured for posterity, or more probably a divorce lawyer. She went back into the house and he said something to the driver, who laughed and slapped him on the back. Thirty seconds later the Beemer rolled off the driveway and that was the end of that.

Except that it wasn't.

Odeerie contacted the client to say he would email the photographs over. She insisted on collecting them in person and paid the balance on the account in cash. Odeerie had been unable to connect Sandra Smith's name with the address she supplied on her new client form. As all he was obliged to do legally was ask for details, not confirm their accuracy, this wasn't a problem. All the same, perhaps alarm bells should have begun to ring before the piece in the *Standard* appeared.

Cheryl Dylan had separated from her husband, Billy, and was bringing divorce proceedings against him. Why was this of interest to the reading public? Mainly because Billy was the only son of Marty Dylan, head of a notorious North London criminal gang. Marty's daughter-in-law was thought to be staying at a safe address with her three-year-old daughter, Caitlin, according to the paper.

Pictures of Cheryl – aka Sandra – and her husband supplemented the piece. As did one of those I had taken in Chingford. Odeerie and I reassured each other that there was no way Billy Dylan could find out who had taken it. Judging by my friend's battered face, we'd been wrong about that.

◆　◆　◆

Odeerie was unsteady on his feet but he made it to the bathroom, where he brushed his teeth, swallowed three paracetamol and changed into a clean tracksuit. His left eye had closed entirely and the lump on his head was the size of a golf ball. In the sitting room, he lowered himself gingerly on to one sofa while I occupied the other.

'Take me through what happened,' I said.

'I told you how they got in?' I nodded. 'When the door was closed, one of them coshed me. Then they bundled me into the office and Billy Dylan asked if I knew who he was and why he was there.'

'What did you tell him?'

'That we had no idea the client was his wife.'

'We?'

'He had a Stanley knife, Kenny. He threatened to slice off my . . .'

Odeerie wrapped his arms around his chest and began to sob. I switched sofas and put an arm across his shoulders. His body quaked while he tried to regain control.

'He's gone, Odeerie,' I said. 'And there's no way he'd have used the blade. Wankers like Billy Dylan chuck out all kinds of bullshit threats.'

'You weren't there, Kenny. He reckoned I was to blame for his little girl being taken away from him.' Odeerie looked at me, tear tracks on his cheeks. 'If I hadn't said what I did, he'd definitely have . . .'

'Erm . . . what did you say?' I asked.

'I told him that, when I found out who the client really was, I insisted on stopping. You carried on behind my back because you needed the money.'

'Did he believe you?'

'I'd be in a lot worse shape if he didn't.'

'So that means you're off the hook because Billy Dylan thinks I'm solely responsible for his wife doing a bunk?'

'At least you know he's looking for you, Kenny – that's something.'

'What did he do after you told him?'

'Kicked me in the head. That's the last thing I can remember.'

'Thanks, Odeerie,' I said. 'Thanks a million.'

'Chances are he'll think we've gone to the police and that'll jeopardise his chances of getting his kid back. He's almost certainly not going to try anything again.'

'Yeah, but if he does . . .'

Odeerie gently massaged the lump on the side of his skull. 'What you need is a minder,' he said. 'Someone to keep an eye on you for the next few days.'

'How am I going to afford that?'

The fat man's expression indicated an internal struggle. Usually it was wind. Thankfully, on this occasion, it represented a financial dilemma.

'Get someone on the business,' he muttered eventually.

'I can hire a bodyguard on expenses?'

'Not a fucking bodyguard, Kenny. Just someone who can handle himself in a ruck, and only for a few days. We're going through a tough patch, remember.'

'Actually, I've got some good news on that front.'

As usual when money was mentioned, I had Odeerie's full attention. It took ten minutes to replay my conversation with Peter Timms.

'Did you give him a new client form?' was his first question.

'I've got his email address. We can DocuSign it.'

'He knows the costs?'

'Timms is minted.'

'Does he really think this Porteus bloke is stalking him?'

'He kind of does and he kind of doesn't. The thing is that it has to be sorted in the next two days.' I told Odeerie about the 'Ten days' phone call and that I had suggested Peter contact the police.

'He shouldn't go anywhere near the bloody police!' he spluttered. 'And I hope you told him about the twenty per cent priority supplement.'

'I wasn't aware we had one,' I said. 'But you can always add it to the quote when you send the contract over.' This suggestion appeared to mollify him.

'How are you going to get to talk to Blimp Baxter?' he asked.

'I'll work something out.'

'It'll take some doing.'

'You think we should turn the job down?'

'Course not. This is a business, Kenny.'

'Yeah, but I don't want us milking it. Peter Timms is my brother's mate.'

Odeerie held his hands up as though he found the idea morally repugnant. 'We'll treat him like every other client,' he said. 'If this Paxton guy has a number, then I'll be able to find it pretty quickly. Did he have any info about the other two boys?'

'Just names. He googled them but nothing came up.'

'Write 'em down and I'll get on to it.'

'You should get checked out by a doctor first, Odeerie,' I said. 'You were spark-out when I found you. At least have an X-ray.'

'I'm fine, Kenny. Go see Dent's apartment.'

Odeerie rose from the sofa with the grace of a sedated rhino and headed straight for the door. 'Gimme a call later,' he said. 'I'll probably have something for you on Clarke and Creighton-Smith and I'll text you Paxton's number if he has one. Actually, I could probably sort out your minder too.'

'You mean someone who's competitive on rate?'

The fat man gave me a wounded look. 'I mean someone decent, Kenny,' he said.

'Yeah, well don't bother about that,' I replied.

'Why not?

'I've already got someone in mind.'

FOUR

Mermaid Court was a complex of red-brick buildings put up in the thirties. According to Wikipedia, its name derived from the fountain in the central gardens, and it was less than a mile from the Palace of Westminster. For this reason it was home to quite a few MPs and senior civil servants. The official entrance was through a six-columned portico on Millbank, although I opted to use the access road instead. Each apartment block was named for a British county. George Dent had fallen from the seventh floor of Surrey House. The east corner of the gardens had more trees and bushes outside it than most – ideal cover for the ghost of a dead magician.

I used the magnetic fob on the key Peter Timms had given me to gain admission. On one side of the entrance hall was a set of pigeon-holes for residents' post. The opposite wall featured a bicycle rack containing several off-road machines. Daylight came through frosted panels in the door and was augmented by three rows of halogen ceiling studs. Had there been an oxygen cylinder and a Sherpa handy, I might have attempted the seven flights of stairs. In their absence I took the lift.

The lock protecting flat 44 would almost have been as easy to open with a pick as it was with the key. I entered a sitting room that was a symphony in brown. At one end of the spectrum was a mahogany coffee table; at the other a set of beige curtains that fell to the floor. The floorboards were varnished pine and the sofa chestnut-coloured leather.

The most interesting thing in the room was a small and well-executed seascape signed with the initials *GD*.

The spare bedroom served as an office. A glass table supported an inkjet printer and a mug filled with pens and pencils. At one side was a mini filing cabinet. The top drawer was thick with opened envelopes and letters. Some had the Mermaid Court address on the front; others had been delivered to the Houses of Parliament.

Presumably the cops had removed anything relevant to their enquiries. All that a quick search revealed was an A4 envelope crammed with receipts, an invitation to a steering committee, half a dozen takeaway menus and several constituency letters, each with a date-received stamp. None were signed *A. Porteus (deceased)*, which would have made things a lot more interesting.

George Dent had fallen from the main bedroom. A twenty-five-metre drop directly on to concrete would be hard to survive. In the absence of a suicide note, and bearing in mind the high levels of alcohol in the deceased's system, the coroner had returned a verdict of accidental death. Only an idiot would believe it. The child abuse images had been category five. Dent would have done the hardest time there was.

Was it possible he could have seen Alexander Porteus from his window? Answer: yes. Could he have fallen accidentally or even been pushed? Also yes. Did I think either event had taken place? Emphatically no.

A key turned in the lock. My instinctive reaction was concealment. Then I remembered that I was in the flat legitimately.

In the sitting room a woman in her mid-twenties was unhooking a large satchel from her shoulder. 'Can I help you?' I asked.

She jumped a couple of inches and her bag crashed to the floor. The top fell open and a Bic biro trundled across the boards. It came to rest against the leg of the coffee table.

'God, you gave me a fright. I thought the place was empty.'

'Sorry about that. My name's Kenny Gabriel. I'm working for Peter Timms. He's George's executor.'

Not a lie in the strict definition of the term, and the woman appeared to have no problem with it. 'Sally Thomas,' she said. 'I was George's constituency assistant. I'm here to pick up any documents he may have left behind after . . .'

The girl's shoulder-length brown hair hadn't seen a salon for a while. She wore no make-up, a pair of jeans and a cable-knit sweater. A slim figure and large hazel eyes made her the perfect candidate for a make-over show.

'Terrible business,' I said, shaking my head.

'Yes.' Sally swallowed. 'Yes, it was.'

I picked up the biro and handed it over. She nodded gratefully and slipped it into her satchel.

'Didn't he leave everything to Amnesty?' she asked.

'Peter is still legally required to take an inventory.'

I had no idea whether this was correct. Thankfully Sally didn't seem to either.

'Actually, George mentioned Peter a couple of times,' she said. 'Doesn't he run Dairy Vale?' I nodded. 'And he's your boss?'

'In a manner of speaking. How long did you and George work together?'

'Almost five years.' Sally's chin wobbled. She pulled a pack of Kleenex from her jeans pocket. 'Sorry about this, but what they did to him was disgusting.'

'What who did?' I asked.

She dabbed her eyes. 'Whoever planted the disk.'

'What disk?'

'The child pornography files were on a disk drive in the toilet cistern. Didn't you know that?'

'To be honest, I didn't really follow the case,' I said. 'Why would anyone plant it?'

Sally tucked the used tissue up her sleeve. She sniffed a couple of times and pushed a rogue strand of hair behind her ear. 'George was doing a lot of work exposing corporate corruption. And believe me, the one thing you don't want to do in this country is cross the establishment. Then again, it might have been the bloody Tories, or even someone in the party. You wouldn't believe the jealousy in politics.'

'How would they have managed it?'

'I told George dozens of times he should get the lock changed. The one he had wouldn't stop anyone who knew what they were doing.'

'What about the coke?' I asked. 'Was that planted too?'

'No. That was his.'

'He told you?' She nodded. 'And you believed him?'

Judging by Sally's reaction, scepticism had crept into my voice.

'Why would he lie?' she asked with an edge to her own.

'Some things no one admits to.'

'George wasn't a paedophile, if that's what you're suggesting.'

'Are you sure?'

'Positive.'

Peter Timms had also been adamant his friend hadn't been sexually attracted to children. Then again, he'd been equally convinced the man wasn't into drugs. Who knows what's really going on with other people?

'Did George ever mention someone called Alexander Porteus?' I asked.

Sally pursed her lips and shook her head. 'Not that I recall. Who was he?'

'Someone he'd met recently.'

'You seem to know a lot about George.'

Her suspicion was understandable. As a result, I decided to pursue a risky and seldom-used strategy – the truth. 'Peter had a few concerns about how George died. He hired me to ask some questions. That's why I'm here.'

'You're a private detective?'

I nodded.

'What kind of questions?' Sally asked.

'Similar to your own,' I said. 'He didn't think George was the kind of guy who'd be into child porn. And he had a few other suspicions.'

'About what?'

'I'm afraid that's confidential,' I said, and moved the conversation forward. 'Did George seem at all agitated before he died?'

'He was under a fair bit of pressure. Which senior MP isn't?'

'Nothing unusual, though?'

'I don't think so. Was Alexander the new boyfriend?'

'George had a regular partner?'

'I don't know about regular, but I think he was seeing someone.'

'He didn't mention a name?'

Sally shook her head. 'George didn't talk much about his personal life.'

I glanced at my watch. The conversation wasn't going anywhere fast and I still needed to arrange some protection before the day got much older. 'God, is that the time?'

'Before you go, Kenny, there's something I wanted to ask.'

'What's that?'

'I haven't got anything to remember George by and he was so proud of his painting. I was wondering whether . . . well, I was wondering if it would be okay if I took the watercolour.'

I'd been surprised that Sally had jumped quite so high when I disturbed her. Now I knew why. The girl had been doing some pretexting of her own.

'Of course I'll send a cheque to Amnesty for whatever the estate thinks it's worth,' she continued. 'And if there's anyone else it's earmarked for, no problem.'

'Not that it's my decision, Sally,' I said, 'but I'm sure George would have wanted it to go to you. Just make sure you tuck it in your bag on the way out. Oh, and if anything else occurs . . .' I handed her my card.

'Actually, there is something,' she said.

'What's that?'

'Oh, nothing important. It's just that we went out one night and got on to regrets . . . You know how it is when you've had a few drinks.'

'Yeah,' I said. 'I know.'

'George said he did something at school he'd felt ashamed about all his life. I asked what it was but he wouldn't tell me. I don't suppose you know?'

'Maybe he raided the tuck shop.'

'It sounded a bit more significant than that.'

I shrugged and said, 'We've all got regrets, Sally.'

'Yes,' she said. 'I suppose we do.'

After departing Surrey House, I sat on one of the memorial benches by the mermaid fountain. Meeting Sally Thomas hadn't changed my mind about Dent's suicide, but it had raised a few questions. Had someone loathed him enough to plant the disk drive in the cistern? If so, then they must have had a bloody big grudge. I made a mental note to check with Odeerie whether the shadow minister had grievously pissed off anyone quite so influential.

The fat man had texted me a number for Simon Paxton, the boy who had organised the cemetery expedition in '79. I called it and was immediately connected to a machine: *This is Simon. I'm unable to speak right now* was the succinct message.

'Hi, Simon,' I said. 'My name's Kenny Gabriel. I was calling about George Dent's death. I'm not a reporter or affiliated with the press. Please call back, it's important.'

I repeated my number a couple of times and killed the call. The wind changed direction and I began to get some spatter from the mermaid. I transferred operations to a bench on the far side of the fountain.

Sitting beside me was a woman with a miniature poodle on her lap. A walking stick rested by her side, and she was swaddled in a tweed overcoat and matching hat. In her eighties, she looked like she was heading for her own memorial bench.

I accessed Baxter Construction's website on my phone. It had all the bells and whistles including hi-res photographs of completed projects from all over Europe. Demolition work had begun at a site south of Blackfriars Bridge. River Heights, an intelligent office and residential complex, was scheduled to open in 2023.

Blimp Baxter was pictured on site with his investors. He was six inches shorter than the other three men and considerably rounder. The face under the hard hat wore an avuncular grin although, if Blimp's reputation was to be believed, there wasn't much the developer would stop at to get his way. He had appeared in court twice accused of financial irregularity. Neither charge had stuck.

There had been rumours in the City that the River Heights project had put considerable strain on Blimp's cash reserves. They'd been denied but had not gone away. Had Blimp bitten off too much even for him to swallow?

Calling a number on a website and expecting to speak to a man worth £1.2 billion was a tad unrealistic. Instead I set myself the task of trying to reach Blimp's personal assistant. Ten minutes and five calls later, I had Daisy Cornwallis, his PA, on the line. 'How may I help you?' she asked in a Roedean accent.

'I'm trying to get a message to Henry Baxter,' I said.

'And your name is?'

'Kenny Gabriel.'

'Is Henry expecting your call?'

'Not that I'm aware.'

Daisy went into termination mode. 'Mr Baxter is tied up in meetings for the next few days,' she intoned. 'However, I'll let him know you called, Mr . . .'

'Gabriel,' I reminded her. 'And could you also let him know that I have some information about George Dent's death he might be interested in?'

'May I ask the nature of the information?' Daisy asked.

'I'm afraid that's confidential,' I said, then gave her my number and cut the call.

Whether either message would provoke a response remained to be seen. Meanwhile I had some personal protection to arrange.

I was about to head for the porter's lodge to drop off the key when the old lady spoke. 'Did you know George Dent?' she asked in a cut-glass treble.

'No,' I said. 'I'm doing some work on behalf of a friend of his.'

'You're aware of what they found in his flat?' I nodded. She held the dog's head between gloved hands and stared into his brown eyes. 'They should cut the balls off nonces, shouldn't they, Alfie?'

'Woof, woof,' Alfie agreed.

FIVE

Forty years ago I arrived in Soho after a sharp disagreement with my parents as to whether I should attend the University of Durham or the University of Life. I paid the rent on my Berwick Street flat-share by doing a variety of jobs until the agency sent me to a place called the Galaxy on Frith Street. The doorman-cum-chauffeur in the club was a guy called Farrelly. A couple of years older than me, Farrelly radiated menace like a five-foot-nine-inch isotope of unadulterated rage.

My time at the Galaxy ended when I discovered Farrelly yanking a barman's teeth. Last year I witnessed him torture someone with a car battery and bite a man's ear off during a scrap. Age had not withered Farrelly, nor custom staled his infinite variety.

Despite this we had parted on reasonable terms. I knew Farrelly was focusing his attentions on a gym he owned in Bethnal Green. I also knew that, as a sideline, he offered a personal protection service. Bearing in mind my problem with a member of what the *Standard* had referred to as 'the most brutal gangland family since the Richardsons', I thought it might be worthwhile renewing our acquaintance.

Farrelly had called his gym Farrelly's Gym. The plastic sign hung over the entrance door of a deconsecrated church. The typeface was sturdy and even the apostrophe looked as though it had been working out. On the outside, it didn't seem like the kind of place where stressed execs consulted their Fitbits every two minutes while wheezing along on digitised treadmills. It didn't seem like that on the inside either.

'You a member?' the guy behind the counter asked.

'Actually, I'm here to meet a friend,' I said.

'No entry unless you're a member.'

'When I said friend, I meant owner.'

The guy probably lived on steroid sandwiches and protein shakes. They'd done wonders for his biceps but not his complexion. Each cheek was acne-ravaged and a pimple on his forehead was on the brink of eruption.

'Through there,' he said, and jerked a thumb the size of a carrot towards the door to his left. 'But you'd better not be pissing me around.'

◆ ◆ ◆

The wall by the entrance was covered in mirrors. Three guys were methodically pumping barbells while gazing at their reflections. A fourth, in a Lycra bodysuit, was lying on a bench straining to raise a heavily weighted bar. The guy standing directly behind him was shouting something that sounded like 'Juju can, Phil. Juju can.'

In the centre of the room were several yellow-painted weight machines. Most were being used by men who may not have been as large as Mr Zit, but who weren't in danger of fading away either. A lissome girl in her twenties alternately punched and kicked a heavy bag. Each decent connection brought forth a satisfied grunt.

At the far end of the room was a stained-glass window. It depicted a heavily bearded Christ wearing a damask robe. In one hand Jesus held a shepherd's crook. Cradled in the opposite arm was an adoring lamb. Above him was a blue sky out of which shone a perfect yellow sun. At least, it would have been perfect had several pieces of glass not fallen from their frames.

Christ was looking downwards at a raised dais. Presumably this was where the altar would have been when the congregants were focused more on matters spiritual than martial. Now the Son of God beheld a roped-off ring in which a pair of men in gloves and headgear were busy thumping the crap out of each other.

Supervising the sparring session was the (not so) Reverend Farrelly.

◆　◆　◆

Back in the day, Farrelly had worn straight-leg Levi's, oxblood DMs and a black T-shirt. Not much had changed. His head had been shaven then. It was shaven now. The muscles in his forearms were coiled together like mating snakes. His gnarled hands looked as though they'd been marinated in vinegar. The imp of death was leaning on the ropes, watching the fighters dance around each other. Judging by the scowl, he wasn't pleased.

I mounted the dais and stood beside him. 'Nice place, Farrelly,' I said.

'Fuck do you want?' he replied.

'Could we have a word in private?'

'Use your jab, Gary. How many times do I have to tell you?' Farrelly shook his head more in anger than in sorrow. From the way he attempted to catch his partner with a series of straight lefts, I assumed Gary was wearing the blue head guard. Not a single punch connected. His coach spat on the floor. 'This *is* private,' he said to me. 'Get on with it.'

'Do you still provide personal protection?' Farrelly nodded. 'Well, I think I might want to hire someone.'

'Who needs protecting?'

'I do.'

'Who from?'

'The husband of one of our clients. He's already beaten up my business partner. Now I think he might be coming after me.'

'Better, Gary. Much better,' Farrelly shouted into the ring. 'Keep moving your feet. Don't let Sammy crowd you in the bleedin' corner.' There followed a further twenty seconds of exchanges before he spoke again. 'How long?'

'I don't know. A week? Maybe two?'

'Twenty-four hours a day?'

'Probably.'

'Week's gonna be five grand.'

'There's no way I can afford that.'

'Better fuck off, then.'

Farrelly wasn't a natural negotiator. People either accepted his initial offer or suffered the consequences. The fuck-off option might also briefly be on the table. Before I could respond, there was a crash behind us.

'Christ's sake,' Farrelly muttered.

A guy had lifted a large disc off a machine and dropped it on the floor. Judging by the way he was loading an even larger weight, he didn't intend to replace the first one on the rack.

'Take a break,' Farrelly instructed the boxers.

He left ringside and walked across the floor of the gym. One by one, the other members stopped working out. The guy who had dropped the weight had settled on to the saddle of the machine and placed his hands on its horizontal bar.

'Get up,' Farrelly told him.

'What?' the guy said.

'You heard me.'

The bloke wasn't quite as large as Mr Zit, but he had several inches on Farrelly. He positively towered over him. At a push, I'd have said he was six-four and eighteen stone. He dismounted the machine.

'Can you read?' Farrelly asked.

'Can I what?'

'Read,' Farrelly repeated. 'Can you read the English language?'

'Yeah,' the guy grunted. 'I can read.'

'Tell me what that says.' Farrelly pointed to a sign on the wall: ALL WEIGHTS MUST BE REPLACED IMMEDIATELY AFTER USE.

The guy shrugged and said, 'I'll do it when I've finished.'

'You'll do it now,' Farrelly told him.

The guy looked down at a forty-five-degree angle.

'I said I'd do it later, granddad.'

'Now,' Farrelly insisted.

The shoulders in the big guy's neck tensed. 'If you want the weight back on the rack, you're gonna have to put it there yourself,' he said.

Every pair of eyes in the gym, including those of Christ and the black-faced lamb, was focused on the two men. What happened next amazed me.

Farrelly backed down.

'Fair enough,' he said, and picked the weight up.

The thick metal disc was the circumference of a bicycle wheel. Farrelly held it chest-high with both hands. He smiled at the guy. The guy smiled at him.

The weight slipped from Farrelly's grasp.

No matter how butch you are, having twenty kilos of steel fall directly on your toes is going to be mortal fucking agony. The guy's screams echoed around the vaulted roof of the gym. He fell to the floor and attempted to grab his crushed foot.

Farrelly calmly replaced the weight on the rack. His victim's screams morphed into sobs. Three of the other members gathered around him. Unless they had a syringe of morphine handy, there probably wasn't much they could do to help.

'Tell Carlos someone's had an accident,' Farrelly told a man who'd been training on a leg press. 'He's gonna need an ambulance.'

The bloke nodded and left via the door I had arrived through.

Farrelly stepped back on to the dais looking no more concerned than if he'd just broken off our conversation to take a piss. 'You still here?' he asked.

'I can't get near five grand, Farrelly. Is there no one else you can recommend? Not as good, obviously, but, you know . . . cheaper.'

Farrelly looked at me intently and sniffed a couple of times. He transferred his gaze to the fighters. The guy in the red helmet was drinking from a taped bottle. His partner had removed his gloves and was adjusting his shorts.

'How much you got?' Farrelly asked.

'Maybe a grand.'

'Gary, over here a minute.'

The fighter in the blue head guard crossed the ring. There was something familiar about his eyes but I couldn't work out what it was.

'This geezer's called Kenny Gabriel,' Farrelly said. 'He's a private detective and he needs a bit of protecting, which ain't no surprise.'

'Pleased to meet you, Mr Gabriel,' the guy said, his voice muffled by the helmet.

'Call me Kenny,' I said to him.

'Now, I know you ain't done this kinda work before, Gary, but it's two months 'til you fight again, so there's no reason you shouldn't earn yourself a few bob.'

'You said I needed to put the hours in.'

'I know what I said,' Farrelly replied. 'But it's only a week and you've got ages to get ready for Saunders. This might not be a bad idea.'

'Whatever you think's right,' the guy said, and removed his helmet.

Forty years fell away in a moment.

SIX

The kid in the helmet was the spit of Farrelly. Not the Farrelly who ran a gym in Bethnal Green in 2016, but the Farrelly who had stood on the door of the Galaxy Club at the arse end of the seventies. His eyes were the same intense cobalt-blue. His hair was in a crew cut. His nose had a bump in the bridge. The vein in his left temple stood out in the same way Farrelly's had when I'd first been introduced to him. Was the guy part of a military experiment? I imagined a platoon of Farrellys yomping across the desert chanting *What's your fucking problem?* and *You're gonna get a twatting*.

'Are you feeling all right?' Farrelly 2.0 asked me.

'Just a bit dizzy,' I said. 'I'll be fine in a minute.'

'Would you like a glass of water?'

'No, thanks. It's passing.'

Indeed, reality was beginning to reassert itself. The only glass that the seventies Farrelly had ever offered anyone was directly to the face. If there was a doctor turning out cloned versions, he hadn't got the formula quite right. As my head cleared, I also realised that Code Name: Gary was five inches taller than his lookalike.

'How about a cuppa?' he suggested. 'Carlos could make you one and stick a couple of sugars in it. Probably dig up a couple of biscuits too.'

Another thing distinguishing Code Name: Gary from the imp of death was his accent. Farrelly sounded like Bill Sikes might have done if he'd been a bit more cockney. Gary was more Thames Estuary than Limehouse Basin.

'Are you two related?' I asked.

'He's my dad,' Gary said. 'We met for the first time last year.'

'Did you know you had a son?' I asked Farrelly.

He shook his head. 'Gary's mum weren't too keen on me meeting him.'

This would have put her in the wise-woman category had she not been insane enough to mingle fluids with Farrelly in the first place.

'When d'you want Gary to start?' he asked.

'Immediately.'

'You mean tomorrow?'

'Right now, if possible.'

Farrelly gave me a sideways look. I'd deliberately withheld Billy Dylan's name in case it pushed up the daily rate. I was about to confess the reason for urgency when Farrelly said, 'He'll need a couple of hours.'

'How about we meet in the Vesuvius?' I suggested.

'That spieler in Greek Street? Thought it closed down.'

'The new owner kept it open.'

'Why did he do that?'

'Because the V is a place of great cultural significance.'

'It's a shithole.'

'Can't it be both?' I asked.

Due to rush-hour traffic it took an hour to get from Bethnal Green to Greek Street. In the back of the cab, I conducted some research on Alexander Louis Porteus. According to Wikipedia, he had been booted out of Harrow at the age of fifteen for drinking and moral turpitude. He must have been a bright bugger as he'd still made it to Oxford.

Shortly after Porteus's graduation, his father died in a road crash and the young Alexander inherited a fortune. He spent a few years in the Alps, but worsening asthma put an end to his mountaineering exploits. Back in London, a brush with spiritualism led to a wider interest in the occult. So much so that, by the late twenties, Porteus had his own church near Broadstairs called the Temple of Selene.

The main tenet of the church had been *to thyne own selfe be trewe.* This was largely interpreted as do a shitload of drugs and bang anything that moves. Many of the disciples were third-tier bohemians and artists, and Porteus became a face in Soho. He bought a house in Dean Street and opened the bookshop in Cecil Court. The former was allegedly used for orgies, the latter raided several times by the authorities.

And so it continued for most of the thirties and forties, during which time Porteus wrote several books on Magick, as he insisted on calling it. The most notorious was a novel titled *The White Tower*, which many scholars considered to be an alchemical treatise on the pursuit of immortality. It was rumoured that *The White Tower* was the book Jim Morrison had been reading at the time of his death. Hand in hand with this rumour was the one that Morrison wasn't actually dead at all.

Thickening the conspiracy stew was the fact that *The White Tower* had been privately published in Paris shortly before Porteus allegedly pegged it from cancer in 1947. That it bore the name William Gifford made no difference. Porteus was wanted by the authorities on a number of charges, and had been keen to remain anonymous.

Photographs accompanied the Wikipedia entry. Two were of Porteus dressed in the robes of the Temple of Selene. They made him look a little camp, as though he were a minor character in a Gilbert and Sullivan production. The third shot was of a different order. It had been taken late in Porteus's life, when his hair had gone and his face had become a fleshy ovoid. His eyebrows had run riot and his ears looked as though they had been inflated and might explode at any moment.

All of which should have made Porteus look like what he was – a silly old duffer high on smack and his own self-regard. Lending the image a chilling aspect was a pair of hypnotic eyes that seemed to leer through the screen on my phone. When the cabbie pulled to a halt on Greek Street and announced that I owed him forty-six quid, I felt as though it had only been a couple of minutes since we'd left the gym.

◆　◆　◆

An Italian expat called Jack Rigatelli opened the Vesuvius club in 1968. Housed in a cellar, the club provided a bolthole for like-minded members to play cards until the early hours. Last year Jack Rig suffered a fatal heart attack. His brother, Antonio, had been intent on selling the building, but had since opted for the rental income from companies prepared to pay through the nose for a Soho address.

The V's ceiling is heavily stained from fifty years of fag smoke and the wall-mounted TV is old enough to be in the Science Museum. On a corkboard behind the bar are postcards from members on holiday in places as diverse as Florida and Fleetwood. Next to it is a jar of pickled eggs that predates decimalisation.

I ordered a whisky and ginger ale from Whispering Nick. 'ON THE SLATE?' he asked after sliding the tumbler across the Formica surface.

'Thanks, Nick. What's the damage now?'

'HUNDRED　AND　TWENTY-EIGHT　POUNDS, THIRTY-FOUR.'

A virus ruined Nick's voice box when he was a kid. His hoarse croak is only audible in a quiet room. Any background noise and he needs his halter mic and speaker. As usual, the volume was cranked up to 11.

'I'll clear it soon, mate,' I promised.

'DON'T BOTHER ME NONE. I'VE GOTTA NEW JOB.'

'Congratulations,' I said. 'What is it?'

'BINGO CALLER.' A rasping sound emerged from Nick's speaker, along with a couple of feedback shrieks. 'YOU GOTTA LAUGH, AINTCHA, KENNY?' he asked before scooping up the box and heading towards his next customer.

I occupied a table and thought about life. I was in my late fifties and had less money in the bank than the average twelve-year-old. Last October the manager of the V had invited me to move to Manchester with her. For several months, Stephie and I had been friends with benefits. She was sexy, intelligent, funny and kind. Only an idiot would have allowed a final chance for happiness to slip through his fingers, which is precisely what I did.

Stephie hadn't called since she left. But then, why would she? A few times I'd picked the phone up; each time I'd lost my nerve. It wasn't the sex I missed so much – although I did miss the sex – as the advice. Stephie called it how she saw it and usually she called it right. What with the Dylans breathing down my neck, I could have used her input.

Gary Farrelly walked into the Vesuvius with a nylon rucksack over his shoulder. 'Sorry I'm late, Kenny,' he said.

'Don't be,' I replied. 'What d'you want to drink?'

'What's that?'

'It's a waga.'

'A what?'

'Whisky and ginger ale.'

'I'll have one of those,' he decided. 'Only without the whisky.'

A whiskyless waga didn't sound much fun, but Gary was probably in training. I returned from the bar to find him gazing around the room.

'Do you come here a lot?' he asked.

'Not as often as I used to,' I said.

'Is it a members' club?'

'After a fashion.'

He gave the V another quick once-over to see if there had been something he'd missed. His perplexed expression suggested not.

'Look, Gary,' I said, changing the subject. 'There's something you need to know about the man I need protecting from.'

'Dad said it was a jealous ex-husband.'

'The husband is Billy Dylan.'

'Should I know him?'

'Basically he's a gangster. His dad's doing time for the Haddon Street robbery and Billy served six months for aggravated assault last year.'

Gary nodded as though digesting this information.

'He also beat the shit out of my business partner,' I added, giving him something else to chew on. 'And he doesn't work alone.'

'Does my old man know about this?' Billy asked.

'I think he probably should.'

'Why's that?'

'No offence, but Farrelly said that you haven't done this kind of work before.'

'It's nothing I can't handle.'

'Maybe,' I replied. 'But shouldn't that be your dad's call?'

I'd avoided bringing Billy's name into proceedings in the gym in case it elevated Farrelly's fee. Conscience had got the better of me.

Gary took a sip of ginger ale. 'I'm a karate black belt and I've worked doors since I was eighteen, if it's experience you're worried about.'

'Did Farrelly find you, or did you find him?' I asked.

'Me him.'

'Must have been a hell of a shock.'

'Yeah, he wasn't expecting to see me.'

I'd meant the other way round, but let it go. After finishing our drinks and saying goodbye to Nick, we left the Vesuvius and headed

west. I used the fifteen-minute walk to extract further biographi-
cal information. Of particular interest was the union between Gary's
mother and father. 'Where did they meet?' was my first question.

'Speed dating,' he said.

'Farrelly went speed dating?'

'So my mum reckons.'

'How long were they together?'

'Only a couple of months. Some bloke asked Mum what she was
doing with an old fart and that if she wanted a decent shag she should
go home with him.'

'And then what happened?'

'Dad ruptured the guy's spleen.'

Thank God Farrelly's isn't the finger on the nuclear trigger. A minor
dispute over fishing quotas and half of Spain would be vaporised. 'So
that was the end of the relationship?' I asked as we rounded the corner
into Brewer Street.

'Yeah, although Mum didn't know she was pregnant.'

'Has she met anyone since?'

'There's been a few boyfriends, but no one's gone the distance.'

'What made you want to track your dad down, Gary?'

'I was thinking of joining the army. If anything happened then I'd
never have known my old man, and he wouldn't have known me. Didn't
seem right somehow.'

'Was your mum okay with the two of you meeting?'

Gary shrugged. 'She came round eventually.'

A significant chunk of Odeerie's business comes from clients wanting to trace their birth parents. I often wondered if they were doing the
right thing. It seemed to have worked out for Gary, though, and I put
this to him.

'Yeah, it's been great,' he said, although the loss of eye contact was
interesting. 'You got kids, Kenny?' I shook my head. 'Married, anything
like that?'

'Nothing like that.'

We walked in contemplative silence until outside the Yip Hing supermarket. 'Mind if I nip in here?' Gary asked. 'I need skimmed milk for my protein shake.'

'Course not,' I said. 'I'll go ahead and stick the kettle on.'

'Can't allow you out of sight, Kenny.'

'Yeah, I get the need for eternal vigilance, Gary, but we're in the middle of the West End and my flat's only fifty yards up this extremely busy road.'

My bodyguard frowned before saying, 'The milk can wait 'til tomorrow.'

'For God's sake, get it now.'

'All right,' he said reluctantly. 'But keep your eye out.'

It was getting on for ten o'clock and there was quite a bit of activity in Brewer Street. A gaggle of Japanese tourists were photographing the exterior of the Glasshouse Stores pub and a stag do wearing T-shirts featuring pictures of the groom was careering towards Regent Street. Pretty much business as usual. I turned the key in the lock. Immediately someone bundled me from behind into the lobby. I sprawled on the floor with the wind knocked out of me. The door closed and I heard a chuckle.

'Hello, Kenny. We've been waiting for you.'

◆　◆　◆

I recognised the first guy as the driver who had dropped Billy Dylan off at his mistress's house. A Crombie overcoat disguised his bulky torso, although it looked incongruous paired with mauve tracksuit bottoms and immaculate white trainers.

His companion was wearing one of those Three Musketeers moustaches that should be made illegal and a plaid shirt. He was smaller than Baldy, but there wasn't much in it.

'I don't know who you think I am, but my name isn't Kenny,' I said.

'Who are you, then?' Baldy asked.

'Raymond Carver' was the first name into my head.

'The author of *What We Talk About When We Talk About Love*?'

'Er, no, a different Raymond Carver.'

'Let me help you, Ray.' Baldy put his hands on my lapels and pulled me up as though I were a rag doll. 'Nah, I reckon you're telling me fibs,' he said, squinting at my face in the low-wattage light. 'You're Kenny Gabriel and we're taking you for a little ride, ain't we, Steve?'

'Where to?' I asked, fear blossoming in my stomach.

'To see our guvnor,' Steve said. 'He wants a word.'

Baldy chuckled again. 'Although that might not be all he wants.'

'Are you the people who beat Odeerie up?' I asked.

'The fat coon?' Steve said. 'Yeah, that was us.'

'And your boss is Billy Dylan?'

Before Baldy or Steve could answer, there was a knock on the door.

'Whoever it is, tell 'em to piss off, Steve,' Baldy instructed his colleague, before saying to me, 'One word from you and . . .'

The knife was four inches long with serrated teeth along its upper edge. The fear in my stomach migrated to my bowels. Steve opened the door a few inches and put his face to the gap. He turned to us with a puzzled expression.

'There's no one there, Lance.'

The door catapulted inwards, delivering a concussive blow to Steve's head. He fell to the floor. Gary stepped over him into the lobby. Baldy pushed me aside and brandished the knife. Gary reached into his jacket and brought out a short black tube. He pressed a catch and two feet of steel shot out.

The two men faced off. Baldy slashed the air. Gary bobbed back. The second time Baldy attempted the manoeuvre, Gary brought the baton down on his shoulder. The knife fell from his hand. I kicked it to the other side of the lobby. Baldy took a deep breath, extended his arms and gestured. 'Come on, cunt, let's go.'

Gary took two steps in and swung. Baldy ducked. The baton struck the wall, releasing a puff of plaster. Baldy lunged into Gary and threw his arms around him. They careered across the tiled floor and slammed into the opposite wall. The baton clattered to the ground. Baldy had Gary in a full bear hug.

I picked up the baton and smacked it across Baldy's calves. He screamed, released Gary, and turned on me. I had a weighty steel rod in my hand. Baldy had a lifetime of gratuitous violence on his CV. There was only ever going to be one winner.

'Let's get out of here, Lance.' Steve was more or less back on his feet. 'Someone's bound to have called the cops.'

Baldy looked at me as though he would have loved to grab the baton and stick it where the sun didn't shine. He pointed and said a single word.

'Later.'

He retrieved his knife and followed Steve through the door. Gary had his hands on his thighs and was attempting to get his wind back.

'Are . . . you . . . okay, Kenny?' he asked. I nodded. 'Should . . . we call the police?'

'No point,' I said. 'How are you feeling?'

'I'm . . . fine,' he said, straightening up.

'How did you know what was going on?'

'I saw them follow you in.'

'Look, Gary, let's call it quits. Billy Dylan's got a small army behind him. You're just one man. Farrelly won't think any the less of you.'

Gary picked up the baton and compressed the steel rod back into the handle with extra emphasis.

'I want to carry on,' he said.

If it weren't for my brother, I'd have to live slightly more out of town than Soho. Somewhere like Dungeness or Whitby. A few years ago his company bought a flat in Brewer Street as a place for visiting clients to stay. Most opted for a decent hotel.

It's fair to say that I haven't stamped my personality on the place. The walls are utility-cream and the furniture looks as though an over-worked PA chose it from an online catalogue. The sofa and armchairs in the sitting room are charcoal polyester, and the dining table has been lovingly carved from a chunk of balsa wood. Throw in four blokes playing cards in their pants and you'd have the perfect safe house.

Gary dumped his bag in the spare room and declined a shot of Highland Monarch Scotch in favour of getting his head down. Competitively priced at £9.99 a bottle, the Monarch doesn't win many blind tastings, so he had probably made the sensible choice. Ten minutes later I could hear snoring from behind his door.

Sleep came less easily to me. A surfeit of adrenaline had much to do with this, although, as usual, the slideshow on the bedroom ceiling was the real culprit.

I watched the years churn over, from the day I arrived in Soho as an eighteen-year-old kid eager for the big adventure to the point when it became apparent that the Road of Excess was scheduled to bypass the Palace of Wisdom.

Opportunities were squandered through arrogance, indolence, fear and frequently a combination of all three. At least I could rerun the slideshow to work out exactly what went wrong and how I could have made infinitely better choices.

Which is pretty much what I did for the next two hours.

SEVEN

I awoke at 7 a.m. and heard a series of grunts and groans coming from somewhere in the flat. Grabbing a pool cue, I went to investigate whatever was happening in the sitting room. I tightened my grasp on the cue and flung the door open. My guest/bodyguard was wearing shorts and a singlet, and knocking out press-ups at a tidy rate. 'Morning, Gary,' I said. 'How did you sleep?'

'Pretty good.' He bobbed up and down another half-dozen times before discontinuing his routine. 'What are you doing with that?'

'Oh, you know, just tidying up a bit.'

'Right.'

'Been awake long?'

'Since five thirty. I went for a run.'

'You ought to have woken me up. I could have joined you.'

'Really?'

'No. Not really.'

Gary mopped his head with a towel. 'What are we doing today?' he asked.

'Seeing my business partner first.'

'To talk about what happened last night?'

'And a few other matters.'

'Actually, I was thinking about that. Billy Dylan blames you for his marriage going tits-up, right?' he asked.

'That's right.'

'What if you persuaded his missus to go back to him?'

'She's in hiding.'

'Isn't that what you do? Find people who've done a runner?'

Which of course was true. It's virtually impossible to disappear without trace in this day and age, particularly with someone like Odeerie on your trail. The fat man usually plays by the rules, but is prepared to go off-piste if all else fails.

'Congratulations, Gary, you're employee of the month.'

'What does that mean?' he asked

'You get to make the coffee,' I said.

Soho used to be a ghost town at eight in the morning. These days it's swarming with millennials marching towards boutique marketing agencies. Occasionally I wonder what advice I'd give my teenage self should I meet him on Wardour Street. Probably nothing that would do any good. Determinists maintain that everything in life is nailed on. It makes for both a depressing thought and a decent excuse.

This philosophical conundrum occupied my thoughts on the way to Odeerie's. I also pondered how likely it was that I'd convince Cheryl Dylan to return to her husband. By the time we arrived at Albion Mansions, my optimism had waned. Billy wasn't the kind of guy to forgive and forget easily, a fact of which Cheryl was presumably aware. Odeerie answered the intercom and buzzed us in. When he came to the door, I couldn't help but react in the traditional manner.

'Fuck me!'

'It's not as bad as it looks,' he said.

'Thank God for that.'

The left eye had closed entirely, its lid purple and grotesquely swollen. The left orbit was badly bruised but still operational. Odeerie's nose had never been a thing of beauty. Now it was in danger of touching his ears. He ushered us into the office. I introduced Gary and covered off the previous night's events.

'Maybe it's time to go to the police,' Odeerie said.

'Won't make any difference,' I said. 'If the Dylans want you, they get you.'

Odeerie didn't dispute the point.

'Anyway, I've got a plan,' I continued. 'Well, it's Gary's plan, actually.'

'Go on . . .'

'We find Cheryl Dylan and persuade her to give the marriage a second chance.'

Odeerie's good eye opened a little wider. 'That's it?' he said. 'That's your plan?'

'Can you think of a better one?' I asked.

The fat man looked sheepish, as well he might. Yesterday it had been a matter of *if* Billy Dylan got to me. Today it was more a question of *when and how*.

'Not right now,' he said, and changed the subject. 'I had a go at the names you gave me. Nothing on Ray Clarke, but quite a bit about Creighton-Smith.' Odeerie referred to a notepad. 'He went to Sandhurst and served with the Blues and Royals for twelve years. After that he joined his father's financial consultancy. That was all good until it was busted for insider trading. Will got off with a suspended sentence, but his old man did four years. The family became bankrupt and had to sell their home in Richmond. Things get a bit sketchy after that.

'Creighton-Smith set up a security company with an old army pal. That went west after two years. He definitely worked for a Chelsea letting agency for a while, and he was in Gibraltar for three years after the crash, although I don't know what he was doing. Currently he's a salesman for a classic-car company based in Mayfair.'

'How did you find all that out?' Gary asked, clearly impressed.

'By knowing where to look,' Odeerie snapped. He wasn't big on giving away secrets of the guild, particularly to people he'd only just met. Gary maintained steady eye contact with him for a few seconds. The fat man looked away first.

'But nothing on Ray Clarke?' I asked.

'He's on the electoral roll as living in Wapping until eight years ago. After that he disappears without trace.'

'Could he be dead?' Gary asked.

'No certificate.'

'Emigrated?'

'If he has then we're shit out of luck.'

'Why d'you want to find these men?'

'I'll tell you later,' I said. Odeerie pursed his lips disapprovingly. 'What's the name of the car dealership?' I asked.

'Mountjoy Classics. Take a look.'

Mountjoy's website showed a range of gleaming cars on plinths in what resembled an art gallery. There was a lot of verbiage about timeless elegance, beauty and craftsmanship. Odeerie clicked on the *Our People* tab. Up came five faces. Will Creighton-Smith's was last.

Mountjoy's senior sales consultant had a receding hairline. A double chin hung over his regimental tie and the bags under his eyes looked as though they had been properly earned. Despite this, there was a rakish charm to the photograph that might carry the day for women of a certain postcode.

'Have you got a home address?' I asked.

Odeerie shook his head. 'I can keep looking if you like.'

'Don't bother. Spend a bit more time on Ray Clarke. If that doesn't work out, start looking for Cheryl Dylan. She's the priority now.'

Odeerie snapped out an ironic salute.

'Is there anything I can do?' Gary asked.

'Have you heard of pretexting?'

He hadn't, and I gave him a brief overview.

'Basically it's lying, then?' he said.

'Only if actors are liars.'

'Why are you telling me all this, Kenny?'

'I'd like you to make a call on my behalf.'

'What sort of call?'

I explained what I was after and what it would involve. Gary had his reservations, although I expected they could be overcome.

It took less than two minutes.

◆　◆　◆

Mountjoy Cars' frontage comprised thirty yards of plate glass with the company's logo etched into it. Inside, the showroom was as bright as an operating theatre. The black-and-white-tiled floor looked clean enough to eat your lunch off. A guy in blue overalls was polishing the windscreen on what might have been a Ferrari. One punter was contemplating a yellow car so low it couldn't have been more than three foot off the ground. Useless for towing a caravan but that probably wasn't top of his wish list.

In the middle of the showroom was a desk, and behind it was a woman in her early thirties. She looked like the human incarnation of the cars: curvy, sleek, classy and expensive. Glossy dark hair framed angular cheekbones. Perfect lipstick might have been applied with a miniature spray gun. 'May I help you, gentlemen?' she asked.

'My assistant called earlier,' I said. 'I have an appointment with Will.'

'And your name is?'

'Malcolm Gabriel.'

The woman consulted a laptop. 'Ah, yes,' she said. 'Will's in the back office. If you and your friend would like to take a seat.'

'He's not my friend, he's my employee,' I said.

The girl reddened. 'Yes, of course,' she said. 'Would either of you like a drink?'

'No,' I said. 'And we don't have all day.'

'In that case, if you could just excuse me for a moment.'

The woman – Caroline, according to her badge – left the desk and sashayed across the showroom on three-inch heels. Gary's eyes followed her every step of the way.

'Was that really necessary?' he asked.

'I'm the CEO of a major ad agency. It goes with the territory.'

Before Gary could comment further, Will Creighton-Smith entered the showroom. An inch or so over six foot, he was wearing a grey suit that had been bought in physically leaner times. The face was grog-blossom pink and the moustache drooped slightly. His hair had thinned out quite a bit since the website photograph.

'Mr Gabriel?' he said. 'Will Creighton-Smith. Pleased to meet you.'

Doubtless Will had googled me. Malcolm and I share a similar build and there's a strong family resemblance. Okay, he looks tanned and distinguished whereas I appear gaunt and desperate, but I had an explanation for that.

'How can I help, Mr Gabriel?' Will asked after shaking hands.

'I'm interested in buying a car.'

'Well, you're in the right place, sport.' Will treated me to a genial chuckle. I parried it with a stony face. 'I'm assuming you're a classic fan,' he continued hastily.

'Not really,' I said. 'I recovered from a serious illness recently. During my convalescence I decided to stop working so hard and have some fun in life. No point in having a fortune in the bank otherwise.'

'Absolutely not,' Will concurred.

'Usually I drive a Volvo but my wife suggested that I treat myself to something more exotic. All the new sports cars I've seen look terribly vulgar.'

Will nodded as though he'd never heard a truer word.

'So that's what led me here today,' I concluded. 'I'm assuming you can help.'

'Delighted, Mr Gabriel.'

'Do call me Malcolm.'

'Delighted, Malcolm. Anything particular in mind?'

'Whatever takes my fancy.'

'Budget?'

I shrugged to suggest that money was almost as vulgar as the modern sports car. Will looked up at the ceiling. I wondered if he were mouthing a silent prayer to whichever automotive god had delivered me to him.

'Perhaps we should look round and see what takes your fancy,' he suggested.

'That sounds an excellent idea,' I told him.

◆ ◆ ◆

There are times when I envy the boys in blue. If you're Inspector Knacker then all you need to do is wave your warrant card under someone's nose and start straight in with your questions. We in the private sector don't have the same luxury. This means that two options present: tell the truth or lie like a bastard.

Mostly I stick to the truth, because people don't mind telling you the last time they saw the woman at number 48 go for a jog. Occasionally it becomes necessary to be more creative with the facts, and sometimes you need to dispense with them entirely.

I'd chosen this option with Will Creighton-Smith as I hadn't fancied walking straight up to the guy and asking whether he'd seen the ghost of a magician that had been bothering a couple of blokes he hadn't seen for the best part of forty years, one of whom was a dead paedophile. At some stage I would have to broach the subject. As we navigated the showroom, I tried to think about how best to do that.

The problem with pretending to be a multi-millionaire interested in buying a six-figure motor is that people tend to become miffed when it transpires you're no such thing.

'And there we have it,' Will said as we stood in front of the only car I could have identified on sight. 'The E-Type's a beautiful old girl who's quintessentially British, wonderfully stylish and a joy to drive. Ticks all the boxes, doesn't she, Malcolm?'

There was a note of desperation in Will's voice. I'd knocked him back on a Porsche, a Lamborghini, two Aston Martins and a Cadillac Eldorado. Time was running out for both of us.

'And Jags represent a pukka investment,' he continued. 'Unlike some of the other cars, they're constantly in demand on both sides of the pond. I don't think she'll be on the floor much longer, so you'd have to decide pretty quickly.'

'It's certainly a wonderful-looking car . . .' I said.

I was pondering what the hell my next move was going to be, when Will frowned and bent over the car's bonnet. The frown hardened into a grimace. He straightened up and shouted to the guy in the overalls, 'Arnold, over here. Now.'

The guy in the blue overalls had been rubbing a cloth over the rear window of a car twenty yards away. He stuffed it into his pocket and trotted over. In his sixties, Arnold was about five foot four with a three-strand comb-over and a chapped nose. 'Can I help, Mr Creighton-Smith?' he asked in a congested tone.

'Tell me what that is,' Will said.

As Arnold examined the car, its gleaming paintwork reflected his features like a distorting mirror. 'Erm, I'm afraid I can't quite see what you mean . . .' he said.

Nor could I. The finish was flawless. Will sighed and shook his head as though Arnold tested his patience on a regular basis. 'For God's sake, man, you aren't required to do much round here,' he barked. 'Is it too much to ask that you don't leave your fingerprints all over the damn cars?'

'I really can't—' Arnold began to say.

Will whipped the cloth out of Arnold's overall and used it to dab at a portion of the Jag that looked every bit as pristine as the rest of the Jag. He thrust it back at him.

'I'm sick of doing your damn job for you,' he said, sounding like an enraged sergeant major. 'Shape up or ship out. Understand?'

'Sorry, Mr Creighton-Smith, but I . . .'

'I said, do you understand?'

Arnold twisted the cloth in his hands and nodded.

'Good,' Will said. 'Now make yourself scarce and don't let me find any more of your snotty paw prints on anything.'

Arnold departed. Will sloughed off the bollocky demeanour he had deployed on him in favour of the unctuous demeanour he reserved for me.

'Sorry about that, Malcolm,' he said. 'Don't know why we keep the idiot on.'

The first rule of pretexting is to stay in character. 'Absolutely no need to apologise, Will,' I replied. 'When people need to be told, they need to be told.'

'My philosophy exactly,' he said, and smirked.

'But you were filling me in about the car . . .'

'Indeed I was.' Will gathered his thoughts. 'Despite her age, the old girl's got some poke,' he said. 'There's a three-point-eight-litre engine in there with two-hundred-and-sixty-five brake horsepower. Get her on a decent stretch and she'll nudge one-fifty. Not that a law-abiding chap like your good self would ever dream of breaking the limit.'

I managed a thin smile.

'But don't take my word for it,' Will continued. 'Go for a test drive.'

Over Will's shoulder I could see Arnold furiously polishing a radiator grille. The lock of detached hair quivered like a straw in the breeze.

'That would be a great idea,' I said.

EIGHT

Will led me to the desk – the gorgeous Caroline had not returned – removed a sheet of paper and laid it before me. 'Just need a few details, Malcolm. Can't let you take quarter of a million quid on the road without knowing your postcode.'

I have an eidetic memory. What goes into my head stays in my head. Usually this puts me ahead of the game, although I've seen a couple of things over the years that I wouldn't mind forgetting. As far as Will was concerned, it meant that I could furnish my brother's details, including: DOB, home address, and both personal and business numbers. Where I came up short was on the driving licence.

'Damn, I've left my wallet in the office.'

'No problem. We don't charge for a test drive, Malcolm.'

Having been franchised to use my first name, Will intended to make full use of it. The high-beam smile was also on permanent duty.

Shame, as I was about to spoil the party.

'My licence is in it.'

A cloud passed over Will's personal sun. 'You really don't have it?' he asked.

'Afraid not. Gary could nip back to the office.' I looked at my watch. 'Although that would take the best part of an hour. Tell you what, Will, let's put this in the diary for another day. I'll swing by when I get back from LA next week.'

'The car might not be around then.'

'That's a shame, but what else can we do?'

Will's dilemma played out on his florid face. In half an hour he could have sold the car to me. If he were on two per cent commission this would put five grand in his pocket. On the other hand, Mr Mountjoy probably had a very strict rule about not letting punters behind the wheel without presenting their licence first. This particular punter was worth a fortune, though, and he was buying a classic car on what was essentially a whim. Malcolm Gabriel could walk out of the door never to return.

Since taking Odeerie's shilling, I've witnessed people grapple with similar issues. Usually it's personal loyalty versus fifty quid in cash. The stakes were bigger this time round, but the decision would be the same. When you get down to it, people are very, very predictable. Will Creighton-Smith was no exception.

'We can waive the licence details, Malcolm,' he said. 'What kind of world is it when two gents can't trust each other?'

'If you're sure, Will,' I said.

'Positive,' he replied.

If I ever make a fortune, which at the time of writing isn't looking likely, then I'll buy myself an E-Type Jag. Appropriately, the example parked on the cobbles at the rear of Mountjoy Classics looked more animal than automobile. The bodywork undulated like firm flesh over trained muscle. Recessed headlights stared imperiously ahead. Put your fingers into the spokes of the wire wheels and you risked them being bitten off. All this and it was painted British racing green. God bless the sixties.

'Looks even better in daylight, doesn't she, Malcolm?' Will said.

'Incredible,' I replied.

'Ever driven anything like this?' I shook my head. 'Well, the thing to remember is that, even though she's fifty years old, there's still a lot of acceleration there.'

Will got into the passenger side of the car; I got into the driver's seat. Not an elegant manoeuvre for either of us. The interior was upholstered in crimson leather faded to surgical pink. At the centre of the wooden steering wheel was a Jaguar's head set against a chequered field. Old-school dials along with toggle switches and an elongated hood made me feel as though I was in a Second World War fighter plane.

We belted up and Will handed me the key. I looked in vain for the ignition until he pointed to it on the dashboard. The car spluttered a couple of times on wakening (don't we all) and then the engine caught. Noise and vibration meant you knew you were in a vintage car, although the chassis felt solid enough. It would have been a shame to damage one of these machines. Almost a crime, in fact.

'How does she feel?' Will asked.

'Amazing,' I said.

'Let's keep it local until you get your eye in and then, if Piccadilly isn't too jammed, we can run her into Knightsbridge.'

'Sounds like a plan,' I replied.

We bumped over the cobbles in first gear until the mews led on to Mount Street. Traffic is always lively in Mayfair, although the morning rush hour was over. I'd managed to get up to third before we reached South Audley Street.

It isn't every day that you get to drive an E-Type around the most exclusive part of town, and I have to admit I was enjoying myself. Unfortunately the fun couldn't last.

There are two ways to get information. First you simply ask for it. If that doesn't do the trick then a pair of twenties usually does. Neither was an option with Will. When several grand's worth of commission disappeared in a puff of exhaust fumes, the chumminess was likely to go the same way. All of which meant that I had to find another strategy. A space opened up and I stepped hard on the accelerator.

The Jaguar leapt forward as though it had spotted an orphaned gazelle. I jerked the wheel to the right and overtook a Volkswagen something-or-other. For about five seconds we were doing forty-five miles per hour on the wrong side of the street, until I corrected the car. Fortunately its braking was superlative, otherwise we would have rear-ended an Ocado delivery van.

Will's eyes were wide and his mouth parted. 'Steady on, sport. This isn't Silverstone.'

'And my name isn't Malcolm Gabriel.'

For a few moments Will struggled to comprehend my words, as though he were back at Hibbert & Saviours digesting a chunk of Virgil.

'Yes, it is,' he said. 'I checked you out online.'

'I look like the bloke,' I agreed. 'But that's as far as it goes.'

I cornered South Street at speed. The Jag's wheels squealed and the car fishtailed before straightening out. A woman carrying a pair of John Lewis bags stared at us as we came to a halt behind a black cab. I kept the revs high and gave her a wave.

'Don't try anything stupid, Will. If my foot slips off the clutch . . .'

'Why are you doing this?' he asked, loosening his tie.

'I'm a private investigator and I want to ask you a few questions.'

He groaned. 'Is this to do with Audrey? Because I promise I'll start the payments again just as soon as I can. You can't get blood out of a damn stone.'

'It's got nothing to do with Audrey,' I said as the traffic started moving. 'I want to ask you about something that happened when you were at school.'

'You mean Hibberts?'

'That's right. Some answers I already know, some I don't. Lie to me and I'll put this thing into a lamppost.'

Will stared at me. 'You're bluffing,' he said.

Builders were renovating a shop in Farm Street. Outside was a yellow skip into which rubble was being loaded via a chute. I manoeuvred the car left and put my foot down. The nearside mirror caught the skip and snapped like a twig. Will stared at the metallic stump in horror, as though it marked a recently amputated body part.

'Fuck me around and the other one goes,' I said.

In truth my heart was probably beating as fast as Will's. Like most spur-of-the-moment ideas, it had seemed a winner at the time. Now I was having second thoughts. Reckless driving, plus fraud, plus criminal damage, plus abduction, wouldn't look too great on a charge sheet.

'What d'you want to know?' Will asked.

'You were at school with George Dent. One night you, George and some other boys broke into Highgate Cemetery.'

'So what?'

'Who else was there?'

'How the hell should I know? It was forty years ago!'

I gave the steering wheel a wobble.

'Try to remember, Will.'

My passenger blew out his cheeks. 'Peter Timms, Simon Paxton and Ray . . . It was probably Higginbottom or something like that. He was a Northern skimp, that much I can remember.'

'A what?'

'Scholarship boy.'

'What about Blimp Baxter?'

'He didn't come in. Useless article was meant to be waiting outside with a ladder.'

'Have you seen him since you left school?'

Will shook his head. 'Why's all this so important to you?'

'George Dent died recently.'

'So I heard.'

'You were still in touch?'

'I saw him at a school event last year.'

'Was Peter Timms there?'

'No, I think he was too busy making ice lollies or whatever it is he does now.'

'Wouldn't have had you down for the alumni society, Will.'

'I like to keep in touch with the old boys.'

'So you can try to flog them vintage bangers?'

Will's hands tightened into fists. His gut hung over his belt but he was still a big bloke and, no doubt, they taught a thing or two about unarmed combat in the Blues and Royals. I fluffed a gear change as we passed the imposing portico of the Church of Christ, Scientist on Curzon Street. The Jag didn't like it. Neither did Will.

'D'you think I'm happy?' he asked. 'Kissing towelhead arse and fluffing up Ivans all day. It should be me test-driving this thing, not the other way round.'

I added casual racism to the list of Will's less endearing characteristics.

'Did you see George Dent again?'

'Why would I?'

Politicians avoid a direct answer by asking a secondary question. Lesser criminals use the same strategy. Will was lying. We halted at a set of traffic lights. I kept my foot on both accelerator and clutch. It brought a pitying look from a motorbike courier and the smell of burning oil began to invade the Jag's interior.

'The man whose tomb you went to that night was called Alexander Porteus.'

'If you say so.'

'Have you heard from him recently?'

'From Alexander Porteus? It may not have occurred to you, sport, but people who've been dead for donkey's years aren't usually interested in Aston Martins.'

'He'd been to see George Dent.'

The look on Will's face was one of genuine surprise. 'Alexander Porteus?'

'Peter Timms saw him too.'

'Believe that and you're mad. Or maybe Timms is.'

'As it happens, I'm with you, Will,' I said. 'Whoever turned up in Peter's garden was masquerading as Porteus.'

'Why would they do that?'

'You tell me.'

'Haven't a clue,' he replied, folding his arms. 'But if you think I had anything to do with it, then you're barking up the wrong tree.'

Will glanced at the remaining wing mirror. I pressed down my foot until the engine was virtually screaming. 'You might be telling the truth about Porteus,' I said, 'but you're lying through your teeth about not having seen George Dent since old boys' day. Level with me or I'll wrap this thing around the next solid object.'

'It's the truth.'

'It's bullshit.'

'Okay, okay,' Will said. 'Just . . . take it easy.'

The lights changed and a tourist bus ahead of us began to move forward. I decreased the revs, gently released the clutch . . .

And stalled.

NINE

I had my seat belt unbuckled before Will could react. Unfortunately I couldn't get the door open quickly enough. Middle-aged men fighting in a sports car is unlikely to become an Olympic event any time soon. There isn't enough space to get a decent swing, plus the gearstick and handbrake hamper proceedings.

Like most scraps, it would probably have gone with weight in the end. Guile and cunning have a role in the martial arts, though. I thwarted my opponent's attempt to headlock me by introducing an index finger into his eye. This brought an anguished roar and I was out of the E-Type far more adroitly than I'd clambered into it.

Will exited the passenger's door seconds later. My advantage was slight, but telling. He pursued me up South Audley Street for thirty yards before giving up.

Decades of smoking means that my lungs are for ornamental purposes only. Adrenaline took me as far Grosvenor Square, where I concentrated on forcing air into my chest and avoiding being sick. An elderly woman asked if I required medical assistance. I gasped something about having a touch of asthma and that I would be okay in a minute or so. She looked doubtful but toddled off.

Eventually I mustered sufficient wind to call Gary and tell him to get out of Mountjoy's showroom before Will made it back.

'Why?' was his understandable response.

'I'll explain later,' I said. 'Meet me in Bar Bernie in Wardour Street in fifteen minutes.'

'Don't go anywhere near your flat without me.'

'Just get a move on before Will shows up, Gary.'

I arrived at Bar Bernie and ordered tea and a toasted cheese sarnie. Miraculously, Bernie's hasn't yet become a Lebanese street-food outlet or vegan optician's. The laminated menu features photographs of burgers and chips taken twenty years ago, and its vinyl seats have been polished to high lustre by the slack backsides of intergenerational stodge enthusiasts. If Bernie's ever does close down, a couple of cardiac units will probably follow suit.

After scoffing my toastie, I checked my phone. No texts or emails from Odeerie, although there was an unattributed voicemail message waiting. The fat man always conceals his number and I expected to hear him telling me that he'd tracked down Ray Clarke. It turned out to be a different fat man entirely.

'This is Henry Baxter speaking. I'm returning your call from this morning and I'd be grateful if you could call me back as soon as possible.'

Blimp concluded by repeating his mobile number a couple of times. I'd rated the chances of him getting in touch at somewhere around zero. Not only had he responded within three hours, but he seemed almost as eager to speak to me as I was to him. I pressed 'Call Return'. He responded on the second ring.

'Baxter.'

'Hello, Mr Baxter,' I said. 'My name's Kenny Gabriel.'

'Ah, yes, you left a message with Daisy. Something about wanting to speak to me about George Dent.'

'That's right. I wondered if it would be possible for us to meet.'

'I'm rather busy. Could you give me an idea as to what you wanted to discuss?'

Blimp sounded tense. Bearing in mind that the developer routinely ate business rivals for breakfast, this was odd. I didn't intend to spoil my chances of a face-to-face meet by satisfying his curiosity on the phone.

'It's rather a delicate issue,' I said.

'Delicate in what way?'

'As I said, probably better to discuss that in person.'

A few seconds of dead air, before Blimp responded. 'You're not a reporter, are you?'

'I'm a private investigator.'

'Acting on whose behalf?'

'Perhaps we could discuss that tomorrow.'

Another silence during which I could almost hear the cogs turning in Blimp's brain. 'How about tomorrow afternoon?' he said eventually.

'What time?'

'Let's say three o'clock. I'm scheduled to be on site at the River Heights development. Know where that is?'

'Blackfriars Bridge where the Corn Exchange used to be?'

'That's right,' Blimp replied. 'Security will tell you where I am.'

And with that, he broke the line. The call had lasted less than a minute, although it had revealed a lot about Blimp Baxter. Specifically that there was something regarding George Dent he was concerned about. It might be a natural disinclination to be associated with a drug-addicted paedophile. Or it might be something else.

There was no way of knowing until the following day, and I was about to call Odeerie for an update on Ray Clarke when Gary entered Bernie's. He sat opposite me at the same time the waitress arrived to collect my plate and ask if I wanted anything else. I said I was fine but that my friend might be interested.

After a cursory glance at the menu, Gary requested a three-egg omelette minus the yolks. The waitress made him repeat the order as though he'd asked for a crocodile sandwich and shook her head as though she doubted if such a thing were possible. 'What's wrong with the yolks?' I asked on her behalf.

'They're not as proteinaceous,' Gary said.

The waitress left, and I moved on to other matters.

'Did you get out of the showroom before Creighton-Smith turned up?'

'Yeah. What the hell happened on the test drive?'

I took Gary through our spin in the E-Type, including its dramatic conclusion.

'Kenny, he'll call the police,' he said. 'Aren't you worried?'

I shook my head. 'Will shouldn't have let me near the thing without checking my licence. He'll keep schtum and source a new wing mirror on the web.'

'Couldn't you just ask him whatever it was you wanted to know?'

'I had to be sure he was telling me the truth.'

'About what?'

I'd told Gary nothing about why I wanted to interview Will Creighton-Smith. There were rules about client confidentiality that I was obliged to respect as a member of the SIA. On the other hand, he was technically an employee of the company, even if Odeerie hadn't exactly welcomed him with open arms. I took an executive decision to give him a synopsis with the caveat that he had to keep his mouth shut.

'So you wanted to know if he'd seen a ghost?' he asked.

'And if he'd had any contact with George Dent,' I said.

'The dead politician?'

'That's right.'

'And had he seen him?'

'They met at an old boys' do last year.'

'But you think he was lying about that?'

'No, that was the truth. He was fibbing about not seeing him since.'

'How d'you know?'

'Instinct.'

Gary scratched his chin. 'You reckon Will might have something to do with Dent's murder?' he asked. A guy eating sausage and chips looked up sharply on hearing the M-word. I gave him a reassuring smile and he returned to his meal.

'For fuck's sake, Gary,' I said under my breath. 'No one's saying George Dent was murdered. What might be interesting is why he committed suicide.'

'You mean someone fitted him up with the porn and the drugs?' he asked. I shrugged. 'How are you gonna find out if they did?'

'Not by talking to Will Creighton-Smith,' I said. 'That door is definitely closed. Hopefully we can have a word with Ray Clarke, though, assuming Odeerie can locate him, that is. And I've just made an appointment to see Blimp Baxter.'

I'd pretty much briefed Gary on my conversation with Blimp by the time our waitress arrived bearing a plate. She waited until Gary and I had moved apart before placing it on the table. 'Three-egg omelette. No yolks.'

'Thanks a lot,' Gary replied. The waitress remained.

'Ain't you gonna try it?' she asked.

Gary unwrapped the knife and fork that had arrived in a paper napkin. He cut a chunk of omelette, placed it in his mouth, chewed and swallowed.

'It's terrific,' he said. The waitress nodded. Having witnessed a man eat a yolkless omelette and pronounce it good, she was ready to go to Jesus.

'You'd better get a move on,' I said, checking my watch.

'Why's that?' Gary asked.

'We've got a date with death,' I told him.

TEN

I was eight years old when my grandfather died. It didn't mean a lot to me other than the fact that I would no longer be required to sit on Grampie Cyril's knee, be given mint imperials, shown the intricate workings of his pocket watch, or told that the country would be far better off if the coloureds were all sent home.

Three decades later I got to take a look at death close up. In his sixties, my father contracted pancreatic cancer. By this time he had ascribed the catastrophe of my youth to the vagaries of character and we were on better terms. I read to him three afternoons a week, usually the books he had loved as a child. We hadn't quite finished *Treasure Island* when Pop set sail for the final time.

My mother took a massive stroke in the checkout queue at Waitrose. The Reaper can be wonderfully ironic. My grief was tinged with relief that I hadn't watched her take the slow trudge into oblivion. I had formed a fear of mortality, particularly my own, that was increasing exponentially as the years progressed. For this reason, visiting a Gothic necropolis wasn't a joyful prospect. But there's no substitute for reviewing the scene of the crime, even if it is forty years after the fact.

The public isn't allowed to wander around Highgate Cemetery unaccompanied. For me and Gary, that meant forking out £24 to take the tour. Around thirty people gathered around Clive in the space where mourners congregated when the place was fully operational. Our guide was a white-bearded gent wearing a panama hat and a purple fleece. He had a posh accent and a lazy, or possibly glass, eye.

It had been drizzling on and off for most of the day. The leaves on the trees were turning colour and their branches dripped arrhythmically as we ascended the path into the cemetery proper. Some tombstones had been subsumed in vegetation; others were perfectly legible.

Periodically, Clive would stop and allow us to gather round him. He would point out features of Victorian funereal design and their significance. Empty chairs spoke for themselves. Celtic crosses represented the pagan tree of life fused to the Christian tradition. Inverted torches marked the extinguishing of the light, and a broken column mourned a life cut short at an early age.

Eventually we arrived at the Mausoleum Porteus. Some of the sepulchres – particularly those in Egyptian Avenue – looked as though they were straight out of a Boris Karloff movie. By comparison, the tomb of Alexander Porteus might have been spun out of icing sugar. Grooved white walls rose up to arched windows glazed in miniature panels of stained glass. The roof resembled a three-cornered party hat.

As we approached, a woman wearing a long grey coat was standing before the building. She moved twenty yards away as the tour group mustered.

'Jeffrey Porteus was a Scottish printer who made his fortune through publishing bibles and religious tracts,' Clive began. 'He subsequently moved to London and invested in the property market. At the time of his death in 1872, Porteus was a very wealthy man, although the mausoleum was built initially for his daughter, Elizabeth, who passed away aged eleven in 1850. Several members of the Porteus family have been interred in the mausoleum. Does anyone know the name of the most notorious?'

'Is it Alexander Porteus?' a Welsh woman in a cagoule asked.

'Indeed it is,' Clive said. 'Porteus was an occultist, prominent in the interwar years. There was a court case brought by other plot owners unhappy about his being buried on consecrated ground. However, the High Court found in favour of the Porteus family and he was interred in the cemetery in June 1947.'

While Clive gave us the lowdown on the black sheep of the Porteus clan, I stole a glance in the mystery woman's direction. Dark-brown hair cascaded over the collar of her coat. She had strong features and a pale complexion emphasised by scarlet lipstick. She was tall, maybe six foot, and in her mid-forties.

'The tomb was designed by Sir George Gilbert Scott, who also created the Albert Memorial,' Clive continued. 'Look through the gaps in the doors and you will see a stone angel bearing Elizabeth Porteus to heaven. For those of you who are interested, the sarcophagus of Alexander is on the far left.'

Although the apertures afforded a restricted view, it was sufficient to take in the floor, the marble panels adorning the walls, the angel with a girl in her arms, and seven sarcophagi. No footprints leading from the one in the far corner.

After everyone who was interested in taking a peek had done so, Clive announced it was time to move on.

'I'm staying for a bit,' I whispered to Gary. 'I'll meet you at the front.'

'Why?' he asked.

'Because I want to, that's why.'

◆ ◆ ◆

Gary walked after the crew while I loitered under cover of a nearby tree. When the coast was clear, I emerged. Disappointingly, the woman appeared to have left. For a few minutes I imagined the scene when the H&S boys had conducted their ceremony. The place was eerie enough by day; it must have been truly terrifying at night.

For the second time, I put my eye to one of the slits. The daylight had decreased and the interior lay in shadow. There was nothing exceptional about Alexander Porteus's sarcophagus. If anything, it was slightly smaller and less ornate than its companions. And yet there seemed to be something luminescent about the marble. Almost as though it was lit from within.

'Beautiful, isn't it?' someone asked. I leapt back from the door. 'God, I'm so sorry,' she said. 'Are you okay?'

'Fine, thanks. Just got a bit of a shock.'

'My fault entirely. I'm here so often I forget how it must affect other people, particularly if you sneak up on them. Not that I was trying to do that, of course.'

From a distance the woman had been attractive. Up close she was truly beautiful. Flawless skin and lustrous hair were impressive enough, but it was the chestnut eyes as wide and bright as a child's that really caught you out.

'What d'you think?' she asked.

'Of the mausoleum? It's an amazing building.'

'Isn't it just,' she agreed. 'Even more so inside.'

'Are people allowed in?' I asked.

'Only family. My name's Porteus. My mother and father are in there, and when the time comes . . .' A dazzling smile finished the sentence.

'Does that mean you're related to Alexander?' I asked.

'He's my grandfather. I heard your guide spouting the usual nonsense about him.' She sighed heavily. 'I've complained God knows how many times, but it never seems to do any good. One idiot even claimed that he was involved in child sacrifice.'

'Which he wasn't?' I asked.

'Of course not,' the woman said. 'The worst mistake Alexander made was criticising Lord Beaverbrook, who called him the wickedest man alive.'

She ran a hand through her thick hair. On one finger was a chunky gold signet ring. A heraldic device had been carved into what looked like a carnelian.

'Sorry, I shouldn't get so vexed over someone who's been dead for seventy years. You must think me a very odd fish.' I assured her I didn't. 'Look, if you're interested in my grandfather and you live in London, then you must visit the shop.'

'Which shop?'

'Porteus Books in Cecil Court? D'you know it?'

'I've walked past a few times.'

'We've got quite a large collection of volumes about my grandfather, if you're at all interested in him. My name's Olivia, by the way.'

'I'm Kenny,' I replied, and we shook hands.

'Well, it was nice to meet you, Kenny,' she said.

'And you,' I replied. I'd spent two minutes with Olivia Porteus, although it felt more like half an hour. The other odd sensation was a suspicion that our meeting had been prearranged. The feeling persisted as I trotted off in search of the tour.

◆ ◆ ◆

Clive had convened the group by the war memorial. I joined at the rear and listened to him detail the number of deaths in the First World War. Most Tommies had been buried close to where they fell, although some had returned to Blighty and subsequently died of their injuries.

'Where have you been, Kenny?' Gary said out of the side of his mouth.

'Talking to Alexander Porteus's granddaughter.'

'The woman in the grey coat?'

'You noticed her?'

'Every bloke on the tour noticed her. What did she—?'

Clive interrupted Gary, asking if we would observe a few seconds' silence in memory of the fallen. We stared at the cenotaph for a minute, after which our guide thanked us for our company, explained that the cemetery relied for its upkeep on donations, and that books and postcards were available in the chapel shop.

The group disbanded, although a couple of people remained to interrogate Clive on the finer points of the Victorian way of death. I intended to wait until they had finished. Gary, however, looked longingly at the gates.

'Kenny, I'm desperate for a slash,' he said.

'So have one.'

'The cemetery toilets are out of order. Nearest ones are in Waterlow Park. It's a twenty-minute walk there and back.'

I shrugged and said, 'What's the problem?'

'I'm shadowing you, remember?'

'Fair enough. Nip behind the war memorial.'

'What?'

'If you want to keep me in view at all times, that's your best option.'

'Or you could come with me to the park . . .'

'I need to speak to that guide,' I said. 'Otherwise it's a wasted journey.'

A couple of workmen were unloading paving slabs off the bed of a low-loader. Clive was having an awkward selfie taken with one of the Japanese tourists. The only other living thing in sight was a large fox lolling on a grassy bank.

Gary looked at the cenotaph. Then he looked at the gates. Then he looked at me. Then he sighed. 'Okay, but wait for me in the road afterwards, Kenny. Do not, repeat do not, go wandering off.'

'I'm not a bloody toddler!'

He didn't seem entirely convinced of this.

'Look,' I said, 'Billy Dylan won't come after me so quickly after last night.'

'How d'you know?'

'Because there's a chance I may have gone to the police. Plus, he knows you're on the job. Billy may be a nutter; he's not stupid.'

'I'm not so sure, Kenny. What if—'

'I've been in this business long enough to know what I'm talking about, Gary. After lunch I'll find a way of getting in touch with him and float the idea of tracking down his wife and kid. Then we'll take it from there.'

'It still seems a bit risky.'

'It's as safe as houses.'

Gary's wince suggested that a bulging bladder might be trumping bodyguard best practice. 'Right, well, see you in a bit,' he said, and walked through the cemetery entrance with a slightly hampered gait. I stared at the fox and the fox stared back. The tourist shook hands with Clive and collapsed his selfie stick. I made my approach.

'I just wanted to say how much I enjoyed your tour.'

Clive's good eye focused on my face while the other sought out a point roughly three inches above my left shoulder. 'Thank you,' he said. 'Is this your first visit?'

'Yeah, but I'll certainly be back. I was interested in the Porteus mausoleum. Do many people visit the cemetery because of Alexander?'

'Not as many as used to.'

'Why's that?'

Clive tugged his beard and considered the question. 'I suppose because he's not so current with young people any more. A few rock bands became tangled up with Satanism during the sixties and seventies. Alexander Porteus was referenced on an album cover by . . . No, can't remember them. I'm more of a Bach man myself.'

'You said that before the Friends of Highgate was formed, there was a lot of vandalism and people breaking into the place at night.'

'I'm afraid there were all manner of appalling things going on.'

'What about séances and black-magic rituals?'

'Do you have a specific interest in Alexander Porteus?'

I held my hands up as though rumbled. 'I've been commissioned to write a book.'

'Really? By whom?'

'If I tell you, would you mind keeping it to yourself?'

Inspired by his comments about the album cover, I dropped the name of a grizzled old rocker that even a man more familiar with the Brandenburg Concertos would have heard of. Clive's eye widened.

'Next time, perhaps I could get a photograph of you and Keith by the Porteus mausoleum,' I added. 'It would look terrific in the book. Maybe on the front cover.'

'He's coming to visit?'

'That's the plan.' I tapped the side of my nose. 'But, like I said, if you could keep it under wraps, I'd be grateful. Perhaps the three of us could take a private tour.'

'I'm sure that could be arranged.'

'Here's my number, Clive,' I said, opting to write it on an old receipt rather than hand over a card with OC Trace and Find inscribed on it. 'Actually, one thing I was interested in were the stories about Alexander Porteus being seen in the cemetery.'

'Er, I'm not with you.'

'I've interviewed several people who claim to have been in the place at night during the seventies and seen his ghost. I know it sounds crazy, but it's come up so often that it's starting to look like more than a coincidence.'

'Probably on drugs,' Clive said gloomily.

'You've never come across anything like that?'

'There was all that nonsense about the Highgate Vampire, of course, but I've never heard anything about Porteus.'

Intriguing though the vampire sounded, I didn't have time to get sidetracked. 'And no one's been in the cemetery recently asking about him?' I said.

'There have been a couple of people who have come on the tour because they're clearly interested in Alexander Porteus and his views.'

'What views?'

'Porteus was a notorious anti-Semite. Many of his ideas seem to be becoming rather popular again, which is a little depressing.'

'Is there anyone who was around in the seventies I could speak to?'

'There's Maggie. She was part of the original group who saved the place. The old girl's in her nineties now, though, and you have to catch her on a good day.'

'Would you mind having a word with Maggie?' I asked. 'I'd be very grateful, and I'm sure Keith would be too. Perhaps he could make a donation . . .'

'She lives in the village. I'll pop round this afternoon.'

I thanked Clive and made for the exit, leaving him to strike up a conversation with the workmen. I was confident he would keep our chat to himself in case it wrecked his chances of escorting a bona fide rock god around the cemetery. If not, it wouldn't matter as long as he pumped Maggie for any Porteus-related incidents.

The guy behind the counter of the gift shop unlocked the gate for me and I ambled on to Swain's Lane. The road was deserted and there wasn't much to do but check my emails while waiting for Gary. Top of my inbox was one from Odeerie.

> Kenny, have found out where Ray Clarke is living
> and what he's calling himself now. Call me when
> you get this.

I was vaguely aware of a white SUV pulling to a halt further down the road. The driver got out, although I was too busy finding Odeerie's number in my address book to take much notice of him. The fat man answered after a couple of rings.

'How are you doing?' I asked.

'Not bad. I've found Ray Clarke.'

'So I gathered. Where's he living?'

'On a Carbury Estate in Wapping. That's not the interesting bit, though. You're not gonna believe this, Kenny, but—'

'Hang on a sec, Odeerie . . .'

The guy who had got out of the car was in front of me. In his early forties, he was wearing a Fair Isle sweater over a pair of chinos. Greying hair was neatly side-parted and he sported a military-style moustache.

'Sorry to interrupt, mate,' he said. 'D'you know if there's a tour about to start? I can't see a sign or anything.'

'It's just finished,' I told him. 'I think that's it for today.'

'Bugger,' the man said.

'You could always try the East Cemetery,' I suggested.

'That one over there?'

There was a hut on the opposite side of the road where tickets were sold. No one was buying any. The driver registered this before looking left and right like a hyper-careful pedestrian. Then he bent down, put his arms around my waist and heaved me across his shoulder.

'What the fuck are you doing?' I shouted.

As the guy approached the SUV, a rear door opened. The car's engine was running.

'Kenny, what's happening?' I heard Odeerie ask. Before I could reply, my kidnapper plucked the mobile from my hand and threw it over the railings.

Gary emerged from Waterlow Park and began sprinting towards the car. I struggled to stop myself from being deposited on the back seat by clutching the rim of the door. Twenty seconds longer and Gary might have made it. The door slammed. My abductor entered the van and turned the key in the ignition. Lance was on the seat next to me.

'Put your foot down, Miles,' he said.

Gary carried on running but no way he was going to catch us. The last thing I saw through the rear window was him hunched over in the road as though about to throw up.

ELEVEN

It was small consolation that Lance had spruced up sartorially since he and Steve had ambushed me in the flat. Then his outfit had comprised a Crombie overcoat over mauve tracksuit bottoms; now he had matched a cream Harrington with a blue denim shirt and black jeans. I guess it's come as you are for retribution, whereas kidnapping is a more formal occasion. Unless this was Lance's murder outfit, of course.

Naturally I had a few questions, where are we going being first, closely followed by what's going to happen to me when we get there, and is all this strictly necessary? Lance instructed me to shut up and that I would find out soon enough.

Lance and Miles weren't in a chatty mood either. Not a word had been spoken by the time we joined the A10 and then the M25. Although the silence was oppressive, at least it allowed me to focus on ways to placate Billy Dylan. Sadly I couldn't improve on Gary's suggestion that I offer to track down his errant wife. Tough on Cheryl, but then she had married the bloke. And besides, if the silly cow hadn't hoodwinked Odeerie, none of this would be happening. Not to me, anyway.

After leaving the motorway, Miles navigated a couple of round-abouts and drove down a tree-lined lane. We pulled to a halt outside a pair of ten-foot gates. A sign that read DUCKETT'S FARM formed an arc between its posts. A security camera swivelled to focus on the SUV. A few seconds later, the gates opened. We sped down a tarmacked track towards the only building on the horizon.

The sprawling bungalow couldn't have been more than twenty years old. There wasn't a grain hopper or a combine harvester in sight. It looked as though the Dylans weren't sowing barley that year. We entered a courtyard, in the centre of which was a red telephone box. Next to it stood a Victorian gas lamp with a wooden parrot perched on top. Outside a double-bay garage was a BMW 7 Series and a superbike with a helmet hanging off the handlebar. Miles parked and killed the engine.

'Get out,' Lance said. 'And remember, you're fuckin' miles from anywhere, so there's no point tryna run for it.'

'Why would I do that?' I asked.

Lance grinned and squeezed my cheek between his thumb and forefinger. 'Because you're shitting yourself, Kenny,' he said. 'And I don't fuckin' blame ya.'

The front door comprised two frosted-glass panels set in a wooden surround. Each had a swan etched into its surface in such a way that their beaks met in the middle. Attached to the brickwork were at least a dozen multicoloured tin butterflies.

When Lance pressed the bell, the first few bars of the theme from *Love Story* sounded out. It was so kitsch that I half expected Barry Manilow to answer the door. Instead it was a stocky woman in her forties with a prominent front tooth.

'Shoes off,' Lance instructed me.

I removed my Hush Puppies and entered. To my left was a large wooden box. Inside were half a dozen pairs of male shoes all at least three sizes larger than mine. I placed my Pups next to a pair of biker boots. Lance followed suit with his Nikes.

'Where's Mrs Dylan, Magda?' he asked.

'Madam in the day room.' Judging by her accent, Magda was Eastern European. She looked at me briefly and with zero interest.

'This way,' Lance said.

We walked down a rose-coloured passage. A pair of elaborate chandeliers hung from the ceiling. Lance bobbed down slightly to walk beneath them. We stopped at the second door on the left and Lance tapped on it. A female voice instructed us to enter.

Perched on a sofa was a small woman in her mid-fifties, wearing a cream broderie anglaise dress matched with a charcoal jacket. Her dark hair had been pinned up and she was wearing hoop earrings. She stood and extended a hand.

'I'm Meg Dylan and you must be Kenny Gabriel. I hope you had a pleasant journey and that Lance treated you well.'

'Very well,' I said. 'Apart from snatching me off the street.'

'Yes, I'm sorry about that. But you probably wouldn't have come otherwise.'

'Probably not,' I agreed.

'Lance, would you ask the others to join us?'

'Everyone?' he asked.

'Yes, including Magda and the boys.'

Having received his instructions, Lance left the room. 'Do have a seat, Kenny,' his boss said. 'I was about to take tea – would you care to join me?'

The sofa was upholstered in lemon fabric and could have accommodated five people were it not for the proliferation of cushions. To Meg Dylan's left was a table bearing a large teapot and a pair of dainty porcelain cups. At its base I noticed a large claw hammer and a green velvet bag.

'That would be nice,' I said, settling into a capacious armchair and trying hard not to stare at the bag and the hammer.

Meg Dylan got busy with the makings, allowing me to take in the room. Three walls were shelved from top to bottom. On each were crowded tiny glass animals and ornaments lit by tiny spotlights. There had to be hundreds of crystal creatures in the twinkling menagerie. We could have been sitting in a Swarovski boutique.

Hanging above the sofa was a family portrait executed in oils. It depicted a man in his late thirties with shoulder-length dark hair, a rock-solid jawline and a tight shirt undone to the navel. Marty Dylan had his arm around a younger Meg Dylan. To his right was his teenage son.

'Ah, I see you're looking at the family portrait.' Meg Dylan poured a golden stream through a strainer into each cup. 'Do you have children, Kenny?' I shook my head. 'Well, they really do grow up so quickly.'

I'd have expected Meg Dylan to be a peroxide blonde wearing a leopard-print dress over a fake tan. Exclude the taste in décor and furnishings and she could have been the wife of an architect, as opposed to the spouse of Marty Dylan.

'Is your son around?' I asked.

'He'll be with us shortly.'

'That's good, because I wanted to clear up all that nonsense in the papers. I'm sure Billy had a perfectly valid reason for visiting—'

Meg held up a hand and cut me off in mid-sentence.

'We can discuss Cheryl in due course.' She handed me a cup and saucer. 'Do you know how hard it is for a woman to run a successful organisation, Kenny?'

'I'm sure it can't be easy.'

'It's terribly difficult. Occasionally you have to make an example of someone, however much you may dislike doing so. It's important to me that you understand that, Kenny. What's about to happen next will be distasteful to both of us.'

The floodgates of my imagination crashed open, engulfing me in all manner of hammer-and-bag scenarios. 'What *is* going to happen next?' I asked

'All in good time, Kenny,' Meg replied. 'All in good time.'

I can't recollect what we chatted about for the next two minutes. I've an idea it had something to do with gardening. Equally it might have been the best way to treat piranha bites or the shortcomings of Icelandic fiscal policy. The small-talk part of my mind was on autopilot while the rest worked on strategies to extricate myself from whatever it was Meg Dylan thought I might find so distasteful. A knock on the door preceded a procession into the room. At its head was Lance, accompanied by Steve and Miles. Three missing links shuffled in next, followed by Magda and Billy Dylan.

I recognised Billy from surveilling his girlfriend's house. He was average height with dark-brown curly hair. He wore a *Videodrome* T-shirt and leather trousers. That a gangster would be into a cult eighties sci-fi movie was peculiar but somehow in keeping with Billy's overall appearance. He resembled a mature student more than a hardened criminal.

The motley group congregated around Meg Dylan's sofa. Although not specifically instructed to do so, I opted to stand.

'Thank you all for joining us,' she said. 'For those of you who don't know my guest, his name is Kenny.'

I offered up a token wave. The only response was a smirk from Lance. Meg Dylan picked up the bag and withdrew something from it. On the palm of her hand lay the separate parts of a broken crystal horse.

'I found this at the back of a shelf this morning,' she said. 'As none of you apart from Magda are allowed in the day room, only one person can be responsible.'

The focus of interest devolved from me to the cleaner. Her eyes were fixed on the carpet, and the cheeks on her slab-like face began to redden.

'Have you got anything to say for yourself, Magda?' her employer asked.

'It was accident,' she said without looking up. 'I no mean break hoss.'

'That's not what upsets me,' Meg Dylan said. 'What upsets me is that you didn't admit what you'd done.'

Or have the nous to throw the fucking thing away, I thought.

'I buy new one,' Magda offered. 'You take money out my pay.'

'They don't make them any more and, besides, that's not the point. What you've done is betray my trust, Magda, and we all know how important trust is.' Meg Dylan paused to stare at everyone in the room. 'So the only thing that needs to be done is decide how to punish you,' she said. 'I've had to think long and hard about this.'

'I buy new hoss,' Magda repeated.

'You can't, you stupid Polish bitch,' Meg Dylan said, her accent slipping several notches down the phonetic scale. 'I've told you that.'

A tear rolled down Magda's face. She knew what was coming would be bad, although she didn't know quite how bad. Meg Dylan held the shattered glass out.

'You're going to eat it,' she said.

TWELVE

Intact, the horse would have been two inches high and four inches long. It might have been possible to swallow each of the three individual pieces whole, although they probably wouldn't navigate Magda's system without surgical intervention. That she would chew each chunk to render it smaller was out of the question. Judging by the way her front tooth was angled, Magda hadn't lived in the golden age of Polish dentistry.

Considerately, Meg Dylan had anticipated this.

'Now, you aren't going to be able to get these down as they are,' she said to Magda. 'So I'm going to give you a little help with that.' She dropped the pieces into the bag and I felt a trill of anxiety at the base of my neck. 'A couple of weeks ago, Billy and I went to see this magic show in town. Actually, it wasn't a magic show, exactly, more of a . . . How did Darryl describe himself, Billy?'

'Said he was a mentalist, Ma.'

'That was it. It's all down to the way you look at things. Most people think you can't eat glass, but that isn't true. To prove it, Darryl ate a light bulb. Can you imagine that, Magda?'

The cleaner rubbed her eyes and shook her head.

'Me neither. Mind you, Darryl showed us how. First of all, you've got to get the pieces really small, otherwise they'll cut your insides to ribbons. He did it by putting the bulb in a bag and smashing it up.'

Meg Dylan handed over the velvet bag and the claw hammer. Magda took them from her as though she were living in a dream. A very bad dream.

'Now, you can crush a bulb in ten seconds, but it's going to take longer when you're dealing with the finest Austrian lead crystal. So I'm going to give you a minute to get these pieces as small as you can.' Meg Dylan held her thumb and forefinger a fraction apart. 'D'you understand that, Magda?' she asked. 'Teeny, tiny . . .'

Although Magda's English wasn't great, a nod indicated she knew what was expected. Meg Dylan reached under the sofa and produced a breadboard.

'Better use this, otherwise you'll ruin the carpet.' She placed the rectangle of wood at Magda's feet. 'Okay, you've got sixty seconds, starting . . . now.'

Magda was generously proportioned and she knew how to swing a hammer. For the next minute we all watched as she beat the living shit out of the remnants of the horse. The sound of crunching glass accompanied by grunts of effort was made even more horrible by the knowledge of what was to come.

'Five . . . four . . . three . . . two . . . one . . . stop!'

The final blow descended after the countdown had finished. Meg Dylan allowed it to pass. Magda was scarlet-faced and sweating profusely. I helped her to her feet.

'Look, if all this is for my benefit, there's no need,' I said. 'You're clearly pissed off, and I know what you're capable of. But I've got something—'

'Well done, Magda,' Meg Dylan said, as though I weren't in the room. She took the bag from Magda and looked inside. 'You know, I think you've every chance of managing this. Mind you, there are a few larger pieces so there's still work to do.'

Lance gestured at me to stand aside. I thought about telling him and Meg Dylan to go fuck themselves. And then I thought again.

Nothing I could do would make any difference to the outcome. What was going to happen was going to happen.

'Get the glass right to the back of your mouth and grind it slowly,' Meg Dylan advised Magda. 'And get lots of spit in there so you don't slice your gums up.'

'I buy two new hosses,' Magda said, a pleading note in her voice.

Meg Dylan picked up one of the teaspoons from the table. 'I'm afraid this isn't entirely clean, although I don't think that's going to matter too much in the circumstances. Maybe start with the smaller pieces first . . .'

Magda opened the bag and peered inside. She poked around like a kid probing a bag of sherbet dip and eventually withdrew the spoon. On it was a small heap of splintered glass. She looked at Meg Dylan as though hoping for a last-minute reprieve. It wasn't forthcoming.

The cleaner opened her mouth and inserted the spoon. She manipulated her jaw from side to side to distribute the shards evenly, and then, tentatively, began to chew. After ten seconds' grinding there was a muffled crack. It was impossible to tell from Magda's wince of pain whether it was a tooth splintering or a chunk of crystal horse. She took a deep breath and carried on chewing.

It was about a minute before she swallowed. Her eyes widened slightly but there was no other reaction. Only when Magda opened her mouth did the damage show. Her gums and teeth were wreathed in blood.

'Urgh, that's disgusting.' Billy Dylan sounded both revolted and delighted, as though watching a gross-out comedy.

'For God's sake, stop this,' I said. Lance's hand detonated against the side of my head. The impact staggered me backwards into an armchair. The room shimmered for a few seconds before returning to focus. I struggled back to my feet.

'I'm so sorry, Kenny,' Meg Dylan said. 'Lance tends to overreact sometimes. Although, to be fair, I did say that you might find this distasteful.'

'Distasteful! It's fucking barbaric.'

Lance looked as though he was about to give me some afters. Meg held up her hand to prevent him. 'Mr Gabriel is a guest, Lance,' she said. 'Although I would remind you, Kenny, that even a guest has certain obligations . . .'

The message was clear: interrupt proceedings again and Meg Dylan would let slip the dogs of war. Billy was grinning broadly and revelling in my discomfort. I looked at the blood covering Magda's chin and opened my mouth.

Absolutely nothing came out.

For the next few minutes I stared at the floor. The sound of grinding teeth was punctuated by the occasional snigger from one of the meatheads. Only when Meg Dylan called time did I look back up. Blood was streaming from Magda's lips, and tears from her eyes. Her grey T-shirt had soaked up a lot of the gore and there were smears on her left arm where she had dragged it across her mouth.

'Lance, get her out of here,' Meg Dylan said. 'The rest of you go back to work, apart from you, Billy. We need to chat to Mr Gabriel.'

The missing links filed out of the room and the door closed. Were it not for the breadboard and the bloodstains on the carpet, it was as if nothing had happened.

Billy Dylan sat on the sofa and stretched his legs out. It was peculiar seeing the contemporary versions of the figures in the painting. And by peculiar, I mean fucking horrible. The buzz in my head felt like a nest of angry wasps.

'Now that's out of the way, Kenny, we can move on to more important matters,' Meg Dylan said. 'You're probably wondering why you're here.'

'I've got a fair idea,' I said. 'Your daughter-in-law approached my partner and asked him to spy on Billy. We realise now it was a terrible mistake.'

'You're dead right it was,' Billy Dylan said.

'Obviously there's nothing we can do to put that right,' I continued with a dry mouth, 'although I'm prepared to make you both a proposal.'

Billy laughed as though I'd just delivered the punchline to an unexpectedly good joke. 'What were you thinking of?' his mother asked.

'Yeah, go on,' Billy said. 'Tell us what it is and then me and Lance'll take you into the garage and make you a counterproposal.'

'Shut up, Billy,' Meg Dylan said. Her son's cackling stopped immediately. 'What did you have in mind, Kenny?'

'Well, obviously Cheryl has gone into hiding with your granddaughter. However unwittingly, I admit that I was to blame to a degree—'

'You were the only fucking reason she left me,' Billy said. 'And in twenty minutes you're gonna seriously regret that.'

'Billy, if you'd kept your prick in your trousers this would never have happened,' Meg Dylan snapped. She closed her eyes and took a deep breath, then opened them again and smiled at me. 'At least listen to what our guest has to say.'

'My partner and I track people down for a living,' I continued. 'We're prepared to find out where she is and give you the address.'

'What if you can't find her?'

'We'll find her.'

'How long?'

'Forty-eight hours.'

Throughout this exchange, Billy had been staring at his mother, open-mouthed. Meg Dylan seemed to be giving my proposal consideration.

'There is a slight problem,' she said.

'What's that?' I asked.

'We already know where she is. The only reason we haven't contacted Cheryl is because of the media coverage. In our line of work, it's a good idea to keep a low profile. It'll go to court eventually and Billy will get custody of Caitlin.'

'Which means you can stick your poxy offer up your arse,' Billy added. 'Can I take him into the garage now, Ma? I need to be back in town by six.'

'Although there might be something else you can help us with, Kenny,' his mother continued. 'Last month, one of our associates disappeared with a large amount of cash. All efforts to locate him have drawn a blank.'

Meg Dylan withdrew two pieces of paper from her handbag and handed them to me. They were copies of a passport and driving licence. The owner was a guy in his late thirties with short brown hair, greying at the temples.

'His name is Martin Gordon McDonald. I'd like you to find him. The documents are fakes, although the photographs are a good likeness.'

'Is the name right?' I asked.

'Ma, we can handle this on our own,' Billy interjected before his mother could respond. 'Dad always says not to bring outsiders in.'

'I think it's a bit late for that, don't you, Billy?'

Billy's head recoiled as though his mother had slapped his cheek. 'That's not fair,' he said. 'You thought Martin was kosher too. Why don't we write the money off and write this wanker off while we're at it. Then we can get on with business.'

I struggled to keep my eyes off the bloodstains on the carpet. All Magda had done was smash an ornament. I'd broken up Billy Dylan's marriage and caused Meg Dylan to be estranged from her only grandchild. The sour bile of fear rose into my mouth.

'No, Billy,' Meg said eventually. 'If it gets out that some toerag took us for a ride, we'll be a laughing stock. We need to cancel bad news with good news.'

Judging by Billy's scowl, he didn't see it the same way. But his mother's word was law. At least, in her house it was.

'If you tell me exactly what happened then your chances are far better than if all I have to go on are these,' I said.

Meg Dylan shifted position on the sofa and crossed her legs.

'You may know that Billy served a short prison sentence recently,' she said. 'He used the opportunity to study accountancy. After he was released, we decided to make use of his skills in the business.'

'Doing what?' I asked.

'A significant part of our operation involves converting large amounts of anonymous cash into less anonymous cash. The challenge lies in finding a legitimate business owner prepared to partner with us.'

'And that's where this guy came in?'

'Billy attended a small-business seminar in the hope that he might do some recruiting. He met a man called Martin McDonald, who ran a training company.'

'What kind of training?'

Meg Dylan looked to her son.

'Business skills,' he said after a long pause.

I wondered why Billy was so reluctant to get the family cash back. Was it embarrassment at losing it in the first place, or some other reason?

'McDonald ran open courses in hotels. He had a serious gambling problem and needed to pay some debts off quickly. He was exactly what we were looking for.'

'How much cash are we talking about?' I asked.

'Why does that matter?'

'Any information you can give me might help.'

'Just short of six hundred thousand,' Meg Dylan said.

'What? You gave him that much on the back of a meeting in a hotel?'

The incredulity in my voice tripped a switch in Billy, for whom this was clearly a sensitive subject. He leant forward and jabbed a finger at me.

'No, I fucking didn't give him six hundred grand. I tried him with twenty thousand and he came back on time with the cash. Next thing we put fifty through his books. Same thing happened. We'd just done a big deal and we had to recycle the money fast. Martin was the best option.'

Billy sank back on the sofa, crossed his arms and scowled.

'Did you check the business out at Companies House?' I asked.

'He used another firm's name and registration number,' Meg Dylan said.

'So this guy's pissed off with six hundred thousand quid and all you've got is two fake documents and a false address?'

'You don't think it's something you can assist with?'

'God, no – this is right up our street.'

'How long will it take you?'

'A month?'

'You mean a week.'

'Slip of the tongue,' I said. 'If, by some chance, it did take a tiny bit longer – which it definitely won't – how would you feel about that?'

'D'you really want to know?' Meg Dylan asked.

'Probably not,' I replied.

THIRTEEN

Returning to London, I tried to come to terms with what I'd witnessed at Duckett's Farm. Informing the police about Magda was risky. The Dylans had more than one Met officer in their pocket. Added to which, Meg Dylan could simply deny anything had taken place. I examined the copies of the passport and driving licence. Although no expert, I would have taken both as kosher. This threw up two possibilities: either Martin McDonald kept world-class forgeries on hand just in case, or he'd commissioned them specifically to fuck over the Dylans.

I'd quizzed Billy Dylan on a few salient points. The seminar had been held at the Burbage Hotel on Great Queen Street in early March. Subsequent meetings with McDonald had taken place at Central London pubs. He'd been invited to the farm and Meg Dylan had run the ruler over him before handing over the first envelope. The six hundred grand had been given to him in a bar at Heathrow Airport. McDonald had probably gone straight to check-in.

Most clients are keen to give you all the information you need, along with a whole lot you don't. Getting it out of Billy Dylan had been like yanking teeth. That his mother didn't want me abbreviated with power tools had clearly put a crimp in his day.

Worst-case scenario: Billy might decide that forgiveness was easier to gain than permission, as far as his mum was concerned. And even if we found McDonald, there was no guarantee that Meg would be as good as her word. She might decide I needed taking care of anyway, what with knowing too much about the Dylans' business.

While driving me to the local station, Miles tunelessly whistled various Adele numbers. It was bloody irritating, although telling him that wasn't an option. Instead I chose a different subject. 'I was wondering about something,' I said, shortly after he slowed for a speed camera.

'Oh, yeah?'

'What happened in the day room . . .'

Miles chuckled. 'Yeah, that was some freaky shit. Even for Mrs D.'

'How long has . . . Mrs D been running things?'

'Since Marty went inside.'

'About four years, then?'

He changed gear and pondered the question. 'It must be about that now. Time flies when you're having fun, eh?'

'When's Marty up for parole?'

'He got eleven years,' Miles said. 'Even with good behaviour, the poor bastard ain't getting out for at least another three.'

'Presumably he still runs things from prison, though?'

'Yeah, but Mrs D's properly in charge. Funny thing is that she didn't give a toss about the business until her old fella went inside. Spent most of her time in Harvey Nicks having her nails done. Lotta people thought Marty goin' away would scupper the Dylans. Ain't turned out like that.'

'She's good at what she does?'

'That's one way of putting it,' Miles said, signalling for a right turn. 'Look, I don't know what's goin' on with you and Billy and I don't wanna know either. But if you take my advice, you'll stay on the right side of Mrs D.'

'What's the story with Magda?'

'How d'you mean?'

'Isn't Mrs Dylan worried she might go to the police?'

'Ain't gonna happen. She's here illegally, and she's fucking terrified of the cops.'

'Does she live in the house?'

'In a caravan out the back. Believe me, it ain't the Ritz, but it's probably better than whatever shithole she was living in in Poland.'

'Aren't Poles allowed to stay in this country by right?' I asked.

'Course they are, but Magda don't know that.'

Miles gave me a wink in the rear-view mirror.

My train pulled into King's Cross just before five. Without my mobile it had been impossible to call Gary, who was, no doubt, wondering what had happened to me. Odeerie probably had a few questions too. He'd been about to divulge something sensational about Ray Clarke when Miles bundled me into the SUV.

The business with Peter Timms and George Dent had taken a back seat compared to the more pressing matter of finding out where Martin McDonald was and what he'd done with the Dylans' cash. The sooner I could get Odeerie looking for him, the better. For that reason, I took the Piccadilly Line to Leicester Square and then walked to Meard Street. The fat man sounded relieved to hear my voice over the intercom; even more relieved when I entered his flat without a heavy limp.

'Thank God you're all right, Kenny' was the first thing he said.

'I'm not all right. I've been with Billy Dylan.'

'Gary told me what happened. I knew he wasn't up to the job.'

'It wasn't his fault. What did the two of you do?'

'How d'you mean?'

'When you knew the Dylans had me?'

'Well, Gary wanted to go to the police, but I said that wasn't a very good idea as they'd just ask a load of awkward questions. I suggested he tell Farrelly what had happened but he was dead set against that for some reason.'

'Okay, so what *did* you do?'

'We thought we'd give it a few hours and assess the situation.'

'Fuck-all, then, basically.'

'That's unfair, Kenny,' Odeerie said with a pained expression. 'Gary said that you were going to tell Billy Dylan about finding his wife and kid, and that you reckoned that would sort everything out.'

'Well, it didn't.'

Odeerie gave me a closer examination in case there was anything small he'd overlooked, like a missing eyeball or a screwdriver in the skull.

'Christ, Kenny, did they use electricity?'

'No, they didn't use electricity. But if you can't find a bloke who's done a runner with six hundred grand, Meg Dylan will plug my dick straight into a wall socket.'

'You mean Billy Dylan.'

'I mean Meg Dylan.'

'What's her problem?'

'She's pissed off because her daughter-in-law's done a runner and she hasn't seen her granddaughter in over a month.'

'I thought you said someone had nicked six hundred grand.'

'They did.'

'I'm confused, Kenny. Can we start again?'

It took ten minutes to relate my afternoon's exploits. Odeerie looked green around the gills and swallowed a couple of times when I recounted the incident with Magda. 'Sometimes you just have to live with the fact that some people get mugged over in life and there's nothing you can do about it, Kenny' was his verdict. 'It sounds as though you did as much as you could under the circumstances.'

And of course he was right. You have to pick your battles – particularly with people like Meg and Billy Dylan. Not that it made me feel any better.

'Can I look at the copies?' Odeerie asked. Despite only being able to open one eye, the fat man was impressed. 'Got the originals?'

'McDonald took them.'

'Shame. There aren't many people who are capable of this kind of work and have access to the right equipment. I know a guy who consults with the Met, but it's hard to tell without the actual documents themselves.'

'You could ask him anyway.'

'True, and it's only going to be one of two or three people, but it might mean talking to all of them.'

'I've got less than a week to sort out two jobs, Odeerie.'

'The Dylans are more important, Kenny. Maybe put the Porteus business on the back-burner. Your brother will understand, won't he?'

'I'll think about it,' I said.

'D'you know where the business seminar was?' Odeerie asked

'The Burbage.'

'McDonald probably had to register to attend. In which case he'll have used an email address. If we get that then it's going to be a whole lot easier.'

'And if we don't?'

Odeerie pursed his lips. 'Then all we've got is his face to go on. I'm assuming that the Dylans checked out the address on the licence?'

'It's a couple in their eighties who've lived there thirty years. Apparently they'd never heard of McDonald and they didn't recognise him.'

'They're definitely telling the truth?'

'Would you lie to Billy Dylan?'

'Only if I had to, Kenny, and there was absolutely no other option.'

'Yeah, right,' I said. 'So if he's using an assumed name, and we can't trace the guy who faked the documents, or find an email address, what's the bottom line?'

'We're stuffed' was Odeerie's professional opinion. A wave of despondency enveloped me. It must have shown on my face, as he quickly dropped the gloomy attitude. 'Look, I'll try with my forgery bloke first thing tomorrow. And I'll call the Burbage and see what day the seminar was on. They often sell the data after these events so it might not be that hard to get hold of his address. Did Billy Dylan tell you anything else about this guy?'

'Like what?'

'Accent? Height? Distinguishing marks?'

I shook my head. 'Said he was average height and sounded as though he was probably from the South-East.'

For a few moments the only sounds were the ticking of a mantel clock and distant street noises. Odeerie shook his head a couple of times as though a persistent fly were buzzing it. Then he pulled a piece of paper from his pocket.

'D'you still want to hear about the scholarship boy?'

'What scholarship boy?'

'Ray Clarke? The guy who went to Hibberts. Although I guess, if you're going to focus on the Dylan job, there's probably no point.'

I took a deep breath and considered the situation. Until Odeerie went to work, there wasn't much I could do apart from sit on my arse and imagine the worst. Added to which would be Malcolm's disappointment if I turned down his best mate twenty-four hours after agreeing to take the job on. No way could I tell Malc why I was quitting, as he'd try to help his kid brother out. And the last thing I wanted was to draw Malcolm into any situation involving the Dylans.

'Go on, then,' I said. 'What d'you know about him?'

Odeerie consulted the paper. 'After they kicked him out of Hibbert & Saviours, Ray Clarke went to live with his parents up North. He took his A levels and came back to London to train as a teacher. He married in his thirties and had a son. Eighteen months ago he contracted motor neurone disease and had to quit his job at a local comp.'

'Where did all this come from?' I asked.

'Social media, mostly.'

'Wasn't that the first place you looked?'

'Yeah, but Ray Clarke isn't Ray Clarke any more.'

'I'm not with you, Odeerie.'

'She's Judy Richards.'

The picture on Odeerie's computer was of a pale-faced, middle-aged woman with short, dirty-blonde hair. She was wearing a blue blouse with a puritan collar and a pair of square glasses. Her smile was slightly strained, as though she had been holding it for several seconds. It was the kind of face you saw behind a bank counter or the reception desk in a civic building. Memorable it wasn't.

There was information about her struggle with motor neurone disease and a link to the MND Association, for which she had raised funds. The disease was progressive and degenerative. It caused muscle-wasting and there was no cure. Half the people who contracted it died within two years of diagnosis, the rest not long after.

I clicked through a few other pictures on Judy's page. In one, she was sitting in a bar with two women her own age. In another she was cradling a marmalade tabby on her lap, and in a third she was sitting in front of a lawn that had a bunch of kids playing on it. Standing behind her wheelchair was a man in his early twenties.

'That's Judy's son, is it?' I asked.

'Yep,' Odeerie replied.

'What's his name?'

'Connor.'

'Wonder how he feels about his old man turning into Widow Twanky.'

'Judy prefers the term trans woman,' Odeerie said a little stiffly. 'And Connor seems fine with it.'

Judging by the way Connor Clarke's hand rested easily on his mother's shoulder, indeed he did. Wide shoulders, blonde hair and gleaming teeth gave him a vaguely Californian appearance. Judy Richards looked as though she could do with half an hour under a sunbed and a course of vitamin D injections. But then I guess motor neurone disease isn't exactly a makeover.

'Why did it take so long to find her?' I asked.

'I had Ray Clarke's name linked to that address. When it switched to Judy Richards, I figured Ray had moved on.'

'But all he'd done was change his name?'

'I'd say he'd changed a bit more than that, Kenny.'

Another click brought up a shot of Judy Richards in front of a minibus clutching a stick of half-eaten candyfloss. The square specs had been replaced by large-frame sunglasses and her smile looked more relaxed.

'What made you realise it was the same person?' I asked.

Odeerie commandeered the mouse. Within a few seconds I was reading an article from a national paper that had maintained a sense of continuous editorial outrage since the Suez Crisis. The piece was titled *Is this really what the NHS was created for?* It detailed how a transvestite called Ray Clarke (aka Judy Richards) was receiving NHS funding to undergo gender reassignment. If that weren't bad enough, Ray was also living on a rent-controlled Carbury social housing estate.

'I found this,' Odeerie said. 'It's the only time both names are linked.'

'When was it printed?'

'Twelve years ago.'

'And Judy's kept a low profile ever since?'

'She posts on Facebook now and again, but that's it,' Odeerie said.

'Anything worth reading?' I asked.

'Like what?'

'A zombie black magician threatening her with death?'

Odeerie shook his head. 'Mostly it's stuff about cats.'

'Friends with anyone interesting?'

'Not that I can see.'

'Okay, I'll visit her. But work on McDonald is all you do, Odeerie. Meg Dylan doesn't fuck around. If we don't deliver, then it isn't just a bonus at stake.'

'I'll call the forgery guy this evening,' he promised.

◆　◆　◆

Dusk is my favourite time in Soho. Developers may be trying hard to turn the place into a retail park, but at sunset there's a crackle of expectation in the air that you can't buy with a charge card. A white witch once told me that it had something to do with ley lines crossing under the Algerian Coffee Stores (no doubt scheduled to become a Costa). Another theory is that the buildings have absorbed the emotions of the personal dramas that have been playing out in the parish since Huguenot refugees arrived in the seventeenth century. Fortunes have been lost, livers destroyed, genius squandered, hearts broken, not to mention John Logie Baird inventing TV in Frith Street.

Perhaps twilight is when the roaring boys and girls return to see what fresh kinds of sin have been invented. Look hard enough and maybe you can see Julian Maclaren-Ross trying to talk his way into the Colony Room, or Soho Pam extracting a 'donation' from the regulars in the Coach and Horses. Quite what they would have made of Spice and Special K was anyone's guess, although I like to think they'd have pitched right in.

I knew I too would become a Soho ghost one day. And if Odeerie couldn't weave his magic, that day wouldn't be too far away. I entered Brewer Street with optimism at low ebb. Even if Odeerie managed to trace Martin McDonald, it didn't follow that he would still have the Dylans' money. And then I would die with McDonald's screams ringing in my ears as Billy and Lance doubled up on the Black & Deckers.

The light was on in the flat, meaning Gary was home. There was little point in my retaining his services now that the Dylans had successfully made their move. I would assure the kid that it wasn't his fault, issue a company cheque that almost certainly wouldn't bounce, and bid him a fond farewell. I opened the sitting-room door to find him wearing a tracksuit and drinking something that looked like methylated spirit.

'Why the hell didn't you call me?' was his first question.

'They threw my phone away. Didn't you see?'

Gary shook his head. 'I knew I shouldn't have left you alone.'

I collapsed into an armchair. 'Yeah, well, we all make mistakes.'

'What d'you mean? You were the one who said there was no chance Billy Dylan would come after you again so quickly.'

'Like I said, we all make mistakes.'

'What happened?' Gary asked.

'Billy's associates drove me to a farm in Hertfordshire.'

'And?'

'I met his mum.'

'You're kidding me.'

'I'm not kidding anyone.'

'Why would Billy Dylan want you to meet his mum?'

'He didn't. Billy wanted to carve me up in his garage. Meg Dylan had a proposition for me. Just as well, otherwise I wouldn't be talking to you now.'

'What kind of proposition?' Gary asked.

'The kind you don't refuse,' I told him.

◆ ◆ ◆

While I related my afternoon's adventures with the Dylans, Gary continued sipping his meths (or it might have been an isotonic recovery drink). When I got to the part where Magda ate the glass, he paled and put the bottle down. The Martin McDonald theft had him leaning forward in his chair.

When I concluded, he let out a long sigh. 'You were right about having my dad put someone more experienced on the job.'

'No, I wasn't, Gary. You sorted Lance and Steve yesterday. Not many would have managed that. And what happened today was entirely my fault.'

'D'you think Odeerie will find this McDonald bloke?'

'Not sure. There isn't much time and there's bugger-all to work with.'

'I don't suppose you're gonna need me any more,' Gary said.

I was glad he'd reached this conclusion before I had to reach it for him. 'The Dylans won't come after me now unless I don't produce the goods on McDonald. Then I'll need a small army to stop them.'

'How about if I helped out with the legwork? If you've got two things on at once, won't you need someone to check stuff out?'

'It's a nice idea, Gary, but—'

'No need to pay me. Just don't tell my old man about today.'

'Can't we say the Dylans have given up?'

'He'll know we're lying.'

'I can't really put you to work for nothing just because you don't want to disappoint Farrelly,' I said. 'Why not tell him the truth?'

Gary folded his arms. 'You and my dad have got history, haven't you?'

'We used to work together a long time ago,' I said. 'And then we ran into each other again last year.'

'How was he back then?'

'Pretty much the same as he is now.'

'How did you know if he liked someone?'

'Easy. He didn't hit them.'

'Seriously, Kenny.'

'What did your mum say?'

'She was only with him a few weeks.'

'But you've known Farrelly almost a year . . .'

'Yeah, although sometimes I think I might as well have met him last Tuesday. The thing is that . . . well, I am his son.'

'It doesn't always feel that way?'

'It *never* feels that way. Don't get me wrong, I'm not looking for him to start hugging me or anything. It's just that it would be good to . . .' Gary trailed off and stared at the floor.

'Farrelly's old-school,' I said. 'Just because he doesn't show it doesn't mean it isn't there. You've got to make allowances.'

'You reckon?'

'Absolutely.'

Gary took a few seconds to digest this information. 'Maybe you're right,' he said eventually. 'It's a bit hard to get through to him, that's all. And look, the reason I want to stay working with you isn't because I don't want to disappoint my dad. Well, not that completely. What you and Odeerie do . . . It sounds interesting.'

'Odeerie spends half his life hunched over a screen and I get told to go fuck myself at least twice a week. Does that really sound interesting to you?'

'The George Dent thing does.'

'That's the exception that proves the rule.'

'It's a no then?'

If I have a weakness – other than rogan josh, indolence, pessimism, fear of heights, the Monarch, an inability to commit to relationships, Marlboro Reds and a dust-mite allergy – it's that I'm not brilliant at saying no to people.

'Until the end of the week,' I said. 'After that, we're quits.'

Gary had bought supplies from the Parminto Wholefood Deli down-stairs. He intended to rustle up a tofu stir-fry and wondered if I felt like joining him. Tofu looks like it started out in life as a yeast infection, but the only thing I'd eaten since breakfast was the cheese toastie in Bernie's. He promised it would be ready in twenty minutes, which was a third of the time it usually takes Domino's to bike round a Meat Feast, so I gave him the nod.

Turns out that tofu also tastes like a yeast infection. Gary frowned when I introduced half a bottle of HP into his subtle blend of Asian vegetables and aromatic spices. After the meal, I told him about my meeting with Olivia Porteus. As far as she was concerned, Alexander had been stitched up by posterity. That may or may not be true, but the old boy was indubitably parked in the family mausoleum and not wandering around back gardens in North London.

What with the excitement of the afternoon, I'd neglected to give Peter Timms the daily debrief included in Odeerie's premier package. There wasn't a whole lot I could tell him apart from that I'd checked out George Dent's apartment and found nothing and interviewed Will Creighton-Smith and discovered nothing. Perhaps he would think bet-ter of the entire thing and call time on what was clearly a pointless project.

Unfortunately I'd left my phone behind in the East Cemetery – or rather Miles had left it there for me – and I couldn't find Peter Timms's card. I knew my brother's mobile by heart, though, and it had only just gone eleven by the time Gary was washing up. Malcolm answered on the third ring.

'Have you given up answering your phone, Kenny?'

Malcolm is phlegmatic by nature. I'd only heard real tension in his voice a couple of times in my life. This made it three.

'I lost it,' I said. 'Is everything okay?'

'Not really,' he replied. 'Peter Timms is dead.'

FOURTEEN

'Let me get this straight, then, Kenny,' DI Paula Samson said. 'The only time you met Mr Timms was two days ago, when he asked you to investigate a ghost who had been stalking him. Is that what you're telling me?'

'Not so much that as to find out if his other friends had seen the same thing.'

'The same ghost?'

'Yeah.'

'Why would that have been the case?'

'The boys played this magic prank when they were at school together. Peter thought it might have something to do with that.'

DI Samson was an attractive woman who looked as though she'd seen her share of trouble. Her complexion had the kind of pallor that came with too much artificial light and not enough sleep. What she needed was a fortnight on the Med, not some eejit blathering on about the occult at eight in the morning.

'It's quite a list,' she said, looking down at the sheet of paper on her desk. 'Have you spoken to Blimp Baxter?'

'Not yet.'

'Simon Paxton?'

'No. The only person I interviewed was Will Creighton-Smith.'

'And?'

'He said that Alexander Porteus hadn't visited him.'

'No ghostly experience reported,' the DI said as she recorded this on the paper. I'd have preferred it had she not kept repeating the word 'ghost' every thirty seconds. It made me feel as though we were in an episode of *Scooby-Doo*. But you can't tell senior officers what to do in their own interview rooms.

'Tell me more about George Dent,' she said.

'I've covered everything Peter told me.'

'Specifically that he saw the ghost shortly before he died?'

'That's right.'

'Were they very friendly?' she asked. 'I mean George and Peter, not George and the ghost.'

'They met every few months for dinner.'

The DI stifled a yawn. 'Did Mr Timms tell you anything about the intruder in his garden?' she asked.

'Only that he looked like Alexander Porteus.'

'Nothing else?'

'He said he made this peculiar howling noise.'

'A barking ghost! You don't hear of those very often.'

Paula Samson's face was poker-straight, although I had a feeling that she was struggling to keep it that way. 'Did he report the incident to the police?' she asked.

'Not that I'm aware of.'

'Okay, I think that's it, Mr Gabriel. Unless you've anything else to add . . .'

'There is something,' I said. 'Peter Timms said that George Dent and he had the same phone call after they'd seen Porteus, telling them that they had ten days.'

Samson looked puzzled. 'To do what?'

'Dent died exactly ten days later, and Timms with only a few hours to go.'

She wrote something on her pad. 'I've made a note of that information, but it does seem that Peter Timms's death was accidental.'

'It's being reported it was a scaffolding collapse at his home. Is that right?'

'I can't comment on that at this stage. Although thanks for *materialising* today, Mr Gabriel – it shows the right *spirit*.'

And they say cops don't have a sense of humour.

I walked out of East Hampstead Police Station into the gloom of a mid-October morning. A mother was dragging her kid to school. I knew how the poor sod felt. The sensible place to be was in bed, not having phonics rammed down your throat, or the piss ripped out of you by the Met.

Malcolm's Lexus was parked on the opposite side of the street behind a squad car. I trotted through the drizzle and got into the passenger seat. He was busy instructing someone about the client meeting he'd deputised them to attend. It was a couple of minutes before the call ended. I passed the time by watching raindrops course down the windscreen and wishing I had a bacon sarnie.

My brother's last instructions were to tell the client that he would join them by ten thirty. 'So how did it go?' he asked me after cutting the call.

'About as well as could be expected,' I said.

'What does that mean?'

'I told the DI about Alexander Porteus. She thought I was off my trolley and so was Peter Timms.'

'She really said that?'

'More or less.'

'Did you mention George Dent?'

'Yep.'

'And the phone calls?'

'And the phone calls.'

'She didn't think that was weird?'

'She thought *I* was weird.'

Malcolm stared at the dashboard as though this was inexplicable news.

'What did you expect, Malc? God knows why I let you talk me into giving a statement in the first place. I must need my bumps feeling.'

'Peter Timms said the ghost was a portent.'

'This isn't *Macbeth*, for Christ's sake. It was an accident. Peter wasn't found dead at the crossroads with a stake through his heart.'

'Neither was Macbeth, if memory serves.'

'You know what I mean.'

'You really don't think it's suspicious, Kenny?'

'It's a coincidence, I'll grant you that. And maybe someone was try-ing to put the shits up him for some reason. But there aren't any such things as ghosts, even Peter agreed with that. The other thing you might want to take into account is the possibility that he didn't actually see anything in the first place.'

'Why would he lie?'

'I'm not saying he did. Just that he was under a lot of stress with the company going through a tough time and his missus bailing. Put an idea in someone's head and sometimes they imagine things that aren't really there.'

Malcolm slipped his phone into his pocket. He was wearing a three-grand suit, a vintage Patek Philippe and slightly too much Eight & Bob cologne. Had he been the one giving a statement, he would have been offered a decent cup of coffee and zero wisecracks. Money talks and it sure as hell gets listened to.

'I don't believe in coincidences,' he said. 'Peter thought something bad was going to happen and it did. He wasn't the type to see or hear things that weren't there.'

'What are you saying, Malc? That someone bumped him off?'

'Maybe.'

'Why didn't they just stick a knife between his ribs?'

'Because it would have drawn attention.'

'And the same person threw George Dent out of a window?'

Malcolm shrugged. The rain was really coming down now, battering the car's roof and windscreen. 'I don't know, Kenny, but something isn't right.'

'Well, I'm sure the police will get to the bottom of it.'

'You said they didn't take you seriously.'

'They thought I was barking mad is what I said.'

Malcolm bit his bottom lip and examined his signet ring. I had an idea what was coming next and I was right. 'How would you feel about carrying on with the job?'

'There's no point.'

'But you've got interviews lined up?'

'Blimp Baxter's agreed to see me and I know where Ray Clarke lives.'

'Then why not follow through? I'll pick up the tab for the last couple of days and pay you for however long it takes to speak to Baxter and Clarke. If they say they haven't seen anything, then fair enough.'

Typical of Malcolm to finish what he started. He could speak four languages fluently and had a judo black belt for the same reason. Not to mention a top-ten ad agency. Only this time he wanted *me* to finish what *he'd* started.

'I'm too busy with another job,' I said.

'Really, Kenny? Because if one of the others has seen the same thing and taken the same call, how are you going to feel if he dies too? And it's only going to take a couple of hours. How important is this other job that you can't spare the time?'

The temptation to tell Malc about the Dylans was almost overwhelming. He looked at me and frowned. 'Are you still taking your meds?'

'Why d'you ask?'

'You seem a bit tense.'

The previous year I'd hit a low patch after my best friend dropped dead. I'd also been involved in a case that ended disastrously. My doctor had prescribed antidepressants. After a couple of weeks I'd thrown the pills away.

'That's between me and my physician,' I said.

'Have you called Stephie?' Malcolm asked.

'What's that got to do with anything?'

'You must miss her.'

'I don't, as a matter of fact. And even if I did, what am I going to say? Sorry I bailed on Manchester and haven't been in touch for nearly a year?'

'You're right, Kenny,' Malcolm said after starting the engine with an aggressive twist of the key. 'No point in trying for some happiness in life when you can sit around feeling sorry for yourself all day.'

'All I'm saying is that—'

'And if something else happens to one of the other guys, then I'm sure you'll be able to live with yourself. When you're busy, you're busy, right?'

'That's not fair, Malcolm.'

My brother flicked the wipers on and checked his mirror. He put the Lexus into drive and edged out of his parking spot.

'Can't you get someone else?' I asked.

'Bit late in the day for that.'

He switched the radio on and began picking up speed.

'No, it isn't.'

The satnav advised a right turn.

'Okay, I'll do it,' I said. 'But only until I've seen Ray and Blimp.'

And that was that. If I hadn't been guilt-tripped into carrying on with the job, then the mayhem that occurred over the next five days could have been avoided.

Brothers. I ask you.

Malcolm dropped me on Oxford Street, where I bought a replacement phone. I checked my messages, one of which was from a tense-sounding Blimp Baxter asking if we could change our meeting to the same time the following day as 'something urgent' had come up. After leaving a message on his machine that this would be fine, I entered the parish via Wardour Street and ordered the bacon bap and tea I'd been longing for since Malcolm had picked me up at six thirty. Both were consumed between Bar Bernie and Albion Mansions. It had just gone nine by the time Odeerie ushered me into his flat. Waiting in the office, as arranged, was Gary. Judging by the atmosphere, Odeerie hadn't warmed to him since their last meeting.

I filled both of them in on my visit to East Hampstead Police Station and subsequent conversation with my brother. The fact that we were still on the clock went a long way to cheering Odeerie up. As did his third breakfast Danish.

'I've always liked your brother,' he said through a mouthful of dough.

'You've never met him.'

'Liked the sound of him, I mean.'

'Don't get too excited. He's only paying until I've spoken to Ray— What's he calling himself now?'

'Judy Richards.'

'Until I've spoken to Judy Richards and Blimp Baxter.'

'That might take a while.'

'No, it won't. I'm seeing Blimp tomorrow afternoon and I'm going to Wapping this morning. That's why I asked Gary to join us.'

Gary was sitting on one of the desk chairs. Odeerie stared at him as though I'd just drawn his attention to a leak in the roof.

'We've got a week to find Martin McDonald for the Dylans,' I said. 'And as I've agreed to spend a bit more time on the Porteus thing, Gary's prepared to lend a hand.'

'He's not experienced and he's not registered,' Odeerie said immediately.

'And he's not working for a paying client either, so it makes no difference.'

Odeerie scowled. What with his eye colour now ranging between gasoline yellow and sphagnum green, it wasn't a pretty sight. He didn't attempt to dispute my point, though. All Gary would be doing was the equivalent of intern work.

'Billy Dylan met Martin McDonald at the Burbage,' I continued. 'We've got a photograph of him, so if Gary goes over there this morning and asks around, then maybe he can pick something up.'

'No point,' Odeerie said.

'What?'

'I just got off the phone to them. They didn't have a small-business seminar in March. In fact, they haven't had a small-business seminar this year.'

'You're sure about that?'

'I spoke to three people, including the conference organiser.'

'Maybe it was booked under a private name.'

'She said the closest thing they've had to a business seminar was a stag do for the Masons at the end of May. And I'm guessing Billy Dylan isn't on the square.'

'Are you sure he said the Burbage?' Gary asked. 'Maybe it was some other hotel.'

It seemed unlikely. When someone pisses off with £600,000 of your unlaundered cash, you tend to remember where you first met them.

'Go to the Burbage anyway,' I said. 'Show McDonald's picture to the barmen and the waiting staff. Check if they've seen him.'

'What if they ask why I want to know?'

'Make something up.'

'Like what?'

'I don't know. Say he's your brother and he went missing in the area. I've got Meg Dylan's number. I'll check if Billy made a mistake and call you later.'

'What d'you suggest I do?' Odeerie asked.

'There's still no sign of McDonald?' I asked. He shook his head. 'Well, according to Billy Dylan he was some kind of business trainer. Maybe you could trawl through training sites for someone who looks like him.'

The fat man sniffed and brushed some pastry crumbs off the upper slopes of his chest. 'We have got other clients, Kenny,' he said.

'Fair enough. I just thought, what with me being six days away from castration at the hands of a bloke you gave my name, home address and inside leg measurements to, you might see it as a priority.'

'I'll get on to this,' Gary said, getting up from his chair. He made his way out of the office, leaving Odeerie and me glaring at each other.

'Where did you find him?' Odeerie asked when the outside door closed.

'He's Farrelly's son.'

'The bloke who used to work for Frank Parr?'

'That's right.'

'He's a straight-up nutter.'

'It isn't hereditary.'

'How d'you know we can trust him?'

'Gary's not hearing anything confidential,' I said. 'And he took on two of Billy Dylan's guys when they jumped me.'

'We're definitely not paying the guy?'

I shook my head. Slightly mollified, he plucked another Danish from the box. 'Well, if it ends in tears, don't say I didn't warn you.'

'Good to know you're looking out for me, Odeerie.'

'S'what friends are for,' he said, and chomped into his pastry.

FIFTEEN

The Carbury Estate in Wapping was a prime example of social housing put up on bomb sites left by the Blitz. Four granite-built blocks faced on to a communal garden occupied by several young mothers whose squealing progeny were racing around the flowerbeds. Each block bore a nautical name that reflected the maritime history of the area. According to Odeerie's research, Judy Richards lived in Drake House.

The front doors on the fourth floor were all coated in emerald gloss. Each had a brass knocker, although I opted to use the bell attached to number 62. It took Judy Richards almost a minute to answer. A grey crop had replaced the blonde bob of the Facebook shot. She was leaning heavily on a stick and wearing a knee-length pleated skirt with a cardigan over a white blouse.

'Can I help you?' she asked.

'Judy Richards?'

'That's right.'

I handed her a card. 'I was hoping to have a chat about someone you were at school with.'

'Who?'

'George Dent, but I'm not a journalist or connected to a paper.'

Judy stared at me full in the face for several seconds before looking down at the card and then back at me again.

'You'd better come in,' she said.

◆ ◆ ◆

The walls in the sitting room were sunflower-yellow. The sofas facing each other had been draped in floral throws. A teak unit held several framed photographs. One was of a smiling couple in their seventies standing outside a garden conservatory. The others were of the same boy at three stages in his life. A gap-toothed toddler beamed at the camera, the adolescent on his bicycle looked more serious, and the graduation photograph showed a handsome young man in a gown and mortarboard.

The final photograph was the one I'd seen on Judy's Facebook page. It had been taken in the Carbury Estate garden and showed her sitting in a wheelchair with the same guy standing behind her. Blue eyes, thick blonde hair, white teeth and a firm jaw gave Connor Clarke a rugged look.

'My son,' Judy said, entering the room.

'He's a good-looking boy,' I said, replacing the photograph.

'Not a boy any more. Connor turned twenty-three last week. Here you are . . .'

'Kenny,' I said. 'Kenny Gabriel.'

'Sorry,' Judy said. 'Sometimes my condition affects my short-term memory.'

She handed me a mug of coffee two-thirds full. Had it been nearer the brim, the tremor in her hand would have caused it to spill.

'D'you see much of Connor?' I asked.

'Every day. He has a flat in Raleigh House, on the other side of the garden. He used to live here, but the place isn't huge, as you can see. The trust placed him at the top of the waiting list. Occasionally I need a little domestic assistance.'

I wondered if Judy's husky contralto had been achieved through force of habit, or whether chemicals and surgery had played a part. If so, they hadn't entirely cancelled her Yorkshire accent.

'I'll be back in a moment, Kenny,' she said.

'Sure I can't help?'

'Absolutely not. Sit down and make yourself comfortable.'

Judy hobbled past a wheelchair charging from a wall socket. I wondered how frequently it saw action. Judging by the time its owner took to reach the door, it would have been indispensable to cover any distance greater than twenty yards.

I settled on to one of the sofas and a marmalade cat padded through the open door. It made a beeline for me and rubbed its head insistently against my shin until I stroked its arched back. My new best friend was purring like a tractor when its owner returned with a second steaming cup.

'Cecil, stop bothering our guest,' she said. The cat gave a plaintive miaow and slunk under my sofa. 'You're not allergic, are you? I'll sling him out if you are.'

'I'm fine,' I replied.

Judy put her coffee on a side table and hooked her stick on its edge. She positioned herself over the sofa and fell into it. 'So, you want to talk about George Dent.'

'If you're okay with that, Judy.'

'That depends what you want to know and why.'

'Do you remember Peter Timms?'

'Yes, I saw the news this morning. Dreadful accident.'

I nodded and said, 'Peter was my client.'

The information had no discernible effect.

'He kept up with George Dent,' I continued. 'They met for dinner occasionally.'

'Is this connected to Hibbert & Saviours? Because I don't have anything to do with the place, and I haven't seen George or Peter in nigh on forty years.'

'I believe you were expelled.'

Judy picked up her mug and took a sip. 'Did Peter tell you that?' I nodded. 'And did he tell you why?'

'Yes.'

'But you're here to talk about George?'

'Actually, I'm here to talk about Alexander Porteus. Have you seen him recently?'

'Is this a joke?'

'Peter Timms didn't think so. And neither did George Dent, apparently.'

'I get the feeling I'm missing a bit of the story here, Kenny,' Judy said.

'Allow me to fill you in,' I replied.

It took ten minutes to relate the information Peter Timms had given me. He had suggested that Ray Clarke had been a star of track and field at Hibberts. No sign of that now. Judy was tall, although her frame was slender and racked by the effects of her illness. All I could detect in the way of make-up was a trace of lippy.

During my story, the cat poked its head out and started nuzzling around my ankles until it realised it was on to a loser and departed the room. The only sounds were the distant shrieks of children playing in the communal garden, and a plane departing or arriving at City Airport. After I'd finished, Judy took a few moments to respond.

'Have you been to the police?' was her first question.

'This morning. They all but laughed me out of the station.'

'Because of the Porteus business?'

'That and a complete lack of evidence.'

'They think his death was an accident?'

'Apparently.'

'And it was *exactly* ten days for both him and George?'

'Give or take a few hours.'

Judy flexed the arms of the reading glasses hanging around her neck a few times. 'Now Peter's dead, who are you working for, Kenny?' she asked.

'I can't reveal that, but it's none of the other boys.'

As my brother was picking up the bill now, my conscience was clear. Well, fairly clear.

'What d'you want from me?' Judy asked.

'First, I wondered whether you'd had any sightings of Alexander Porteus, although I'm guessing that's not the case.' Judy shook her head. 'Do you believe you saw a ghost that night in the cemetery?' I asked.

'No, it was too solid to be a ghost. Having said that, there was something . . .' Judy produced a handkerchief from the sleeve of her cardigan. She dabbed her lips lightly before replacing it. 'What did Peter Timms say?'

'Couldn't make his mind up. On the one hand he thought it was someone pranking you. On the other he also seemed to think there was something supernatural about it.'

'And Creighton-Smith?'

'Didn't give a damn one way or the other.'

A faint smile from Judy. 'Will wasn't overly blessed with imagination,' she said. 'I imagine he's running the family business and on his way to his first coronary.'

'Actually, Will's selling second-hand motors. Although you're probably right about the heart attack.' Judy frowned. 'The family business tanked,' I explained. 'He works for a classic-car company in Mayfair.'

'Poor old Will,' she said with a straight face.

'Have the other boys contacted you recently?' I asked.

Judy shook her head. 'One thing I learned about the upper classes at Hibberts is that they're bloody ruthless. That's how the system perpetuates itself. If one of the pack falls, the rest abandon it and move on.'

'Were you a pack member?' I asked.

Judy chuckled. 'I was a skimp, Kenny. D'you know what that is?'

'A scholarship boy,' I said, recalling Will's use of the term.

'That's right. Hence I failed to make the grade on two levels. Firstly I was poor, which the gentry despises; secondly I was clever, which makes them suspicious.'

'You were unhappy at Hibberts?'

'Not entirely. There was one exception to the rule – at least I thought there was – and I was good at games, which gave me a degree of kudos.'

'Why did you go?' I asked.

'My parents were all for it.' Judy's eyes flicked to the photo of the elderly couple. 'They thought it would give me advantages they didn't have. When the interview panel heard my accent, I was sure it would be an automatic refusal. By the time I was offered a place it was impossible to say no.'

'How old were you?' I asked.

'Fourteen.'

'Must have been tough.'

'It was. If I'd stayed in Doncaster, things might have turned out differently.' Judy paused for a moment and seemed to think about this. 'Then again, perhaps they wouldn't. Maybe we all end up where we're meant to end up.'

This vaguely melancholic sentiment hung in the air. There were a few questions I still wanted to ask Judy. One took precedence over the others.

'You said there was an exception to the rule about your being unhappy,' I reminded her. 'What was that, exactly?'

'George Dent,' she said.

Which was when the outside door opened.

SIXTEEN

Connor Clarke had the broad shoulders, narrow hips and swollen biceps of a natural athlete. He was wearing faded jeans and a checked thermal shirt. His blonde hair was an inch or so longer than in the photograph on the bureau, and a pair of thick-framed black glasses leavened out the jock look with a hint of geek.

Presumably Judy didn't receive many visitors, as he performed a double take on seeing me perched on the sofa. 'Connor, this is Kenny Gabriel,' she said. 'He's a private investigator.'

Connor didn't appear thrilled to see me but he observed the social niceties. After giving Judy a kiss on the cheek, he turned to me and we shook hands. 'Don't think I've met a private investigator before. Sounds exciting.'

'Actually, I'm more of a skip-tracer. It's less exciting.'

'Trying to track people down?'

'Pretty much.'

'And that's what Judy's helping you with?'

'It's about an old school friend, Connor,' Judy interjected.

'As long as that's all he's asking about.'

Connor gave me a hard stare before turning to Judy. He crouched beside her and asked, 'How are you feeling?'

'Not so bad, Con.'

'Any dizziness today?'

Judy shook her head.

'Did you take your meds?'

'Yes,' she said.

'And ate something straight afterwards?'

'I managed a glass of milk.'

'You've got to eat solids, Judy, even if it's just half a bowl of cereal. Remember Dr Anderson said the pills would absorb better that way.

'I'll try tomorrow.'

'Promise?'

'I promise.'

Judy was rewarded with a kiss on the forehead. Connor stood up. 'I'll put another hour in and then make us something nice for lunch,' he said. Judy smiled and nodded. Her son scowled at me. 'You won't be taking much longer, hopefully. As you can see, Judy's energy levels aren't great right now.'

'Only a few more minutes,' I said.

'Just make sure that's all it is.'

He left the room without a goodbye. It had been short and not particularly sweet, at least not as far as I was concerned. Connor's attitude to his ailing parent had been of a different order. Who would comfort Kenny in his declining years? Supermarket Scotch and daytime TV, probably. Always assuming I could afford them both.

'Sorry about that,' Judy said. 'Connor lived through some unpleasant stuff with the media. It's made him very protective.'

'When you transitioned?' I said, hoping that was the correct verb.

'That's right. Certain papers weren't very happy with the NHS funding my procedure. In the end I had to send him to stay with my parents.'

'What about his mother?'

'Returned to Australia after we divorced.'

'Didn't she want to take Connor with her?'

'Pam made token noises but she wasn't at all maternal,' Judy said. 'When I threatened a legal challenge, the towel was thrown in pretty quickly.'

'I take it Connor doesn't know about what happened at Hibberts?'

'Is there any reason he should?'

'I suppose not,' I said. 'You were talking about George Dent . . .'

Judy's right leg twitched several times, as though an electrical charge had passed through it. She held her thigh steady for a few moments before responding. 'Hibberts was like most public schools. Lots of adolescent boys keen to experiment but lacking girls to collaborate with.'

'They experimented with each other?'

'For the vast majority, it's just their hormones bubbling over. Once they have access to the opposite sex, that's an end to it.'

'But not George Dent?'

Judy shook her head. 'George was properly gay. He hid it well and he didn't take part in any fumblings in the cricket pavilion or after lights-out in the dorm. Incredibly disciplined, when you think about it.'

'Did he confide in you?' I asked.

'After a fashion. I've known I was in the wrong body since I was five. You become very observant when you carry a secret round all the time. It must be a little like being a spy. Constantly on the lookout in case someone susses you.'

'And George was in the same boat?'

'He sensed there was something different about me and that it wasn't just my flat vowels. George was a decent runner and we used to train on the Heath. One afternoon we took a break by the ponds. Some guys were swimming and George said that, on the whole, he thought he might prefer boys to girls. I said that, on the whole, I might prefer to *be* a girl than a boy. He asked me what I meant, and that was that.'

'Quite brave of you to confide in each other.'

'Actually, we'd come close a couple of times before. It was just a matter of getting across the line, to use a running metaphor.'

'And afterwards you became friends?'

'More that it took the friendship to a different level.'

'Did George persuade you to go into the cemetery?'

'He asked if I'd go along. Have you spoken to Simon Paxton?'

'Not yet.'

'Are you going to?'

'Perhaps.'

'Simon was peculiar, even then. When he looked at you it was as though he knew what you were thinking. He scared me shitless, if you'll excuse the expression, although he and Will seemed to get on well enough, which was a surprise.'

Judy dabbed her mouth with the hankie. It's tough to imagine any man in his mid-fifties as a sixteen-year-old; when he's wearing court shoes and a pleated skirt, it's tougher still. Life changes us all. It had changed Judy Richards more than most.

'I don't understand why you agreed to go to the cemetery,' I said. 'Weren't you worried that you'd be expelled?'

'I think at some level that's what I was hoping for. Although it might not have been, had I known how it would affect my parents.'

'They were upset?'

'Devastated. Can you imagine how it must feel to have your son set up for life, only to have him throw it all away?'

It didn't take much imagination, what with having done pretty much the same thing to my own parents. 'How did they react?' I asked.

'It would have been better had they bawled me out, told me that I'd flushed my prospects down the toilet and never forgiven me.'

'But that's not what happened?'

Judy adjusted her position on the sofa and rolled her head around her neck. I wondered if the cause of her tension was physical or emotional.

'They were very understanding and said that everyone makes mistakes in life. Of course, that made it infinitely worse. But if it was excoriation I was after, then it was in no short supply at the local comp.'

'The kids gave you a tough time?'

'And the teachers. You can't blame them, I suppose. I'd turned my back on state education and then come scuttling back when I couldn't hack it with the rich kids. At least, that's what it must have looked like.'

'But you passed your exams?'

'Just about.'

'And became a teacher yourself?'

'Not immediately. Dad got me a job in customer accounts at the water board.'

'Were any of the H&S kids in touch?'

'A letter from George arrived out of the blue one day about six years after the cemetery incident. He'd just come down from Oxford and was working as a researcher for the Labour Party.'

'What did he want?'

'To apologise for what happened that night. He said it had been playing on his mind and wondered if I wanted to meet up.'

'Did you?'

'What was the point? Our lives were as different as different could be. George was contributing to international policy documents and I was trying to explain to pensioners why their bill was £6 higher than it had been last quarter. I was clever, Kenny. If I'd stuck Hibberts out for a couple more years . . .'

Judy stared at her lap as though her alternate future were playing itself out there. 'What did you do with the letter?' I asked, to bring her back to the here and now.

'Resealed the envelope and sent it back,' she said.

'And that was the last you heard from George Dent?'

'Not quite. When my gender reassignment hit the news, he sent me a note saying that if there was anything he could do to help I should get in touch.'

'But you didn't?' Judy shook her head. 'How did you get from the water board to working as a teacher?' I asked.

'My grandfather died and left me a few thousand in his will. I used it to move back to London and study for a PGCE.'

'Couldn't you have done that locally?'

'Probably, but there were other things in my life by then that were made considerably easier by living in a big city.'

'And you've been a teacher ever since you qualified?'

'Until my illness retired me.'

'Always in London?'

'Yes. It's not been a bad life, and I've had Connor, which has been wonderful. A few years more would have been nice, but that's not going to happen. I've made my peace with the world and I intend to enjoy whatever time I have left.' Judy's voice had thickened and her eyelids began to flutter. 'I'm afraid that's as much as I can manage, Kenny,' she said.

'It's been useful,' I said. 'Thank you.'

'Would you mind assisting me to the bedroom?'

Helping Judy up was an awkward manoeuvre. Eventually she was on her feet. Our journey across the room was laborious. Her energy levels had depleted to the point that she was virtually a dead weight. We entered the passage like contestants in some kind of tragic three-legged race. She nodded at a door and I toed it open. Cecil the cat shot out and headed for the kitchen. God knows how he'd got in there.

Judy's bedroom was small and neat. The dressing table looked as though it had been purchased in IKEA, the wardrobe made from MDF sometime in the eighties. The walls were lilac and a jute rug protected the floor. Artificial citrus notes came from a scent bottle on the table that had three sticks poking out of it. It smelled as though we had entered an ersatz lemon grove.

Lowering Judy on to the bed felt like depositing a corpse into a shallow grave. She was unconscious before her head hit the pillow. On the bedside table were two photographs. One was of Connor when a toddler, the second of a boy who had probably just entered his teens. Ray Clarke's smile wasn't quite as broad as his parents'. After everything Judy had told me, perhaps there was a reason for this.

I looked from the image of a curly-haired adolescent with everything before him to a woman living on the bones of her arse and who probably wouldn't be around at all in a year's time. One of Odeerie's favourite axioms sprang to mind.

Life is shit and then you die.

SEVENTEEN

The first thing I did after leaving Judy's flat was spark up a Marlboro. It felt good to have cool autumn air on my face and smoke hitting the back of my throat. I hung over the balcony wall and watched Connor Clarke clipping one of the trees in the garden. A couple of the young mums were also casting glances in his direction.

My conversation with Judy hadn't been particularly illuminating, although at least she hadn't seen Porteus's ghost. If he hadn't been troubling Blimp Baxter either, then I could report this to Malcolm and concentrate on finding Martin McDonald.

I stubbed out my fag at the bottom of the stairs and dropped the butt into a litter bin. I was trying to work out how to use my new phone when someone shouted my name. Connor Clarke was beckoning me into the garden.

I hopped over the small wall and made my way across the grass. Connor was standing under a beech tree holding a pair of long-handled secateurs. He laid the tool down and removed his gardening gloves. 'I wanted to apologise, Kenny. I was rude to you earlier and there was no call for it. Judy's all I've got and sometimes that makes me more suspicious than I ought to be. Can we start again?'

Our handshake lasted longer than the one twenty minutes earlier.

'I left Judy in her bedroom sleeping,' I said. 'She seemed pretty exhausted. I hope that wasn't entirely my fault.'

'I'm sure it wasn't,' Connor said. 'She's been doing really well recently but the exhaustion can still come out of a clear blue sky. That's something we'll have to get used to until she's better.'

'I understand your mother has motor neurone disease,' I said, before realising my error. 'Sorry, it's just that—'

'It's an understandable mistake, Kenny. And Judy's more my mother than my birth mother ever was. She asked me what I wanted to call her when she transitioned. I opted for Judy and that's what it's been ever since.'

'Even so, it must have been a bit odd for you.'

Connor pursed his lips, as though this was something he had never considered. 'At first, perhaps, but the change was gradual. And children adapt pretty quickly.'

'I suppose so,' I said. 'What's the prognosis for Judy's illness?'

'She should be fully recovered in six months or so.'

'Is that what the doctors say?'

Connor smiled. 'Doctors are fools.'

'You sought a second opinion?'

'Wouldn't you, for someone you love? We need to put more work in but it will all pay off in the end. It's simply a matter of time.'

I wondered if Connor and Judy had approached some kind of quack faith healer. There was no shortage of charlatans prepared to take cash from the desperate. If so, Judy had seemed far less confident of a happy outcome than her son.

Connor tucked his gloves into his pocket and scratched the back of his neck. A pair of crows took off from the tree behind him and cawed their way into the air.

'The garden looks nice,' I said. 'Do the other residents pitch in?'

'No, it's just me. I'm taking an MSc in horticulture and the trust subsidises my rent if I put in a few hours every week.'

Connor stared at the leaves covering the grass. Years in Odeerie's employ have taught me the value of shutting up, particularly when it appears that someone wants to get something off his chest. I sensed that was the case with Connor. I was right.

'Judy's been getting hate mail,' he said. 'A lot of it's about her illness being God's punishment. I wondered if that was the reason you were seeing her . . .'

Connor's fishing was understandable. Judy's claim that I was interested in an old schoolmate hadn't sounded a hundred per cent credible, even if it was half-true. But I'd guaranteed the woman confidentiality, so I nodded and refused the bait.

'I don't suppose you have any experience of that sort of thing?' he continued. 'On a professional level, I mean.'

'How many letters has she received?' I asked.

'The fourth came a few days ago. There's been the usual Internet trolling but that didn't bother her too much. The letters really seem to get her down.'

'Have you spoken to the police?'

'What's the point? There weren't any physical threats, just a lot of crazy shit about burning in hell and quotes from the Bible.'

'Did you keep the letters?' I asked.

Connor shook his head. 'Judy wanted them destroyed.'

'Were they sent through the regular mail?'

'Yes.'

'If things escalate then it's a good idea to have the previous communication if the police need to act,' I said. 'Although it's probably just some saddo getting his kicks.'

'Thanks for your advice,' Connor said. 'I'll bear it in mind. Will you want to see Judy again, or did she tell you what you needed to know?'

'I think that's it for now.'

'And it's really nothing we should be worried about?'

I was wondering how to field this question when a little girl saved me the bother. She was fiddling with the door handle on the gardener's hut. The size of a small garage, it had been given a mock-Tudor look completely at odds with its surroundings. Connor trotted over and picked her up.

'There's lots of sharp tools in there, Maisie,' he said. 'You've got to be careful.' The kid was delighted at being swept off the ground. Even more delighted when Connor deposited her across his broad shoulders. 'Shall we take you to Mummy?' Maisie nodded enthusiastically. 'Sorry again for being so short,' Connor said to me.

'Not a problem,' I replied.

He smiled and trotted back to the swings, with Maisie squealing as though on a fairground ride. I returned to my phone. There were two messages. My brother's required no reply. I'd asked whether he could arrange for me to visit Peter's house. He was confirming that Peter's ex-wife would be there all day.

The second was from Sally Thomas, whom I'd met in Mermaid Court and given permission to take the painting. She answered almost immediately. 'Hello, Sally, it's Kenny Gabriel. You left a message . . .'

'Thanks for calling me back,' she said.

'Pleasure. How can I help?'

'There's something I'd like to show you.'

'What is it?'

'Photographs. I'd prefer not to go into details on the phone. You never know who might be listening in.'

'Presumably it's something to do with George.'

'That's right.'

'Look, Sally, if it's the kind of thing they found in his bathroom then you really ought to go to the police.'

'It isn't.'

'Can't you give me a hint, at least?'

'I'd rather not. Is there somewhere we can meet?'

'Where are you now?'

'Foyles.'

'How about Bar Bernie in Wardour Street at one o'clock?'

'See you there,' she said.

◆　◆　◆

On my way back to Wapping Tube station, my phone rang, displaying Gary's name. Hopefully it was good news from his visit to the Burbage Hotel.

'Did you find anything?' I asked.

'Sod all' was his disappointing answer.

'Who did you talk to?'

'Concierge, bar staff, waiters, porters, you name it.'

'And you showed them McDonald's photograph?'

'Yeah, I told them it was my brother who'd gone missing, like you said. One of the bar staff started crying and said that her sister disappeared last year and they still haven't found her. I felt like a right piece of shit.'

'Welcome to my world, Gary.'

'What d'you want me to do now?' he asked.

'I'm seeing someone in Bar Bernie at one. Why don't we meet in the Vesuvius later and we can work something out. Assuming you want to carry on, that is . . .'

'Will it involve me lying my arse off?' he asked.

'That depends on what Meg Dylan has to say,' I replied.

◆　◆　◆

I'd hoped that the next time I spoke to Ma Dylan it would be to hand over Martin McDonald's address and the name of the bank in which he had deposited her cash. Admitting that I was no further down the road wasn't a happy prospect. Usually I'm hoping I don't get someone's voicemail. This time it was the other way round.

She answered on the second ring.

'Hello, Kenny. Have you got some news for me?'

'Er, not exactly, Mrs Dylan.'

'Do call me Meg.'

'We checked out the Burbage, Meg.'

'And?'

'They have no record of the business seminar where Billy met Martin McDonald. In fact, they haven't had that kind of event this year.'

'Are you sure?'

'We spoke to the conference organiser.'

Silence.

'So I was just wondering,' I continued, 'whether Billy might have got the name of the hotel wrong. There are quite a few in that area.'

It must have sounded as unlikely to Meg Dylan as it did to me. 'Let me have a word with him,' she said. 'How are your other leads coming along?'

'Nothing concrete yet,' I said. 'But it's early days.'

'Not really, Kenny,' she replied sweetly. 'You've only got six days left on the job. After that, I'm afraid the penalty clause will have to be invoked.'

My sphincter dilated and my scrotum tightened. 'I'm sure we'll have good news for you soon,' I said in a voice distinctly higher than its usual register. 'There are a couple of leads.'

'That's wonderful,' Meg Dylan said. 'Billy will return your call sometime this afternoon. Have a great day, Kenny.'

'Drop dead, bitch,' I said.

To the dialling tone.

◆ ◆ ◆

Trinity Road was a five-minute walk from Hampstead Tube station. Most of its Georgian houses had three storeys, and I passed four English Heritage blue plaques on my way to number 38. Wooden shutters obscured most of the box windows. There were boot scrapers, lamp holders, fire plaques and even a couple of sundials.

Five million would buy you something decent, although you'd have to fork out at least another three to go top of the market. Peter Timms's house was yellow-brick and had black-painted iron railings outside, with a flight of steps running up to the front door. I pressed the bell and waited.

The woman who answered looked to be in her late forties. She had bobbed blonde hair and she was wearing a black polo-neck sweater and jeans. On her feet was a pair of incongruous yellow trainers with green flashes. Delia Timms looked as though she had been crying for a long time and was only just keeping it under control now.

'Can I help you?' she asked.

'My name's Kenny Gabriel,' I said. 'My brother spoke to you earlier.'

Delia took several seconds to recall the conversation. 'Yes, Malcolm said you might come round. You're some kind scaffolding expert. Is that right?'

What I know about scaffolding could be written on the back of a beer mat, leaving room for the Old Testament and most of *Paradise Lost*. Malcolm hadn't thought it appropriate to bother Delia Timms with stories of ghostly portents, though.

'More an accident investigator,' I said.

'The police experts think it was a loose bolt.'

'Almost certainly they're right, but you know what insurance companies are like. Often they try to invalidate claims due to misadventure.'

A frown came over Delia's face. 'You're saying that Pete came back from a DTI function and decided to shin up thirty feet of scaffolding in his dinner suit?'

'That's what *they* might suggest. I assume he was carrying life cover . . .'

This gave Delia pause for thought. Money usually does for most people. She ran a hand through her hair and said, 'Well, I suppose there can't be any harm, although it's just a lot of poles and stacked planks now.'

'Great,' I said. 'How do we get round there?'

◆ ◆ ◆

We entered a passage through a locked gate. To the right was the exterior of the house, to the left a high wall separating it from the property next door. The passage led on to a decent-sized garden. Mostly it was well-tended lawn, although there were two mature oak trees, in one of which was lodged a sturdy-looking tree house.

'After we broke up, Pete preferred to use the granny flat,' Delia Timms said. 'This is the easiest way to access it.'

We had stopped by a door that, judging by the different brickwork, had been built into the property in the last couple of decades. Lying on his back was a headless garden gnome. Apparently Peter Timms hadn't been the only fatality last night. A few yards away, scaffolding poles, joints, pins and planks had been neatly arranged.

'What time did your husband get back?' I asked.

'I think about ten o'clock,' Delia said. 'The man next door heard the taxi pull up. Five minutes later there was an almighty crash. The neighbour can see into the passage from up there.' She pointed at a window under the eaves of the house next door. 'One of Pete's legs was stretched out from under the scaffolding, and he called the emergency services.'

'Was the scaffolding arranged above the door?'

'That's right. The wall needed repointing.'

'Did the police take anything away?'

'I don't think so.' Delia consulted her watch. 'Look, I don't want to appear rude, Kenny, but as I'm sure you can imagine, arrangements need to be made . . .'

'No problem,' I said. 'I'll let myself out when I'm done.'

'Will you tell Malcolm if you find anything amiss?'

'Of course,' I said, 'although I wouldn't concern yourself too much about that. And I'm sorry for your loss. Peter seemed a decent man.'

Delia's eyes brimmed. 'The divorce had got really unpleasant,' she said, 'but that was only the bloody lawyers. I just hope Pete knew I didn't . . .'

'I'm sure he did,' I replied.

Delia Timms nodded, retraced her steps and closed the gate. Not for the first time I felt less than splendid about lying for a living. I distracted myself by focusing on the accident site. If someone had collapsed the rig then I didn't see how. Had they been on top of the structure, they'd have come down with it.

Peter Timms had told me the door leading to the neighbour's garden had been locked the night he saw Alexander Porteus. It still was. It would have taken a decent-sized key that I'd bet pounds to peanuts had been long since lost, even if the mechanism hadn't rusted. The wall was twelve feet high. For anyone other than Spider-Man, it would have taken a ladder or a rope to scale.

Unless Alexander Porteus had walked straight through it, of course. Had Peter Timms really seen the shade of a black magician ten days ago?

After checking the door, I took a few shots of the garden and the granny-flat window on my phone. Then I walked back to the side of the house where the scaffolding was stacked. I noticed the gnome's head lying under a rhododendron bush and fished it out. He was a cheerful-looking fella with a white beard and a red hat. I stood his body up and balanced the head on his shoulders. He looked grateful and I decided to pump him for information. 'What happened last night, mate?'

Nothing from the gnome.

'Was it an accident, or did someone do him in?'

Nothing from the gnome.

'Did you see Alexander Porteus too?' I asked.

'Is your name Kenny?' he replied.

◆ ◆ ◆

My surprised cry caused the man to jump a couple of inches. In his late forties, he was wearing a pair of Lycra shorts and a top made from the same material. His baseball cap bore the Adidas logo and a water bottle was clipped to a thin belt around his waist. A runner, unless I was very much mistaken.

'Geoff Cracknel,' he said. 'I own the place next door. I was just checking on Delia and she said that you were taking a look around. Sorry to give you a start.'

'No problem,' I said. 'I was just . . .'

Having a chat with a decapitated garden gnome didn't seem the ideal way to finish the sentence. Instead I rose from my crouch with the usual stifled moan. Geoff removed his cap to reveal a mass of sweat-drenched grey curls.

'Delia says you're an accident investigator.'

'That's right. My brother, Malcolm, was friends with Peter.'

'The police have already been.'

'Are you the person who called them last night?' Geoff nodded. 'Did they interview you this morning?' He nodded again. 'I don't suppose they mentioned anything suspicious?'

'Why d'you ask?'

'Peter said he'd had an intruder a couple of weeks ago.'

Geoff uncapped his bottle and took a swig. I suspected it was more to give him the chance to think than hydrate. 'Are you suggesting foul play?' he asked.

I shrugged and said, 'There must be a fair few burglary attempts in a neighbourhood like this.'

'Not really. Security's high, which means you'd have to be either very skilled or very stupid to attempt a break-in.'

'But it does happen?'

Geoff replaced the cap on his bottle and prodded the watch strapped to his wrist a couple of times. 'Something occurred to me when I was running. Perhaps I ought to have mentioned it to the police.'

'What was that?' I asked.

'Before the scaffolding gave way, I heard a shout.'

The revelation was a disappointment. Most people have something to say when half a ton of scaffolding falls on their head. Assuming they get the chance to say anything at all, that is. I put this point to Geoff.

'I don't mean immediately before,' he replied. 'More like ten seconds.'

Less disappointing.

'Was it a sentence or a word?' I asked.

'Just a shout, as though he'd been surprised by something. But if it was the scaffolding working loose, surely he would have had time to jump away.'

True enough. Even if he'd caned the hooch at his DTI do, ten seconds would have been more than sufficient for Peter to take evasive action.

'You sure it was that long?' I asked.

Geoff nodded. 'I was on a conference call to the States. Otherwise I'd have checked it out immediately.'

'And you didn't mention this to the police?'

'I said there was a shout, but they didn't seem to think it was relevant.'

'Did you emphasise the time delay?'

'Not really. D'you think I should call them?'

'Might be an idea,' I said.

EIGHTEEN

The older you get, the narrower life becomes. The opportunities of youth begin to slough away in your thirties. If you're not doing what you want to do by forty, then hopefully you've got enough cash to anaesthetise yourself with hi-tech juicers, mid-range BMWs, wearable technology and heritage vinyl. One day in your fifties, you'll look into the mirror and wonder why your old man is staring back at you.

A decade later, the juicer's been replaced by nasal-hair clippers and the BMW traded in for something half the size that knows how to parallel-park itself. You're also taking a keen interest in Alzheimer's research. From there on in, it's just a matter of what's going to kill you and when oblivion is scheduled to arrive.

In the New Year, my doctor had suggested that I swap antidepressants for sessions with a cognitive behavioural therapist. Greta encouraged me to combat negative thinking. En route to Wardour Street, I gave it a shot. If I failed to find Martin McDonald, there would be no need to worry about a ripening prostate or a softening brain. Nor would I be routinely humiliated in a rest home by work-experience teenagers on Ritalin. By the time I entered Bar Bernie, I was at least two notches above suicidal.

Sally Thomas, the secretary I'd gifted George Dent's watercolour to in Mermaid Court, was tucking into a mug of coffee and reading a volume of Tony Benn's diaries. She looked smarter than at our last meeting. Her brown hair was in a ponytail and she'd put a bit of slap on. That and the trouser suit led me to wonder if she was going somewhere special. I slid on to the opposite bench in the booth.

'Hey, Kenny,' she said. 'How's it going?'

'Oh, you know . . . How can I help you?'

Sally closed the book and placed it in a small pink rucksack. From it she took an A4 envelope and placed it on the table.

'I'm assuming these are the photographs,' I said.

'That's right.'

I reached for the envelope. Sally covered it with her hand. 'You have to promise not to say where you got them.'

'I promise.'

'And that you won't sell them to the press.'

'Would they be interested?'

She nodded. 'They're of George.'

'Can I show them to anyone?' I asked.

'If it helps find out who framed him.'

'You think the photographs might do that?'

'Maybe.'

'So why not take them to the police?'

'Because I don't trust them.'

'You could make copies.'

'I already have.'

Sally took her hand off the envelope and I looked inside. In two of the images, George Dent was hunched over a coffee table with a rolled twenty up his nose. It was poised over a line of white powder. In the third shot there was another guy on the sofa. This companion was staring directly into the lens of what was clearly a concealed camera. The light wasn't great but it didn't need to be. I recognised the face immediately.

'Where did you find these, Sally?'

'They were taped inside the lining paper at the back of the watercolour. I didn't notice the envelope until I went to hang it up. Even then I almost missed it.'

'Have you any idea why they were there?'

'You can tell the camera's hidden. Someone's trying to blackmail him.'

They were the kind of photographs you saw first in tabloids and then plastered across celeb sites. Usually taken in sting operations by journos 'acting in the public interest'. Only these didn't seem to have made it on to the editor's desk. I slipped the pictures back into the envelope.

'What d'you want me to do with them?'

'You said your client thought George was innocent.'

'How do pictures of him taking drugs prove that?'

She leant forward in her seat and said under her breath, 'Because maybe it was the same person who planted the child abuse pictures in his flat.'

'Maybe,' I said. 'And maybe not.'

'Whoever's in the picture with him has to be a suspect.'

'D'you know who it is?' Sally shook her head. I treated her to a protracted sigh. 'Tough to track someone down from a photograph.'

'You're not interested, then?'

'I'll show them to my associate and see what he can come up with.'

Sally's extended bottom lip made her look like a disappointed eight-year-old whose dad had bought the wrong doll at Christmas. But there was no point in telling her the truth. She'd only want to know what I intended to do, and I hadn't decided that yet. Unkind not to offer up something, though.

'Odeerie might get lucky,' I said. 'How about I keep you in the loop?'

'I expect to be kept in the fucking loop,' she snapped. 'I'm the one who gave you the photographs. And who the hell's Odeerie?'

'A guy I work with. He's good with stuff like this.'

Sally frowned and said, 'Maybe I ought to take them to the police.'

'Give me a couple of days,' I replied. 'If I haven't been able to sort anything out then, by all means, go to the Met.'

'I suppose so.' Sally glanced at my watch. 'Is that the right time?'

'Actually, it's five minutes slow.'

'Shit!' She grabbed her bag and coat.

'Off to something important?' I asked.

'Job interview.'

'Really? What are you going for?' I asked.

She was halfway to the door before I finished the sentence.

I had almost an hour to kill before I needed to meet Gary. It was enough time to eat a burger and chips and check in with Odeerie. The fat man's phone went straight to mail. I was halfway through a Quarter Pounder when my mobile began ringing with a withheld number. I answered expecting Odeerie. 'You're in big trouble, cunt' wasn't his usual opening.

'Thanks for returning my call, Billy,' I said.

'Why are you bothering my mum?' he asked.

'Because I didn't have your number and there's something I needed clearing up.'

'In future you speak to me directly. Got it?'

'It'll be a pleasure,' I said.

'About this hotel. Why did you think it was the Burbage?'

'You told me it was.'

'Yeah, well I might have got that wrong.'

'Because there's so many hotels running business seminars?'

'There are, as it goes,' Billy said. 'And I visited a shitload before I found someone who was right for us. If it weren't the Burbage, it must have been some other place.'

'Okay, give me a couple of possibilities and I'll check them out.'

'It was months ago, for fuck's sake. I can't remember where I went.'

'And the pubs you met McDonald in?'

'Same thing.'

'What about the airport? Are you sure it was Heathrow and not Gatwick? Or are you a bit confused about that one too? I mean, it was only half a million quid.'

'You know, I'm gonna love ruining you,' Billy said, and cut the call.

I pushed away my half-eaten burger. It had been satisfying but unwise to tell Billy how I really felt. Fail to locate Martin McDonald now and I was in very deep shit indeed. I took a swig of tea and checked my watch.

Just enough time to visit a certain esoteric bookshop.

◆　◆　◆

In the early twentieth century, Cecil Court was home to the British film industry when many of the Victorian-era shops sold film stock and cameras. Since the war it has been colonised by antiquarian bookshops. The majority retain their original frontages. These and the converted gas lamps lend the alley a vaguely Dickensian feel that brings tourists flocking in to purchase first editions that could be bought for half the price around the corner on Charing Cross Road.

The sign for Porteus Books was picked out in gold lettering. Several volumes arranged in its plate-glass window were vintage, although the majority had been recently published. Titles included *Harness the Power of the I Ching* and *Vishnu Speaks!* and *Secrets of the Kabbalah*. Prayer beads, incense burners, images of Ganesh, and temple bells were also displayed.

The smell inside the shop combined the sweetness of incense and the pulpy smell of new books. Directly opposite me was a rack with the top-ten bestsellers that month. Number one was something called

Angels Watch Over Us. Other volumes were arranged across shelves cat-egorised into the world's major delusional systems.

Behind the sales desk was a man in his early thirties. He was wear-ing a blue corduroy jacket over a polo shirt and jeans. Were it not for a three-inch golden ankh around his neck, he could have been manning the reference section at a local library.

'I'm looking for Olivia Porteus,' I said.

'Are you the chap collecting the Navajo fertility fetish?'

'Er, no. My name's Kenny Gabriel.'

'Oh, right. Well, she's downstairs.'

I thanked the assistant and trotted under an arch with a picture of a garlanded Maharishi Mahesh Yogi attached to it. The atmosphere was different in the basement. Partly this was due to the subdued lighting and the exposed brickwork. Mostly, however, it was the stock and the way it had been laid out.

Half the floor space was filled with glass cabinets. Items had been arranged as though in a museum. In the nearest, I could make out a black scarab on a chain and a silver disc bearing a pentangular symbol. Bookcases went from floor to ceiling along the wall to my right. Their shelves held leather and cloth volumes. The categories were the same as those on display upstairs with one exception: ALEXANDER PORTEUS.

A couple of Porteus's books had elaborate gold tooling on the spines. Others were slim and plain in comparison. Seventy years ago, the author had padded around this cellar in person. It may have been this thought, or the comparative coolness of the room, that caused my skin to stipple.

I was scanning the old boy's oeuvre when his granddaughter entered through a propped-open door. Olivia Porteus was wearing a navy-blue dress with dark woollen tights and black boots. Chestnut hair, which had been loose when I met her in Highgate Cemetery, was piled on her head and secured with a pencil.

'Oh, hello,' she said. 'You're the cemetery man, aren't you?'

'Kenny Gabriel,' I said.

'Did Rodney send you down?'

'Yes. I hope that's okay.'

'Of course it is.' Olivia deposited the half-dozen books she was carrying on a nearby chair and we shook hands. 'Would you like a coffee?' she asked.

'I'm fine, thanks,' I said. 'I was passing and thought I'd pop in.'

'Good,' she said, and smiled. 'What d'you think of the place?'

'It's a lot different down here than up top.'

'We get the more serious collectors and bibliophiles in the basement. Many of them come especially from Europe or the States. Let me get you a seat . . .'

Olivia removed the books from the chair and fetched a stool from the other side of the basement. Despite my protests, she perched on the stool and I took the chair.

'Is there anything specific I can help you with?' she asked. 'Or is this purely a social visit?'

'Actually, there was something. When we met at the cemetery . . . I wasn't there just for the tour. I had a specific reason for attending.'

'Which was?'

'Research.'

'You're a writer?'

'I'm an investigator.'

'A psychic investigator?'

'Not exactly.'

Olivia's forehead furrowed. I took a deep breath and plunged in.

'Some boys performed a magic rite when they were at Hibbert & Saviours School forty years ago. A figure materialised and chased them away. They're concerned he might have returned. They seem to think . . . Well, they seem to think it was your grandfather.' A Piccadilly Line train rumbled along the track that ran forty feet beneath us. 'Obviously it's someone posing as him,' I added when the noise had abated. 'At least, I assume it is.'

'May I ask how you know these people?'

'One of them employed me.'

'Is your client still being bothered by my grandfather?'

'Not any more. He's dead.'

A bell tinkled upstairs as someone entered the shop. A cool breeze wafted across the basement. Olivia might have felt it too as she wrapped her arms around herself.

'How did it happen?' she asked.

'He was crushed under falling scaffolding and one of the other boys committed suicide.'

'Had they both seen Alexander?'

'They seemed to think so.'

'Were they the only boys involved?'

'There were six all told.'

'Have you been in contact with the others?'

Before I could respond, there came a commotion from upstairs. Something fell to the floor with a loud thump. The sound of raised voices followed.

'You can't just march in here and do this, Sebastian,' from Rodney the shop assistant.

'I'll do whatever I fucking well like,' from someone with more finely chiselled vowels. 'Hand the money over, you little shit.'

Olivia was hurrying across the basement before I was out of my chair. I arrived at the top of the stairs to find that a rail-thin man in his late thirties had joined Rodney behind the counter. Sparse blonde hair had been combed back on the guy's head. His cheeks were hollow and there was a corona of red spots around his lips. He wore a pinstriped suit jacket over a V-neck T-shirt and faded jeans. Around his neck was a knotted silk scarf.

The till was open. A slew of notes covered the counter and a couple of tenners were on the floor. Olivia was staring at Blondie and he was staring back at her. He looked surprised; she looked pissed off.

'What are you doing, Sebastian?' Olivia asked.

'I wanted to borrow a couple of hundred, that's all.'

Sebastian's adenoidal voice grated on my ears.

'You know the procedure,' Olivia said patiently. 'You get your allowance every month. If you need more then you get in touch with me first.'

'Do you have any idea how humiliating it is to beg my sister for money?'

'*Ask*, Sebastian,' she said. 'There's a difference.'

Sebastian folded his arms. 'Not when it's my money, there isn't.'

'We've been over this a thousand times.' The aggression in Olivia's voice had been replaced by an emotional catch. 'Please just leave.'

'Not until I get what I came for.'

Sebastian began gathering the notes up from the counter. Rodney looked at Olivia for an indication as to what he should do. She seemed close to tears.

'I think you should go,' I said.

Sebastian looked up. 'And you are?'

'That doesn't matter.'

'Take the cash, Sebastian,' Olivia said. 'We'll discuss this later.'

Her brother's smile revealed two uneven ridges of beige teeth.

'There we are, man who doesn't matter. Best keep your nose out of family business.'

Sebastian took seconds to collect the rest of the money. He stuck the notes in the inside pocket of his jacket. Then he scooped the pound coins from the till and did the same with them. 'Sorry to clear you out, sis, but you know how it is.'

'Yes, Sebastian,' she said. 'I know exactly how it is.'

Olivia's compressed lips suggested disapproval verging on anger. Her eyes communicated a different message. A composite of sadness, pity, shame and despair.

'Right, well, I'd better be off,' Sebastian said, unable to hold his sister's gaze. 'I'll let you know how much is here, Liv, and you can deduct it from my allowance.'

The door opened before Sebastian reached it. A bearded fifty-something guy wearing a grey trilby and a black leather coat stood aside and allowed him out. He looked from Olivia to the till and asked, 'Is everything all right?'

'Yes, of course,' she said. 'Were you looking for anything specific?'

'The name's Jenks. You said my fertility fetish would be available today.'

'Unfortunately there's a problem, Mr Jenks,' Rodney chipped in. 'The fetish was impounded in customs after a last-minute appeal by the Navajo Nation.'

'Why don't you come downstairs and we'll see if we can get to the bottom of this, Mr Jenks,' Olivia suggested. 'Rodney, could you put the kettle on?'

Rodney closed the till and left to do his duty. The disappointed Jenks trudged towards the stairs. Olivia drew a sleeve across her face.

'I'm sorry you had to see that, Kenny,' she said. 'Thanks for trying to help.'

'No problem,' I said.

'I need to sort this fetish business out,' she said, 'but if you're free tonight, why don't you come round for supper? We can carry on our conversation then?'

'That would be great,' I said. Olivia smiled.

'Seventy-five Dean Street at seven,' she said. 'My name's on the bell.'

Olivia's invitation had lightened my mood. For the first time in months – if not years – the streets of Soho didn't feel like a rat run. The workmen tearing up the pavement on Old Compton Street seemed a cheery bunch of artisans and I didn't send a French tourist in entirely the wrong direction for Trafalgar Square.

Sebastian could do with a slap or three but that was hardly his sister's fault. You can choose your friends but not your family and all that. I suspected Seb hadn't raided the till to fund a trip to Holland & Barrett, but it wasn't any of my business. As long as he didn't show up at Dean Street that evening, it was good enough for me.

Even the Vesuvius mid-afternoon couldn't dampen my spirits. A couple of the regulars stared at the racing on the TV with expressions that suggested fortune wasn't smiling upon them. Whispering Nick was peering at a copy of the *Sun* as though it were the Rosetta Stone. The smoking ban was being accorded the usual level of respect, and a pall of blue haze hung over the place.

Gary was waiting at one of the tables. 'How are things?' I asked.

'I've had better mornings,' he replied. 'You?'

I told him about my meetings with Judy Richards and Sally Thomas.

'Who were the photographs of?' Gary asked. I reached into my pocket and laid them on the table. 'No way! Will Creighton-Smith blackmailed George Dent?'

'Unless he doesn't know the camera's there either.'

Gary picked up one of the images. 'Nah, he knows all right,' he said. 'You can tell Dent hasn't got a clue, though. Shouldn't you go to the police, Kenny?'

'Maybe,' I said, and changed the subject. 'The Burbage was a total wipeout?'

Gary sank back in his chair and sighed. 'No one recognised the picture. Billy must have met McDonald in a different hotel.'

'Or he didn't meet him at all,' I said. 'I spoke to him earlier and he reckons he can't remember any of the pubs they visited either.'

'Why would he lie?'

A good question, for which I had no answer. Meg Dylan would have given her son pretty much anything he asked for. And while six hundred thousand was a fortune for anyone on the right side of the law, it would hardly break the Dylan bank.

'There's some kind of scam going on,' I said. 'But I don't know what it is and I don't know how to prove it.'

'Has Odeerie found anything?'

I shook my head. 'He would have been in touch.'

Joie de vivre began leaking out of me like gas from a ruptured pipe. Supper with Olivia Porteus was all well and good, but if I didn't find Martin McDonald I'd be food for worms by next weekend. Gary waved his hand above our table in a vain attempt to dispel the cigarette smoke. 'What d'you want me to do next?'

'How about keeping an eye on Billy's place in case McDonald shows up?'

'What are you gonna do?' he asked.

'See a man about a camera,' I said.

◆ ◆ ◆

Of the many things unavailable in the Vesuvius – a full-bodied claret, intelligent conversation, veal carpaccio on a bed of seaweed, change for a fifty – the lack of a mobile signal is the most irritating. The club's pay-phone is so shot that you have to bang the handset on the bar a couple of times and scream into the microphone for anyone to hear a word you're saying. As what I had to discuss with Odeerie was of a confidential nature, I decided to put my call in to him from outside the club.

It took ten minutes to cover off the morning's events. Unsurprisingly, the fat man became very excited about the George Dent and Will Creighton-Smith photos.

'Will was blackmailing him, then?' he asked.

'Looks that way.'

'And that might have given him a reason to plant the child porn.'

'Apart from it doesn't make any sense,' I said. 'Why tip the police off? He couldn't make any cash that way. Plus I think Will's more of an opportunist than a planner. Something like that would take some organising.'

'You're just going to let it slide, then?'

'Of course not. I'm going to see him this afternoon. Any luck going through the trainer sites for McDonald?'

'No one looks anything like him,' Odeerie replied. 'I've run his name past a few membership organisations and they've got no record of him either.'

'I think there might be a good reason for that.' I took Odeerie through my theory that Billy was pulling some kind of number on his mother.

'Why bother?' was his first question.

'Maybe he's diverting money to another project.'

'Such as?'

'Drugs? Guns? Whores?'

'All he'd have to do is ask.'

'Gambling debts?'

'What kind of idiot threatens Billy Dylan?'

Odeerie had a point. Not many criminal activities would bring a blush to Meg Dylan's cheek and Billy was at the top of the gangster food chain. A rival might take him out in the street with a MAC-10, but no one would put the squeeze on.

'Well, he was lying through his teeth about not remembering where he met McDonald,' I said. 'And Gary didn't find out a thing at the Burbage.'

Odeerie sniffed. 'Doesn't surprise me.'

'What have you got against the kid?' I asked.

'How about you've only known him two days and he's never done this kind of work before? Added to which, he's only just out of nappies and his old man's a fruit loop. Apart from that, he's totally perfect.'

'He's working for free,' I reminded him.

'It won't be free if he spills his guts to the police or the press.'

'Meaning?'

'I got a call from a bloke this morning asking if we were investigating George Dent's suicide, because if we were then he might have some information.'

'What did you tell him?'

'That we might be interested.'

'Which basically confirms we're on the case.'

'What else could I say, Kenny?'

'Yeah, I s'pose,' I said. 'What did he give you?'

'Nothing. Just said he'd be in touch.'

'Did he say when?'

'No.'

'What did he sound like?'

'Middle-aged and posh.'

'And you think he might be a journalist?'

'Soon as he knew I was on the job, he put the phone down.'

'A reporter would have carried on asking questions.'

'Not if he knew I wasn't going to give him anything.'

'It makes no sense, Odeerie. If Gary had given the guy info, he wouldn't need to confirm we were working on the case. It must have been something else. Plus we need all the help we can get on this.'

'I hope you don't regret bringing him in, Kenny. That's all I'm saying.'

'Gary'll be in touch for Billy Dylan's address,' I said. 'I've asked him to keep an eye on his place in case McDonald puts an appearance in.'

The fat man grunted.

'In the meantime, I want you to focus on Billy's background. He did six months in Longmill Prison last year. That's where he took his bookkeeping course.'

'So what?'

'What kind of accountancy qualification do you get after six months? You'd barely know how to switch a calculator on.'

'How am I going to find out what Billy Dylan got up to in the nick?'

'Use your imagination.'

'Thanks, Kenny, that's really helpful,' Odeerie said. 'And by the way, has your brother signed his new client form? Because I've had nothing back yet.'

'He's good for the money,' I said.

'It's not just that,' Odeerie said. 'We need to have the right—'

'Sorry, mate,' I said, 'you're breaking up. I'll call you later.'

I called Mountjoy Classics to make sure Will would be available and was told by Caroline that it was his day off. I informed her that I had a valuable item that needed to be delivered to him personally and did she have his number? Will answered like a man roused from a deep sleep.

'Mr William Creighton-Smith?' I asked in a snotty accent.

'Er, yes, that's right,' he said, sounding a bit more together. 'Who's this?'

'My name is Jeremy Danvers. I'm calling from LJ Couriers. We have a package that we've tried to deliver to your workplace. Unfortunately we've been informed it's your day off.'

'What kind of package?' Will asked.

'I believe it's a promotional gift from the Porsche car company. However, it is high-value and we do need you to sign for it personally.'

'Could you deliver it to my home address?'

'Do you reside in the London area?' Will confirmed he did. 'Stay on the line a moment and I'll check with our courier if he can redirect.' I put Will on hold for a minute and lit a ciggie up. 'As long as you're going to be home in the next hour,' I said after a couple of tokes. 'Could you give me the address and the postcode?'

'No problem,' Will said. 'Have you got a pen handy?'

NINETEEN

According to the plaque above its main entrance, Brundle Gardens had been built in 1924. Had the red-brick mansion block been situated in Kensington or Chelsea, it would have been prime real estate. Two hundred yards from Kilburn Tube station, however, and the squirearchy wasn't desperate to bag a weekend pied-à-terre.

After our ill-fated test drive, I'd planned on never having to see Will Creighton-Smith again. Now I was rocking up to his flat with an envelope of incriminating photographs. Safe to say that he wasn't likely to cut me a slice of Battenberg and ask if I wanted one lump or two with my Earl Grey.

Set against this was the fact that I had the whip hand. Any sign of retribution and I could take the snaps to the local cop shop. Although Will and I might not be hugging each other like brothers in arms, at least the conversation would be civil.

A workman was repairing the intercom panel. He overrode the lock and allowed me into the building. Its lobby smelled of curry and disinfectant. Carpet tiles curled at the edges like stale sandwiches and a couple of the spotlights in the ceiling had popped. I entered the lift and pressed the button more in hope than expectation.

The machinery juddered before ascending. A sign claimed that it could hold eight people max. I had my doubts about that. The same carpet tiles that graced the lobby had been used on the third floor. Plaster walls were chipped and scuffed. It was incredibly warm, although there wasn't a radiator or a heating duct in sight.

'Exodus' by Bob Marley & the Wailers was playing at volume in the flat opposite the lift. Its thumping bass accompanied me down the corridor. The numbers on the doors had been painted in black above spyholes to see who was calling. I rapped on 312 and waited for an answer. There was no answer. I pushed the door. It opened.

Will had probably nipped out for a pint of milk or a gram of coke. He might not be entirely delighted to find me kicking back on his sofa but there wasn't much he could do about it. Cut up rough and I'd wave the photographs under his nose.

I've accessed a few places clandestinely in my time. There's always a buzz of excitement cut with a sense of voyeurism and the fear of discovery. I felt a tingle in my spine as I entered the sitting room. Nets hung over a large bay window overlooking the street. They hadn't been washed in a while but admitted sufficient light to illuminate the room. A bookcase held several military memoirs and the collected works of Chris Ryan and Tom Clancy. Interspersed with the paperbacks were framed photographs of Will.

In one he was sat on the hood of an armoured vehicle. There were sweat stains on his singlet, and a khaki hat had been pushed back on his head. Muscles bulged in his arms and his moustache bristled like a bog brush. Faded writing read *Granby '91*.

Another featured Will with two other guys on bar stools holding up steins of beer. In a third he was lined up in a regimental photograph behind a small but flamboyantly horned antelope. The last looked to be the most recent. Will was in front of an expensive-looking villa wearing Ray-Bans, white shorts and a polo shirt. His belly was on the march and his hairline in retreat. The smile looked a trifle strained.

A sofa faced a serving hatch. This was where George Dent and Will had been sitting when they were snorting bugle. Open the hatch slightly and a camera could be left behind it, programmed to take interval shots.

A hand clamped itself around my mouth from behind and something pinched the side of my neck hard. A dozen fireworks blossomed and faded into darkness.

And then the darkness faded too.

◆ ◆ ◆

I was lying on my back in a large enamel bath. My hands had been fastened beneath me. My socks had been removed and my feet secured with swathes of electrical tape. They were in an elevated position between the taps. A towel was fastened tightly around my mouth and nose to the point that I could only just about breathe. All that emerged when I tried to speak were muffled grunts.

'You're awake,' Will Creighton-Smith said. 'That's good. I was worried I might have done you some permanent damage before I got the chance to do you some permanent damage. If you know what I mean.'

I struggled to part my wrists and ankles. The best I could manage was to slide my feet off the taps. Will leant over and put them back. He was wearing a grey T-shirt that struggled to make it over his stomach and a grin that turned mine over.

'Not so cocky now, are we, sport?' he said. 'D'you know how much it cost me to get that wing mirror replaced? Five hundred quid, that's how much.'

I said that I'd repay the money. Will leant over and put his ear to my mouth. I attempted the sentence again. All the extra volume did was increase the level of distortion through the towel.

'Sorry, still couldn't catch it. Tell you what, when all the fun and games are over we'll see what you have to say then. If you've got anything to say at all, that is.'

The problem with having incriminating photographs in your jacket pocket is that you have to be able to access your jacket. Mine was hanging two feet above me from a plastic hook. Next best thing is that you tell the person who's trussed you up that the photographs exist and where they are. No chance on that front either.

Will perched on the side of the tub. 'Actually, I'll level with you,' he said. 'What's going to happen to you now probably won't kill you unless you've got a dodgy ticker. Have you got a dodgy ticker?'

I nodded vigorously.

'No, I don't think you have,' he said. 'And if you have, then never mind. I'll dry you off and tell the medics you took a heart attack.'

Fear engulfed my body. My limbs shook involuntarily as though the temperature in Will's bathroom had suddenly dropped by ten degrees.

'God, that takes me back,' he said. 'In the eighties we'd give the odd Paddy a washing if he didn't tell us what we wanted to know. They used to shiver like fuck as well. Ulster was a shit posting, but it definitely had its compensations.'

Will shifted position on the bath. I could hear the faint sound of Bob and the Wailers knocking out 'Could You Be Loved?' I've never been much of a reggae fan.

'Most of the Provos were like you,' he continued. 'Full of the blarney and all that rebel toss. Until they'd had a washing, that was. Then they were just a bunch of spud-munchers, begging for it all to stop.

'You'll get fifteen seconds. Don't 'fess up and you'll get more. It'll be fucking horrible and afterwards you will do absolutely anything I ask, from giving me a blowjob to jumping out of the window.' Will smiled. 'That was the option we used to give the Micks. The window, I mean; not the blowjob.'

He got up from the bath. I heard a tap filling a container. He reappeared holding a small plastic watering can with the words BABY BIO embossed on its side.

'You'll feel like you're dying,' he said, 'and if we go on long enough that's what'll happen. Don't think you're tough enough for that, though, are you, sport?'

I held my breath as the towel covering my nose and mouth became sodden. Suddenly and inexplicably my lungs were full of cement. My body spasmed as the pressure in my chest increased to the point where it must surely implode. The pressure mounted. And it kept on mounting. And then it mounted some more.

As my brain began to shut down, it transmitted a series of unconnected images: a baby crawling across a floor; a tree alone in a snow-covered field; an astronaut bouncing across a lunar landscape; men and women streaming out of factory gates; a snake with a mouse in its jaws; Stephie throwing her head back and laughing.

When the towel was pulled away, it was as though my system had been shocked into stasis. And then oxygen rushed into the void.

'Enjoy that?' Will asked.

I tried to reply but couldn't.

'Thought not. Laughing on the other side of your face now, aren't you? So, what's it going to be, sport? More of the same, or do you want to tell me why you were asking all those questions the other day?'

'In . . . my . . . jacket,' I gasped.

Will frowned and pulled it off the hook. He removed the envelope from the inside pocket and examined the photographs. His eyes widened and his jaw dropped.

'Get me out of here,' I said. 'Right now.'

◆ ◆ ◆

Will had to help me into the sitting room. It took ten minutes and several whiskies before the shock began to subside. Once, when I was having root-canal work, the drill slipped. It was mildly uncomfortable compared to being waterboarded. Despite the Scotch and the blanket around my shoulders, I couldn't stop shaking.

Will defended his actions by saying he'd almost lost his job as a result of my clipping the Jag's mirror. When my teeth stopped chattering, I called him a variety of names, many of which began with the first three letters of the alphabet.

I'd have carried on indefinitely if it hadn't been necessary to get down to business. Will was sitting on the sofa and I was on a bentwood chair. I spread the photographs on the coffee table between us.

'What's going to happen now is that I'm going to ask you a series of questions which you're going to answer immediately, without any hesitation. So much as scratch your arse and I take copies of these straight to the police. Understand?'

Will nodded.

'Okay. First up is why are you and George Dent snorting coke together, and why did you photograph the occasion?'

'George came to Founder's Day last year,' he said. 'He caught me having a line in the Gents and asked if he could join me.'

'Were any of the other cemetery crew there?'

'Only George.'

'Did he say if he'd spoken with any of the other boys?'

'He mentioned that he saw Timms now and again.'

'What about Blimp Baxter?'

'Nothing about him. The main thing he wanted to know was whether I could source him some coke.'

'Which I'm guessing you could?'

'I fix a few mates up now and again.'

'From the goodness of your heart?'

'No, I need the money. And so would you if you had my ex-wife's lawyers on your case. That was why . . . Well, that was why I took the photos.'

A wave of nausea came over me and I broke off my interrogation to take a few breaths to steady myself. 'How much did you ask for?'

'Twenty thousand.'

'Which he paid?' Will nodded. 'Did you go back for more?'

'George said that if I asked for seconds he'd take the pictures to the police.'

'Why leave them with him in the first place?'

'I wanted to give him something to think about.'

'Did you believe him about reporting you?'

'Absolutely. There was something rather desperate about old George. But then, you often hear about kiddie-fiddlers being unable to live with themselves, don't you? Probably why he did a header out of the window.'

'How long did you supply him for?'

Will hesitated. I looked at the photographs.

'About three months,' he said immediately. 'But this was last year.'

'Sure?'

'Sure.'

'Did he talk about anything in particular?'

'Like what?'

'A new boyfriend, maybe?'

'God, no. All he wanted to do was get his gear and piss off as quickly as possible. It was all I could manage to get him to do a line for the camera.'

I drained the last of my whisky, poured another and lit a Marlboro. Judging by Will's expression, the flat was a smoke-free zone. I blew a stream across the table and changed the subject. 'Why did you go to the cemetery in seventy-nine?'

'God knows. Because it was a laugh, probably.'

'Ray Clarke says you were friendly with Simon Paxton.'

'I wouldn't put it like that, exactly . . .'

'How would you put it?'

'I used to hang round with Paxo because he was a freak. He was obsessed with all this magic stuff, and he had a thing about death.'

'You mean he liked reading about it?'

'I mean he liked killing things. Paxo would buy mice in the village pet shop. He'd put each one into a plastic bag and watch it suffocate. He seemed fascinated with the point at which something . . . ends.'

'Did you get a kick out of it too?'

'The first couple of times. After that it got boring. There's only so often you can watch a mouse snuff it. Unless you were Paxo, that was.'

'Why do you think he chose you?'

'It was like some sort of initiation thing. Afterwards we were . . . What's the word?'

'Complicit?' I suggested.

'Probably. And Paxo could be good company when he felt like it. Although that changed after the cemetery.'

'In what way?'

'It weirded us all out, but it affected Paxo most. He blew his A levels because he got so into all that magic crap. All you'd ever see him doing was reading a book by that Porteus bloke.'

'What was it called?'

Will shrugged. 'It was forty years ago.'

'*The White Tower*?'

'Actually, that does ring a bell. Paxo carried the bloody thing around wherever he went. Right up until they expelled him.'

'Was he depressed?'

'The opposite, if anything. He had this superior look on his face, as though he knew something you didn't. It pissed the other boys off and one day he copped a decent hiding off a few of them. The more they put the boot in, the more the crazy bastard laughed. He was begging them not to stop in the end.'

'Was he okay?'

'In the san for a couple of days but it was just cuts and bruises. There was no repeat performance, mind you.'

I'd found out what I needed to know and time was moving on. I gathered the photographs together.

'If you don't mind me asking, what's your interest in all this?' Will said.

'Peter Timms hired me to make a few enquiries.'

As Peter was dead, there was no longer any need for client confidentiality, although the main reason I'd dropped his name was to see Will's reaction. It landed like a ton of bricks.

'Timms?' he said. I nodded. 'Why was Timms so interested about what happened in Highgate Cemetery? He was with us, for fuck's sake.'

'It was more about a few things that had happened since.'

'Such as?'

'George Dent's suspicious death.'

'He killed himself. What's suspicious about that?'

'George was high on drugs when he fell, Will.'

'I hadn't supplied him for months.'

'So you said.'

'It's true. He jumped because he was going down for the child porn and I had nothing, repeat nothing, to do with that.'

No one likes being associated with child pornography. Even allowing for this, Will's denial seemed particularly vehement.

'I believe you,' I said. 'Apparently George had seen someone who looked like Alexander Porteus and Peter wondered if it might be someone playing mind games.'

'Why would anyone do that?'

'I've no idea and neither did Peter.' Will looked authentically blank. 'A pile of scaffolding fell on him last night. The police think his death was an accident.'

'But you don't?'

'I'm not sure,' I said. 'George Dent reported seeing Alexander Porteus and died ten days later. Now Peter Timms is dead and he saw Porteus too. Both of them went on your cemetery expedition. Makes you think a bit, doesn't it?'

Judging by Will's expression, it certainly did. I got to my feet and he rose from the sofa. 'Erm . . . What d'you intend to do with the photographs?'

'Nothing, if you've been telling the truth.'

'I swear to God, I have,' he said. 'And all that business in the bath. You do understand? Working at Mountjoy's might not be much, but it's all I've got . . .'

I'd lied to Will about who I was and put his livelihood at risk. Perhaps it had been unwarranted. Having reached this conclusion, I kicked him directly in the balls. The breath was driven out of his mouth in a whoosh, and he sank to his knees.

'Thanks for the Scotch,' I said, and saw myself out.

TWENTY

I left Brundle Gardens like a man walking on stilts. Judging by the tremor in my hands and the smell on my breath, the guy distributing the *Standard* probably thought I'd been on the piss since breakfast. The story on page five made for interesting reading.

Work on the River Heights development had been suspended. Foundation excavations had uncovered an Anglo-Saxon burial ground. The project was already behind schedule due to a protracted, and ultimately futile, bid to have the old Corn Exchange protected. Hopefully the discovery wouldn't affect the meeting Blimp and I had scheduled for the following day.

There was no sign of Gary when I got back to the flat. Either he was stationed outside Billy Dylan's apartment complex or he was in the gym knocking out star jumps. I had a long shower and a quick rummage through my wardrobe (grey chinos, blue Oxford shirt, white T-shirt, black corduroy jacket) before setting off for Dean Street.

Olivia Porteus's eighteenth-century town house was one of only a handful in Soho that had been spared the developers' attentions. Three storeys high, it retained its original frontage, including arched windows with white frames that contrasted sharply with dark brickwork. The building was sectioned from the street by iron railings and its front door was an imposing slab of wood at least ten feet high.

Attached to a wall was an intercom, underneath which was a key-pad and four buttons with names next to them. Three of these were companies. The one at the top was labelled *O. Porteus* in handwritten script. I pressed it and waited. And then I pressed it again. And again. I'd begun to suspect that Olivia had had a better offer when her voice came over the speaker.

'Is that you, Kenny?'

'Er, yeah. Am I too early?'

'Bang on time. Come up the stairs until you reach the top.'

An electronic lock clicked open. I entered a roomy entrance hall. Its walls were covered in classical murals. Satyrs pursued nymphs through olive groves. A unicorn reared up in front of a toga-clad man reclining on a throne. Most spectacular was the painting to my left, depicting a pair of soldiers clutching spears and standing guard over an urn around the rim of which ran a line of Greek script.

Two doors led off the first landing: one to a company called Zeto-Chufti PR, according to the Perspex nameplate; the other had FPTN Ltd. inscribed on a shiny brass plaque. The second floor belonged exclusively to Jeremy Harcroft Associates. Olivia Porteus was wait-ing at the top of the third flight of stairs wearing a pinny with the OXO Cube logo across it. I handed over the bouquet and wine I'd bought.

'Hope it's okay,' I said wheezily. 'Didn't know what you were cooking.'

'Spot on,' she said. 'And these smell heavenly. Do come in.'

Olivia installed me in the sitting room while she attended to some-thing in the kitchen. Bearing in mind that her grandfather had once called it home, I'd been anticipating something fairly spectacular. A gallery of crystal skulls, perhaps, or Anaglypta wallpaper embossed with a '666' motif. That it appeared to have been furnished by Heal's was both a relief and a disappointment.

The sofa and chairs had been upholstered in dark-blue hessian and a huge lump of coral occupied the fireplace. The chandelier might have been in situ during Al's time; an industrial zinc bookcase most certainly hadn't been. The most exotic volume was a copy of Omar Khayyam bound in green leather. Alexander Porteus's signature scrawled across the title page gave me pause for thought.

A far smaller bookcase held a dozen volumes. Presumably these were more precious, as glass doors protected the cabinet. A couple of the books were leather-bound, although most were covered in faded cloth. Five had Porteus's name on the spine; a few were by authors unknown to me, and the rest unattributed.

Where the doors met was a brass lock. Small splinters of wood indicated that it had been recently forced. I was wondering if Olivia had lost the key when she came back into the room with the flowers in a vase. 'Don't they look beautiful?' she said. 'They must have cost a fortune, Kenny – you really shouldn't have.'

'My pleasure,' I said. 'This is a lovely room.'

'Thank you.' She placed the vase on a side table. 'Dinner will be fifteen minutes.' A mouth-watering aroma had accompanied Olivia in from the kitchen. My last proper meal had been Gary's tofu stir-fry. Hopefully whatever Olivia was cooking would expunge it from my memory. 'Do have a seat,' she said.

I occupied one of the armchairs while Olivia settled on the sofa. Jeans and trainers had replaced the dress. Her hair remained up, as it had been in the bookshop when Sebastian had made his eventful visit.

'Before we eat, I want to apologise for my brother's behaviour,' Olivia said, as though reading my mind. 'That way we'll enjoy our evening more.'

'There's absolutely no need,' I replied.

'That's kind, Kenny, but you deserve an explanation, particularly after you stood up for me. Sebastian has some issues . . . Actually, he has a drug problem, is the plain truth of it. Often he needs money at short notice to score or to pay off debts. I'm not sure what this afternoon was about.'

'It can't be easy for you,' I said.

Olivia shrugged. 'He's my brother. I want to help him.'

'Has he tried rehab?'

'Half a dozen times. It looked as though the last session had done the trick until a few months ago. Seb's fine until he falls in with the wrong people.'

Olivia stared at the fireplace and tried to harness her emotions. For a moment I thought they would run away with her. Eventually she succeeded.

'I'm sorry, Kenny, it's just that Sebastian overdosed last year. If his neighbour hadn't called round unexpectedly, chances were he would have died.'

'Have you spoken to him since this afternoon?'

'Yes, Seb's always very apologetic. He tries to do the right thing, it's just that . . . Anyway, you aren't here to listen to me launder the Porteuses' dirty linen.'

True enough. I changed the subject. 'Did your grandfather use to have the whole house?'

'He did,' Olivia replied, 'although I let the other floors to businesses, as you probably saw. Alexander dissipated the family fortune, I'm afraid. He was a remarkable man but not astute. The shop and the building were all that was left after my father died. Sebastian wants me to sell this place and give him half the money.'

All roads seemed to lead to Sebastian Porteus.

'But you're not keen?' I asked.

'I'm afraid it wouldn't do him any good. Our father was of the same opinion. He created a trust fund, of which I'm the executor. Half the money from the rental incomes goes into it. If and when he controls his drug problem, I'll dissolve the trust and give Seb his money.'

'And the shop?'

'Dad left it to me solely. Another sore point for Sebastian.'

Olivia's mobile rang. She fished it out of her pocket and looked at the screen. 'Sorry, Kenny, I'm not sure who this is. I'd better take it just in case.'

'No problem,' I said, and she accepted the call.

'Olivia speaking . . . Yes, that's right . . . No, I'm afraid the shop's closed at the moment. Tell me the title and I'll probably know whether we have it in stock.'

Her tone became diamond-hard.

'That book *is not* by my grandfather . . . I don't care what you've been told – Alexander Porteus did not write *The White Tower* . . . Then why don't you ask your alleged expert to track down a copy and do not, repeat do not, call me again.'

Olivia cut the call and almost threw the phone on to a nearby table. That her grandfather might not be the author of *The White Tower* was potentially interesting.

'Problem?' I asked.

'Just some idiot after a first edition of *The White Tower*.'

'It's a novel, right?'

'If you can call it that.'

'What's it about, exactly?'

'A necromancer who uses human sacrifice to extend his life. What makes it doubly irritating is that it's the major reason people think my grandfather went down the same route, which he most assuredly didn't.'

'Must be annoying,' I said.

'Very.' Olivia looked at her watch, and her expression changed from furious to concerned. 'Whoops! I'd better get back to the kitchen.'

'Smells like you're doing a great job,' I said.

'Let's hope you aren't disappointed,' she replied.

◆ ◆ ◆

The beef chasseur was delicious. Olivia served it up in the sitting room, along with the bottle of Tempranillo I'd bought. The prandial conversation was mundane, probably a necessary rebalance after the revelations about her brother. We spoke about how much Soho had changed over the last couple of decades, movies we'd both seen and the different countries Olivia had grown up in.

Over pudding (white-chocolate lava cake) we shifted gear through books, recycling, the ubiquity of digital media and whether the Brexit vote would result in an early general election. I wondered when we would get on to the subject of Alexander Porteus and the reason I was taking an interest in him. It arose when we vacated the dinner table for the sofa by the window.

Olivia had put some Miles Davis on the system, turned the lights down and lit half a dozen candles. We were each cradling a venerable Armagnac.

'How did it go with the fertility fetish?' I asked.

'Badly, I'm afraid,' Olivia said. 'Looks like it might be going back to the States.'

'Sad for Jenks.'

'Yes, he had rather set his heart on it.' She took a sip of brandy. 'Before my brother's interruption, we were talking about my grandfather.'

'We were,' I agreed.

'And that two of your clients had seen him shortly before they died. May I ask who they were?' Death having removed the need for confidentiality, I was able to supply the information. 'But you're still looking into it?' Olivia asked.

'My brother was a friend of Peter Timms's. He asked me to carry on.'

'Why's that?'

'Because Malcolm thinks it's peculiar they both died after seeing your grandfather's ghost. Or at least what they took to be Alexander Porteus's ghost.'

'What d'you think?'

'They probably saw something.'

'Why did they assume it was him in the first place?'

I took Olivia through the 1979 excursion into Highgate Cemetery. She winced a couple of times, especially when I covered off the bit about the recitation from Porteus's book. 'What's happened to the other boys since?'

'One's done very well in business and the other's selling used cars. Life's been a bit tough on the third, and the fourth is a recluse.'

'It might sound like a cliché from a horror movie,' Olivia said, 'but it's dangerous meddling in the occult, especially when you're young.'

'You think it really was your grandfather?'

'It might have been,' she said, 'although it's not always as simple as that. Dark spirits can manifest in an almost infinite number of guises.'

It was getting on for eleven by now and things were getting lively in the street below. A glass shattered, followed by a shout and shrieks of male laughter.

'Assuming it was your grandfather or . . . a dark spirit . . . would there be any reason why nothing else happened for the best part of forty years?'

'Probably because it needed one of the original participants to bring it about.'

'By performing another ritual in Highgate?'

Olivia shrugged. 'Wherever they were, the person involved would need to know what they were doing. May I get you another drink, Kenny?'

While Olivia poured us each a refill, I thought about the man who might be capable of inviting her grandfather to put in a second appearance. Was Simon Paxton conjuring the ghost of Alexander Porteus to kill his former classmates?

Each glass was a third full of brandy. Olivia handed me one of them. 'Maybe you're right,' she said. 'There's probably a perfectly simple explanation for the deaths.'

'That's what the police think.'

'There we are, then. Demonic possession is extremely rare. You should tell your brother he's wasting his money and your time.'

Olivia's perfume and the brandy combined to produce a heady bouquet. We clinked glasses and sipped our drinks.

'How long have you been a private detective, Kenny?' she asked.

'About six years,' I said.

'What did you do before?'

'I was in the music business.'

'Managing bands?'

'Something like that.'

Actually I served in Cheapo's Records on Rupert Street before it was replaced by a particularly charming bureau de change. Other jobs in my portmanteau career have included: cavity-wall insulator, pest controller, pharmaceutical-trial volunteer, walking-tour guide, artist's model and journalist. Fortunately Olivia didn't ask for a CV.

'Married? Kids?' was what she did ask.

'Neither,' I said. 'How about you?'

'I was married for a couple of years to a lawyer, but it didn't take. Some people aren't meant to tread the usual path.' Olivia took a hit on her brandy and left a faint lipstick smudge on the glass. She kicked off her shoes and said, 'I've a feeling that's the case with you, Kenny.'

'Why's that?' I asked.

'Private investigator is a bit of an outsider's job, isn't it? Looking in from the margins of life, trying to work out what's going on and why.'

This made the day-to-day sound a bit more glamorous than it actually is. More often I'm standing on the margins of an NCP trying to work out where a missing Merc has been parked. No point going against the flow, though . . .

'Yeah, it can get pretty lonely sometimes,' I said.

'That's a shame. No one around to cheer you up?'

'Not right now.'

Olivia squinted. 'Although I'm guessing there was someone . . . ?'

'Yeah, there was,' I said. 'But that's all over and done with now.'

Olivia's thigh was touching mine; her arm draped along the sofa behind my neck. 'You have an amazing aura,' she said. 'Has anyone ever told you that?'

'Not recently,' I replied.

'Although yours is tinged with black, which isn't a good sign,' Olivia continued. 'That means there's a degree of negativity or something troubling you.'

'Really?' I said.

'Really,' she replied. 'Perhaps I could help with that . . .'

Olivia took my glass and placed it on the floor. Her kiss was tantalisingly brief. She pulled away and appraised me like an antiques expert assessing a piece of Meissen porcelain. 'No, I'm afraid it hasn't made that much difference,' she said. 'I could give it another go if you wanted me to . . .'

This time the kiss was twenty seconds long. Our tongues intertwined, and various parts of my neural system that had been dark for a long time lit up. Abruptly, Olivia pulled out of the clinch and gave my aura another once-over.

'Mmm . . . It's a bit better,' she said. 'But if we're going to sort it out entirely, we're going to have to try a lot harder. Do you want to try harder, Kenny?'

'Absolutely,' I said.

TWENTY-ONE

Fair to say that I'm not an early bird. Usually the only thing that gets me up before nine is a groaning bladder or Odeerie insisting I travel to a distant part of the Tube network at a client's behest. The morning after Olivia Porteus 'cleansed my aura' was no different. For a few seconds after waking, I wondered whose room I was in.

Exposed brick walls had been painted white. Over one was arranged a series of antique prints featuring brightly coloured parakeets. Another bore an intricately woven kilim. The furniture comprised a pine chest of drawers, a dressing table and a free-standing wardrobe. Light streamed through diaphanous curtains. The dressing table was strewn with scent bottles and lotion pots, indicating that I was in a woman's room. My brain immediately supplied the owner's name. It also served up carnal highlights from the previous night. Sadly the space beside me was unoccupied.

It had been a habit of Stephie's to depart before I woke. Another had been never to refer to the fact that we'd slept together in the first place. This didn't always make for an easy life, and I hoped Olivia wouldn't pursue the same line.

My clothes had been neatly folded on a chair. I put my pants and T-shirt on for modesty's sake, and took a leak in the bathroom. A new toothbrush lay on the basin. After putting it to use, I entered the kitchen and found a scribbled note under a Kellogg's box.

Hi Kenny, hope you slept well and help yourself to
breakfast. Give me a call this afternoon. Olivia xxx

Over a bowl of cornflakes, I reviewed the night's events. At my time of life, the old chap is unpredictable – sometimes he's game; sometimes he isn't. Fortunately the booze had helped rather than hindered. And Olivia Porteus naked fully delivered on the promise of Olivia Porteus clothed.

That a beautiful woman had succumbed in double-quick time to a wizened geezer fifteen years her senior didn't strike me as unusual. Never underestimate the male ego, is all I can tell you. I followed a second bowl of cornflakes with a coffee. Olivia had washed the dinner things and left them to drain. I was busy transferring the cutlery into the appropriate drawer when a key turned in the front door. Assuming Olivia had left something behind, or even better felt unable to stay away from her demon lover, I wandered into the hallway to be met by the sight of Sebastian Porteus.

Difficult to tell which of us was the more surprised. Sebastian had been anticipating an empty flat, and I'd been expecting his sister. As my T-shirt didn't quite cover my pants, probably Seb received the bigger shock. 'Who the hell are you?' he asked.

'Kenny Gabriel,' I said. 'We met in your sister's shop yesterday.'

'You and Olivia slept together! How long has this been going on?'

'None of your fucking business' is what I wanted to say. 'She's gone to the shop' is what I did say. He sighed, shook his head and marched into the sitting room. I popped into the bedroom and pulled my chinos on. When I joined Sebastian, he was busy searching a drawer in a bureau. 'Does Olivia know you're here?' I asked.

'What's that got to do with you?' he replied.

'Maybe we should call her.'

'Feel free.' Sebastian slammed one drawer closed and opened another.

'Are you looking for cash?' I asked.

'No. Not that it would be any of your business if I were. My sister is happy for me to come and go as I please.'

He pulled out a red velvet box and opened it. Inside was a set of Apostle spoons. He snapped it closed and carried on rooting. He looked worse today than he had yesterday. His hair was greasier, and stubble covered his chin like mould on a Petri dish. Another box was opened. This one contained several pairs of cufflinks.

Seb swore under his breath. A leather photo album was examined briefly before being discarded. Next out was a narrow cardboard box fraying at the edges and held together with an elastic band. Sebastian snapped the band and opened it up.

'Yes!' he said triumphantly.

My brother collects vintage watches. A favourite is a Rolex Prince for which I know he paid a mint. The one Sebastian was holding looked to be in superior condition.

'Did that belong to your grandfather?' I asked.

'What if it did?' Sebastian turned the winder and grinned. He put the watch back into the box and slipped it into the pocket of his coat. Then he closed the drawer and got to his feet. 'I'm wearing it to a function this evening, if you must know,' he said.

The only function Sebastian was likely to attend was the Smackheads' & Crack Dealers' Ball, with carriages at 3 a.m. or whenever the Drug Squad kicked the doors down. The Rolex would be sold within the hour. He knew it and I knew it.

'Why are you looking at me like that?' he asked.

'Because you're lying,' I said.

Sebastian's face contorted into a rictus of rage. He took a couple of steps towards me. 'Say that again and I will fuck you up.'

'You're lying,' I repeated.

For a couple of seconds, I thought he might actually follow through. What would have happened then was anyone's guess. Which was precisely why Sebastian backed down. The only type of fights he picked were those in which victory was assured.

'The reason your teeth aren't on the floor right now is because I don't want my sister upset,' he said. 'And, while we're on the subject, stay away from Liv.'

I rolled my eyes. Sebastian grinned. It was hardly a Colgate smile, but then crack isn't cut with fluoride.

'Don't say I didn't warn you,' he said.

After which cryptic warning, he departed the flat.

◆ ◆ ◆

On the way to Brewer Street, I wondered whether to call Olivia and tell her that Sebastian had stolen their grandfather's watch. In the end I opted not to. For one thing, the arsehole had been right: it really wasn't any of my business. For another, it was too late to do anything about it now. Seb would probably sell the Prince for a fraction of its true value and blow the swag on assorted pills and powders.

My plan was to take a shower and change into fresh clothes before heading off to meet Blimp Baxter at the River Heights development. I decided against calling his PA to see if our appointment was still in his diary. After the discovery of the medieval burial ground, there was every chance he might want to postpone it again. Far better to turn up regardless and hope that Blimp would still spare me some time.

Gary was in the kitchen piling chopped fruit into a juicer I didn't recognise. He looked like he could do with the vitamin C. Dark circles were spreading under his eyes and his skin was looking a touch waxy. 'Where have you been?' he asked.

'Someone invited me round for supper. I ended up spending the night.'

'You didn't think to tell me?'

'Why would I?'

Gary put the lid on the juicer and flicked the switch. Its blades screamed as they tore through the fruit. 'Because Billy Dylan might change his mind about taking you out,' he said over the noise. 'And he could have changed it last night.'

'Weren't you watching his place?' I asked.

'Doesn't mean he couldn't have got someone else to do it.' Gary took the lid off the juicer and transferred its contents into a glass. 'Where were you, then?' he asked.

'With Olivia Porteus, the woman from Highgate Cemetery.'

Gary looked as though he were about to make a comment, but changed his mind.

'How long were you outside Billy Dylan's place?' I asked.

'Until nearly midnight. It was bloody freezing.'

'Any joy?'

'He went out at four and came back around eight.'

'Anyone with him?' Gary shook his head. 'What about visitors?'

'It's hard to say because he lives in a complex. There's thirty apartments. You don't know who's visiting who. That bloke who came at you in the flat picked him up and dropped him off.'

'Lance?'

'That's him.'

'Anyone with them?'

'Not unless they were in the boot.'

Gary knocked back the rest of the smoothie and began rinsing out the glass.

'Why are you still here?' I asked.

'How d'you mean?'

'You should have been outside Billy's place for the last three hours.'

'I have to go back?' he asked.

'Yeah, you do, Gary. Hanging around like a spare prick at a wedding is what this job's all about. Or didn't I explain that to you?'

'What'll you be doing?'

'Talking to Blimp Baxter, hopefully.'

'He's the property developer, right? The one who has that show on TV?'

'And who held the ladder when the boys went into the cemetery.'

'Maybe you could take over from me when you're done.'

'That's not the way it works. As I'm a skilled operative, it's important that I'm deployed where my skills are of best use.'

'Shagging Olivia Porteus, you mean.'

'We all contribute to the cause in our own way, Gary,' I said. His eyes rolled. 'But if you want to quit, then all you have to do is say . . .'

Gary placed the glass on the draining board. He stared at the taps intently, as though trying to turn them on with the power of thought alone.

'All right, then,' he said eventually. 'But if nothing happens today, can I contribute to the cause by doing something indoors?'

'We'll see about that,' I said.

'And I'll probably stay at my flat if it gets late. It's only a couple of Tube stops away from where Billy lives. If there's anything unusual, I'll give you a call.'

'Fair enough,' I said. 'Good luck.'

◆ ◆ ◆

After showering, I googled Blimp Baxter's River Heights development, specifically regarding discoveries of archaeological significance. The search returned half a dozen results, a couple of which carried more than a whiff of schadenfreude.

According to the *Post*, a workman had noticed a skull and called the police. The cops concluded that the remains were ancient and the Association for British Archaeology had applied to have work suspended. Blimp said that, while he fully appreciated the need to excavate, it was important that activity be resumed as soon as possible in order that homes could be built to alleviate the housing crisis.

The *Post* pointed out that the cheapest apartment would go on sale for 3.8 million, so it was unlikely the average Londoner would benefit from the River Heights development. It was indicative of the media's ambivalent attitude to Blimp. He had taken over his father's modest construction business after leaving school and within twenty-five years turned it into a billion-pound global company.

On the plus side, he fronted a TV show called *Elevator Pitch!*, in which young entrepreneurs explained their idea to him in the time it took the lift to travel from the Shard's ground floor to its summit. If Blimp thought it had potential, the contestant made the second round. If not, he told them why in no uncertain terms.

Cross Oliver Hardy with Caligula and you more or less had Blimp Baxter. Spray the result in Teflon and you'd be closer still. No one had got anything to stick to Blimp, although plenty had tried. He'd been accused of bribery, physical assault, sexual excess (two-day orgies, according to the *Mirror*) and a flagrant disregard for planning laws. If a loophole existed, you could be sure Blimp's lawyers would find it. That hadn't been the case with River Heights. Not yet, at least.

I wasn't looking forward to asking Blimp whether he had seen the ghost of Alexander Porteus. So much so that, when my phone rang, I half hoped it would be his secretary calling to de-schedule our meeting. It wasn't.

'Is that Kenny Gabriel?' a male voice asked. I confirmed it was. 'It's Simon Paxton here. You left a message on my machine.'

'Thanks for calling me back, Simon,' I said, sitting bolt upright and giving the call my full attention. 'I wanted to speak to you about George Dent.'

There was a silence on the line. I was about to check we hadn't been disconnected when Paxton spoke again. 'Are you a reporter?' he asked in a clipped voice. 'Because if you are, then I have no interest in continuing this conversation.'

'I'm a private investigator,' I said.

'Working for whom?'

'Initially Peter Timms. And now for my brother, who was a friend of his.'

'I don't understand.'

'Peter died a couple of days ago.'

Again there was no immediate response from Paxton, although I could hear a dog barking in the background.

'I'm sorry if that's come as a bit of a shock,' I continued. 'It was in the papers. I assumed you knew.'

'It's not a shock,' he said. 'I haven't seen Peter in forty years.'

'And George Dent?' I asked.

'What are you investigating, exactly?' Paxton replied.

'Peter thought the child pornography and the drugs in George's flat had been planted by someone who had a grudge against him.'

'What kind of grudge?'

'That's what I'm trying to find out.'

'Who else have you spoken to?'

'Ray Clarke and Will Creighton-Smith. And I'm about to talk to Blimp Baxter.'

'Just a moment, Sappho!' Paxton said, following more barking. 'And you want to see me too?' he asked.

'If you know anything that might be useful.'

'Be here tomorrow round four p.m.'

'Can't we speak on the phone?'

'It isn't safe,' Paxton replied, which was kind of interesting. 'The nearest station is Middlemere,' he continued. 'You'll need to hire a taxi to Zetland House from there. Oh, and one other thing, Mr Gabriel . . .'

'What's that?' I asked.

'Be careful,' he said, and cut the call.

TWENTY-TWO

Walking from Brewer Street to Albion Mansions, I wondered what Simon Paxton had to tell me that couldn't be said over the phone. Of course, the guy could just be a world-class paranoiac. According to Peter Timms, his former schoolmate had been in and out of various mental institutions. I might travel all the way to Suffolk only to be told that I needed to be careful as MI5 were monitoring my thoughts.

One person who was taking extra precautions was Odeerie. 'Are you alone, Kenny?' he asked after I pressed his intercom buzzer.

'No, I've got Jon Bon Jovi, Prince Philip and the Dalai Lama with me,' I said. 'Can you let us in, please? His Holiness is dying for a piss.'

'Very amusing,' Odeerie said.

Usually when I reach the fat man's door, it's ajar. Not this time. Odeerie peered at me over a chunky safety chain. He squinted to my left and right as much as the angle would allow. 'Is the password *pizza* or *donut*?' I asked.

He gave me a sour look before unhooking the chain. Beethoven's Second Symphony was playing through a small but powerful speaker in the office. Odeerie pressed 'Pause' on his phone and the music stopped. I occupied one of the corduroy sofas while Odeerie descended on to its unfortunate companion.

'You look tired,' I said. 'Are you sleeping okay?'

'I was up working most of the night,' he said, rubbing his face.

'On what?'

'Billy Dylan and Longmill Prison.'

'Did you speak to someone?'

'Yeah, the governor said he'd email his file over.'

'That's a joke, isn't it?'

'Of course it is, Kenny. What I actually did was spend five hours hacking into the UK prison database. And if anyone finds out about it, I'll be featuring on the database personally, so this stays strictly between you and me.'

I made a zip motion across my lips.

'Including Gary Farrelly,' he added.

'Fair enough,' I said. 'What was on Billy's file?'

'Mostly just cell transfers and medical issues. He kept his nose clean and got three months off his sentence.'

'Anything about who he was hanging with?'

'Nothing specific.'

'What about his cellmate?'

'Cons get their own cells at Longmill. It's like the bloody Dorchester.'

'And his accountancy course?'

'Actually, you were right about that,' Odeerie said.

'He didn't finish it?'

'He didn't start it.'

I gave a low whistle. 'So the little bastard did lie to his mother.'

'Looks that way. Although he did take a course. Guess what it was . . .'

'Plumbing?'

'Nope.'

'Bookbinding?'

'Nope.'

'Taxidermy?'

'What?'

'Just tell me the name of the course, Odeerie.'

'Acting.'

'Acting!'

The fat man smirked and shook his head. 'It's the biggest doss there is. Just pretend you're a tree, or improv some bullshit about life on the wrong side of the tracks, and it's a big tick in the self-improvement box when it comes to parole. Half Longmill signed up. Basically it's bleeding-heart liberals and third-rate luvvies who want to boost their egos and milk the taxpayers for a few quid.'

'You've been reading the *Daily Express* again,' I said.

'It's true, Kenny.'

'That's as may be, but it doesn't help me any. You're sure there wasn't anyone in Longmill doing time for fraud?'

'Not who looked anything like McDonald.'

'Oh well, it was worth a shot.'

'How much longer do you have?'

'Five days.'

'Why not just piss off for a few months until it all blows over?'

'Because for one thing it won't blow over, and for another all they'll do is cut lumps off you until you tell them where I am.'

'What if I don't know where you are?'

'Then they'll cut lumps off you for fun. Billy Dylan might believe I carried on looking for his wife when you told me to stop, but that doesn't mean he won't do you for second best if he can't get hold of me.'

Odeerie's hand reached for the eye that had taken a pasting. It may have been healing but the memory was raw. And while I could theoretically take a one-way trip to the arse-end of nowhere, the fat man couldn't even step on to his balcony.

'Looking on the bright side,' I said, 'a lot can happen in seventy-two hours.'

The Corn Exchange had stood at the junction of Blackfriars Road and Southwark Street since 1885. Experts called it a fine example of Victorian industrial architecture. Blimp Baxter called it a barrier to the growth of London as a global city. The developer won the day and demolished the place in four months.

Fifteen-foot steel barricades surrounded the site. Peep through the gaps and you could see a level area of ground the size of a football pitch. Positioned at the entrance was a Portakabin with a notice that read ALL VISITORS REPORT TO SITE OFFICE attached to it. I climbed the half-dozen steps and rapped on the door. A huge Sikh in a Parka opened up. He was wearing a blue turban and had a black beard that reached halfway down his chest. 'Can I help you?'

'My name's Kenny Gabriel. I've an appointment with Blimp Baxter.'

The Sikh unclipped a radio from his belt and flicked a switch. 'Boss, you there?' he asked. A few seconds of dead air before Blimp responded.

'What d'you want, Adesh?'

'Bloke at the gate says he's got a meeting with you.'

'Really? What's his name?'

'Kenny Gabriel.'

'Oh, yeah, the investigator,' Blimp said without enthusiasm. 'Bring him out.'

'Sure thing, boss.' Adesh clicked the walkie-talkie off.

'Must be a lot quieter since all this blew up,' I said.

'Yeah, everyone's on standby,' he said.

'Still being paid?' I asked.

Adesh nodded. 'Once your schedule's out of whack it costs a fortune. Not to mention the aggro from the Mayor's office.'

'What have they found?'

'Some kind of burial ground. At first they thought there was just a couple of skeletons. Now it looks as though there's bleedin' dozens of 'em.'

None of the three hard hats in the Portakabin was large enough to fit me. As a result, I accompanied Adesh across fragments of brick and broken glass like a man balancing a galia melon on his head. A white tent had been erected forty feet away from a pile driver. If Adesh was correct, and the Association for British Archaeology got its way, the machine wouldn't be seeing any action for a while.

Inside the tent, two men were standing beside a trestle table on which lay a number of dingy items. A patch of earth had been excavated to about three feet. It revealed a pair of brown corroded skeletons. One was hunched in a foetal position, the other stretched out on its back. Disconcertingly, its skull had been placed between its feet. I tried to focus on the two people in the room with a bit more padding on them.

Blimp Baxter's jowly cheeks were cratered with acne scars, although for a guy in his mid-fifties he had an impressive head of dark-brown hair. His blue eyes were as hard as an eagle's and had caused more than one contestant on *Elevator Pitch!* to dry up entirely on the journey to the Shard's summit. Wearing a grey business suit, he was wagging a finger in the face of a man sporting a sky-blue fleece and a pair of glasses that made his eyes appear large and owlish.

'Are you out of your mind?' Blimp asked the archaeologist. 'We're two months behind schedule as it is without having to let you lot loose with teaspoons and toothbrushes.'

'I fully understand your concern, Mr Baxter,' he replied. 'And of course we will bear in mind this is a construction site.'

I admired his sangfroid. Not many people kept calm when Blimp got in their face.

The tycoon glanced in my direction. 'I'll be with you in a couple of minutes,' he said, and returned his attention to the archaeologist. 'How many more of those do you think there are, Spencer?' he asked in a much less bollocky voice.

'It's hard to say but the GPR results indicate numerous anomalies in the substrata. That means there could be as many as another thirty burials.'

Blimp rubbed his chin and appeared to give this some thought. 'Who else has seen the results apart from you?' he asked.

'I'm the only person,' Spencer said, 'although I've shared the information anecdotally with colleagues. It's really very exciting.'

'Yeah, yeah, I get all that,' Blimp said. 'But what if the equipment was faulty?'

'It's in excellent working order.'

Blimp put an arm around Spencer's shoulder. The archaeologist looked slightly bewildered at his sudden change in demeanour.

'Here's the thing, Spence,' Blimp said. 'My company puts buildings up all over the world and we probably don't pay enough attention to the archeological heritage we might be destroying. I'm guessing that's a concern to someone like you?'

'Absolutely,' Spencer replied.

'Of course it is,' Blimp nodded empathetically. 'Actually, I've been thinking that what we need is to retain a consultant we could fly into each site, and pay a fee of . . . oh, I don't know . . . maybe twenty thousand? Starting with this site, of course.'

It was as outlandish a bribe as I'd heard. What made it even more audacious was that Blimp had made it in front of a third party. Clearly it wasn't the fact that he might be witnessed taking a bung that bothered Spencer, though. He stared at his shoulder as though Blimp's hand were a turd.

'Even if I did say the equipment was faulty, Mr Baxter, which I have absolutely no intention of doing, the tests would simply be rerun.'

'And if I just bulldoze away?' Blimp asked. 'What then?'

'As a Stop Notice has been issued, you would be committing a criminal offence that, in this instance, would almost certainly carry a jail sentence.'

Blimp shook his head. 'People like you make me puke,' he said. 'Who the hell cares what happened five hundred years ago?'

'Eleven hundred,' Spencer corrected him.

For a moment I thought Blimp was going to hang one on him. His jaw became rigid and his shoulders tensed. Although he probably had sixty per cent less adipose fat on him, I'm not sure Spencer would have come out on top if it came to a scrap.

'Oh, just fuck off, why don't you?' Blimp said eventually.

'As long as we're clear about the situation, Mr Baxter.'

Blimp's eyes were a pair of death rays, but he kept his trap shut. Spencer picked up a cagoule from the trestle table and walked out of the tent. Blimp breathed heavily for a few seconds before reaching inside his suit for a silver hip flask. 'Want some?' he asked.

'No, thanks,' I replied.

Blimp drained the flask and screwed the top back on. Then he jumped into one of the graves. The skeleton's ribcage fractured on impact like a bag of twigs. Blimp brought a polished brogue down hard on each femur. One cracked sharply like a banger; the other gave way with a groan. The portly developer gave it some afters before stamping repeatedly on the tibia as though putting out a fire.

He picked up the yellow skull with the tips of his fingers and held it at waist height. Eye sockets through which London light had filtered over a thousand years ago gazed sightlessly up at him. It looked as though Blimp was starring in an avant-garde production of *Hamlet* and about to launch into the famous soliloquy.

'You fucking cunt,' he said, and drop-kicked it.

The parietal bone hit the roof of the tent and crashed down on to the trestle table, where it disintegrated. Teeth from the jaw sprayed in various directions, an incisor bouncing off my hard hat. The rest of the skull was reduced to myriad fragments.

The effort left Blimp red in the face and panting in a cloud of skeletal dust. After brushing some of it from his shoulders and hair, he clambered out of the grave.

'What d'you want to talk about?' he asked.

TWENTY-THREE

What with it being chilly in the tent (not to mention covered in fragments of Hengist, or whatever name Blimp's victim had answered to in life), we made our way to the Portakabin. Blimp told Adesh to wait outside. I was surprised Blimp needed a minder who could probably uproot trees with his bare hands. Good to see he was an equal-opportunities employer, though.

The cabin contained two desks, a Calor Gas heater, a mini fridge and not much else. A large whiteboard had been partially expunged of dates and text. After Adesh had left, I hung my tiny hat on a rack by the grimy window. Blimp sat behind one of the desks, sparked up a small cigar and inhaled deeply.

'Let's start with who you are and what you do,' he said. I handed over a business card. 'Skip-tracers run people to ground, don't they?'

'I'm acting more in an investigative capacity.'

'Connected to George Dent, my PA said.'

'That's right.'

'For whom are you working?'

'I'm afraid I can't reveal that,' I said, not wanting Malcolm – technically now my client – linked to the investigation in any way.

Blimp snorted. 'Drop the bullshit, old boy.'

'It's a professional requirement.'

'Is it really? Well, suit yourself, but I don't have all day . . .'

Quite why a man up to his oxters in dead Anglo-Saxons and over-run charges had the time to see me at all was surprising. As he had, I jumped straight in.

'Before he died, did George Dent contact you at all?'

'Our professional lives occasionally brought us together. Industry events and that kind of thing.'

'I was thinking of something of a more personal nature.'

Blimp blew out a column of blue smoke and shook his head. 'I don't go in for all the old-school-tie rot. I'm grateful to Hibberts for one thing and one thing only, which is teaching me that it's a dog-eat-dog world.'

'You didn't enjoy your time there?'

'That's an understatement.'

'But you were friendly with George?'

'Who told you that?'

'Peter Timms.'

The name had no discernible effect on Blimp.

'Have you been in touch with any of the others?' he asked.

'I had a chat with Will Creighton-Smith.'

'Good God, what's that buffoon up to now?'

'Selling vintage cars.'

'Yah, I heard his old man crapped out on the business. Must have been hard for Smith. What did he tell you about George?'

'They'd seen each other a couple of times.'

Blimp raised his eyebrows. 'Wouldn't have thought they'd have been particularly simpatico. Or has Will jumped the fence in his old age?'

'What fence?'

Blimp blew an air kiss in my direction.

'You mean, is he gay?' I asked.

Blimp shrugged. 'Wouldn't surprise me. Always thought he was too butch to be true.'

'Weren't the pair of you friends?'

Blimp rested his cigar on the edge of the desk and leant forward. 'Ever heard of the remora fish?' he asked. I shook my head. 'It attaches itself to the underbelly of a shark and lives off the fragments of food it doesn't ingest. The shark has its skin kept in good condition and, because of that, it tolerates the situation.'

'You were a remora fish to Will's shark?'

'Pretty much. I helped him get what he wanted and generally played the useful idiot. In return I wasn't relentlessly bullied, which is what usually happens to fat kids in places like Hibberts.'

'What about the trip to Highgate Cemetery?'

'What about it?'

'Did Will involve you in that?'

Blimp picked up his cigar. Perhaps the nicotine had helped reduce his stress levels. Certainly he appeared to have become more relaxed during the course of our conversation. 'He asked me to find a ladder to get them in and out.'

'But someone spotted you.'

'Did he tell you that?'

'Actually, it was Peter Timms. Or should I say the late Peter Timms.'

'Have you been in touch with any of the others?'

'All bar Simon Paxton.'

'What's the Northern skimp doing these days?'

'Ray Clarke? He's a retired teacher.'

'That who you're working for?'

I shook my head.

'Well, he kept quiet about what happened that night, which was decent.'

'Sounds as though you quite liked him,' I said.

'Clarke got to Hibberts through guts and hard work. I respect that. The rest of us had wealthy parents and knew just enough to pass the Common Entrance Exam.'

Blimp ground his cigar butt out on the floor and looked at his watch. 'Is there anything else?' he asked. 'Because wonderful though strolling down memory lane is, there are a few things I need to attend to.'

'Before he died, George Dent said that he'd seen Alexander Porteus.'

'Who?'

'The man whose grave they visited in the cemetery. The person they said appeared when they were performing the ritual.'

'So what?' Blimp said. 'He was off his head on booze and drugs. Probably thought there were pink spiders crawling over the ceiling most nights.'

'Peter Timms saw Porteus a few days before he died too.'

Blimp frowned. 'How d'you mean, *saw* him?'

'In his garden, late at night.'

'Maybe he'd been at the same stuff Dent had.'

'I don't think so.'

'Is that what you wanted to know?' Blimp said incredulously. 'Whether a dead man's been tailing me?'

'I take it that's a no, then?'

'Of course it bloody well is. Whoever is paying you to look into this must be very rich and very stupid. Some public-school boys bit off more than they could chew forty years ago. There's nothing to investigate. End of story.'

As though to emphasise its owner's point, Blimp's phone buzzed. He looked at the screen, sighed and pressed 'Accept'.

'Hello Leonid, how are you? . . . Yes, I just finished speaking with the man ten minutes ago . . . I did try but it's not quite so easy in this country . . .'

Blimp held the phone away from his ear as something incomprehensible blasted out of the earpiece. 'I'm afraid you'll have to repeat that in English,' he said. 'Yes, I'm attending to it, Leonid, but I can't work miracles . . . Very well, I'll come round in person—'

Whether Blimp had intended to say more was immaterial. Leonid had cut the call. Blimp returned the phone to his pocket, looking every minute of his fifty-three years.

'Right, I've got to go.' Blimp rose from the chair. 'If you take my advice . . .' He looked at my card for a prompt. 'If you take my advice, Kenny, you and your client will let well alone. Otherwise who knows what might come out of the woodwork.'

Blimp's counsel carried a warning note. I also got the impression that something I'd said had put his mind at rest. The reason he'd made time to see me was that he wanted to find out what I knew – or didn't know.

'Oh, and one other thing,' he said on his way to the door. 'I've a feeling a break-in at the site tonight might lead to an appalling act of desecration . . .'

'Someone might destroy one of the skeletons?'

'You never know.'

'Perhaps you should step up security,' I said.

'First thing tomorrow,' Blimp replied.

◆ ◆ ◆

I picked up two voicemail messages after leaving the River Heights site. The first was from Olivia, suggesting I visit the bookshop that evening. The second was from Connor Clarke, asking that I get in touch. Neither sounded too relaxed.

'I hope you don't mind me contacting you, Kenny,' Connor said when I returned his call.

'No problem. How can I help?'

'You remember I told you Judy had been receiving hate mail?' he asked.

'Has there been more?'

'This morning. Thank God she was in bed and I got to it first. It's the same handwriting, but it's a lot crazier. I wondered if you'd mind taking a look and giving me your professional opinion. I can take a photo and email it . . .'

'Probably better I see it in person,' I said.

'If you're sure,' Connor said. 'I don't want to put you out or anything.'

'How about nine tomorrow morning?' I suggested.

'Could you come to my flat?' Connor asked. 'I'd rather not disturb Judy if she's sleeping and obviously I don't want to talk in front of her if she isn't.'

'Of course not,' I said. 'Oh, and Connor, it might be a good idea if you stay with Judy tonight, just to be on the safe side.'

'You think this guy might be serious?'

'It's just a precaution,' I said.

And I hoped it was.

TWENTY-FOUR

I made my way to Leicester Square and popped into the Porcupine for a drink. Porteus Books closed at 6.30 p.m., which was when Olivia had suggested I pitch up. It gave me half an hour, and I'd just ordered a large waga when my phone rang with Gary's number. 'Kenny, I've got him,' he said.

'McDonald?'

'Yeah, we've just come out of Angel Tube . . . He's walking . . . down St John Street.'

Gary sounded slightly out of breath. Bearing in mind his fitness level, it was likely due to excitement than exertion. 'Where did you pick him up?' I asked.

'Outside Billy's complex in Docklands. I didn't see him arrive, so he must have come in through the car park. Anyway, he walked out the front door half an hour ago and headed straight for the DLR. I didn't get the chance to call you . . .'

'Try not to lose him,' I said. 'Did you get a photograph?'

'On my phone . . . Not sure what the quality's like, though . . . Haven't had a chance to look at it yet . . . Kenny, I'm going to have to go. There's people everywhere and I don't want to lose him.'

'That's fine, Gary,' I said. 'Take plenty of photographs and make a note of any address he goes to. Oh, and one more thing . . .'

'What's that?'

'You're a star.'

◆ ◆ ◆

Had the Porcupine been less crowded, I'd have shouted that the drinks were on me. Instead I bought another waga and a bag of Doritos, and instructed the barman to keep the change. If Gary lost McDonald, the photograph of him emerging from Billy Dylan's building should be proof enough that the pair were in cahoots. Even a double dose of mother love wouldn't be enough for Meg Dylan to ignore the obvious.

Kenny was off the hook.

I sank my waga and trotted down the Charing Cross Road. A decent meal, followed by a spot of leg-over, and my delivery from the forces of darkness would be complete. Rodney was displaying the Closed sign when I reached Porteus Books in Cecil Court. 'Oh, hello again,' he said. 'How are you?'

'Good, thanks. Is Olivia around?'

'Downstairs with a client. Don't think she'll be too long. Although, be warned – she's not in the best of moods.'

'Sebastian?'

Rodney nodded. 'He came round this morning.'

'After money?'

'Probably. At least he didn't lift it straight from the till this time.'

'Rodney, can I pick your brains about something?' I asked.

'Pick away.'

'Have you read a novel called *The White Tower*?'

'Yonks ago.'

'What's it about?'

'Basically some black magician whose assistant kills his victims for sacrificial purposes to keep his master alive. It was quite notorious back in the day. People thought it contained a message about how to achieve immortality.'

'Does anyone know who William Gifford was?'

'Is this going back to Liv?' he asked. I made a zipping motion across my lips. 'Porteus was based in Paris at the time it was printed,' he continued. 'Some professor in the States ran a computer analysis on the style. He's sure it's him.'

'What do you think?'

'Whether it's by Alexander Porteus?' Rodney shrugged. 'To be honest, I haven't read any of the old boy's other books, so I've got nothing to compare it with. Mind you, the program the prof used was ninety-eight per cent accurate.'

'How do I go about getting a copy?'

'Bound to be something online. Although I wouldn't tell Liv you're reading it. Not if you want to stay between the sheets, that is . . .'

Olivia emerged from the basement accompanied by a man in his sixties wearing a tweed suit and a mane of grey hair that fell to his shoulders. 'So nice to have met you, Professor O'Connor,' she said. 'I'll let you know when the book arrives and we can arrange a time for you to pick it up.'

The pair shook hands and Rodney let the prof out of the shop. The smile left Olivia's lips. She stared at me as though I were an anthrax carrier.

'I'm amazed you have the nerve to show your face.'

'What? I thought you said we should meet at six thirty.'

For a moment I thought Olivia was going to tell me to sling my hook. Then she turned on her heel and marched downstairs. Rodney gave me a baffled shrug before I followed his boss.

Olivia lost no time getting down to it. 'Well, now you're here, at least I get to say what I think of you to your face,' she said, hands on hips.

'Look, I don't know what this is about, but I'm sure we can—'

'You've really no idea?'

'None at all.'

Olivia shook her head in wonderment.

'Why don't you just tell me what's wrong?' I said.

'Sebastian popped in this morning. He said that he came round unannounced and found you rooting through the bureau—'

'He said *what*?'

'When he checked to see if anything was missing, he found our grandfather's Rolex was gone. If you've sold it, Kenny, then you'd better contact whoever took it off your hands and tell them it was stolen property.'

'Of course I haven't sold it!'

'Then return the watch and that will be that. Sebastian doesn't want to go to the police and nor do I. To be honest, I'm just embarrassed that . . . Well, let's just say I'm very embarrassed and leave it there, shall we?'

'I'm not surprised Sebastian doesn't want to involve the police,' I said. 'He's the one who took the watch.'

This drew a sardonic smile from Olivia. 'He said you might try something like that,' she said. 'Seb has his problems, but at least he isn't a liar.'

I took her by the shoulders and forced her to look me in the eye. 'D'you really think I'd steal from you, Olivia? And if I had taken the watch, why would I turn up here?'

'I wouldn't have noticed it had gone missing for months. During that time you could have got away with God knows how many other things.'

'Has anything gone from the flat before?' I asked.

No answer.

'Something portable you could pawn or sell in a pub?'

Still no answer.

'Perhaps you convinced yourself that you'd just mislaid it . . .'

A small tear formed in the corner of her left eye. 'Last month some-one forced the lock on the book cabinet in the sitting room. My grand-father's notebooks were taken.'

'Did you report it to the police?'

Olivia shook her head.

'Because you didn't want to get Sebastian into trouble?' I asked.

'It might not have been him,' she said. 'No dealer would take them without proof of ownership. I've put the word round but no one's been approached.'

'Does Seb have any interest in Alexander Porteus?'

'None whatsoever. So, you see, it might well have been someone else.'

'Olivia, you need to stop conning yourself about your brother. It's not doing you any favours and it's not doing him any either. Sebastian needs professional help.'

'Seb's been in clinics,' she said, the tears flowing freely now. 'He always ends up relapsing.'

'Maybe it's just a matter of finding the right kind of therapy,' I said.

'There is something . . .' Olivia dabbed her eyes with a tissue. 'But it's drastic and I don't know whether it's the right thing or not.'

'Drastic in what way?'

'It would mean a residential stay and cost a fortune.'

'If it means Sebastian recovers then it's got to be worth considering.'

Being cooped up behind a razor-wire security fence and given kale juice enemas six times a day would do Seb a world of good. Just think-ing about it made me feel a whole lot better. I put an arm around Olivia's shoulders.

'I know what you think of Seb,' she said, 'and I can't blame you. But he really was the sweetest little boy. The drugs changed him overnight.'

Yeah, right. Course they did.

'All the more reason to take drastic action,' I said, pulling her closer. 'How does Sebastian feel about going into rehab again?'

'Oddly enough, he's amenable to it, with a couple of provisos.'

Olivia pulled me in and delivered a lingering kiss. She broke it off, looked in my eyes and then repeated the process. First Gary's news and now this.

It just kept getting better and better.

Over a pair of lobsters in J Sheekey, the tension between Olivia and me began to thaw even further. After dessert, she suggested returning to her flat for a nightcap. Second time round, the sex was less frantic and more considered. Olivia put the safety chain on the door, which meant that Seb couldn't barge in unannounced. A jolly good time was had by all – unless Olivia was faking a jolly good time, that was.

As she was attending a two-day conference in Edinburgh the following day and had an early start, I volunteered to trail back to Brewer Street. She kissed me goodbye and promised to call from her hotel. At 1 a.m. the main thoroughfares of the parish were still fairly busy. The backstreets were quieter.

No message from Gary, which seemed peculiar. The last time I'd spoken to him, he'd had Martin McDonald in his sights. I thought about calling him but he was probably asleep back at his own flat, which was nearer Docklands, and what difference would a few hours make? It had been a long day and tomorrow promised to be longer still.

I turned into a deserted Brewer Street looking forward to getting at least six hours. I'd just fished my keys out when the car started up. After a couple of throaty revs, it pulled out and accelerated hard.

First it was on the opposite side of the road.

Then it was on my side of the road.

Then it came straight at me.

One option was to run across the street. If the driver jerked the wheel in time, I was roadkill. If not, he was hardly likely to throw the Ford Focus into reverse and back up over me. I abandoned this risky option in favour of running like crazy in the opposite direction. Had it not been for a lamppost and a rubbish bin, I'd have been toast. The driver swerved to avoid the former; the latter caught under the bumper and seriously reduced his speed. When it slid out, he floored the accelerator again.

Thank God Zorba's Magz & Vidz was still open.

The door had been wedged in order that its more bashful punters could make a swift entrance and exit. I hurtled through the multicoloured streamers and careered into a rack of corporal punishment DVDs. The green Focus roared off, leaving me writhing around on the grubby carpet trying to force air into my appalled lungs.

'Looking for something special, are we, sir?' the guy behind the counter asked.

TWENTY-FIVE

I only had a fleeting glimpse of the driver. Probably male and definitely wearing a baseball cap would be the best description I could give the police. In time they might have run through CCTV footage and found a licence plate. Assuming it was a serious attempt to take me out, the car would almost certainly have been stolen. I'd have to spend several hours in the cop shop explaining why someone might want to murder me to a bored DS who'd probably wish they'd succeeded.

Prime suspect was Billy Dylan. I'd been stupid to tell him I was close to finding Martin McDonald. Assuming Billy was still in league with McDonald, the best way to ensure it remained a secret was to put me in a hospital or a morgue.

Were there any other suspects? I pondered the question while soothing my nerves with a quintuple Monarch and a chain of Marlboros. I'd come up with jack shit on the Porteus front. Unless my brother was trying to take me off the case without hurting my feelings, it wasn't connected to that. Other than Billy Dylan, the only person I'd royally pissed off in the last few days was Will Creighton-Smith.

And so I felt doubly satisfied that Gary had a photo placing Billy and McDonald together. It got me off the hook as far as Meg Dylan was concerned, while dropping the apple of her eye in the clart at the same time.

Sleep seemed an unlikely prospect and I decided to search for *The White Tower* online instead. It took ten minutes to locate a Wicca site from which I could download a regular copy for a tenner or an annotated version for twice the amount. Following Rodney's less-than-glowing review, I clicked on the budget option.

The White Tower featured a nobleman living in an unnamed city and dying of an unspecified disease. The former sounded like Paris; the latter was a dead ringer for lung cancer. And the count was a romanticised description of Alexander Porteus.

The count's enemies had brought him low through cunning and deception. Now he was face-to-face with eternity in a tall building by a river. That was until our hero was visited by the demon Asmodeus, who informed him that, if he wanted another ten years on the planet, he must follow his instructions to the letter.

Primarily these involved sacrificing his enemies after certain incantations and rites had been recited both pre- and post-slaughter. The count accepted the deal, for which I had some sympathy. His enemies were a shower of shits. Too weak to carry out the attacks himself, he co-opted his amanuensis, Simeon, to do the dirty work.

The book dragged, particularly when it got into specifics, and I could see how people thought the novel was little more than a handbook in disguise. Several sections were printed in French and Latin.

Simeon nailed his master's first victim with a garrotte and the second with a dagger to the heart. Asmodeus then required Simeon to present himself to the universe and perform a jig of some description. At least that's what Google Translate reckoned *sautiller* meant. Whoever had penned it, *The White Tower* was a crock.

I closed my laptop and fell into a doze. My last conscious thought was whether Gary had been able to supplement the picture with an address.

Four hours later, I woke to the sound of the shutter being raised on the Parminto Deli. After a certain age, no man should fall asleep in an armchair after downing half a bottle of Highland Monarch. My head felt as though it had spent four hours in a tumble dryer and my legs almost buckled when I attempted to stand.

Knowing Gary's penchant for the early start, I gave him a call that went straight to voicemail. I allayed my anxiety with the thought that he had probably turned his phone off while working out in the gym. I sent a text asking for an update as soon as, and headed for the bathroom.

It was 6.45 a.m., which meant I had just enough time to shower and drink a litre of black coffee before packing my bags for the trip to Suffolk. I'd arranged to meet Connor Clarke at nine to take a look at Judy's hate mail. That gave me ample time to make it across town to Liverpool Street station. It was going to be a long day.

The Carbury Estate looked less welcoming than on my last visit. Then it had been bathed in autumn sunshine. Now it was lacquered in drizzle and no kids were playing on the swings in the central garden. Connor Clarke answered the door wearing a lumberjack shirt over tracksuit bottoms.

'Oh, hello, Kenny,' he said. 'How are you?'

'Good, thanks,' I said. 'We did say nine a.m. . . . .'

'Absolutely. I was writing an essay and lost track of time. Do come in.'

The layout of Connor's flat was identical to Judy's. Four doors led off a central passage that culminated in a sitting room. A cheap wooden table supported an open laptop and a pile of textbooks. A pair of black vinyl chairs on steel legs might have been rescued from a skip. The floorboards were bare and unsanded.

'It's a bit basic,' he said, which was putting it mildly.

'Must be good to have your own space, though,' I replied.

'It has its advantages, particularly if you want to have someone back. Judy was happy for me to have visitors but it could be a bit, you know, awkward.'

'Of course,' I said. 'How is Judy?'

'She's visiting her friend Patti this morning. It's a palaver and the taxi costs a fortune, but it's good for her to get out of the flat.'

'It must be hard for both of you,' I said.

'There are certain challenges,' he replied. 'But we're meeting those.'

'Actually, I'm a bit pushed for time. Perhaps I could see the letter . . . ?'

'Of course,' Connor said. 'Have a seat and I'll get it.'

I occupied the chair nearest the window. A damp patch above the fireplace was speckled with mould and the light bulb was unshaded. The only thing that smacked of personality was a four-foot cactus in an earthenware pot. Connor returned holding a plastic envelope. He removed the letter and laid it on the table. It had been handwritten on a sheet of quality paper. He moved aside to allow me a closer look.

> Abominator,
>
> The Architect punishes you for your sins, although your suffering now will be as naught compared to that in the eternal place. You and your kind transgress His natural law. For that you shall burn in The Pit. Now is but a taste of what is to come. He will render your flesh and grind your bones. Understand that I am His Righteous Servant. He has risen me to deliver justice in the earthly realm. As with the others, so with you. Know that I will contact you again in 10 days.
>
> SP

'You said there'd been others,' I said after reading it.

'That's the fifth,' Connor replied.

'All signed SP?' He nodded. 'And the language and handwriting were similar?'

'Pretty much. They were pretty abusive and it was all in that kind of biblical style. This is weirder, though. There's all that business about delivering justice and being in touch again in ten days. D'you think he's serious?'

'When did it arrive?'

'Yesterday.'

'Have you seen anyone unusual about the estate recently?' Connor shook his head. 'Has Judy been behaving oddly at all?'

'Not that I've noticed.'

'Would she tell you if anyone was making physical threats?'

Alarm filled Connor's eyes. 'Why wouldn't she tell me?' he asked.

'She might not want to worry you.'

'You think I should show her this, don't you?'

'At the very least take it to the police. There's someone called DI Samson at East Hampstead Police Station. Tell her I sent you.'

'Okay, I will,' Connor said, 'although I'd still prefer not to involve Judy. She's been making fantastic progress and I'm worried this might set her back.'

'That might not be necessary,' I said.

Connor's gaze drifted back to the letter. He ran his hand over his chin and shook his head. 'Some people are really fucked up,' he said.

'Half the world,' I replied.

Before leaving Connor's flat, I photographed the letter. 'The Architect' had a slightly Masonic ring to it. The rest simply read like standard extracts from the *Book of Nutter*. *He has risen me up* was perhaps an allusion to Porteus coming back from the dead. And, of course, the initials

SP were those of Simon Paxton – and probably a couple of million other people. But it was the ten-day line that was most concerning.

Hopefully it would be enough to persuade Paula Samson to take some action, although there was no guarantee. If anything happened to Judy, at least I'd made every effort to prevent it. Quite why the threat had been delivered by letter this time, I had no idea. But then, I had no idea as to who the hell was behind the threats either.

Perhaps Simon Paxton would be able to enlighten me.

On my way to Wapping Tube station, I pulled my phone from my pocket intending to see if Gary had deigned to call. Odeerie's name was displayed on the screen. His message requested an urgent response.

'What's up, Odeerie?'

'Gary's in St Michael's Hospital.'

'How bad is it?' I asked.

'Very bad,' he replied.

TWENTY-SIX

I stepped out of the lift and followed the signs to the Intensive Care Unit. Behind the reception desk was a black woman in her fifties wearing a light-blue uniform. A pair of thick-framed glasses hung from her neck. She finished inputting something into a computer and asked how she could help.

'I'm here to see Gary Farrelly.'

'Are you a family member?'

'I'm his employer.'

'Only immediate family members are allowed to visit.'

'Perhaps you could let his father know I'm here.'

The woman took my name and instructed me to take a seat. While she conducted a brief phone conversation, I drew some water from the cooler. The only other person in the waiting area was a middle-aged man in a high-vis jacket reading a copy of *Chat*. He looked up and registered my presence before refocusing on the magazine.

I was drawing a second cup when a guy around my age with thinning blonde hair and a white coat stepped through a pair of swing doors. The woman nodded towards me and he approached.

'Mr Gabriel?'

'That's right.'

'My name is James. I'm the senior ward nurse. Mr Farrelly is happy for you to see his son but I'd appreciate you keeping your visit brief.'

'How is he?' I asked.

'Gary's in an induced coma. The consultant is hoping this will allow the swelling on his brain to decrease. Then he may decide to operate.'

'What if it doesn't decrease?'

'You'd need to ask the consultant about that.'

'I'm asking you, James.'

'I really can't comment on—'

'Individual cases,' I said, finishing his sentence. 'I get that, but in general, when you've seen this kind of injury, what's been the outcome?'

Shakespeare maintained there was no art to find the mind's construction in the face. It didn't apply in James's case. His eyes dropped and his lips tightened. 'It's fifty-fifty,' he said. 'Gary could come out of the coma with very little adverse effect.'

'But on the other hand . . .'

'There could be a degree of brain damage.'

'What type of damage?'

'Loss of motor function, usually. He may experience localised paralysis or struggle with his speech. Although physio can do a lot to help with that.'

'Is there a chance he might not come out of it at all?'

'I think that's unlikely, but I can't say for sure.' The memory of Gary knocking out press-ups in the flat came into my mind. 'Are you okay?' James asked.

I swallowed and nodded.

'I'll take you through,' he said.

◆ ◆ ◆

Gary was in a bay at the end of the ward, his bed in a slightly elevated position. A Perspex tube led from his mouth. It bifurcated into a pair of units that were presumably keeping his lungs inflated. Half a dozen electrodes fed from his chest into machines that pulsed and bleeped. A fine mesh of wires covered his shaved scalp like an alien creature harvesting his thoughts. I felt an irrational desire to tear it off.

Farrelly was sitting on a chair beside the bed. He was staring so intently at his son's immobile face that he didn't notice our arrival. James coughed. Farrelly looked up and I saw bewilderment in his features for the first time in forty years. This wasn't anything he could stare down or pummel into submission.

'I'd be grateful if you could bear in mind the time,' James said.

'No problem,' I replied, and he left.

Farrelly stood. 'Thanks for coming,' he said.

'What have they told you?' I asked.

'Just gotta wait. His mother's on holiday in the States. They still haven't managed to track the poor cow down to tell her what's happened.'

For thirty seconds the only sound was the systematic sigh of the piston in the oxygen machine and the staccato pulse of the heart monitor. At any moment one might stop and the other go into overdrive. It was horrible and then some.

'How d'you know Gary was in here?' Farrelly asked.

'The police got the office number from a card in his pocket. Odeerie picked the message up this morning. How did they get in touch with you?'

'One of the cops uses the gym. He recognised Gaz from there.'

'What do they think happened?' I asked.

'Mugging,' Farrelly said. 'He was probably on his phone and they came up behind him. Fuck knows what he was doing in Islington.'

I could have told Farrelly that Gary had been following Martin McDonald. That the reason he was in hospital was down to me. Farrelly would probably have gone for me there and then. On the other hand, if he found out at a later date that I'd said nothing, the consequences could be far worse and potentially terminal.

'Gary said you'd been giving him some bits and pieces. Said some bloke had nicked his boss's cash and you were tryna find him?'

'Something like that,' I said.

'What happened to the fella who wanted to give you a hiding?'

'That all blew over.'

As though it doubled up as a lie detector, the frequency of the electronic beeping escalated, as did the sine wave on the screen. Gradually it resumed its previous beat and pattern. Farrelly reached out and needlessly rearranged Gary's sheets.

'You know what I said when he first turned up at the gym?' I shook my head. 'Told him if he was looking for a handout then he could piss off. Thank fuck he didn't listen to me. Thing is, now he might never know . . .'

'I'm sure he knows, Farrelly,' I said, thinking back to the conversation Gary and I had had when I'd returned from the Dylans'. 'Not everything needs to be spelled out.'

Farrelly and I had got through nigh on sixty years apiece without picking up any human baggage. At least, that was the way it had been. Now we were two middle-aged geezers in a hospital ward, wondering what it all added up to.

James brought us back to the here and now.

'The consultant is on his way down,' he said, 'so it would be a good time to end your visit, Mr Gabriel. Assuming that . . .'

'No problem,' I said. 'Farrelly, I'm really sorry.'

'Ain't your fault,' he said. 'But when I find out who did this . . .'

Farrelly's period of introspection had gone. Once again he looked like a psychotic gargoyle carved by a crazy mason. He may never know that Billy Dylan was responsible for what had happened to his son – unless I told him, that was.

And while I would have liked to see Farrelly's wrath descend on Billy Dylan's head, chances were it would also fall on mine for putting Gary in harm's way.

Not the easiest choice I'd ever made.

◆ ◆ ◆

St Michael's was founded in the early nineteenth century. Additions have been made to the original building over the years. Lifts, escalators and stairs link each part of the hospital complex, although you have to have your wits about you to navigate the place efficiently. The ICU has no direct exit on to the street. In order to leave the hospital without triggering half a dozen alarms, it's necessary to cross into the Duke of York Memorial Wing via an elevated walkway and to descend a further two floors using a lift or the stairs.

What with the shock of having seen Gary in a coma and the dilemma of whether to confess to Farrelly that I was indirectly responsible for putting him in it, I didn't pay much attention to the other two passengers in the lift.

Only when Woman A asked Woman B if she knew whether the pharmacy was open did recognition dawn. 'I'm afraid I don't,' she replied in a familiar accent.

'Someone said there's a chemist's nearby,' Woman A said. 'I don't suppose you know where that is?' Woman B murmured that she had no idea about that either.

I turned and saw Judy Richards.

◆ ◆ ◆

The canteen looked like an airport departure lounge. Huge circular lights were suspended from a high ceiling and the floor had been laid with polished beech-wood panels. The walls were decorated in soothing pastel shades and the tables covered in linen cloths. Add a departures board to the mix and we could have been in one of the snootier cafes at Gatwick rather than a major London teaching hospital.

Judy was wearing a navy jacket over a V-neck sweater and pair of cream slacks. Maroon lipstick and blue eyeshadow made her look five years older than she actually was. Thus far, the conversation had been limited to the excellent quality of the drinks and how busy the canteen was. Judy had asked why I was visiting St Mick's but not shared any information in return. She made an adjustment to the control panel of her electric wheelchair and dabbed a trace of cappuccino from her lips.

'How are your investigations progressing, Kenny?'

'Slowly. Something else is taking up a lot of time at the moment.'

Judy fingered the large onyx pendant hanging around her neck from a silver chain. 'You're probably wondering why I wanted to have a coffee,' she said.

True enough. I was also curious as to why Judy had lied to her son about visiting her friend Patti that morning. 'When you asked if I'd seen Alexander Porteus, I'm afraid I wasn't . . . Well, I wasn't entirely honest,' she continued.

'You have seen him?'

'Porteus is dead, Kenny.'

'Someone pretending to be Porteus, then.'

Judy's head twitched involuntarily a couple of times. She closed her eyes for a couple of seconds, took a deep breath and opened them.

'The day before you visited, something odd happened. It was one thirty in the morning and I was having difficulty sleeping. The flat was stuffy, so I went on to the balcony for some air . . .'

'And you saw something?'

'Someone. They were in a cloak standing under the trees in the garden doing this odd jigging routine, with peculiar hand movements.'

'Was his face visible?'

'I wasn't wearing my glasses, so I can't even be sure it was a man.'

'And then what happened?'

'I had a coughing fit. When it was over, whoever it was had disappeared.' Judy smiled and took a sip of coffee. 'Look, it was probably someone who drank too much at a fancy-dress do and was a bit out of it. You get all sorts on the estate.'

The insouciance would have been more convincing had her free hand not been gripping the armrest of her chair so tightly that the knuckles were showing.

'Did you get a phone call shortly afterwards?' I asked.

'No,' Judy said. 'Why d'you ask?'

'No particular reason. Why didn't you tell me you'd seen Porteus when we met?' The last question was tacked on quickly in the hope that Judy wouldn't pursue the matter of the call further. Fortunately she didn't.

'I lead a quiet life, Kenny. And whoever it was, they weren't trying to spook me. It was pure chance I went on to the balcony.' Judy pulled her jacket together and fastened the button. 'My coughing jag only lasted a few seconds,' she said. 'When I looked up again, Porteus— the person wasn't there.'

'Behind a tree?'

Judy shook her head. 'I went back into the flat and turned the lights off. Then I put my glasses on and watched for half an hour. The only living things I saw were a couple of foxes.'

'So you don't think it was the ghost of Alexander Porteus but you don't think a real person could have moved so fast? Does that about sum it up?'

'I suppose,' she said quietly.

'Then what are you going to do?' I asked.

'I've no idea.'

'At the very least speak to your son.'

'It would only worry him, and what's the point in doing that?'

Judy knew about Porteus. Connor knew about the latest threatening letter. I was aware of both but would betray at least one confidence if I squared the circle. The scenario was tougher than one of the case studies in my SIA ethics exam.

'Did Connor ask you anything about my visit?'

Judy nodded.

'What did you tell him?'

'That an old school friend had come into some money but that the solicitor was struggling to find him. That's why they brought you in.'

'And he swallowed that?'

Judy shrugged. 'He didn't ask any more questions.'

Which, of course, isn't the same thing, although if Connor had any suspicions, he would almost certainly have tried to quiz me further that morning. 'Do you and he share everything with each other?' I asked.

'What twenty-three-year-old tells his parent everything?'

'Okay, but you don't keep any secrets from him?'

It was as close as I could get to edging towards the fact that Judy had lied through her teeth about going to see Patti. Had she told me that she levelled with her son about everything, there wouldn't have been much more I could do.

She shifted in her chair and made her choice.

'You remember that Connor said I was making great progress . . . ?'

'Isn't that true?'

'Perfectly true. Just not for the reasons he thinks. I've been coming here every week for the last four months to take part in a drug trial.'

'Is it doing any good?' I asked.

'It's made a noticeable difference to my condition, but it won't cause any change to the outcome. And I don't want to give Connor false hope.'

'You think he has that?'

'Con has a tendency to think that if he puts his faith in something it will inevitably happen. In certain respects he's quite naïve.'

I recalled what Connor had said to me in the garden about his mother getting better in a few months. At the time I'd wondered if Judy had been seeing a quack. Now it looked as though her son wasn't quite the full ticket.

'I've explained that I'll get very sick eventually and that he probably won't be able to look after me, but he just says that everything's going to be fine and changes the subject. When I'm gone . . . Well, I wonder what will happen to him. I'm the only person in his life, and mostly he works on his own.'

'No girlfriend?'

'There was someone a couple of years ago. She was an older woman but it all seemed to be going fairly well. Then, almost overnight, it fell apart.'

'D'you know why?'

'No, but I don't think he ever really got over her. Connor's too trusting when it comes to people, which is another thing that keeps me awake at night.'

'What about his mother?'

'Lives in Melbourne and doesn't give a shit.'

A waiter advised us that the cafe would be closing for an hour and that, if we wanted anything else, now was the time.

'Can't you get someone else to explain to Connor what's going to happen?' I said when he'd left. 'Maybe it would be easier for him if it came from a third party.'

'You really think so?' Judy asked.

I saw an opportunity to kill two birds with one stone.

'Why not ask him to move back in for a week or two? If there's any-thing peculiar about Porteus— about the person you saw in the garden, then at least you'll have someone around who can provide security. And during that time you might find an appropriate moment to tell him about the drug trial.'

Judy twiddled with her pendant again and frowned. 'We'll see,' she said and then added, 'D'you really think some crazy person is coming after me, Kenny?'

'I don't know,' I said. 'But there's one thing I've learned recently.'

'What's that?' Judy asked.

'Better safe than sorry.'

TWENTY-SEVEN

I stared at the afternoon rain lashing Odeerie's office window. The fat man drummed his fingers on his desk. Occasionally he halted the timpani to shake his head; occasionally it would be a protracted sigh. It was bloody irritating and I'd have told him so under normal circumstances. These were not normal circumstances.

'I might have been a bit hard on the kid,' he said, giving the desk a rest for a few seconds. 'But it was never personal.'

'So you said,' I replied.

'He just wasn't experienced.'

'You mentioned that too.'

'I don't blame you, Kenny. I blame myself.' Odeerie raised a hand as though refuting any potential disagreement. 'I've been in this business twenty years. Surveillance is an art, and it takes practice.'

'You had me at it on my second afternoon.'

'That was different. You're naturally furtive.'

'Fair enough. I'll tell Farrelly it's your fault and give him your address. The pair of you can sort it out between you.'

Odeerie shuddered.

'That's what you did with me and Billy Dylan,' I said.

'Only because it was a matter of life and death.'

'And you think this isn't?'

'You don't know the kid was fucked over by Billy. The police think he was mugged and they know what they're talking about.'

'I thought the police were a bunch of muppets?'

'With regard to freedom of information issues they can be a bit short-sighted,' Odeerie said. 'But not when it comes to random acts of violence.'

'It's too much of a coincidence. One minute Gary's on Martin McDonald's tail; the next he's battered to a pulp.'

'Yeah, but if McDonald knew he'd sussed him, why didn't he just peg it?'

'Because Gary had photographs.'

'Stick a bullet in him, then.'

'This is London, Odeerie. No one carries a gun around just in case. Gary was picked up by Billy's goons and given a pasting. They made it look like a mugging because they don't want a murder inquiry on their hands.'

'You can't be sure it was Billy's lot.'

'Yeah, and maybe some punter's hand slipped on the steering wheel last night, and maybe you'll win Rear of the Year. Theoretically possible but very unlikely.'

Odeerie looked as though he was about to respond, but didn't. Instead he began drumming his fingers again. I gazed out of the window into a gunmetal sky and tried not to visualise Gary Farrelly's bloated face and the machinery keeping him alive. I failed on both counts. The fat man resumed our conversation.

'D'you think Farrelly could take Billy Dylan down?'

'Either that or die trying.'

'Why not tell him?'

'Think about it . . .'

Odeerie didn't need long. 'Because he'll be after you too?' I nodded. 'Can't you say Gary acted without permission? Even if he comes out of the coma, he'll probably have significant memory loss. It's a chance worth taking, Kenny.'

Having made his suggestion, the fat man removed a bag of onion rings from his desk drawer. He tore it open and began munching the contents. The sound was less irritating than the drumming, although there wasn't much in it.

'When are you off to Suffolk?' he asked.

'I'm not going. I need to watch Billy's place in case McDonald goes back.'

'Of course he won't. They know you're on to them.'

'Maybe, but I can't just bugger off to East Anglia while he's in hospital.'

'That's exactly what you should do. You're no good here and it gets you out of harm's way if they try a repeat performance of last night.

'And you can carry on billing Malc for my time.'

'*And* it'll take your mind off things.'

The chances of me getting within half a mile of Dylan or McDonald without being spotted were nigh on zero. If they made me, I'd probably wind up in the bed next to Gary's. Visiting Simon Paxton still didn't seem right, though.

Odeerie's next question was a bit left-field. 'What kind of mobile did Gary use?' he asked.

'Does it matter?'

'Humour me.'

'I think it was an iPhone.'

'Got the number?' I nodded. 'And an email address?'

'Yeah, but his phone was nicked, remember.'

'Did he have an iCloud account?'

'No idea.'

'If he did, his mobile might have been set to automatic upload.'

It took a few moments for Odeerie's point to register. When it did, I felt a surge of excitement. 'Which means the photographs would be on it?'

'As long as he had a connection.'

'Brilliant! We'll at least have one shot of McDonald coming out of Billy's apartment and there might be loads more.'

'Don't get too excited, Kenny. Gary might not have had an iCloud account and his phone might not have been set to upload. Plus, Billy Dylan isn't stupid. He could have thought the same thing and deleted them already.'

'Wouldn't it be hard to hack the account?' I asked.

Odeerie nodded. 'Virtually impossible, unless you've got the password.'

'But not completely impossible?'

'No, but the less information I have, the longer it's going to take. Is there anyone who knew Gary well and might be able to give us a steer?'

'Only Farrelly, and I can't really ask him.'

Odeerie appeared lost in thought for a few moments. 'Never mind,' he said. 'I'll check out his social media profile and see what I can pick up.'

'Anything I can help with?'

'Go and see Simon Paxton.'

'Yeah, maybe you're right.' I got up from my seat and made for the door.

'Why don't you kip here tonight, Kenny?' Odeerie suggested. 'They probably won't have another shot at you after last night, but you never know.'

'I'll take my chances,' I said. 'You'll keep me up to speed?'

'Course I will. It's probably not going to be quick, though. I might have to run a brute-force program. That could take days to work, if it works at all.'

'We don't have days, Odeerie,' I said.

'I know,' he replied.

After leaving Odeerie, I called Simon Paxton and left a message saying that I would be arriving at the same time but a day late, and to contact me if that was a problem. Then I wandered the parish for a while. I wasn't in the mood for the Vesuvius and Nick's crap jokes, or the regulars' hilarious questions about whether I'd tracked down Lord Lucan yet. The rain became heavier and my brolly began to disintegrate. I took it as a sign that I needed the solace of alcohol and drifted towards the French House. Perched on a bar stool, I watched a gloomy afternoon morph into a gloomy evening over a series of moody wagas and al fresco Marlboros.

In the *Standard* was a story about how the burial site at the River Heights development had been desecrated and a skeleton destroyed. Blimp Baxter suspected it was the work of Londoners disaffected by a decision to prioritise the capital's dead over the capital's living. The Association for British Archaeology was of the opinion that it was mindless vandalism and insisted a twenty-four-hour guard be mounted.

It seemed as though Blimp would have to suspend activity for a few months at least. This meant that he and his investors would likely lose a significant amount of cash that, according to the paper's financial pages, could run into tens of millions. If it didn't wipe Blimp out, questions would certainly be asked about Baxter Construction's asset base, in addition to those that had been posed already.

Eventually I broke free of the French's gravitational pull. Although still fairly early, I walked down Brewer Street like a GI traversing the Mekong Delta. No ambush had taken place by the time I reached the flat, where I heated up a double pepperoni pizza and washed it down with a bottle of Newcastle Brown.

After eating I rang St Michael's. There was no change in Gary's condition. I asked if his father was with him and was told that he was. The temptation to tell Farrelly that I not only knew who his son's attacker was but also where he lived was a strong one. Specifically how he would respond I had no idea, but it would be swift, violent and definitive. Instead I thanked the nurse and hung up.

I put a ska compilation on the hi-fi and spent the next twenty minutes flicking through the latest *Private Eye*. As night properly gathered, Malcolm's comment about Stephie dominated my thoughts. The train had left the station as far as our relationship was concerned, but what was the harm in giving her a call?

I set my phone to block ID and dialled Stephie's number. She answered immediately. 'Jake, for God's sake, be patient! I'll be down in two minutes.'

My opening line died on my lips.

'Jake, is that you?' Stephie asked.

Still nothing from me.

'Who *is* this?' she said.

Whatever I said after a five-second silence would sound weird. Thanking God that I'd had the foresight to withhold my number, I pressed the 'Disconnect' button. If Stephie ID'd the call then she'd hopefully think it was a telemarketing bot.

As usual before retiring to bed, I downed a large Highland Monarch. Unfortunately the cheapest Scotch money can buy didn't send me straight to the land of nod. The same old existential questions jostled for headspace with those of a more recent vintage, and one in particular held sleep at bay.

Who the hell was Jake?

◆ ◆ ◆

At eight o'clock the next morning, I put a call into Simon Paxton. If the letter Connor had intercepted was to be taken at face value, then I only had a few days to find out who had sent it to Judy and why. Paxton's line rang for two minutes without me being invited to leave a message. Over an espresso, I debated whether it was worth going at all.

As there wasn't a lot to do in town other than serve as a moving target, the answer was yes. I called Odeerie to see if he'd had any luck with Gary's iCloud account. He told me not to be so bloody impatient. A second call revealed that Gary had remained stable overnight; a third summoned an Uber to ferry me to Liverpool Street station.

If you're a bit down in the mouth, my advice is don't travel through East Anglia. The landscape is pancake-flat and the sky goes on for ever. It's as though the entire region has been specifically created to give you an existential crisis. If it hadn't been for the buffet car then I'd probably have called the Samaritans at Hatfield Peverel. Thank God for the consolations of Stella and Pringles.

I changed at Ipswich and forty minutes later the train pulled into Middlemere, a village about five miles inland from the North Sea. Constructed from yellow brick, the Victorian station had a crenulated wooden canopy that protected a pair of stout oak benches with cast-iron frames. Window boxes held well-tended shrubbery, and *Jas. Oliver* of Woodbridge had supplied the station clock, probably around the time it first opened.

Three passengers alighted. A sixty-something gent in a waxed jacket marched through the open barriers as though he owned them. A girl weighed down by a gigantic yellow rucksack followed less stridently. I brought up the rear. A woman in a Prius picked the gent up, and the girl boarded a bus. The only cab on the rank was a twenty-year-old Honda Civic with more filler in her than Joan Collins.

I put my bag in the back and instructed the driver that my destination was Zetland House. 'Never heard of it, mate' was his unsettling response. 'Got the postcode?'

'It's a biggish place by the sea,' I said, after realising I hadn't.

My driver's sunglasses and leather driving gloves made him look like a member of the Stasi. They were augmented by a skinhead haircut. 'Is it a hotel?' he asked.

'Actually, it's a private residence,' I said. 'Hang on a minute . . .'

I reached for my phone, intending to search for a shot of the house. No signal. Fortunately the name appeared to have rung a bell with my driver. 'Hang on . . . D'you mean the place up on Carlton Point?'

'No idea,' I said. 'It's owned by a man called Simon Paxton.'

'Ah, right – I know where you're after,' he said. 'Major Gerald used to own it. Bloke who's got it now's a bit of a weirdo, ain't he?'

'I think that might be his reputation.'

'You sure it's still there?'

'Er, I hope so.'

'Only one way to find out.'

At the third time of asking, the Civic's engine caught and off we went.

We travelled down a dual carriageway for two miles before Ricky, the driver, turned into a lane barely wide enough to accommodate his car. Being driven ten miles above the speed limit by a man in black glasses wasn't relaxing. 'Place has been falling into the sea for ever,' he said as we swerved in and out of a lay-by to avoid a head-on with a tractor. 'Used to be a churchyard up there but that went over in the seventies. My old fella reckoned you could find bones on the beach after a storm.'

'Can't they take measures to prevent coastal erosion?' I asked.

Ricky chuckled. 'If there's enough cash they can. Places like Southwold, they put up sea defences. No one gives a toss about Carlton Point.'

'What else is on the cliff?' I asked.

'Might be few chalets left from the holiday camp, but the Denes went over the edge years ago. Apart from that, it's just your mate's house.'

We passed a small copse at around fifty and took a bend almost on two wheels. Reflexively I grabbed the edges of my seat.

'You all right?' Ricky asked.

'Yeah, just that we went round that corner a bit sharpish.'

'Don't worry. Ain't no speed cameras on this stretch.'

Ending up in a spinal unit had been more of a concern than three points on Ricky's licence. As a sign indicated it was only a mile to Carlton Point, I decided to keep this to myself and pumped him for more information.

'You said Simon Paxton was a bit weird.'

Ricky gave me a sideways glance. 'I've heard people say he's not the friendliest. Likes to keep himself to himself, if you know what I mean.'

'Nothing wrong with that, is there?'

'Course not. Just means you get talked about.'

For the last few hundred yards, tall hedgerows had bordered the road. These disappeared and suddenly we were in the middle of farmland that stretched to the horizon on either side. A lighter tone in the sky suggested the sea lay ahead.

'And to be fair to the bloke,' Ricky continued, 'he is miles away from the nearest village. S'not like he can just nip out for a pint.'

'Does he get many visitors?' I asked.

'Put it this way, there's two taxi drivers in Middlemere and you're the first person I've taken to Carlton Point since the Denes closed. So unless they're all going up there with Bob Yallop, I'd say he don't get much company.'

Zetland House was shielded from view by half a dozen mature poplars. Only when we were within a hundred yards of the place could I see three chimneys rising from the roof. Ricky halted outside a pair of tall iron gates.

'That'll be eight forty.' I handed a tenner over and told him to keep the change. 'How long you around for?' he asked.

'I'm not sure.'

'Only, if you tell me what time you need to go back to the station, I could come and fetch you. You won't get a signal out here.'

'Mr Paxton has a landline,' I said. 'I can call and let you know.'
'Suit yourself,' he said before pulling away.

◆　◆　◆

Zetland House was a two-storey building with a Gothic portico around the front door. Mock turrets rose up from each corner of the roof and a brass sundial had been cemented into the wall above the portico. The stonework beneath the gutters was stained and one of the ground-floor windows had been patched with hardboard.

Multiple slates were missing from the roof. The sunken garden was so overgrown it now only recessed a few inches. The gate's hinges were shot and it took an effort to open one of them a couple of feet. I squeezed through the gap and walked down a compacted track. I pushed the bell and then banged on the front door.

No one answered. Simon Paxton couldn't hear me, or he wasn't home. I peered through the downstairs windows. One room had been completely cleared; the other had a random collection of furniture in it, including a chaise longue, a bamboo hatstand, a linen press and a dead yucca plant.

At the rear of the building the sound of the sea was more pronounced. What had once been a sizeable garden was now a field. Fifty yards from the cliff edge, a sign advised that proceeding further was hazardous. Seagulls wheeled and shrieked in the misty air. I shouted Paxton's name a couple of times to no avail. It was beautiful and it was cold. After a minute or so, I turned back to the house.

As Ricky had said, Simon Paxton could hardly nip out to the pub, so he had to be somewhere. A pair of French windows led into a library with scores of books arranged over built-in shelves. The fireplace had a modern convection heater in a marble hearth, and a neatly folded blanket was draped over a leather sofa. The side table bore a coffee cup and an ashtray with a packet of fags beside it.

The doors were locked but it would have been the work of a moment to flip the latch with my picks. I'd just fished them out when someone spoke. 'Who are you and what are you doing?' he asked.

I slipped the picks into my pocket and turned. The man was about five foot ten. He was wearing a blue Parka over a Fair Isle sweater and a pair of brown corduroy trousers. The breeze tousled his thick grey hair.

Oh, and he was pointing a shotgun at me.

TWENTY-EIGHT

Simon Paxton held the weapon at waist height. No doubt he could still hit the target should he wish to. Bearing in mind that he'd invited me to see him, it was quite a welcome. I decided to introduce myself and remind him of his obligations as a host.

'Simon Paxton?'

'Who are you?'

'Kenny Gabriel. I called to say that I'd be a day late.'

I was relieved to see the gun lower a few inches. Paxton looked thoughtful. 'The private detective?' he asked. 'Looking into George's death?'

'That's right.'

'I took you for a vagrant trying to snatch some cash or find a place to sleep.'

Perhaps I needed to refresh my wardrobe. The opportunist-thief look wasn't in that season. It was more high waists and primary colours.

'How about I show you a card?' I said.

'That won't be necessary.'

Paxton broke the barrel and laid the gun over his arm. He approached me and held a hand out. 'I was after rabbits,' he said. 'Place is overrun with the bloody things and they make good eating. To be honest, I'd forgotten you were coming.'

'I did call this morning but there was no reply.'

'Must have been out. Let's go inside.'

Simon led me through a door at the side of the building into a passageway that smelled of damp. Fleur-de-lis wallpaper was peeling and the runner was down to the threads in places. After removing cartridges from the barrels, he opened a gun cupboard and placed the shotgun into the rack.

'Used to belong to my uncle,' he said, as though responding to my unanswered question. 'Must get round to applying for a licence.' He locked the cupboard and put the key ring into his pocket. 'Did you drive down?'

'I took the train.'

Simon nodded, pulled off his Parka and hung it on a peg. 'You'd better come through to the library,' he said.

We continued down the passage to a door that opened into the room I'd been about to slip the latch on five minutes earlier. Simon ushered me through.

'Coffee or tea?'

'I'm fine, thanks,' I said.

'I'd offer you something stronger but I keep no alcohol in the house.'

Shame. After the incident with the gun – not to mention the fact that Zetland House was refrigerator-cold – a treble malt would have gone down nicely. Simon crossed the room to switch the convection heater on. Then he sat on the sofa and took a cigarette from the pack. I followed suit with my Marlboros. He lit them both.

Where to sit was a dilemma. The only alternative to the sofa was a wing chair twenty feet away. It was a bit distant for the confidential chat I'd been hoping for. In the end, I occupied the opposite end of the Chesterfield.

'I take it you know the circumstances of George's death?' I asked.

Simon nodded. 'How did Peter die?'

'Crushed under some falling scaffolding after a night out.'

'An accident?'

'I'm not sure. Peter reported seeing the ghost of Alexander Porteus not long before it happened, as did George.'

At the mention of Porteus's name, Simon's lips pursed as though he'd experienced some acid reflux. 'You know what happened in the cemetery?' he said.

'I've had reports from Peter, Ray, Will and Blimp. I also know that Ray was expelled afterwards and you . . . erm . . . went off the rails a bit.'

'Who told you that?'

'Mostly Will, or at least he supplied the detail.'

Simon took a long drag on his cigarette, tilted his head back and expelled the smoke in the general direction of a dusty chandelier.

'What's Ray Clarke up to?'

'He's had a sex change and goes by the name of Judy Richards.' Simon gave me a sharp look. 'You really didn't know about that?' I said.

'Why would I? When did you speak to Blimp?'

'A couple of days ago.'

'That must have taken some doing. What did he say about George?'

'He'd bumped into him a couple of times through work, but that was it.'

'And was Will any more illuminating?'

'Not particularly. He didn't keep up with him.'

'Yes, well, hardly birds of a feather, were they?' Simon stubbed his cigarette out in the glass ashtray. 'What do you want from me?' he asked.

'Anything that could cast light on whether George was set up or not.'

'And whether Peter was murdered?' I shrugged. 'Who are you working for now?'

'My brother, Malcolm.'

'What's his interest in all this?'

'He was a good friend of Peter's and he's suspicious that both he and George reported seeing Alexander Porteus before they died. *Do* you have any information?'

'I might. Although I'm not sure what it's worth.'

'Only one way to find out . . .'

I extinguished my fag and sat upright, intending to convey the sense of a man focused and ready to get down to business. There was a scratching sound at the door.

'Hold on a moment, Kenny.'

Simon crossed the room. As soon as he opened the door, a large black Labrador leapt up at him. Simon's demeanour changed immediately. 'Hello, Sappho,' he said. 'How are you? She's had a touch of distemper,' he explained to me, and returned his attention to the dog. 'But you're feeling a lot better now, aren't you, sweetheart? D'you want to go walkies?'

Judging by the thumping tail, the answer was affirmative.

'You can stay here if you like,' Simon said to me.

'I'll come with you,' I replied, and Sappho barked impatiently.

'Okay, but you'll need something a little bit warmer than just a jacket. I'll see if I can dig out a sweater. We're about the same size.'

Sappho snuffled around me, decided I wasn't that interesting and scampered down the passage after her master. In their absence, I checked out the library shelves. There were leather-bound sets of Walter Scott and Dickens and single volumes from Somerset Maugham and authors who had largely fallen out of fashion.

Other shelves held books on birdwatching and the flora and fauna of East Anglia, and there was an entire collection of bound *Punch* magazines stretching from 1880 to 1948. The last shelves I looked at held books solely on religion.

There were five bibles – the oldest dating to 1657 – and three books of common prayer. At least ten volumes were bound in stiff vellum and printed in Latin or German. More contemporary was a work by Émile

Durkheim and a complete twelve-volume edition of *The Golden Bough* by James Frazer. I was leafing through volume three when Simon and Sappho returned.

'Found something decent?' he asked.

'*Taboo and the Perils of the Soul*,' I quoted from the book's spine. 'Not exactly an airport novel.'

'I bought the esoteric stuff years ago. It really doesn't interest me any more. Here, this should just about fit you. Not the height of fashion but warm enough.'

Simon passed me a thick woollen jumper with a roll-neck collar. 'Thanks,' I said and replaced the volume. In doing so, I noticed that all the religious books were pristine, whereas the others, including the Dickens, had a fine layer of dust on them.

'Are you ready?' he asked.

'Absolutely,' I said.

TWENTY-NINE

Simon's sweater came down almost to my knees but I was glad of its warmth. We retraced our steps to the back of the house and then down a track running parallel to the sea. A path from the house to the beach had been swept away. Now the quickest way down was via a ravine.

Sappho would bound ahead and then turn with an expression that conveyed impatience at our desultory progress. Simon explained that, when Zetland House had been built in 1880, it had been a mile inland. Interesting but not as interesting as the information he'd been about to supply about George. At least, I hoped it wasn't.

You had to watch your step in the ravine; the way was thick with bushes, rocks and marram grass. Conversation abated until we arrived on the shore. Sappho gambolled joyfully into the sea while Simon and I resumed our chat.

'First let me give you some background,' he said as we trudged over the pebbles. 'After the business in the cemetery, I had a breakdown. My parents took me to several psychiatrists but none of them did any good. By my mid-twenties my behaviour had become so erratic that our relationship disintegrated entirely.'

'They disowned you?'

He nodded. 'I was violent and abusive. Eventually I spent a few months in prison for shoplifting. On my release, my father gave me five thousand pounds and said that he and my mother, and my sister, never wanted to see me again. If George hadn't intervened, I don't know what would have become of me.'

'Intervened in what way?'

'He tracked me down, paid my rent and opened an account at a local store.'

'Why did he do that?'

'Partly because it was in his nature. But I think on some level it was George's way of making up for what happened to Ray. He always felt terrible about that.'

'Helping you was a way of expiating the guilt?'

'To an extent,' Simon said. 'I owe him a hell of a lot.'

'What did the shrinks think?'

'About my mental health issues?'

I nodded. 'They came on pretty quickly?'

'Not really,' Simon said. 'I'd been prone to fixations for years; it was one of the reasons I became so obsessed with Alexander Porteus.'

'What did they diagnose, specifically?' I asked.

'The consensus was bipolar disorder. George arranged for me to see someone in Harley Street who prescribed the appropriate medication.'

'So this would have happened even if you'd never seen Porteus?'

'If you believe the professionals.'

'What do you believe, Simon?'

A flock of seagulls took off as Sappho chased them. They shrieked irritation at being disturbed, while she woofed disappointment at not making a kill. Simon picked up a rock and threw it into the water. 'It was Porteus,' he said. 'He took great delight in corrupting young men by convincing them that they could achieve incredible things if they became his disciples.'

'Did any of them succeed?'

'Most ended up in jail. A couple became bankrupt and committed suicide. Somebody once said the devil doesn't come dressed in a red cape and pointy horns. He comes as everything you've ever wished for.'

'Don't think I've come across that one.'

'Sometimes it's referred to as the law of attraction. What they don't say in the self-help books is that what you wish for may not come from the anticipated source.'

I still wasn't sure how this related to Alexander Porteus, although, from the way Simon picked up his step, it appeared this was his final word on the matter. We had covered a hundred yards more beach before conversation resumed.

'How did you come to live at Zetland House?' I asked.

'It was my Uncle Gerald's. My sister and I visited in the holidays. When he died, the place was left to me along with a decent chunk of cash. It was quite a surprise. I hadn't seen him in twenty years.'

'You didn't think of selling the place?'

'I wouldn't have got much of a price; the erosion was pretty bad even back then. If it had been saleable, I'd still have lived there. It might seem a solitary life to you, Kenny, but I've got Sappho for company and she's all I need.'

I was wondering whether a Labrador might ease my metropolitan ennui when Simon stopped in his tracks. At the foot of the cliff was a pile of rubble. Among the bricks and concrete lay a bulky figure. Simon beat me to the spot by thirty seconds. Sappho was busy running in circles and barking furiously.

'It's the chip shop man,' Simon said. 'He must have gone over last night.'

The figure was a man-sized plastic fisherman complete with beard, cape and sou'wester. He was holding the upper portion of an enormous yellow cod. Its tail had fractured and was lying a few feet away, as was the bowl of the fisherman's pipe.

'There used to be a holiday camp,' Simon explained. 'They demolished the buildings a few years ago.' He bent down and retrieved the fragment of pipe. 'Looks like they forgot about him.' He slipped the bowl into his pocket and stared at the clifftop. 'Nothing lasts,' he muttered, to me and the world at large.

'No,' I replied. 'At least, not if it's any good.'

A flurry of dirt and pebbles rolled down the cliff.

'Should we be standing here?' I asked.

'Probably not,' Simon decided. 'Come on, Sappho,' he said, and the three of us retreated to the safety of the compacted sand.

'Did you see George again after you moved into Zetland House?' I asked.

'He was a regular visitor until six months ago.'

'George didn't mention he saw you to Peter.'

'Nor did he mention that he saw Peter to me. George was naturally secretive, even at school. He'd spend most of his time on the headland painting when he was here.'

'What did the two of you talk about?'

'Nothing profound. I think he found it an easy place to relax from work. Particularly when his career took off.'

'Did you ever discuss what happened in the cemetery?' Simon shook his head. 'Not even when he visited for the last time?' Another headshake. 'And George didn't email or speak to you on the phone before he died?'

'About what?'

'Maybe the court case?'

'No, although I did attempt to contact him a couple of times. In the end I assumed that he was either too busy or too ashamed to talk about it.'

'You think the abuse images belonged to him?'

'Why wouldn't they?'

'He told Peter and his PA they'd been planted.'

'And the drugs?'

'He said they were his.'

'I've no idea about the images,' Simon said after a moment's reflection. 'George was a fantastic friend to me, but when it comes to that kind of thing . . .'

He didn't need to finish the sentence. You only had to open the paper to read that the most unlikely people turn out to be paedophiles. There was one more question I needed to ask, and I wasn't looking forward to asking it.

'George and Peter saw Alexander Porteus before they died.'

'So you said.'

'Well, I was wondering whether . . .'

'What?' Simon asked.

'. . . you'd seen him too.'

I might as well have asked if Sappho had been spayed, for all the reaction I got.

'No,' Simon replied. 'Although I'm not surprised he appeared to George and Peter.'

'Why's that?' I asked.

'We brought him back across the great divide and now he's returning the favour. Except that it's the other way round, of course.' He darted a look at me. 'Many religions believe that those who have passed reappear to fetch us to the other side. Sometimes it's people who loved us . . . and sometimes it isn't.'

We walked on in silence for another twenty yards. The sky had become ominously grey and Sappho appeared to be losing her enthusiasm for the walk.

'Might be an idea to head home,' Simon suggested.

'Suits me,' I said. The wind off the sea was biting. 'Is that it about George?' I asked, disappointment creeping over me in addition to hypothermia.

'Not quite,' Simon replied. 'About three months ago, he called out of the blue. Said he'd been feeling down and would I mind him visiting for a week.'

'Down about what?'

'He told me that he'd agreed to something politically unethical and that he deeply regretted it. Naturally I asked what it was and George said it was better I didn't know as it might place me in a dangerous situation.'

'Dangerous was the word he used?'

Simon nodded. 'Virtually all he did was sit in the library and smoke, or go on to the beach and stare at the sea. I asked if he could put things right. George said possibly but that it would mean disgrace and the end of his career.'

'And you've no idea what it was?'

'None whatsoever. Although he left saying that he'd decided to take some action. When I heard that he'd committed suicide, I wondered if that was what he meant and whether the child pornography was what he'd been referring to.'

'How would telling you about those put you in danger?'

'I don't know.'

Presumably Simon wasn't aware that Will had blackmailed George over the drugs photographs either. That would have meant the end of George's political career, although it didn't sound particularly 'unethical'. Not unless it wasn't Fair Trade cocaine.

'Is that why you agreed to see me?' I asked.

'You said that you were investigating whether George committed suicide or was murdered,' Simon replied. 'And I suppose there's always been that question at the back of my mind too. Even if I did keep telling myself it was rubbish.'

'Why not go to the police?'

'With what? It wasn't as though George gave me names or details. When I heard that you were looking into the case, though, it seemed like a way to talk to someone who wouldn't look at me as though I was crazy.'

Sappho was by our side, tongue lolling and exuberance entirely departed. She looked up at Simon and whined. 'Nearly home, girl,' he said, and patted her head. 'Have you found out anything that might point in that direction?'

I thought about telling him about Will and the photographs, but decided against it. 'Not really,' I said. 'What you've told me is interesting, but I don't think it brings me any closer to finding out if anything suspicious happened to George.'

'Then you'll close your case?' Simon asked as we approached the ravine.

'Yes,' I said. 'I think that's probably that.'

Back at the house, I refused Simon's offer of coffee and used his phone to call a taxi. During the twenty minutes it took to arrive, he told me that the council had served a compulsory purchase order and that he had to be out in a year. Dealers would strip the place of its more desirable fixtures and fittings, after which it would be demolished. He and Sappho intended to buy a bungalow a couple of miles up the coast with the compensation money.

Bob Yallop had been dispatched instead of Ricky to pick me up. His Jetta was in far better shape than Ricky's Civic, although the same couldn't be said for Bob himself. Shoulder-length hair was thinning to the extent that his scalp shone through, and his gut hung over his belt as though it had territorial designs on his thighs.

One thing Bob did have going for him was that his driving was a sight less bowel-curdling than Ricky's. I was relaxed enough to try to make sense of the info Simon had given me. George Dent had operated in too murky a world for a humble skip-tracer to penetrate. Tomorrow I intended to call Malcolm and admit that I'd drawn a blank. At least I could concentrate on bringing Billy Dylan to book.

Unlike his colleague, Bob wasn't much of a talker. Only when we were on the dual carriageway did he strike up a proper conversation. 'You been up to Zetland House, then?' was his opener.

'That's right.'

'What's happenin' to that old place?'

'It's being torn down in a few months.'

'Bloke what lives there movin' out, is he?'

'No, they're demolishing it with him still inside, Bob' is what I wanted to say. 'I think that's the general idea' is what I did say.

My driver nodded as though, on balance, this was probably the wisest course of action. I hoped it would be the end of our chat. I was disappointed.

'Don't see him down the pub much.'

'Is that right?'

Bob changed down into third and overtook a bus. 'The major liked a drink,' he said, and returned to the slow lane. 'You'd see him in the Crown most nights.'

'Each to his own,' I said, hoping that platitudes might do the trick.

'Course, he was a sociable man,' Bob continued. 'Not like the bloke who lives there now. What's his name again?'

'Simon,' I said. 'Simon Paxton.'

'That's right. I remember that woman asked if I knew him.'

'Erm, what woman was that, Bob?'

'Took her up there 'bout a month ago,' he said. 'Usually don't remember fares, but I remember her all right. She looked like that cook on telly what's always swinging her jubblies around and lickin' her fingers.'

'Nigella Lawson?'

'Yeah, that's the one,' Bob said as he took the turn into Station Road. 'Course, I'm not saying it was Nigella Whatsit, just that it looked like her. She had the same kind of hair and you should have seen the rack on her. Mind you, this bird was taller . . .'

'What kind of accent did she have?'

'Posh. Same as Nigella.'

'How old?'

'Late thirties. Early forties, maybe.' Bob turned on to the station concourse and parked. 'Why you so interested in her?' he asked.

'Oh, just that it sounds like someone Simon and I used to work with, although he didn't mention that Olivia had been to visit. How long did she spend at the house?'

'Don't know. I only took her up in the mornin'. Thought Ricky might have pulled the return job but he said he didn't. Maybe your pal drove her back.'

Bob consulted his meter. 'That's eight fifty, mate,' he said.

I got my wallet out and instructed Bob to make out a receipt for a tenner. He took the note, scrawled something across a small pad and tore off a sheet.

'There you go,' he said. 'Say hello to your lady friend and tell her Bob Yallop's always happy to give her a ride, if you know what I mean.'

'Yeah, I'll be sure to do that, Bob,' I said, and opened the door.

'You know, there was one other thing . . .'

'What's that?'

'She had this fancy ring on. Red stone with some sort of carving in it. That the sort of thing your friend used to wear?'

'Yes,' I said. 'Exactly that sort of thing.'

◆ ◆ ◆

For a good twenty minutes on the train, I pondered why on earth Olivia hadn't mentioned her visit to Simon Paxton. I hadn't mentioned him by name when I'd told her about the Highgate Cemetery incident, but it still seemed extraordinary. Presumably there was a perfectly rational explanation that I'd hear when she returned from Scotland.

Eventually my brain slipped into neutral as I watched the darkening East Anglian landscape flash past. The carriage was empty and greenhouse-warm. Combined with the hypnotic rattle of the wheels, it began to make me feel sleepy. I allowed a two-day-old copy of the *Ipswich Advertiser* to fall on to my lap, closed my eyes and began to dream.

It was almost dark on the beach. The moon was high in the sky and the tide had advanced over the pebbles until it was within yards of the fisherman. In a few minutes, the water would float him free of the shingle and bear him out to sea.

Wait any longer and I would be carried away myself. I wished the fisherman bon voyage and hoped that we would meet again some day. The stub of pipe fell from his lips and he muttered something through his beard. I put my ear closer to his mouth and he told me who had murdered George Dent.

THIRTY

Odeerie's arms were folded tight and his lips screwed together in a sceptical grimace. 'Seriously, Kenny,' he said. 'You really think that's what happened?'

'Positive,' I replied.

The fat man blew out his cheeks and shook his head. It had just gone 8 a.m. I'd had four hours' sleep. The Seven Dials Bakery had called to say that Odeerie's delivery of breakfast croissants was running late. Fair to say we were both a little tetchy.

'Blimp Baxter blackmailed George Dent to get his plans passed for the River Heights development, and then George decided to go public with it?'

'That's right. As part of his remit for Urban Development, George chaired the Inner City Planning Committee. Blimp's application to have the Corn Exchange demolished was denied twice and then the committee changed its mind.'

'How many sat on it?' Odeerie asked.

'Nine,' I said.

'What was the split?'

'Six for, three against.'

'Then it wasn't George's vote that carried the application?'

'No, but he was the chairman and the most senior politico. You know how that world works, Odeerie. George probably did a little quid pro quo with a couple of the other members.'

'All to prevent the drugs photos from getting out?'

'And ruining his career.'

Odeerie's arms disengaged. He glanced at his watch and scratched his head. 'But you said that Will took the photographs.'

'Almost certainly at Blimp's suggestion. If Blimp could get some kind of leverage on George then he could use it to get the application passed.'

I took my laptop from my bag, opened it up and placed it before Odeerie.

'This is the Old Hibbertians website. Tell me what you see . . .'

Odeerie squinted at the screen. 'A bunch of middle-aged blokes holding up champagne glasses,' he said. 'Is that what I'm meant to see?'

'The two standing by the left of the statue are Blimp and Will.'

'So what? They both went to Hibberts.'

'Will said that he hadn't seen Blimp in forty years.'

Odeerie sat back in his chair and sucked his teeth. 'Maybe he forgot.'

'Who's going to forget meeting Blimp Baxter? And when Will admitted to blackmailing George Dent, he was definitely worried about something. That something was his link to Blimp.'

'Baxter paid Will to blackmail George Dent?'

'Exactly. When Will mentioned to Blimp that he was supplying George Dent with coke, Blimp saw an opportunity. It wasn't about cash. It was about allowing the River Heights planning application to go ahead.'

'Then I'm not surprised he was worried about you finding out,' Odeerie said. 'He could do four years straight off the bat for regular blackmail. A lot longer if the connection to Blimp was revealed.'

The doorbell rang. Odeerie couldn't have hauled his arse out of the office any quicker had his trousers been on fire. Les croissants étaient arrivés.

I rubbed my hands over my face in an attempt to banish the tiredness. After arriving back from Suffolk, I'd spent an hour searching online for the River Heights application. RIBA reported that it had been passed at the third time of asking.

Checking the Hibberts site had been a shot in the dark. On finding the photo of Will and Blimp, I'd emitted a whoop of delight that was probably audible in Piccadilly Circus.

Odeerie returned to the office carrying a cardboard box. 'I'd offer you one, Kenny, but there's only six.'

Odeerie virtually inhaled the first croissant. The second received a couple of cursory chews. After dispatching the third, he asked, 'Where did you get this theory?'

I could have told him that a fibreglass fisherman revealed it to me in a dream.

Or . . .

'It was a subconscious thing,' I said. 'You know, when your mind connects the dots without you being aware of it and then suddenly you have the answer.'

'What about Alexander Whatshisname?' Odeerie asked. 'How does that fit in?'

'Simon Paxton thinks he and the other boys set up some kind of supernatural connection with Porteus in the cemetery.'

'What do you think?'

'He might be right.'

'Stone me, Kenny. You are joking.'

'Not everything can be explained rationally.'

Odeerie screwed his face up and looked at the final three croissants. 'Maybe you should have one of these,' he said grudgingly. 'Your blood sugar must be low.'

Simon Paxton's theory did sound a little less convincing in Odeerie's office, complete with brushed aluminium desks and humming computer stack, than it had on a windswept Suffolk beach. No point arguing the toss, though.

'Leave Porteus out of the mix and then does it make sense?' I asked.

Odeerie considered the question. 'So, for argument's sake, let's say that Blimp did get Will to set George up with the drugs photos and he passed the River Heights application to stop them getting out. Then George changes his mind and tells Blimp that he's going to the press about what happened. Why does Blimp plant the porn and the drugs in his flat?'

'So that George would be discredited. Blimp wanted to neutralise him if he went ahead with his threat to reveal that he'd been blackmailed to pass the River Heights development in the first place. Who would believe someone who'd been charged with being a paedophile and a drug user?'

'After which George tops himself?'

'Or he was murdered by Blimp just to make completely sure.'

Odeerie grunted. 'And he killed Peter Timms?'

'Either that was a genuine accident or Blimp thought George must have told him something.'

'So Blimp Baxter, billionaire property tycoon and TV personality, also moonlights as a serial killer? That's really what you're going to the police with, Kenny?'

'I probably don't have enough proof,' I admitted.

'You don't have *any* proof,' Odeerie corrected me through a mouthful of dough.

'But what if I convince Will that I know everything?' I said. 'Then he might confess to the cops in return for a good word at sentencing.'

'And if you're wrong?'

'Then I look like a twat.'

'Yeah, well, that wouldn't be the first time. Look, I think you're in danger of making one and one add up to three here, but there's probably no harm in giving Creighton-Smith a prod and seeing which way he jumps.'

While Odeerie concentrated on his breakfast, I called Will on his mobile. It went straight to voicemail. My next call was to Mountjoy Classics, where a man who sounded in a hurry said that Will hadn't turned up for work that morning. I asked if he had rung in sick and was told he hadn't.

'Not there?' Odeerie asked after I hung up.

'No. And he's not called them either.'

'Bit odd, isn't it?'

'Yeah, maybe,' I said. 'How's the password thing doing?'

Odeerie wandered over to a desk on which were a large screen and a keyboard. He tapped a couple of keys and said. 'It's seventy-four per cent of the way through the program.'

'What does it do, exactly?'

'Tries out every letter and numerical combination it can to obtain a password. The parameters I've set mean that it'll be finished in about four hours.'

'And it'll have cracked it by then?' I asked.

'Not necessarily. Depending on the length and complexity of the password, it can take weeks or months to get right. Years, even.'

'We've got forty-eight hours.'

Odeerie's silence said it all.

'Let's wait until your program finishes,' I said. 'If that doesn't produce the goods then I'll come up with . . . you know . . . another plan.'

We sipped our coffee. I wondered what the hell the other plan might be. I had a fair idea that that was on Odeerie's mind too. As there wasn't much I could do about the Dylans, I focused on my other problem instead.

'I'm going to call Blimp and set up a meet. I'll tell him I've got proof he blackmailed George and that I'll stay quiet if he gives me fifty grand.'

'It's an incredibly good plan, Kenny,' Odeerie said. 'In fact, the only fly in the ointment I can see is that you don't actually have any proof.'

'I'll take the wand. If he tries to bargain, I can take the recording to the police.'

The 'wand' was a digital recorder disguised as a fully functioning pen. I used it when interviewing people. Usually I didn't bother telling them that the chubby biro I was scribbling away with could also hold six hours of conversation.

'Wouldn't be admissible in court,' Odeerie pointed out.

'I know, but at least the cops will do some digging off the back of it.'

'Or arrest you for attempted blackmail. Blimp's a player, Kenny. Screw him over and he won't like it.'

The fat man had a point. Calling Blimp out wasn't without risk. But if I didn't give it a shot, I'd never know. I reached for my phone again.

After six rings I prepared myself for Blimp's voicemail and was taken aback when I got the man in person. 'Blimp Baxter,' he said, sounding as tired as I felt.

'Blimp, it's Kenny Gabriel—'

'What the hell do you want?'

'A meeting.'

'About what?'

'The photographs you and Will took of George Dent snorting coke.'

'Don't know what you're on about, old boy.'

'And it's not just the pictures.'

'You're full of shit.'

'Fair enough. I'll take it all down to West End Central and see what the duty sergeant thinks about it. Maybe the papers would be interested too . . .'

'Hold on, hold on,' Blimp said. Silence for a few seconds, after which, 'I live on Regent's Park Road. Can you come at eleven p.m. tonight? I'm having a couple of people round, but they'll be gone by then.'

I said I could and took the details.

I hadn't expected Odeerie to give me a round of applause after I'd reported Blimp's sudden change of heart about meeting up, although I had expected something. Instead he pursed his lips and shook his head. 'Just because he's agreed to meet doesn't mean he'll tell you anything' was his disappointing verdict.

'Maybe not, but it means I'm right.'

'I don't know, Kenny. I've got a seriously bad feeling about this. If he did kill George Dent and Peter Timms then he won't draw the line at you.'

'Here's what we'll do,' I said. 'If I haven't called you—'

An electronic parp interrupted me. Odeerie waddled over to the workstation, clicked the mouse a couple of times and rapidly entered something on the keyboard.

'What is it?' I asked.

'The force program's nailed the password.'

A series of photographs showed a bunch of people in what looked like a restaurant, followed by half a dozen shots of two guys sparring in the ring at Farrelly's Gym. Then we got to three in a row that had been taken outside Billy's apartment block. The third clearly showed McDonald walking out of the door.

'Bingo!' Odeerie said.

'Except that Billy could say the photo was taken before he went missing,' I said.

'No, he can't,' Odeerie replied. 'The time and date are embedded in the image, and there's a log on the iCloud upload. Hang on . . .'

He clicked and the final two shots appeared on the screen. The second had a slightly tighter focus.

'Christ, what was Gary doing at a theatre?' I asked.

'I'll expand the picture,' Odeerie said.

On the window of the Cock & Bull Theatre pub was a poster advertising the current production. Next to the poster were photographs of the cast.

One of whom was Martin McDonald.

THIRTY-ONE

I had called Olivia on the journey back from Suffolk and again after arriving at Liverpool Street station. On each occasion there had been no reply. That she hadn't returned my calls seemed peculiar. As Porteus Books was only a five-minute walk from Odeerie's, I decided to look in on her in person. I also needed time to think after seeing the final photograph on Gary's iCloud account.

At 9.15 a.m. things are slow in the occult book trade, especially on a Sunday. When the bell tinkled, Rodney looked up from his iPad like a medium roused from a trance. 'It's Kenny,' I reminded him. 'Is Olivia in today?'

Putting aside the tablet, Rodney gave me his full attention. 'She's visiting Sebastian in hospital,' he said, 'although he might have been discharged by now. Anyway, she definitely isn't coming in.'

'What happened?'

'Overdose.'

'Heroin?'

'Neediness.' Rodney sighed. 'God, I'm such a bitch. Seb swallowed thirty paracetamol yesterday afternoon. At least, that's how many he said he took.'

'He tried to kill himself?'

'Except that half an hour afterwards he called Liv and she got an ambulance round to him. Does that sound like a suicide bid to you?'

'He was faking it?'

'You might say so – I couldn't possibly comment.' Rodney yawned and examined his fingernails.

'Has he tried anything like this before?' I asked.

'Only half a dozen times. Basically, Seb reaches for the bottle when he isn't getting enough attention from his big sister.' Rodney gave me an arch look. 'Or he thinks someone is getting more. Tell me, how *are* things with you and Liv?'

'I should call her,' I said, ignoring the question.

'Spoilsport.' Rodney handed me a key. 'You can talk privately on the office phone,' he said. 'I'm sure Liv won't mind under the circs.'

'Thanks,' I said, and headed for the basement.

Olivia's office was about half the size of a domestic garage. Dozens of books were piled on shelves and virtually every other available space. Some had pieces of paper or Post-it notes tucked into their pages. Others had been packed into envelopes, presumably ready to be sent out to collectors.

Amidst the chaos was a desk bearing a closed laptop and a vintage push-button phone. A large brass frog weighted down several documents and papers. I sat on a rickety bentwood chair and called Olivia's number.

'Hi, Rodney,' she said. 'Everything okay?'

'Actually, it's Kenny,' I replied. 'I dropped in to see you and Rodney let me use the office phone. Apparently Sebastian took an overdose . . .'

'Yes, he did,' she replied. 'Although it looks like he might have become confused and not swallowed quite as many pills as he thought, thank God.'

'Why did he do it?' I asked.

'Things were getting too much for him and he was starting to drift back to his old life again. And he was upset about the business with the watch.'

'The one he accused me of nicking?'

'Seb wasn't in his right mind, Kenny,' Olivia said sharply. 'He's asked me to apologise to you.'

'Where is he now?' I asked.

'We're at my flat. He'll rest here for a few days.'

Fucking wonderful.

'Look, Kenny,' Olivia continued, 'how about supper tomorrow? I'd suggest tonight, but I don't want to leave Seb on his own.'

'No problem,' I said. 'I've got to work anyway.'

'Okay, I'll give you a call and we can sort something out. Oh, and Kenny . . . afterwards . . . there's always your place, isn't there?'

'There certainly is,' I replied. 'Actually, there's something else I wanted to ask—'

'I'm afraid it'll have to wait. Sebastian's due at the doctor's in half an hour.'

'No problem,' I said. 'See you tomorrow.'

◆ ◆ ◆

My next call was to Farrelly. While pondering how to open what might be a tricky conversation, my eyes fell on a printout of a rare-book auction listing the lots on offer, specifically those of Alexander Porteus. The reserve on most was less than £200, although for one volume it was £6,500 – *The White Tower* by William Gifford.

According to its description, the novel was in fine condition and number 123 of 1,000 copies privately printed in Paris in 1947. It also said that many scholars considered William Gifford to be the pseudonym of Alexander Porteus. The scholars in question clearly hadn't consulted Olivia.

And yet the entry had been highlighted. Perhaps I'd ask her about it tomorrow, or perhaps I'd steer clear of anything to do with Alexander bloody Porteus, focusing my efforts instead on getting her back to my Brewer Street love salon.

If I didn't get on and call Farrelly, there was a good chance I never would. He wasn't going to like what I had to tell him, but he deserved to know. I also needed his help in confronting the people who had nearly killed his son.

Gary's condition was the first thing I enquired about after he answered the call.

'Better than he was. They've done something to reduce the swelling.'

'That's wonderful news, Farrelly. I'm really pleased.'

'Yeah, well, he ain't out of the woods yet. That the only reason you called?'

'Actually, there was something else I wanted to discuss . . .'

'Get on with it, then.'

'Are you doing anything this evening?'

'Why d'you wanna know?'

'I wondered if you fancied the theatre . . .'

THIRTY-TWO

On my way back to the flat I pondered two things. Firstly, how to break the news to Farrelly that I'd played a part in putting Gary into hospital. Secondly, what was the best way to approach my meeting with Blimp Baxter?

The Blimp dilemma was whether to go straight in and demand money to keep schtum about George Dent, or to extend the conversation in the hope that he might incriminate himself on the wand. As far as Farrelly was concerned, all I could do was cross my fingers and hope for the best.

Moments after I'd arrived at this conclusion, my phone started vibrating. 'I was beginning to think you were avoiding me, Kenny,' Meg Dylan said. 'You know you've only got tomorrow left . . .'

'Yeah, I know,' I said.

'I do hope that you aren't going to bring bad news. Not after I put so much faith in you. Although I'm not sure Billy and Lance are of the same opinion.'

'We haven't got anything,' I said. 'But we're still working on it.'

'Now, that is a shame,' Meg Dylan replied. 'Even if you don't meet with success, Kenny, it would be a mistake to make me come looking for you.'

'It'll be sorted by Tuesday,' I said and cut the call.

Night had settled over Brewer Street by the time I ordered a cab for my rendezvous with Farrelly. Popular opinion has it that the pubs of Islington are full of human rights lawyers agonising over whether to have the grilled monkfish or the veal casserole with their Château Margaux. That might well be true for some of the borough's establishments. It isn't for Ye Olde Mitre on Essex Road.

All six of the pub's TVs were tuned to Sky Sports and the closest thing you were likely to get to a wild-rice supersalad was a bag of pickled onion Monster Munch. It was noisy, it was crowded and hopefully three or four of the regulars might pull Farrelly off me should things not go entirely to plan.

I ordered a waga and tried to distract myself by watching a football match. A penalty had been missed to a chorus of delighted jeers shortly before Farrelly arrived. He joined me at the bar and refused the offer of a drink.

'This isn't a fucking theatre,' was his first observation.

'Yeah, the place we're going to is on City Road,' I said. 'I thought we should meet in here to discuss a few things first.'

'What kinda things?' he asked, looking around. 'You said that you knew who did Gary. Just show me who they are.'

'Actually, it's not quite that simple.'

Farrelly moved his shaven head closer to mine. 'Why not?'

'I think the people responsible are probably the Dylan family. But the only way I can find out for sure is by talking to someone in the play we're going to see.'

'You mean Marty Dylan?' I nodded. 'Ain't he in Brixton nick?'

'The business is being looked after by his wife.'

'Why would she have Gary beaten up?'

I took a deep breath. 'You're not going to like this, Farrelly. All I'm asking is that you let me finish the story before you . . . Well, let me just finish the story.'

It took fifteen minutes to cover off how I'd initially wanted Gary to protect me from Billy Dylan and how events had led to his being in hospital. 'Basically, it's all my fault,' I concluded. 'And I'm incredibly sorry for what's happened to Gary. What I want to do now is find out if Billy really was responsible.'

Farrelly stared at me for what felt like the best part of a fortnight but was probably ten seconds. Someone scored in the match. Judging by the groans and obscenities directed at the screens, it wasn't the Mitre's preferred team.

'So, let me get this right,' he said slowly and deliberately. 'You come into my gym with some story about a bloke who's miffed because his missus has done a bunk and he thinks you're to blame. That bloke is Marty Dylan's son but you don't think it's worthwhile mentioning the fact?'

'Actually I did—'

'And then you let my kid, who has had no experience of this kind of work, walk straight into a shitstorm and get his lamps kicked out. That about right?'

'I told Gary in the Vesuvius who the client was and that he should let you know with a view to getting someone more experienced on the job.'

'What did he say?'

'Gary thought he'd be letting you down.'

Farrelly nodded a couple of times, as though acknowledging a voice in his head that was issuing instructions. Very precise instructions.

Next Time Round was a comedy about three students who resolved to meet every five years after leaving university. Given that it was one step up from am-dram, I expected it to be dreadful, and yet several times found myself laughing aloud along with the rest of the audience. At least until Farrelly glared at me.

We were in row eight of the Cock & Bull Theatre pub. Occasionally I could hear the fruit machine paying out in the bar below. The play started at seven thirty to a full house, probably due in part to the poster on the pub's window featuring a four-starred review from *Time Out*. There were also black-and-white shots of the actors: Maddie Malone, Tom James and Sean Hicks (aka Martin McDonald, the guy who had absconded with the Dylans' cash).

The play's final line was delivered, after which there was a blackout. When the lights went up, the actors took a curtain call. The audience clapped enthusiastically, with the exception of Farrelly and myself. All three actors cast curious glances in our direction. Sean Hicks gave no sign of recognition.

The punters headed for the stairs that led to the bar. When they had dispersed, Farrelly and I crossed the stage. We walked down a dimly lit passage towards a room from which came the sound of voices. Farrelly turned the handle and in we went.

Maddie Malone was sitting in front of a mirror removing her make-up. Tom James was tapping something into his mobile, and Sean Hicks had just taken off the jacket he had been wearing in the final scene.

'You two shut the fuck up,' Farrelly instructed Malone and James. 'And you,' he said, pointing at Hicks, 'are gonna answer some questions.'

'I have absolutely no idea who you are,' Hicks said. He was about five-ten with a bit of a gut and skinny legs. I'd have said late thirties, although thick brown hair meant that he could easily pass for ten years younger.

'I'm Gary Farrelly's old man. Name ring any bells?'

'Absolutely none whatsoever,' Hicks replied.

'Gary came here the night he was beaten to shit half a mile down the road,' Farrelly said. 'My mate reckons you had something to do with it.'

Hicks frowned. 'Yes, I think I did hear about that,' he said slowly. 'Is your son the poor chap who was mugged?'

'Yeah, except that he weren't mugged. The bloke you're working for nicked his phone and almost put him in the bleedin' morgue.'

'And who am I meant to be working for?' Hicks asked.

Farrelly looked in my direction, as did Malone and James.

'Billy Dylan,' I said. 'The pair of you scammed a fortune from his mother.'

'What?' Hicks said.

'You heard,' Farrelly replied.

'I can assure you that I've never heard of Billy Dylan, and as for me scamming anyone's mother . . . Well, that's just absurd.'

Hicks threw his jacket at Farrelly's head and raced for the open door. I extended a foot and he went down like a sack of spuds. Seconds later, Farrelly had him in a headlock.

'Er, maybe not quite so tight, Farrelly,' I said.

Reluctantly he decreased the pressure long enough for Hicks to draw breath.

'I can explain everything,' he used it to gasp.

◆ ◆ ◆

An hour after Farrelly and I had finished with Hicks, I was en route to Regent's Park Road in the back of a cab. Fortunately the traffic was light, as it was going to be a close call to make Blimp Baxter's house by 11 p.m. I'd tested the wand a couple of times and was fully prepped for my second great coup of the evening.

When the cabbie dropped me off with five minutes to spare, my heart was beating like a jackhammer. If I didn't relax then I'd take a coronary before reaching Blimp's front door. I gave the bloke twenty quid and focused on my breathing.

The three-storey, white-stucco house had been built in the early nineteenth century. Plain architectural lines leant the place a touch of class that was sadly lacking in its owner. The front door was at the top of a flight of stone steps. I rang the buzzer and gazed up at a security camera. No response, so I rang again. A minute passed and I began to suspect that Blimp either couldn't hear the buzzer or had forgotten I was coming and hit the sack. I pulled out my phone and called to let him know I was on his doorstep. After half a dozen rings it went to voicemail.

It's amazing how many people fit state-of-the-art surveillance cameras but spend a tenner on the front-door lock. Even for a rank amateur, the Yale pin tumbler was a piece of piss. I keep a set of picks in my wallet 'purely for emergencies, officer' and had taken several lessons from Professor YouTube on how to use them.

First I inserted the tension wrench and applied moderate pressure. The diamond reach pick went in next and connected with the first pin in the cylinder. Thirty seconds later, the fifth succumbed and the door opened.

A security light bathed the entrance hall in a dull amber glow. The alarm panel on the wall to my left looked as though you might need a degree to operate it. I waited for it to howl like a banshee and was (mostly) relieved when it didn't. The hairs on my neck were standing to attention. My mouth was as dry as a snake's.

The hall led directly into a large sitting room. I flicked a switch and a row of ceiling lights came on. So did a pair of smoked-glass standard lamps. The walls were papered in purple silk. Three large sofas faced a wall-mounted screen large enough to be used in a multiplex. On the hearth of a moulded fireplace was parked a vintage pedal car that had probably been some kid's pride and joy in the fifties.

No sign of a tubby property developer.

Off the sitting room was a passage. A series of black-and-white photographs featuring Louis Armstrong, Dizzy Gillespie, Miles Davis, Billie

Holiday and John Coltrane ran along both walls. I'd pegged Blimp to be more of a Phil Collins fan than a jazz aficionado. Hopefully I wasn't creeping the wrong address.

The first room I checked was an office with enough tech in it to rival Odeerie's. Pinned to a corkboard were aerial photographs of the River Heights development and an invitation to an investors' function. I checked the invite in case it was where Blimp was currently kicking back. The gig was in three weeks' time.

Next up was a small bathroom, which meant I had only one more door to look behind before I checked out the first floor or cut my losses and buggered off.

I flicked four switches in quick succession and found myself in a games room. A pinball machine bleeped and rang as the electricity travelled its circuits. Bakelite panels glowed into life on an antique Wurlitzer. The jukebox ground into action and resumed playing 'Only the Lonely' by Roy Orbison from the middle eight.

In one corner was a cocktail bar and on the walls a series of Spy cartoons featuring billiards champions from back in the day. Nearby was a rack of cues. Three were missing. The centrepiece of the room was a snooker table. Its lights must have been operated by the pull next to the rack, as the baize was in relative darkness. Something was in the centre of the table that I couldn't make out. For a moment I thought it was a crash helmet. Then my eyes accustomed themselves to the light.

I was looking at the head of Blimp Baxter.

◆ ◆ ◆

Blimp's head listed slightly. One eye was closed; the other pointed upwards as though trying to view something on the ceiling. His tongue protruded slightly, giving the impression that his last act on earth had been to blow a raspberry. Surprisingly there didn't appear to be a great deal of blood. The only other evidence of recent decapitation was a spatter pattern against the oak-panelled wall.

'Only the Lonely' finished. The Wurlitzer clicked, whirred and played the next selection. I've always found 'My Boy Lollipop' a bloody irritating song. My nervous system kicked in and I circumnavigated the snooker table on my way to the jukebox, doing my best to ignore its grisly load. The distraction of Blimp's head, combined with the meagre light and squelchy carpet, hindered my progress, although it was the corpse that caused me to stumble and fall.

Adesh, the huge Sikh I'd met at the River Heights development, lay with his legs partly under the snooker table, a dark stain on the front of his turban. Blood and brain matter had seeped over the carpet through the pulpy mess at its rear.

I scrambled back on to my feet, wiped my hands on my jeans and continued to the jukebox, desperate now to end the fucking song. In the end I pulled the plug from the socket and Millie Small's voice slowed, deepened and eventually stopped. I leant my head against the cool glass screen and tried to prevent my brain from going into meltdown. It came up with a delightful thought: what if the killer was still in the building?

At the opposite end of the room was a set of double doors. My hands refused to purchase on the doorknobs. I gave them an extra wipe and a low click rewarded my second effort. I'd been hoping for a fire exit. Instead I found myself in a small antechamber with a glass roof. A white telescope was inclined upwards at a forty-five-degree angle. Had anyone been peering through it, they would probably have been able to see every crater on the full moon that provided my only source of light.

Occupying an armchair was Blimp's torso. This was where he had been decapitated. The carpet and chair were sodden and his shirt glistened in the moonlight. Protruding through a tangle of flesh at his neck was a nub of crimson-specked ivory. During the process his bowels had evacuated. The stench of shit and blood was overwhelming. I bent double and heaved my guts up.

Several deep breaths cleared my head. On the cream wall above Blimp's body had been daubed words in what looked like Cyrillic script and, I was pretty certain, his blood. Accompanying them was a symbol of a crudely drawn fish in a circle.

'Oh, Kenny,' someone said. 'What am I going to do with you?'

THIRTY-THREE

Connor Clarke was wearing a pair of spattered yellow overalls. In his right hand was a glistening brush. His face was streaked and his blonde hair matted with blood. Asking whether he was responsible for Blimp's death seemed a tad unnecessary.

'The words mean *death to those who cross us* and the fish symbol is the calling card of a notorious Ukrainian crime syndicate,' he said. 'The Krev also like beheading their victims to send a message.' Connor assessed the graffiti like an artist taking stock of a work in progress. 'It's not really finished, but it's good enough,' he decided. 'With a bit of luck, the police will conclude that you disturbed the killer.'

The vintage revolver he drew from his overall pocket had a metal belt loop dangling from the grip. Its steel barrel seemed almost comically long. Above the muzzle was a ridge to aid the shooter's aim. From ten feet it would scarcely be necessary.

'Sorry, Kenny. I really did try to keep you out of this.'

'How?' I asked.

'The threatening letter to Judy, for one thing. I called your business partner and asked if he'd be interested in hearing some information about George Dent. He said he would, which indicated you were investigating his death. That meant you and your partner needed misdirecting. At least for a while.'

And, of course, he was right. I had seen the letters *SP* and immediately thought of Simon Paxton.

'Why would I be suspicious of you?' I asked.

'Judy saw me in the garden after I'd returned from Peter's house. Did she tell you about that?' My silence provided the answer. Connor smiled. 'But you didn't connect it to me? Perhaps I overestimated you, Kenny.' He looked at the wall clock.

'What you've achieved is amazing,' I said quickly. 'I'd be fascinated to hear how you managed it . . .' Nothing works every time in life, but flattery comes close. Most normal people fall for it. Hopefully the deranged would be no exception.

'Why not?' Connor said after mulling it over. 'If anyone was coming, they'd be here by now, and another half-hour won't make much difference.'

◆ ◆ ◆

Back in the games room, Connor flicked a couple of switches that activated a set of extra spotlights. The drinks bar was ten foot long with four high stools against it. On two shelves were a dozen bottles and as many glasses. I poured a large shot of Jim Beam into a tumbler. My hand was shaking so much that almost as much booze went over the side as went into the glass. I held the bottle up. Connor shook his head.

He sat on the edge of the snooker table while I occupied one of the bar stools. I intended to make my drink last as long as possible in the hope that providence might somehow save the day. Blimp's head with its waxy grey skin and protruding tongue suggested that providence had left the building.

'Mind if I smoke?' I asked.

'Go ahead,' Connor replied.

He laid the revolver on the wooden rail of the snooker table. I reached into my inside pocket and pressed the button on the wand. No matter how the next few minutes played out, at least there would be a record of our conversation.

I pulled out a packet of Marlboros and lit one up.

'Where shall I start?' Connor asked.

'The absolute beginning,' I said.

'That would be almost a year ago, when I discovered a dozen photographs tucked away at the back of a drawer in Judy's flat. They were of the same three boys wearing school uniform. One was of Judy but there was no clue as to who the other two were. The blazers all had "H&S" embroidered on the pocket. It didn't take long to discover which school they'd been taken at.'

'Why not ask Judy?'

'Because clearly she didn't want me to find the photographs. Instead I contacted the man who runs the Hibberts alumni society and gave him a story about having found some photos belonging to my deceased father. Matthew was in the same year as Judy and identified George Dent and Peter Timms immediately. We met for lunch and he told me about how, in 1979, some boys were seen running from Highgate Cemetery. Judy was the only boy caught but the other kids in the school knew exactly who had entered the cemetery with him. The headmaster asked that the culprits identify themselves. George Dent and Peter Timms didn't say a thing. The others you could understand staying quiet, but George and Peter were Judy's best friends when they were at Hibberts, according to Matthew.'

'So this is all about revenge for the boys keeping quiet and allowing Judy to be expelled from Hibbert & Saviours?' I asked.

'In truth, it was more curiosity to begin with. I did some research and found out that George was a regular at a bar in Camden. I made sure I bumped into him and we became friendly. Or at least, George thought we did.'

I lit another cigarette off the first and ground the butt out on the carpet. What with there being a human head lying on the snooker table and a corpse stretched out on the floor, there didn't seem much point trying to hunt down an ashtray.

'I knew from Matthew that Simon Paxton had been obsessed with Alexander Porteus at school and that was why the boys had visited the cemetery,' Connor continued. 'I decided to play a few mind games by calling George and pretending to be Porteus delivering a warning from beyond the grave.'

'How did he react?' I asked.

'It terrified him. After a couple of calls he was really freaking out. I asked him over dinner what the matter was and he couldn't wait to tell me how he'd entered Highgate Cemetery forty years ago and seen the apparition of Alexander Porteus. The story was fascinating. So much so that I began to read the Master's works.'

'Including *The White Tower*?'

'Indeed, and when I did the scales fell from my eyes, Kenny. Once you fully accept the doctrine of being true to yourself, there's no need to worry about petty morality. As the Master says, *A sated body leads to unity of mind and purpose.*'

'Except that it's a work of fiction,' I said. 'Alexander Porteus died of lung cancer in 1947 and was brought back to England and buried in Highgate Cemetery.'

Connor smiled in the way that certain people do when they're about to put you right on climate change or why the World Trade Center really went down. I recalled what Judy had said about his tendency to see the world in terms of absolutes.

'The service was conducted using a weighted coffin,' he said. 'The Master was secretly interred in the family vault in 1958 after suffering a heart attack in Madrid.'

'Even if that's true, I still don't understand why you did all this.'

'Have you read the *Tower*?'

'I know what it's about. A magician's assistant dispatches his master's enemies in order to buy his boss an extra—'

And suddenly I knew exactly why Connor Clarke had murdered four people and was about to do the same to me unless I got very lucky in the next ten minutes.

'All this is for Judy, isn't it?'

'Can you think of a more appropriate way to punish the people who ruined her life than by sacrificing them to extend it?' Connor asked.

'Which is why you pushed George out of the window?'

'He was so pissed that he barely knew what was happening. The same went for Peter Timms. In his case, all I had to do was hit him over the head with a scaffolding pole and then collapse the rig on top of him.'

'How did you access his house?' I asked.

Connor chuckled. 'That's when I knew the Master was truly guiding my hand. George asked if I was looking for extra gardening work and introduced me to Peter. He was in the office all hours and gave me the back-door key and the alarm code. That night, all I had to do was wait until he came back. Afterwards I hid in the tree house until everyone had left.'

'Is that what you did after he saw you in the garden?' I said.

'Of course. I wondered if Peter might work that out.'

'What would you have done if he had?'

Connor's shrug spoke volumes.

'Did the Master also insist that you wander around dressed up like him?' I asked.

'No, I'll admit that was pure self-indulgence. It scared George so much that I thought I might as well use it on Peter.'

'But not Blimp?'

'No point. Baxter isn't— wasn't the imaginative type.'

Connor looked sideways at Blimp's head. For a moment I thought he was about to stretch out a hand and ruffle his hair. Thank Christ that didn't happen.

'In Baxter's case, I had to play the long game and take my chance when it arrived,' he said. 'I thought it might be months until that came round. Adesh was with Blimp everywhere he went. And then I recalled a quote from my Latin class at school. "*Quis custodiet ipsos custodes?*"'

'"Who guards the guards?"'

'I'm impressed, Kenny. The trick wasn't trying to find a way past Adesh; it was more about how I could work with him to get to Baxter.'

'Adesh was in on this?'

'Not knowingly. Adesh was a karate instructor, so I joined his club and got to know him. He told me that the day job was looking after Blimp Baxter. I said I was a huge fan of *Elevator Pitch!* and was there was any way I could meet him?'

'Adesh invited you here?'

'With his boss's permission. Things weren't looking too good at River Heights and Blimp was getting paranoid about his impatient Ukrainian investors. He didn't like going out and he and Adesh played snooker most nights. If the project went under, Blimp intended to skip the country.'

'Meaning you had to act quickly?'

Connor nodded. 'It also provided a good scenario for me to kill him without arousing the suspicions of the police. All the surveillance camera will show is a man in a baseball cap with a rucksack on his back whose face can't be made out. I don't think they'll be slow to suspect a professional assassin, probably acting on behalf of the Krev.'

'And Adesh?' I asked. 'Don't you feel any guilt about him?'

'*Guilt is for the weak and the foolish,*' Connor said in what I was beginning to recognise as his quotation voice. '*The strong man is untroubled by conscience.*'

Connor stretched an ache out of his left arm. The action caused his sleeve to roll up and reveal a familiar-looking gold oblong strapped to his wrist.

'Where did you get that?' I asked.

'The watch? From our mutual friend Sebastian Porteus. The Temple of Selene presented it to the Master in 1928. Rather elegant, don't you think?'

'Seb stole it for you?'

'There were certain things I wanted from his sister's private collection that she wasn't likely to sell to me. All of which meant the only alternative was to steal them. Or, better still, have Sebastian steal them on my behalf.'

'What kind of things?'

'The Master's notebooks, primarily. I wanted to possess something that he had written with his own hand. The watch was a bonus.'

'And Sebastian said no problem, Connor, I'll nick it for you?'

'Not quite, although Seb would have done virtually anything for someone who could supply him with a few rocks of crack on a regular basis.'

'So next it's Simon and Will?' I asked.

'That's the plan. After taking care of you, of course . . .'

'Because you think murdering them—'

'Sacrificing, Kenny.'

'Because you think sacrificing them will somehow help Judy? Is that how it works? Every time you knock one of them off, she gets another six months?'

'Of course not. There are complex rites that must be observed. But the bottom line is that Judy can use her left hand again and only needs the chair for distances. If you'd known her longer, you'd be amazed.'

'There's a reason for that,' I said.

Connor frowned. 'What are you talking about?'

'Judy was in St Mick's when you thought she was visiting her friend Patti. She volunteered for a drug trial there a few months ago.'

Connor grabbed the revolver and took a couple of paces towards me.

'If this is some kind of strategy, Kenny, it really isn't going to work. Judy's recovery has nothing to do with any drug trial.'

'Then why not call and ask her about it?'

'Because there's no point and I don't have the time.'

'Connor, listen to me,' I said. 'I'm speaking to the person you were before you found the photographs and read the *Tower* – the person who knows that killing people helps no one, least of all Judy. Put the gun down and we'll call the police.'

The look in Connor's eyes faded as though the wattage of his madness had begun to wane. I walked slowly towards him with my hand outstretched. For a moment I thought he would hand the gun over. Then the craziness generator kicked in again.

He grabbed my arm and dragged me towards the snooker table. He bent me over it so that my torso was on the baize and my stomach resting on the cushion. He slotted the plug into the wall and once again 'My Boy Lollipop' was on the jukebox, presumably to mask the sound of the discharging gun.

People often say that they've looked death full in the face. I was doing it literally. Without tension in the muscles, Blimp's flesh had sagged, giving him a mournful expression entirely in keeping with events. His tongue had extended a further centimetre from his teeth and turned the colour of a ripe aubergine.

The eye that had been focused on the ceiling had realigned and was staring directly at me. The metallic smell of blood and early putrefaction drifted into my nostrils like the first whiff of mustard gas across the trenches. In a moment Connor would pull the trigger and I would wake up on the wrong side of no-man's-land.

'Kill me now and you'll never know what really happened in the cemetery,' I shouted over the sound of the heavy bass of the Wurlitzer's speaker. The song continued for a few seconds and I waited for oblivion.

'What d'you mean?' he asked.

'I saw Simon Paxton a couple of days ago. He said something about Judy and Alexander Porteus that you really need to hear.'

'Tell me.'

'Turn the jukebox off first.'

The Wurlitzer was ten feet or so away from the snooker table. Just about the right distance for what was my one and only chance. Connor turned and killed the song.

'Go on, then,' he said. 'What is it?'

'Catch!'

Blimp's head sailed through the air. Connor reactively dropped the gun to grab it. I took my chance and ran like hell. The corridor was ten yards long. I had three left to travel when Connor exited the games room. One round shattered the frame containing Billie Holiday's photograph. Another thudded into the lintel of the door.

In the sitting room I careered into a standard lamp. Its glass shade exploded like a grenade on impact with the floor. All I had to do was make it across the hallway and out the front door to freedom. Except that the bastard lock had re-engaged.

I twisted it left and right but the latch refused to move. Connor trampled over the shards of glass in the sitting room. Reason asserted itself over terror. The button above the handle unlatched the lock. I pressed it down, heard a click, and threw the door open.

Connor's final shot was his best effort. It whined through the air a few inches from my left ear and shattered the window of a passing night bus. Maybe it had taken out a passenger. Maybe it hadn't. I wasn't hanging around to check.

For the second time in a week I raced death down a city street. The best I could manage when my lungs said no more was to drag myself behind a parked Range Rover and wait for the inevitable. Running footsteps approached and slowed.

'Are you all right?' I looked up into what I had assumed would be the muzzle of a gun and the raging face of Connor Clarke. Instead I was staring at a man in his mid-twenties wearing a tweed sports jacket and a concerned expression.

'You dropped this,' he said.

I accepted the wand as though it were the key to the universe and burst into tears. The guy put a hand on my shoulder and said that everything was going to be okay.

Five minutes later, I heard the first siren.

THIRTY-FOUR

There were eleven marked and four unmarked police vehicles outside Blimp's house. The exterior was illuminated by three floodlights running off a generator in one of the vans. Crime tape stretched between a pair of squad cars to mark the road as off limits. Photographers prowled like dingoes with telephoto snouts while reporters tried to cajole officers into answering questions. It was organised chaos with the sense that something major had happened hanging in the chill night air.

A medic had wrapped me in the kind of space blanket that you usually see around the shoulders of marathon runners. He had also given me a shot to calm my racing heart. The PC who had been first into the games room had received the same treatment. I suspected a couple of the other officers would be spending the night with a bottle of vodka for company when they came off shift.

DI Paula Samson entered the ambulance. When we'd last met in East Hampstead Police Station she had appeared tired. Now the woman looked positively exhausted.

'Hello, Mr Gabriel.'

'Call me Kenny,' I said.

'How are you feeling, Kenny?'

'Not fantastic.'

'That's to be expected after what you've been through.'

'All of which could have been avoided.'

Samson's pallid cheeks coloured. 'I'm sorry I dismissed your concerns so lightly when you gave your statement,' she said. 'It just all seemed a bit out there.'

There was no point in playing kick-the-dog any further. Samson would have enough shit to shovel when the case came under review.

'You're sure the man you interrupted was Connor Clarke?' she continued.

'Positive.'

'And this is his address?' The DI held out her notebook.

'That's right. Connor's father lives in the opposite block. I don't have the number on me, although you could probably find it easily enough from your records.'

'What's his name?'

'Judy Richards.' Samson looked up. 'The guy used to be called Ray Clarke,' I explained. 'He changed gender a few years ago.'

'I need a full statement,' Samson said. 'I could interview you in hospital but that would take time . . .'

'He should be taken in,' the medic muttered.

'I don't need to go to hospital,' I said, to the guy's visible disapproval.

'Great,' Paula Samson said. 'One of the neighbours is letting us use her kitchen as a temporary incident room. Are you okay being interviewed there?'

'Has she got anything to drink?'

'We could ask,' she said.

'Then I'm happy,' I replied.

Paula Samson led me up a set of stone steps into a house that wasn't as large as Blimp's but which could still have accommodated a family of nine. She shepherded me into a brightly lit kitchen in which two other officers were working. One was wearing a uniform and sitting at a pine refectory table hunched over a large laptop. The other was leaning against an Aga cooker while talking into his mobile.

Samson introduced me to the uniformed officer and gave her Judy's address. She nodded and left the room. We sat at the table and Samson produced a pad. She said that, on reflection, alcohol was probably a bad idea as I'd just been medicated for shock. Served me right for swerving a ride with the medic.

Over the next hour, I took Samson through the story of my involvement with the case, from meeting Peter Timms to the point at which I had dashed from the house of horror, as the tabloids would no doubt soon be calling it. She stopped me a couple of times to ask questions. Of specific interest were the whereabouts of Will and Simon and the precise exchanges I'd had with Connor in the games room. The download from the wand saved time with this. Samson listened with fascination and paused the laptop occasionally to clarify a muffled exchange.

The interview was coming to an end when the female officer returned. She whispered into Samson's ear. The officer nodded at me as though apologising for the secrecy. Then she scooped up her laptop and left the kitchen.

'Connor Clarke's holding Judy Richards hostage,' Samson said.

'Christ, what does he want?' I asked.

'To talk to you,' she replied.

◆ ◆ ◆

It took fifteen minutes to reach the Carbury Estate, sirens screaming and lights flashing. During the journey, Paula Samson liaised with the armed response team. From what I could gather, the police negotiator had made contact with Connor, who had refused to allow Judy to leave the flat until he had spoken to me first.

'There's no danger,' Samson assured me as we pulled on to the access road to the estate. 'You won't leave the car and armed officers are in place. The negotiator will tell you how to play things.' She looked directly into my eyes. 'Sure you're okay with this, Kenny? You've been through a lot tonight.'

'Yeah,' I said, 'I think so.'

Virtually all the lights in the estate were turned on apart from those on the landing where Judy Richards lived. An officer with a megaphone was instructing residents to remain in their flats until such time as it was safe to leave.

Four cars and a van with heavily tinted windows were parked in a semicircle on the north side of the garden. Five bulky officers stood next to the van, dressed in black with a variety of tools hanging from Kevlar vests. The only one not holding a snub-nosed rifle approached our car. He got into the back seat next to me.

'Kenny Gabriel, this is John Gallen,' Paula Samson said. 'John's a negotiator attached to SCO19. He's been talking to Connor.'

'Pleased to meet you, Kenny,'

Gallen didn't look much more than thirty, although the Harry Potter-style glasses probably took a few years off him. He removed his black cap and we shook hands.

'Connor sounds reasonably calm,' he said, 'although, in light of earlier events, that may not mean much. Can you describe his demeanour tonight, Kenny?'

I gave Gallen a potted version of events supplemented by Judy's take on her son's impressionable nature. Paula Samson added a couple of things she'd heard on the wand.

'Ordinarily we wouldn't ask someone to do this,' Gallen said when we'd finished. 'But a conversation with you is the only thing Connor's requested.'

'I'm fine with it,' I said.

'Just a few guidelines before we call him. If he asks for anything, don't say yes or no. Just ask him to tell you more. That's your key phrase: *tell me more.*'

'Got it,' I said.

'If he makes a yes-or-no demand, say that you'll refer it to me and keep on talking. It's important that you don't sanction anything, Kenny.'

'No problem.'

Gallen removed a pair of headsets from a rucksack. Paula Samson gave me a reassuring smile from the passenger seat of the car. Gallen plugged both headsets into what looked like a supersized mobile phone.

Connor Clarke answered on the third ring.

'Hello, Connor, it's John. Kenny Gabriel's with us. Before I put him on the line, I need to talk to Judy.'

'She's still sleeping.'

'Any chance you could wake her up, mate?'

'I need to speak to Kenny first.'

Gallen grimaced before nodding to me.

'Hello, Connor, it's Kenny.'

'Are you okay?' he asked.

'Yeah,' I said. 'I'm good.'

'I'm sorry for what happened.'

'That's all in the past, Connor. We need to focus on the future now.'

Two hours ago I'd been running from a house while someone took potshots at me. Now I was exchanging pleasantries with the man whose finger had been on the trigger. Weirder still was Connor's voice. He sounded like a frightened six-year-old.

'You were right about Judy taking the medication,' he said. 'That's what was making her better. Porteus tricked me.'

'How about you come down and we sort this out, Connor?' I said.

'What will happen to Judy when I'm not around?' he asked.

'She'll be looked after.'

'Will you make sure?'

'Absolutely.'

A long silence. So long that I wondered if Connor had cut the call.

'Okay,' he said. 'I'm coming out now.'

'That's the sensible decision, Connor,' Gallen interjected. 'Open the door very slowly. Step on to the balcony without your weapon and lie flat on the ground.'

The three of us stared up at the third floor. The door opened and Connor came out with his hands in the air. An armed officer emerged from the entrance to the walkway. He repeatedly shouted a phrase that I couldn't make out.

Connor reached for something. Three rounds discharged from the cop's gun. Connor slumped to the floor. The officer approached and stood over him.

'Oh, fuck,' John Gallen said.

Half my age and twice as fit, Gallen and Samson raced up the steps of Drake House. By the time I arrived, the pair of them were standing above the body of Connor Clarke. Three members of the SWAT team looked on, their guns pointing to the cement floor. One had removed his helmet and was taking deep breaths in what seemed to be an effort to calm himself.

'Did he discharge a round?' Gallen asked the officer holding Connor's gun.

The guy shook his head. 'It was empty.'

Judy Richards cradled her son's head while making a feral keening noise that was as old as time and always meant the same thing. Paula Samson offered a comforting arm. It was pushed away almost violently. Judy's eyes met mine without comprehension. Her disease would carry her off in a few months' time.

But in truth she was already dead.

THIRTY-FIVE

Samson detailed a driver to take me home. It was 5 a.m. and the streets were virtually deserted. Drizzle was falling and the rhythmic sweep of the car's wipers dispelled the silence that would have necessitated conversation. Just as well as I wasn't in the mood for small talk. Gazing through the rain-spattered passenger window, I reflected on what had taken place in Blimp's house and on the Carbury Estate.

Maybe Connor had been right about Porteus tricking him. Shakespeare contended that 'The evil that men do lives after them; the good is oft interred with their bones.' Had the 'Master' perverted a vulnerable mind decades after his death?

I asked the officer to drop me in Oxford Street. From there I walked down Poland Street, across Broadwick Street and into Lexington Street. The only people I saw were a man sleeping in the doorway of the Star & Garter and an oriental woman in a kimono trundling a huge pink suitcase behind her.

It was dawn when I got into the flat. I turned on the radio and poured a third of a bottle of Monarch into a tumbler. Blimp Baxter's death was competing for air space with a profit warning from a supermarket chain and beating it hands down.

I switched the radio off, sparked up a smoke and drank my Scotch. Farrelly would be picking me up at noon. We were due at the Dylans' at 2 p.m. Whatever happened there couldn't compete with the carnage in Blimp's games room.

After my Scotch and a couple more fags, I intended to make my way to Bernie's for a massive fry-up. Then I'd call Odeerie for a debrief session, and would probably have enough time to look in at Porteus Books to see Olivia. Oddly enough, someone was pressing my buzzer repeatedly. Except that it wasn't odd.

According to my watch, it was 11.47 a.m.

◆ ◆ ◆

Farrelly's usual expression is that of a man who's just been told he's two minutes late registering a significant lottery win. That morning, there appeared to be something slightly more relaxed about him. The muscles around his jaw weren't as tightly clenched, and his eyes weren't trying to bore twin holes into my forehead.

'I've been ringing that bleedin' bell five minutes,' he said, and then sniffed the air around me. 'You reek of booze and fags' was the verdict. 'I hope you haven't forgotten what's going down today?'

'I haven't forgotten, Farrelly,' I said. 'Where's Hicks?'

'In there.' Farrelly nodded to his ancient Volvo. There appeared to be no one inside. I pointed this out. 'He's in the boot with a sock in his gob,' Farrelly informed me. 'And you'll be in there with him if you don't stop yawning.'

'Sorry,' I said. 'Didn't get to sleep until six.'

Farrelly shook his head as though words failed him.

'Couldn't you lay off the sauce just one night?' he asked.

'It was a work thing. Give me five minutes to freshen up.'

'Freshen up? We're on our way to a straightener, not dropping in for tea at the Women's fucking Institute.'

Despite this, Farrelly appeared to have made a sartorial effort himself. T-shirt and jeans had been forsaken in favour of a black sports jacket over a white shirt and grey slacks. On his feet were a pair of polished loafers.

'I was at the hospital this morning,' he said to explain the unusual garb. 'Gary's mum was there, so I reckoned I'd make a bit of an effort.'

'I hope she appreciated it,' I said. 'How is Gary?'

The corners of Farrelly's mouth appeared to be twitching. Had I not known better, I would have said he was attempting to smile. Or trying hard not to.

'He's awake,' he said. 'And he's talking.'

◆   ◆   ◆

Farrelly granted me ten minutes to shower and change, after which I'd better be in the bastard motor or he'd slice my fucking ears off. I beat the deadline by thirty seconds. He started the engine and turned into Regent Street.

'Gotta bad headache,' Farrelly said after I requested more details on Gary's condition. 'Apart from that, he's fine.'

'When will they discharge him?'

'Coupla days, probably.'

'Does he remember anything about what happened?'

'Yeah, he does, as a matter of fact. Says it was two chancers after his phone. One of 'em must have been tooled up.'

'Not Billy Dylan?'

'Don't look that way.'

'Why didn't they take his wallet, then?'

'Toerags probably got disturbed.'

I took a few moments to digest this information. It seemed like a coincidence that Gary had been mugged so soon after tracking Hicks to the theatre. But coincidences do occur, which is why we have a word for them.

'If Billy wasn't responsible for what happened to Gary, then why are you still coming to the Dylans'?' I asked Farrelly.

He shrugged and replied, 'Said I would.'

'But you won't do anything rash?' I asked. 'Best for all concerned that everything passes off nice and easy.'

'Scout's honour,' he said as we crossed Oxford Circus.

'How long has Hicks been in the boot?' I asked.

Farrelly consulted his watch. 'Two hours.'

'Have you checked on him?'

'He'll be fine so long as he don't panic.'

'What if he does panic?'

Farrelly made a face as though I'd wondered what might happen if it started raining.

'Where did you keep him overnight?' I asked.

'At my place, like we agreed.'

'He's all right, isn't he, Farrelly?'

'Why wouldn't he be?'

'Because you can get a bit carried away sometimes.'

Farrelly indicated left and turned on to the Marylebone Road.

'I did heat up a screwdriver on the stove,' he admitted.

'Please don't tell me you've blinded him.'

'Course I ain't. What d'you take me for?'

A borderline psychotic with a penchant for torture was the answer. Probably not the best time to mention it, though.

'I wanted to see if there was anything about Billy Dylan that he didn't mention in the pub last night,' he continued.

'And was there?'

Farrelly nodded and reached into his jacket pocket. He produced a memory stick and threw it on to my lap.

'He gave me this,' he said. 'You wouldn't believe what's on it.'

Farrelly parked in a lay-by a hundred yards along the road from the Dylans' farm. He popped the trunk to reveal Sean Hicks lying in a foetal position. His hands and feet were restrained and there was a gag over his mouth. He was wearing the same suit he had worn on stage the previous night. Farrelly unfolded a five-inch lock knife, the sight of which made Hicks's eyes bulge a bit.

'I'm gonna cut you loose,' he said. 'Don't try nothing because you're two stone overweight and we're in the middle of bleedin' nowhere. Understand?'

Hicks nodded. Farrelly sliced through the nylon ties.

'The other thing is I don't want no chat. We're taking you in to see the Dylans and we're taking you out again when we're done. Nothing bad's gonna happen unless you piss me off by talking too much.'

Again Hicks signalled his understanding. Farrelly removed the gag and pulled an argyle sock from his mouth. Hicks coughed and spluttered and asked whether we had any water. 'What did I say about talking?' Farrelly asked.

'Here,' I said, and handed him a bottle of Evian. Hicks drank every drop and could probably have downed a gallon more. His circulation was shot, which meant it was four or five minutes before he was able to walk properly. We arrived at the gates to find a man wearing a quilted jacket and a beanie hat standing in front of them.

'We're here to see Meg and Billy Dylan,' I said.

'Your name Kenny?' he asked.

'Yeah, and this is Sean Hicks, aka Martin McDonald.'

'And who's this one?'

'Farrelly.'

'Farrelly what?' the guy asked.

'Just Farrelly,' I said.

'Yeah, well, I've gotta search you before you go through.'

The guy was about six-two and large enough to need his own post-code. Hicks and I raised our arms and submitted to a search. When it came to Farrelly's turn, he handed over the lock knife.

'That's all I'm carrying,' he said.

'Still gotta pat you down,' the guard replied.

'You ain't laying a finger on me, son.'

For a few seconds the men stared at each other in an effort to gauge which way it would go if it came to it. Logic dictated that the younger, heavier, taller man would win hands down. Logic isn't all it's cracked up to be.

'Whatever,' the guy decided, and pushed the gate open.

We didn't have to ring the bell, since Lance opened the front door as we approached. A Hawaiian T-shirt wrapped itself around his momentous shoulders and the stubble on his scalp glistened like blue steel. His eyes fell on Hicks.

'Well, well, if our old friend hasn't come back to see us. Billy's gonna love meeting you again, sunshine. Hope you've got his money.'

'Can we come in, Lance?' I asked.

'And Tweedledum and Tweedledee too!' He opened the door wide. 'What a fun afternoon we're all going to have.'

Sean Hicks trailed Lance down the passage as though it led to a scaffold. I wasn't feeling too sensational either. I was delivering exactly what Meg Dylan had asked me to. How pleased it would make her was another matter.

When we entered the day room, mother and son were on the sofa. Billy's jaw dropped a couple of inches when he saw Hicks. Meg squealed with delight.

'You found the bastard!' she said. 'Well done, Kenny.'

'Thanks,' I said. 'His real name is Sean Hicks.'

'May I offer you a drink?'

I shook my head.

'Is this your business partner?' Meg asked.

'More of an associate,' I replied. 'Farrelly, this is Meg Dylan.'

Farrelly grunted a response. The crystal animals seemed to fascinate him. In the car I had told him about my last trip to the farm, although mere description couldn't do justice to the hundreds of twinkling creatures.

'Are you a Swarovski fan?' Meg Dylan asked him.

'No,' Farrelly grunted.

If the bluntness surprised her, Meg didn't show it. Lance grimaced and folded his arms as though something he had eaten for lunch was giving him trouble.

'Well, I suppose that's our business concluded, Kenny,' his employer said. 'You've fulfilled your side of the bargain and you're free to go.'

'Don't you want to know how we found Sean?' I asked.

'I'm sure we can extract that information from him in person.'

Meg Dylan gave Hicks a glance that could have stripped paint. He looked as though his legs might give way. Mine weren't rock-steady either. For a second I was tempted to abandon the stupid bastard to his fate.

'That's not going to happen,' I said. 'We'll tell you how and why Sean took your cash, who you can get it back from, and then the three of us are leaving.'

'You'll do what you're told,' Lance said.

'We'll do what we bleedin' well like,' Farrelly snapped back at him.

'Now, now, Lance,' Meg Dylan said soothingly. 'Let's hear what Kenny and his friend have to say before doing anything hasty.'

Farrelly winked at Lance. It didn't improve his mood any.

'Billy told you that he and Sean met at an event for small businesses when he was looking for someone to launder money through,' I said. 'But that was a lie.'

No response from Billy despite a quizzical look from his mum.

'The truth is that he and Hicks met in Longmill Prison,' I continued. 'Billy always fancied himself as an actor so he joined one of the classes Sean was teaching. Billy wasn't the next Al Pacino, but one of the homework exercises was to come up with a scene the group could act out the following day and his wasn't half bad.'

'He's talking shit,' Billy said, although his voice carried zero conviction.

'Sean encourages him to write the entire script. It turns out to be a blinder, so much so that Sean sends it out to a few contacts in the industry. Sure enough, there's interest from investors, but it's a high-concept idea, and no one wants to come on board unless there's already a decent chunk of money in the pot. In theory Billy has access to a fortune, but he won't get his hands on it if he tells his mum he wants to make a movie. Instead he and his co-producer cook up this fantastic idea. Tell you what, Sean,' I went on, 'why don't you take it from here?'

Hicks's cheap suit was less crease-resistant than tinfoil. His dark hair was greasy and his jowls rimed with stubble. He looked like crap but he was still an actor.

His shoulders straightened and he took a deep breath.

'The first thing I want you to know, Mrs Dylan, is that none of this was my idea. Billy said that he knew how to get the money and that it would just take a minor piece of subterfuge. I insisted that we pay every penny back out of the film's profits.'

'You lying bastard,' Billy said.

'Shut up,' Meg replied.

'But what he said is totally—'

'I said be quiet!'

'Billy suggested I use my acting skills to pose as a businessman eager to launder money,' Hicks continued after his co-conspirator had sunk back on the sofa with a sullen scowl. 'He had the documents forged to give the impression things were on the level. Then you gave us the six

hundred thousand and . . . well . . . you know what happened after that.'
Hicks's head inclined in penitential fashion. 'I realised that we'd made
a terrible mistake and wanted to return the cash,' he said. 'Although
Billy insisted that it wasn't something that you'd really miss in the grand
scheme of things and that we should push ahead with the project.'

Bearing in mind that he'd had Farrelly waving a red-hot screwdriver
in his face, followed by over three hours in the boot of a car, it was a
bravura performance from Hicks. Not that Billy Dylan appreciated the
finer points.

'Has all the money gone?' his mother asked.

'You've got to look at it as an investment—'

'I said, has the fucking money gone?' she said.

'There was no other way to raise the cash,' Billy said. 'Read the
script, Ma. Once you've seen it, you'll realise that—'

'You think I give a toss about your poxy script?'

Billy crumpled as though he'd been punched in the gut. I almost
felt sorry for him. Then I remembered that he'd beaten the shit out of
Odeerie.

'Okay, you can leave now,' Meg Dylan instructed me.

'Not without Hicks,' I replied, and pulled the flash drive out of
my pocket.

'What's that?' she said.

'Billy gave Sean access to his laptop when they were working
together. He copied the drive in case there were any creative differences
down the line. There's all manner of fascinating stuff on there: names,
cash transfers, account numbers . . .'

Billy put his head in his hands.

'How much d'you want?' Meg Dylan asked.

'Nothing,' I said, and tossed the stick to her. 'Although if anything untoward happens to me or Sean, then a copy gets emailed to
the police.'

Meg thought about it, although not for long. 'You've been clever, Kenny, but watch your step. If that gets out, you'll wish you'd never been born.'

'Keep your side of the bargain and it's going nowhere,' I said. 'Oh, and we're taking Magda too,' I added. 'Assuming she wants to come, that is.'

Meg Dylan stared at me as though my ears were melting. 'What d'you want that Polish slag for?' she asked.

'Just get her in here,' Farrelly interjected.

Meg nodded at Lance, who reluctantly left the room. For the next five minutes things were a bit strained. Billy stared daggers at Hicks, while Meg's expression suggested that she was thinking how, or perhaps whether, she was going to tell her husband about all this in the next visitors' session at Brixton.

Farrelly recommenced his inspection of the menagerie, occasionally picking up one of the animals and holding it to the light. I wondered how things could go wrong (at least a dozen ways) and what we could do if it did (basically fuck-all).

Magda looked disconcerted when she entered the room. The last time I'd visited she'd ended up chowing a mouthful of broken glass. Her English wasn't sensational and it took five minutes to explain to her that my brother was willing to provide her with a job and a place to stay. If she wanted to leave, then it would mean packing immediately. I wasn't entirely sure if she believed me or not, but it didn't seem to matter. 'I get my things,' she said, and headed for the door.

'Hold up a minute,' Farrelly said.

The giltwood chair was the only classy piece of furniture in the room. If it was reproduction then it was an excellent reproduction. If genuine, it had been hand-carved by a master craftsman the best part of two centuries ago.

Farrelly upended it and splintered a leg free with the heel of his shoe.

'I reckon you're due some compensation, luv,' he said to Magda.

She had no idea what he was talking about and nor did I. That was until Farrelly entered the gallery containing the crystal menagerie and brought the chair leg down on to one of the shelves.

Lance bellowed and charged across the room. It was the same strategy he had used against Gary in the lobby of my flat. Farrelly Senior was a different proposition.

Ducking low, he stabbed the chair leg hard into Lance's ribs. The big man gasped and fell to his knees like a penitent in chapel. Farrelly brought the improvised club down on his skull. We wouldn't be hearing from Lance again that afternoon.

Farrelly wiped the chair leg and handed it to Magda. A smile spread across her face and she went to work. When all the shelves had been taken care of, she began to stomp the animals into splinters, grunting with the effort. Whatever indignities had been visited upon Magda during her incarceration with the Dylans – and no doubt there were many – they were at least partly exorcised during a fifteen-minute orgy of ecstatic destruction. But it wasn't Magda's efforts that had me transfixed.

Meg Dylan's face was the best show in town.

THIRTY-SIX

The return journey was a quiet one. Magda had a vacant expression, and appeared stunned by the enormity of her actions. Sean Hicks stared listlessly out of the window, and I fought against exhaustion. Dropped off first was Hicks, who lived in a block of flats on Green Lanes. Before releasing the central locking, Farrelly turned to face him. 'Fetch the copy of that stick thing to my gym tomorrow afternoon,' he said. 'If I'm not there, leave it with the big geezer on reception.'

'What copy?' Hicks asked. 'The only one I had was on my key ring.'

'The one you gave to Farrelly last night?'

He nodded.

'And I handed over to Meg Dylan,' I said, and sighed. 'So the only thing keeping us all alive, we don't actually own any more?'

'Don't bleedin' tell no one,' Farrelly instructed Hicks.

'Of course I won't,' he said. 'Can I go now, please?'

Farrelly released the central locking system and Hicks got out of the car.

'Actually, I wouldn't mind some fresh air,' I said. 'I'm feeling a bit sick.'

After exiting the Volvo, I caught up with Hicks.

'Christ, what now?' he said. I showed him a picture of Gary on my phone.

'Did this guy come to see the play?'

'He did, as a matter of fact,' he said, after taking a moment to examine it. 'Same row you two were in. I remember thinking he didn't fit in with the usual crowd.'

'Was Billy Dylan around that night?'

Hicks nodded. 'We were going to talk about some changes to his script after the show. He and Lance left just before the final curtain, though.'

'Did they say why?'

'No, I just got a text from Billy saying that something urgent had come up and that he'd call me to rearrange.'

'Right,' I said, and couldn't help but ask, 'Was his script really that good?'

'Yeah,' Hicks said, 'it was.'

'What was it called?'

'*Graveyard Zombies*. I know what you're thinking – just another crap zombie movie. But this one really did have some class. It was kind of a satire on—'

'That wasn't what I was thinking.'

'Oh, okay.'

'However good it was, Sean, you need to forget about the film and Billy Dylan.'

Hicks's face indicated this wouldn't be a problem. I said goodbye and trotted back to Farrelly's car. 'What were you talking to him about?' he asked.

'Just emphasising that he really needs to keep his mouth shut,' I said.

'You ain't gonna puke?' Farrelly asked.

'No,' I replied. 'I ain't gonna puke.'

My brother had agreed that Magda could temporarily bunk in with his housekeeper and cook, both of whom lived in the servants' quarters of his house in Fulham. Farrelly waited for me while I led her to the front door.

The housekeeper answered the bell. Annie greeted Magda by name and said how pleased she was to meet her. I handed her rucksack over and said to Magda that I would drop by to see her in a day or two. She nodded and followed the housekeeper through the door. I was halfway back to the car when I heard footsteps behind me.

Magda's hug was brief and powerful. She muttered something in my ear in Polish, and then barrelled back up the stairs before I could request a translation.

'I didn't get no fucking hug,' Farrelly said when I rejoined him in the car. I extended my arms. 'Behave yourself,' he said. 'Your brother must have a bob or two. That place is bleedin' enormous. How come he made a bundle and you're broke?'

'Malcolm has talent.'

'Means sod-all if you don't do nothing with it.'

'Yeah, but you've got to have it in the first place.'

Farrelly turned his gaze from the house to me. 'You've just fronted out Billy Dylan and got that poor mare out of shtook.'

'And your point is?'

'You spend too much time peering up your own arsehole.'

'Did you get that in a fortune cookie?'

Farrelly took the kind of deep breath that parents often do when their kids are properly irritating them. 'Your nut needs sorting out,' he said.

'You applying for the job?' I asked.

'Don't bleedin' tempt me,' he replied.

Farrelly dropped me off outside the flat. I invited him in but he was keen to get to St Michael's before visiting time was over. I asked him to give Gary my best and tell him that I'd be in to see him soon. Ten minutes later I was pondering his advice over a black coffee laced with a shot of Monarch, and half a dozen stale Jaffa Cakes.

Did I spend too much time examining my own fundament? My therapist had emphasised the importance of challenging negative assumptions. I told her that I'd blown the chance of leaving Soho with the only woman I'd ever loved, which was the pure truth any way you sliced or diced it. Greta had asked why I couldn't begin another relationship. And to be fair, that's what had happened.

Olivia and I were in the very early stages, but it might lead on to something longer-term. If it didn't, then at least it was taking my mind off Stephie.

And perhaps Farrelly had a point about my career. I might have been barking up the right tree for the wrong reason with Connor Clarke, but at least Will and Simon were still alive as a result. And Meg Dylan would be keeping Billy on a short leash for the foreseeable future. My ringing phone interrupted the positive-thinking binge.

'Hello, stranger,' I said to Olivia.

'Sorry, Kenny,' she said. 'Things have been hectic. How are you?'

'Not bad. How was Edinburgh, by the way? I forgot to ask.'

'Edinburgh?' she repeated as though I'd said Leningrad. 'Oh, yes, Edinburgh was fine. Sorry, it seems ages ago now. Do you still want to meet tonight?'

'Assuming you do,' I said. Olivia sounded as knackered as I felt.

'I think that would be best,' she said, which was odd.

'How about something to eat? There's a new Thai place on Frith Street looks like it might be pretty decent.'

'Actually, I think a drink would be better, if that's okay with you,' she said. 'And I won't be able to stay too long, I'm afraid.'

'Why's that?' I asked.

'I promised to help Seb with his packing.'

'Where's he going?'

'Arizona.'

◆　◆　◆

The Coach and Horses is an old-school boozer that hasn't changed its décor since the early seventies. Everyone prepared for the worst when Norman Balon, its tyrannical landlord, retired. Fortunately all the new owner did was install an upright piano. The oak panelling remains, as do the red vinyl bar stools, the signs promoting Skol lager and Double Diamond, and the feeling that Jeff Bernard or Peter Cook might stagger through the door at any moment.

After ordering a large waga, I occupied the only free table in the place, on which lay a discarded copy of the *Standard*. Predictably its front page carried the sensational news of Blimp Baxter's death and the subsequent shooting of his suspected killer. He had been named as Connor Clarke and there was a picture on page two.

It was the photo taken in the garden at the Carbury Estate. Connor was standing behind Judy's wheelchair with a broad smile on his face. A man who looked less like a serial killer you would be hard-pressed to find. And yet, as the report pointed out, he was also being linked to the deaths of three other people.

Olivia arrived wearing the same grey coat she had worn when we'd met in Highgate Cemetery. Only when she sat down did I notice the shadows under her eyes. I went to the bar for drinks and returned to find her reading the paper.

'This is horrendous,' she said. 'D'you think it was some kind of sex thing?'

'It was a bit more complicated than that.' I took a sip of my drink. 'Connor thought he was keeping his father alive by killing Blimp. He murdered three other men for pretty much the same reason.'

'You sound as though you knew him.'

'Read paragraph three.'

'"The suspect was interrupted by a man thought to be in his late fifties, who is currently helping police with their enquiries." That was you?'

'That was me.'

'Christ, Kenny. What happened?'

Olivia's G&T remained untouched throughout my account. Her hand flew to her mouth when I got to Blimp's head on the snooker table, and I took it easy on the adjectives from there on in. Connor's obsession with her grandfather and *The White Tower* didn't get much of a reaction, although, after she expressed her general shock and sympathy at my ordeal, it was the element we wound up discussing.

'I suppose that wretched book will start selling again,' she groaned. 'An auction house is listing it as being written by my grandfather. I've demanded they either remove it from sale or state that William Gifford is the real author.'

All of which explained why I'd seen the title highlighted in the catalogue on her desk.

'A friend of Connor's father had his life destroyed by *The White Tower* forty years ago,' I said, and took a sip of my waga. 'His name's Simon Paxton.'

'You're joking! I went to see him.'

'Really?' I asked, choosing not to reveal that so had I. 'Why was that?'

'He had some books he was looking to sell. A few were first editions by my grandfather and Simon wanted to see if I was interested.'

'Were you?'

Olivia nodded. 'He had to move out of the house and was selling everything off. At least, that's what he told me.' She pulled her coat tighter around her shoulders. 'Kenny, you don't think there was any other reason he wanted to meet?'

'Probably not,' I said. 'It makes sense that if you have rare books by an author you'd go to the dealer who specialises in his works.'

Some tit on the piano was trying to initiate a sing-song.

'I can barely hear myself think,' Olivia said after glancing at her watch. 'D'you mind if we go outside? There's something I'd like to discuss.'

In the past, when women have announced the need for a discussion, it's usually been about my drinking, plans for the future, unsuitable friends, thoughts on children, attitude to Catholicism, perspective on tracker mortgages or tendency to sarcasm. Given that Olivia and I were technically only on our third date, it was unlikely to be any of the above. And yet I still had a sinking feeling as we made our way outside.

The Coach had provided a few benches for the use of smokers. The only other taker on a parky night was a ginger geezer in his seventies hunched over a pint of Guinness. Olivia sat with her back to him and got straight down to it.

'You know I told you on the phone that Sebastian is checking into the Cedars rehab unit for three months?'

'The place in Arizona?'

'That's right. Well, the thing is . . . the thing is that I'm going too.'

'To make sure he doesn't back out? Probably a good idea—'

'Actually, I'll be living there.'

'Erm . . . I'm not with you, Olivia.'

She sighed and ran a hand through her hair. 'The Cedars places heavy emphasis on the need for family support. Seb and I have dual nationality, which means I can go to the States with him. We're flying out tomorrow.'

'For the whole three months?'

Olivia nodded. 'After that, we plan on living in America full-time. Seb thinks a fresh start is just what he needs.'

'Sure, but isn't selling up a bit drastic?' I said. 'Why not go to Arizona until the treatment's finished and see how things are then?'

Olivia took my hand. 'My mind's made up, Kenny. If I'm not there for Seb, there's a real chance he won't make it. You do understand that, don't you?'

Had I mentioned that Sebastian had been stealing from Olivia on behalf of Connor Clarke, it might have made a difference. But I had an idea that there were some things about her brother that Olivia would have to find out for herself. Maybe that would happen in Arizona and maybe it wouldn't. Time alone would tell.

'If you've made your decision then you've made your decision,' I said at around the same time a car drew to a halt on the opposite side of the road.

The horn tooted and Olivia looked up. 'There's Seb now,' she said. 'Let's keep in touch, Kenny.' She gave me a brief kiss, trotted over the street and got into the car. Her brother looked out of the driver's window and grinned. Actually, grin doesn't even nearly describe it. Triumphant leer would be nearer the mark.

As the green Ford Focus pulled away from the curb and headed north up Greek Street, I realised that I'd done Billy Dylan a disservice. Although undoubtedly a piece of shit in human disguise, Billy hadn't tried to run me down in Brewer Street.

Sebastian Porteus had been responsible for that.

THIRTY-SEVEN

Two weeks after Blimp's murder, an arcade owner in Brighton contacted Odeerie. The guy suspected his staff were filching cash from the machines and wanted someone to keep the place under surveillance. Said person would need to pass for the kind of loser who might realistically spend three hours a day playing slot machines. Odeerie showed him my photograph and I was hired on the spot.

I was travelling on the 9.21 from Victoria and had fallen into a light doze when I felt a tap on my shoulder. The young woman looked familiar but I couldn't place the face. She was wearing a dark-blue skirt with a matching jacket, and had a chop cut that accentuated delicate cheekbones.

'It's Kenny, isn't it?' she asked. I admitted it was. 'Don't you remember me?' was her next question.

'Afraid I can't quite place the face,' I said.

'It's Sally,' she said. 'Sally Thomas. I was George Dent's constituency secretary. The last time I saw you was in that greasy spoon in Soho. I gave you the photographs of George and the other man taking drugs. You said that you'd try to find out who it was and get back to me. Only that didn't happen . . .'

'Sorry,' I said. 'Life got a little hectic.'

'Likewise,' she replied. 'Mind if I sit here?'

When we had first met in Mermaid Court, she had looked like a member of the Amish community. Now Sally could have posed on the front of *Elle* when it was carrying a dress-for-success feature. 'I'm guessing you got the job?' I said.

She nodded. 'Trainee account manager for Brass Neck PR. I'm seeing a financial services company in Haywards Heath today. How about you?'

'Working with a new entertainment client.'

'Anyone I might have heard of?'

Had my client been Sony, I might have been tempted to break the OC Trace and Find confidentiality commitment. As it was the Klondike Kabin, I wasn't.

'Afraid I can't reveal details,' I said, and tapped the side of my nose.

Sally nodded her understanding.

'Well, at least I turned out to be right about George,' she said, 'even if it wasn't a sinister plot and just some random headcase. Weird that he went after Blimp Baxter and Peter Timms as well, though.'

'Not that weird,' I said.

Sally frowned. 'What does that mean?' she asked.

I'd shown DI Samson the photographs of George snorting coke and told her that Will had confessed to blackmailing him to prevent their release. She'd said that she'd look into the matter. When I added that I thought it had actually been part of a wider conspiracy, including Blimp, to have the River Heights scheme passed, Samson had not unreasonably asked for proof. I'd been forced to admit that it was simply a hunch.

All of which meant that I wasn't jeopardising an investigation if I told Sally what I was pretty much certain had happened. And that's precisely what I did.

'Wow,' she said. 'The bastard totally screwed him.'

'Except there's no evidence.'

'What about the photographs? And Will's still alive. Why can't the police arrest him and get a confession?'

'Because all he has to do is deny the shots were taken in secret and that he ever used them to extort George. The fact that he hasn't been charged means that's probably what he's done.'

'How about if I posted the photographs and the story online anonymously?'

'What good would that do?'

'George's reputation would be salvaged.'

'I wouldn't advise it,' I said. 'Someone might trace the source.'

'So Will gets off scot-free?'

'Looks that way,' I said as the train began to decelerate.

'Why am I even surprised?' Sally said, shaking her head. 'You know, I got into politics so I could change people's lives. Everything just comes down to money and luck in the end. At least in PR I get to wear decent clothes and don't have to listen to constituents bitch about immigrants all day.' She got to her feet and shouldered her bag. 'Nice seeing you again, Kenny. At least, I think it was.'

'You too, Sally,' I replied. 'Good luck with the job.'

◆ ◆ ◆

I'd been in the Klondike for a couple of hours when one of the staff members opened up a machine with a key he wasn't supposed to have. He removed handfuls of coins from the well in full view of his colleague. Tim and Craig were in it together, as the client suspected. I took half a dozen photographs of the pair in action while pretending to text someone on my phone and then emailed them to Odeerie.

Mission accomplished, I walked along the seafront, collar turned up against the chill wind, and mulled over what Sally had said. Did happiness come down to money and luck? Not really. However often you hit the jackpot in life, you're still obliged to pump your winnings back into the machine. Rich or poor, lucky or unlucky, we're all fucked in the end.

I'd just finished a punnet of chips and was about to follow up with a stick of candyfloss when my phone rang. I chucked the carton and accepted the call.

'Is that Mr Gabriel?' a man asked.

'Who's calling?'

'Clive Palmer from Highgate Cemetery. I took you on the tour a few weeks ago when you were researching the book.'

'Yes, of course,' I said. 'Although I'm afraid now the band's on tour again, Keith's gone a bit cold on the idea.'

'That's a shame, but it wasn't why I was calling. You asked if I'd have a word with Maggie, who worked with the Friends of Highgate Cemetery.'

Indeed I had. Maggie was the woman who might, or might not, be able to shed some light on the nocturnal sightings of Alexander Porteus. My heart rate quickened.

'Did you manage to speak to her?' I asked.

'I did, as a matter of fact,' Clive replied. 'It took longer than I expected as she's been in hospital with a touch of pneumonia. Lucky to survive, really. Almost anything can carry you off when you're in your nineties—'

'What did Maggie have to say?' I asked impatiently.

'Well, it's quite interesting. Apparently the Friends employed a Turkish labourer called Tolga to clear the more persistent undergrowth. He didn't speak much English but was devoted to the cemetery, according to Maggie.'

'Okay,' I said, feeling a tad disappointed. 'And does Tolga know something?'

'Sorry, I'm not explaining myself properly,' Clive said. 'Apparently Tolga was upset by the vandalism. So much so that he took to wearing a cloak and wandering around at night to scare the vandals away.

Judging by Maggie's description, he was the spitting image of Alexander Porteus.'

'So it was almost certainly Tolga the boys saw . . . I mean the reports were about.'

'It does sound very likely,' Clive said. 'No one had a clue what he was up to until the police saw him coming out of the gates at dawn one morning. Of course, Maggie made sure he stopped . . . Are you still there, Mr Gabriel?'

'Yes,' I said. 'Thanks for calling me back, Clive.'

'Not at all,' he said. 'If and when Keith decides to go ahead with the book, I thought it might make for a rather interesting chapter.'

'I'll be sure to mention it to him,' I said.

I emerged from the Tube at Oxford Circus and entered Soho via Argyll Street. It was getting on for 7 p.m. Points failure on the return journey from Brighton meant that I didn't have time to go back to the flat before meeting Gary Farrelly in the Vesuvius. With all the excitement of Blimp's murder, it had been a couple of days before I'd got round to visiting St Mick's, by which time he had been discharged.

Gary hadn't responded to my attempts to contact him and I was beginning to think I might not see him again. Then he had texted and suggested meeting in the Vesuvius. Perhaps the blow to his head had caused lasting damage after all.

Early evening, the V isn't particularly crowded. A couple of the regulars were playing cards, and a thirty-something newbie in a bomber jacket was staring mournfully into an empty glass. Whispering Nick was flicking a duster on a stick around the fixtures and fittings. He looked like a chimpanzee attempting to use a fishing rod. 'What are you doing, Nick?' I asked.

'What the fuck does it look like I'm doing?' he croaked.

'Cleaning the place, only it can't be that.'

Nick inspected one of the lights. Not gleaming, exactly, but at least some of the dust had been redistributed. 'Antonio's found a manager,' he said. 'Thought I'd better tidy up a bit before they get here. S'pose you want a drink?'

'Actually, I popped in for some financial advice.'

'Really?'

I raised my eyebrows. Nick responded with a sarcastic smile. He mixed me a waga and laid it on the bar.

'What's the new manager like?' I asked.

'GOT LOTS OF EXPERIENCE,' Nick said after plugging in his speaker.

'What, in a place like this?'

'S'WHAT ANTONIO RECKONS.'

'Bet they'll be a pain in the arse.'

'YOU NEVER KNOW, KENNY. YOU MIGHT BE PLEASANTLY SURPRISED.'

After which elliptical comment, Nick turned his attentions to the guy in the bomber jacket who had realised that his glass wasn't likely to refresh itself. I decamped from the bar to a table and flicked through a copy of the *Metro*.

Gary walked in when I was halfway through a piece about how the NHS was on the point of collapsing. His hair was shorter and he looked a touch paler than on his first visit to the V three weeks ago. That apart, there wasn't much difference. We hugged, which is something I don't do every day and which certainly caused Nick to perform a double take.

'Looking good, mate,' I said. 'Have you been given the all-clear?'

'More or less. I'm seeing the consultant tomorrow. Get the nod from him and I can stop taking the meds completely.'

'Fantastic. Fancy a drink?'

'No, thanks. I'm meeting a couple of friends at King's Cross in an hour.' Gary cleared his throat. 'I read about what happened to Blimp,' he said. 'Were you the bloke who disturbed Connor Clarke in his house?'

'That was me.'

'They kept your name out of the papers.'

Which was true. Odeerie had been all for telling the press that Kenny Gabriel of the OC Trace and Find network (network!) was responsible for tracking down Connor Clarke and available for all investigatory work, location no object. Not fancying the hassle, I'd put the kibosh on it and the fat man hadn't stopped grumbling since.

'So Clarke was just a nutter, then?' Gary said.

'Actually, it was a bit more complicated than that . . .'

I told him about how Connor had been subsumed into Alexander Porteus's twisted world and how reading *The White Tower* had deep-fried his mind. I also mentioned how Sebastian Porteus had tried to mow me down in his car.

'Why did he do that?' he asked.

'Olivia was the only person who took his bullshit seriously and he couldn't bear the idea of losing her. At least, I think that was the reason.'

Gary grunted. 'Sounds like you had a lucky escape, Kenny.'

'From Connor or the hit-and-run?'

'Both.'

'Actually, I thought it was Billy Dylan who was trying to kill me because I'd told him that we'd found Martin McDonald. Same way that I thought he'd given you a pasting in Islington. Although I wasn't entirely wrong about that, was I?'

A few moments' silence concluded with the sound of the lavatory flushing.

'How did you know?' Gary asked.

'That it was Billy? Because Sean Hicks said that he and Lance left the theatre shortly after you did, and because your wallet got left behind. No mugger would have taken your phone and not bothered with the cash and the cards.'

'Are you gonna tell my old man?' he asked.

'Why didn't you?'

'Because he'd probably have taken Billy Dylan out.'

'I think that's a fair assumption,' I said.

'And what would have happened then?' Gary asked.

'Marty Dylan would have gone after Farrelly big time.'

'Which is why I told Dad that it was a pair of chancers who got lucky.'

'Although it was definitely Billy?'

'Yeah, it was him all right,' Gary said. 'I don't know who the other guy was because he got me from behind.'

'You did the right thing,' I said. 'Even if it does mean that Billy gets away without being punished.'

Although he bore a strong resemblance to his old man at the same age, I had never felt the same level of menace emanating from Gary. Until now, that was. Something hard in his pale-blue eyes made the atmosphere in the V feel distinctly chilly.

'I don't know about that, Kenny,' he said.

'How do you mean?' I asked.

'I'm taking a few months off to go travelling.' He leaned across the table and all but whispered in my ear. 'But when I get back, I've gotta feeling that something tragic might happen to Billy Dylan.'

Gary held my gaze for a few seconds before breaking into a shit-eating grin. It was as though a hypnotist had clicked their fingers in his face.

'You know, I'd still be interested in working with you and Odeerie,' he said. 'Maybe I could look you up and see how you're fixed.'

'No problem,' I said. 'Odeerie sends his regards.'

'Yeah? I got the feeling he didn't like me much.'

'The fat man doesn't like anyone.'

Gary chuckled and checked his phone. 'I really need to make a move,' he said, and got up from his chair. 'Look after yourself, Kenny.'

After he left, I spent a few minutes trying to recall an elusive proverb about fathers and sons. Eventually my memory served it up.

The apple doesn't fall far from the tree.

◆ ◆ ◆

The problem with drinking in the same place for forty years is that you become nostalgic. Every nook and cranny of the Vesuvius holds a memory. Since I first walked into the place, there have been all manner of riotous nights and milestone celebrations with people who are now dead or as near to it as makes no difference.

Back in '85, the V's oldest member was Harry Cosgrove. A surly old geezer, he sat at the bar and knocked back vodka and tonics and didn't have a good word to say for anyone, including himself. When he didn't come in for a week, Jack Rig visited his bedsit in Stepney to see how he was. Unable to get a response, he and the landlord had entered the flat. Harry was hanging from the sitting-room door with an empty bottle of Stoli at his feet and a squadron of flies buzzing around his head.

What I ought to have done was warn the guy in the bomber jacket to get the hell out while the going was good. But what was the point? I wouldn't have taken a blind bit of notice had Harry C. offered me the same advice. If you're bound for the land of the lost then nothing stops you getting there. And if your name isn't on the ticket, it isn't on the ticket.

I asked Nick for a supersized waga and prepared to get pissed.

I was halfway down my fifth of the night when the intercom buzzer went. Nick pressed the release and twenty seconds later someone walked into the Vesuvius who I hadn't seen in twelve months, one week and two days.

'Hello, Kenny,' Stephie said. 'How've you been?'

EPILOGUE

Tolga leans against the wall and catches his breath. What would have happened if the last boy had fallen back down? Ever since he's started scaring the crazies out of the place, Tolga has wondered what he would do if they didn't run away from him. But that didn't happen tonight. The kids were terrified.

Of course, the team fixing the cemetery wouldn't approve. They're nice people, particularly the tall one, Maggie, who's in charge. But the trouble with nice people is that they don't like to cut corners. In Britain everything has to be done *by the book*.

He begins walking back to the hut where his tools are stored. The first time he wore the cloak was three months ago. Two crazies were trying to force one of the doors of the catacombs. Tolga made a growling noise like a dog. He had never seen grown men run so fast in his life.

He stops by the grave that is like a small house with a peculiar roof on top. It's the place the crazies seem to be attracted to most. He'd once looked through the slit in the door during the day. Stained glass bathed the inside in beautiful light, although the tomb in the corner had a glow all of its own that Tolga found unsettling.

He collects the candles the kids dropped. They probably just came into the cemetery for a dare. You don't care about much apart from girls and having fun at their age. The boys will soon forget what happened tonight. That's the way it is when you are young.

ACKNOWLEDGMENTS

I would like to thank:

Deborah Manship, Melanie Newman, and Kiare Ladner for being fantastic first readers.

The Thomas & Mercer team, particularly Jane Snelgrove, Jack Butler and Russel D. McLean, for all their hard work and invaluable editorial input.

Veronique Baxter at David Higham Associates.

ABOUT THE AUTHOR

Born in Liverpool, Greg Keen got his first job in London's Soho over twenty years ago and has worked there ever since; his fascination with the area made it a natural setting for his books. *Soho Dead*, the first in the Soho Series of urban-noir crime novels, won the CWA Debut Dagger in 2015. Greg lives in London.